Praise *for* Lynne Hugo

"Skillfully constructed and impressively written... a near-poetic quality."
—Betsy Willsford, *Miami Herald,* on *Swimming Lessons* (coauthored with Anna Tuttle Villegas)

"I suspect that every woman who reads it will find something of an 'of course, I understand.'"
—Carole Philipps, *Cincinnati Post,* on *Swimming Lessons*

"...bittersweet and rewarding."
—*Publishers Weekly* on *Swimming Lessons*

"Beautiful in its use of language and unsettling in its observations, this story was the worthy recipient of the River Teeth Literary Nonfiction Book Prize."
—*Library Journal* on *Where the Trail Grows Faint: A Year in the Life of a Therapy Dog Team*

"Wow!...a must-read for anyone interested in...the basic human need to nurture and be nurtured."
—Mike Nobles, *Tulsa World,* on *Where the Trail Grows Faint: A Year* ... *Dog Team*

"A lovely writer...H ... d soul enough to do ...
—Jo Gibson, *O* ... *Trail Grows F* ... *Therapy Dog Team*

"The novel builds to the climactic trial scenes...moving."
—*Publishers Weekly* on *Baby's Breath* (coauthored with Anna Tuttle Villegas)

Lynne Hugo

Lynne Hugo has published seven previous books, including fiction, nonfiction, poetry and a children's book.

A recipient of fellowships from the National Endowment for the Arts and the Ohio Arts Council, Ms. Hugo makes her home in southwestern Ohio with her husband and brilliant (maybe slightly spoiled) Labrador retriever, a certified therapy dog and one of the subjects of *Where the Trail Grows Faint: A Year in the Life of a Therapy Dog Team*, which won the River Teeth Literary Nonfiction Book Prize. Her most recent novel was *The Unspoken Years*, published by Harlequin NEXT. Her every day includes a hike with her Lab in a nearby forest. Nature and wildlife conservation are among her passions, as are exuberant reunions with extended family and old friends, and time with her own family. She's also engaged by politics, vegetarian cooking, horseback riding and novels that provoke intense discussion with her book group. There's more information on her Web site, www.lynnehugo.com.

THE NEXT NOVEL™

LYNNE HUGO

GRACELAND

GRACELAND

isbn-13:978-0-373-88113-0
isbn-10: 0-373-88113-4

This edition published by arrangement with Harlequin Books S.A.

TheNextNovel.com

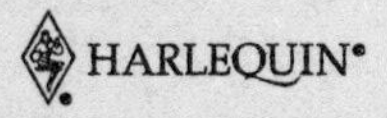

PRINTED IN U.S.A.

For my beloved friend,

Barbara Keller Eshbaugh

Acknowledgments

An excerpt from *Graceland* was first published in *Women's Words* in January, 1998. Permission to reprint is acknowledged with gratitude, as is support provided by The Ohio Arts Council during the preparation of the manuscript.

Dr. Robert Zipco generously gave information and guidance regarding kidney disease and dialysis, which was essential to the accurate portrayal of each. His help was of inestimable value.

Tara Gavin's editorial sensitivity and sensibility are extraordinary. My great thanks to her, and to my agent, Susan Schulman. My gratitude also to Sean Mackiewicz, editorial assistant. Special thanks to Alan, Brooke, David, Ciera and Robert deCourcy, Frederick Hugo and Jan Fuller for unflagging interest and support.

CHAPTER 1

Even though I am the oldest, I've always been in the middle, stuck between my sisters like the fulcrum of a teeter-totter, keeping each safely balanced. Perhaps it became a habit, and in the years since I escaped home I've brought the role on myself, rather than what it seems: the noose of the inescapable circle of fate.

The thing is, I never see it coming. I always believe that I am on the cusp of being able to live out in the open, and say what I really mean. Twenty-one years ago, when I was a breath under eighteen, I got married to change everything. I had to get out from between Madalaine, born after me, and Ellie, the youngest, who's like a fern frond that withered unaccountably before it ever unfurled. I also got married to get out from between Mama and Daddy, who needed a full-time mediator to decide who had failed to pay the electric bill on time, whose fault it was that the Dodge on the street was slumped over a flat tire or the butcher had given Mama a soup bone with no meat on it again. I thought it would all be different, that I could make life be different.

I was fourth in my class. I could have found a way to college or at least to work in some faraway city, instead of marrying Wayne in such a misguided hurry, and my life would have turned on a different dime. In fairness, nobody told me I couldn't, but nobody said I could, and nobody from my family ever had. The idea was as likely as a rosebush springing up in the desert on its own. So I've worked as a secretary for Dr. Hays for the whole of my married life, and watched his patients grow up or grow old, be newly born or newly dying. Of course, I tend to hear the suffering parts of their lives, and I remind myself that surely they have ice-cream sundaes and birthdays and Christmas mornings, too. "Toughen up, Lydia,"

Dr. Hays said to me when he found me crying over Mrs. Kinsey's spina bifida baby the same day Mr. Davis, who was a bird-watcher, had a stroke that took away his vision.

He has a point. I know what life can dish up for breakfast: my own brother, the real oldest child, is retarded. I call myself the oldest, because I was expected to be in charge and to take care of my sisters and Charles. Someone might think that Charles was what I wanted to escape, but that's not true. He is the nicest and happiest member of our family. Mama fusses about him, and Ellie fusses *at* him every hour of the day while she carries her basset hound around and mourns for Elvis, but Charles just gives everyone his lolling smile and lets them go on. He claps with Vanna for every letter of *Wheel of Fortune*. Of course, Mama does, too, so maybe that doesn't prove anything about Charles. Madalaine married early, like me, but Mama and Daddy have their oldest and youngest living with them forever in their eye-blink of a house in the part of Maysfield for people who are poor but white. The truth is, I have no idea who takes care of whom: Ellie complains like a squeaky door; Mama hardly budges from her chair; and Daddy disappears to the Toyota plant—Kentucky's notion of hope—while Charles watches television. They all live in the same house we grew up in and have canned soup and grilled-cheese sandwiches for supper every night. There's nothing I can do about it except feel bad, but I do that really well.

I should have climbed on happiness's coattails and stayed on them when I had the chance even though Wayne Merrill was a good man when I married him, and still is. No woman in her right mind could take that away from him. So what if he parks himself in a La-Z-Boy and falls asleep holding the remote control every night after supper? I started taking some classes when Claire got into high school, and I read in our bedroom at night while Wayne flips between channels in the living room. He's never said a harsh word to me. He deserves to be loved.

When I first got this same fifteen-point diamond that I've

worn ever since on my left hand, God gave me as clear a sign as he did Moses that I was going to pay for being in such a hurry to get out. Wayne took off for two weeks to the south of Kentucky to help his uncle, who'd broken his leg, oversee a tobacco harvest. While he was gone, I stayed in Maysfield and had the thought—so distinctly that it was like someone else's voice in my head—that if he didn't come back it would be all right with me. I'd hardly dated anyone else, and it occurred to me that I might like to, and I even knew who I wouldn't mind going to the diner with. Tommy McDonald, with his flashy grin and confident swagger, had honked and waved mightily at me the previous week.

Maybe it wouldn't have made any difference, though. Sometimes it's hard to distinguish one man from another. After I was married, some mornings I'd start to call Wayne *Daddy*, when I saw him in his coveralls, silently wolfing his bacon, eggs and buttered toast before he pecked me on the cheek and left for the plant an hour before it was time for me to get to the office. His hands are big and chapped like Daddy's, and his face has the same flat expression as the other men's. He's grown himself a beard to hide behind, but it makes him stand out instead because it has a reddish tint that doesn't match his hair—an ordinary medium-brown mixing itself into early gray—or the various mix of his unruly eyebrows. Another man, one I thought was unique, left me just as weighted with worry and alone in my own skin, so, in the end, maybe it would have made no difference at all who I'd married.

What turned out to matter was Claire.

"*Et voilà*," I say sarcastically as I detail the insertion of a new roll of toilet paper onto the holder with slow, exaggerated motions. I've come out of the bathroom to prove my point that once again he's left it empty. He looks up from the television more confused than wounded. He wouldn't talk to me this way, and I'm often ashamed of myself for doing it, an emotion that's on the losing side of a bout with irritation. Of course, he doesn't know what "*et voilà*" means. I wouldn't either except that I've been surreptitiously studying Claire's French books since her freshman year. My pronunciation is likely off even though I practice with the section called *Say It Right!* Hints in each chapter. Maybe even Claire wouldn't know what I was saying, though she probably wouldn't miss the intonation. She's enough like me that his ways get on her nerves, and in a smaller way then, I'm in the middle and arguing with her about the merits of what makes me crazy. Wayne's a good father, though, and after it seemed that we'd not have a child, I know that to him she wears the wings and sneakers of Love, even if he's not the sort to display it on his face or speak of it.

I've been addressing invitations to Claire's graduation party to members of his family and mine, and twice Wayne's asked, "Did you send one to Uncle Jimmy?" Another time he said, "What are we getting Claire?" though he's a man who for seventeen years has never known what we were giving her for Christmas until the paper and ribbons were in tatters on the floor. So I know that her graduation next month is getting to him as much as to me, but we'll never speak of it. I certainly can't talk to either of my sisters. Ellie's not had a child, though she thinks her dog is just as important and says she'd die to save him like any mother. Madalaine is so bitter about Bill leaving her that nobody else can dare to have a care of her own.

I knew a man named John Rutledge, the type to replace the empty cardboard roll, who talked and read books and told jokes within jokes, tossing up funny lines one after another like some brilliant juggler. It was partly that that drew me to him and partly that he made me believe I was a beautiful woman, nothing like what I'd seen in any mirror, even the ones that can be expected to dissemble, like that of a mother's eye. My hair was a lush, shining espresso so rich it circled around both auburn and black, my eyes much bluer, my face less round, my nose straighter, my breasts bigger. When we were apart, I never once thought that I'd be all right if I never saw him again.

It was by loving John that I knew I had never loved Wayne, and that's the only piece of knowledge I can't forgive John for giving me. But, then, maybe I ruined him, too. He was married; I was married. He gave me up before I gave him up, but in the end maybe the order didn't matter, regardless of how much I thought it did. We let each other go. It was the right thing to do, but I still miss him.

I think of sending John one of these invitations, but it is pure whimsy. The impulse comes from the notion that I could tell him that this is killing me. "John," I'd say into the softness of his sweater aching with the mixture of his cologne and cigarettes, "she has been all I've had for so long, the point of everything. When she walks across that stage, raising her is over. She's going away to college. What's left? Look at her, fair-skinned and tall, her hair dark like mine, but those big, deep brown eyes instead of my ordinary blue ones. She's what I wanted to be. I used to wear my hair the exact way she does when I was her age, can you believe that?" I wrap a short curl around my finger and pull on it hard when I think of him.

"Your eyes are not ordinary, Lydia. How can you say that? You're nuts, you know? I love your eyes. They're like patches of sky in October, you know how the sky turns that pure blue? Periwinkle, I think that's the color." How could a woman not fall in love with a man who will use the word *periwinkle*?

I can imagine John chiding me that way because he did once, when I said I was just a secretary. "You can take classes and get a degree, you can figure out what you want to be on your own. You really don't have to work for Dr. Hays until one of you dies, you know," he said. That's what I tell myself when I wonder what will become of me, but today I imagine John saying it again, telling me I will be okay when Claire leaves. It's easier to believe that way.

CHAPTER 2

"I don't see why Lydia keeps inviting me to these things," Ellie says, examining the mail scattered on the kitchen table. "Was it Daddy brought the mail in? 'Cause sometimes Charles drops something. Is this all there was? She knows I can't leave Presley. You and Daddy'll be at the party, I suppose, so there won't be anyone to watch him." A Hallmark invitation, *Please Come* printed in fancy script above a bouquet of bright balloons and a mortarboard hat, flutters from her hand back onto the table as she tosses it aside. Dust motes float like separate loose irritants in the late afternoon light as it enters the kitchen beneath the yellowed shade, half-pulled and revealing a small tear and several brown spots.

"Take him with you," Mama says from her recliner in the patchwork living room. "You always do."

"Well, I'm not going to this time. He hates being tied up, and Madalaine's kids tease him. It's not fair. Is it Presley?" Ellie's tone becomes a tender wheedle as she bends to scratch the loose skin behind the basset's ears. She follows her mother's voice into the living room in three steps. "I don't ask her to tie her kids up when they come here."

"Might not be a bad ider," Mama chuckles in a conspiratorial tone. The flesh of her bare arms emerging from her sleeveless shirt is enormous and dimpled, almost luminous in the darker corner of the room. A safety pin holds the top of her blouse together where a button is missing. Ellie is torn between correcting Mama's pronunciation and capitalizing on a rare chance to criticize Mama's prize grandchildren openly.

"She really ought to teach them better manners. All that

roughhouse and hollering jangles my nerves. Presley is much better behaved."

"Presley's all right for a *dog*." Mama lands heavily on the last word and draws it out. She loudly blows her nose, its bulbous tip exaggerated with redness, and then awkwardly tosses the crumpled tissue toward a paper grocery bag open near her chair. It misses, tumbling on the floor by several others.

"Shut up Mama. He *has* feelings, you know. And by the way, the word is pronounced *idea*."

Charles, intent on the television, laughs from the couch and claps for *The Price Is Right*. His glasses are halfway down his nose again, his graying hair askew as he chews the Juicy Fruit gum that Lydia brought him. Usually Ellie takes it away and chews it herself because Charles leaves a sticky mess of it on every table in the house, but Lydie has started tucking it in his pants pocket when Ellie isn't looking. Then he gets to have it unless Ellie takes his pants to wash them, and whatever was left of the pack glues his pocket together in the dryer. Well, Charles can just wear them that way, Ellie's decided. Too damn bad. It should hardly be her job to check Charles's pockets with everything else she has to do.

"Thaaz righ, idea, idea, ider. Seventeen thousan' dollar."

Mama ignores Charles and narrows her eyes at Ellie. "So says you, Miss Fancy Pants High Horse." She holds up a wrist and flounces it. Her layered chin rearranges itself against the bottom of her neck.

Ellie is disgusted as she often is. "Charles, for God's sake. This is a stupid rerun. You've *seen* it." Then to Mama, she changes the subject, anticipating a chance to win back the high ground. "Did you remember to tell Lydia that she has to take Charles to the doctor Tuesday at four?"

"You take 'em."

"I have told you over and over that in the first place I have to work, and..."

"Lydie works later 'n you," Mama taunts.

"Lydia works for someone who will let her off just whenever she wants. And you know I can't drive on Dixie Highway. Those turning lanes, off this way, then that way…I *can't*, you *know* that. Why do we have to have this conversation every other month?"

Mama snorts. "Git me a Coke, will you?" She says *git* deliberately, Ellie can tell, knowing how it irritates her daughter.

"Get up and get it yourself." Ellie's retaliation feels cheap, but still she puts her shoulders back and walks from the living room to her bedroom instead of into the kitchen, where the linoleum is cracked and chipped down to the black glue in spots and two of the stove burners haven't worked for three or four years. Ellie's bedroom is festooned in pink with white gilded furniture that she bought and paid for herself because it put her in mind of Lisa Marie's room in Graceland.

"That dog's about as fat as Elvis when he keeled," Mama shoots just before the slam of Ellie's door tallies her bull's-eye. "Charles," she says, then repeats, louder. "Charles! Get me a Coke, will ya?"

"Seventeen thousan' dollar…" he says without moving.

The sun has set and Ellie emerged from her room to heat the soup when Madalaine arrives with a foil-covered Pyrex dish, her ten-year-old in tow. The screen door into the kitchen slams from the vacuum of the May breeze, and Ellie jumps.

"Hello Maddie, hi Jennifer," Ellie says, composing herself deliberately.

"Hey Auntie El, where's Presley?" Jennifer, so blond she looks out of place with her dark-haired mother, ducks her head around to glance into the living room.

"Please, Jennifer, I've asked you nicely…"

"Sorry. Aunt Eleanor. Where is Mister Presley?" The girl's voice is sassy as she enunciates with exaggerated precision.

"Jen…" Madalaine warns her with the syllable. Then she

aims her voice at her sister, gesturing with her chin toward the living room. "How is she? Is the cold better?"

"What do you care?"

"Don't start with me, El. Look, I brought you a meat loaf." Madalaine holds it out, trying to distract her sister.

"Well I'm sorry. It's very nice for you and Lydia, isn't it? I'm the one left to take care of this freak show."

"For God's sake." Madalaine speaks with the frustration of the long weary in a conversation that repeats itself like hiccups. "Does it ever occur to you that I have problems too? My husband's child-lover is about to give birth. Does it occur to you that Jennifer and Brian are affected by that? That *I* am affected by that? How do you think I feel about *my* life these days? Geez, hand me a rag. This counter is covered with grease." She swipes at the discolored space next to the stove, noting that the stove itself is equally dirty. When she tries to flip on the light over the chipped sink, nothing happens. "How do you see anything around here? That light was burned out last week."

"At least you had a chance. You *had* a husband. It's not my fault if you didn't take care of him." There are faint lines across Ellie's forehead and deeper ones that connect her nose to the corners of her mouth, but her long brunette hair is fixed much the way her niece, Claire, fixes hers, which is with the sides pulled up and fastened in the back, the rest hanging loose. Ellie fixes hers with a bow, whereas Claire uses a plain tortoiseshell barrette. Today's pink bow bobs as Ellie flounces her hair with a girlish gesture related to the way she has taken to cinching in her belts two holes more tightly than would be comfortable.

Madalaine is overcome with indignation for a fleeting moment, then her eyes fill. "Bitch," she says under her breath. "Jennifer, come on, we're going."

Jennifer is in the living room teasing the dog with a handkerchief that Charles left on the end table. Presley is becoming frenetic, dashing back and forth between Charles and the television as Jennifer waves the handkerchief toward his face. "It's mine and you can't have it," she taunts. From her recliner, Mama chuckles but her throat breaks it into a cough. A moment later, Jennifer's thin arm is wrenched upward and startled, she looks up into her mother's teary face.

"I said, we're going. Leave the damn dog alone." The upward pressure of Madalaine's grip makes it awkward for Jennifer to get her feet underneath her, but her mother does not loosen her hand.

"Bye, Maw Maw," Jennifer says, scarcely above a whisper. She'll take on Auntie El, but she knows not to cross her mother when she's crying again.

Her mother is still sniffling when she and Jennifer reach the car, so Jennifer gets into the back seat of their blue Chevy. She looks out the side window as Madalaine sighs, blows her nose into a Kleenex and starts the car.

"I didn't mean to pull on your arm that way, baby," Madalaine says into the rearview mirror.

"It's okay," Jennifer says to her own faint reflection. She's told her mother that she wants her nose straightened, made as straight and small as Christina Uhlman's. Not one cheerleader at her school has a big nose, and she is afraid hers will even keep growing until it looks like her mother's family's. All of the Sams sisters have faces and noses something like Maw Maw's.

"No, it isn't. Aunt Eleanor can just be...difficult, you know how she is. Tonight she said something mean and it just, well, my feelings got hurt."

"Like Daddy hurts your feelings?"

Madalaine pauses, considering whether or not there is any similarity. "I guess so. I mean, well, see, Ellie thinks that her life is just *so* hard, you know? Like it's my fault that she never got married. But we both know the real reason..." Jennifer had once confided to Madalaine her theory about the real reason a man never proposed to Auntie El, which is Auntie El's nose, even more like Maw Maw's than Aunt Lydie's or her mother's.

"She told me that when Aunt Lydie got married she threw her bouquet to you, but when you got married you threw yours to someone else so she'd have to stay with Maw Maw and Poppy and Charles," Jennifer says.

"Uncle Charles," Madalaine corrects automatically, then her voice changes. "She *told* you that? God, I don't believe her. When did she say that to you?" Madalaine didn't wait for an answer. "She doesn't need to stay there. I've told her a million times to get her own apartment. Maw Maw and Poppy are still okay, they can take care of Charles."

"But Maw Maw is so fat..." Jennifer says cautiously. "Will you get fat like Maw Maw when you're old?"

"Absolutely not. Do you see me getting fat now? She's always been fat. It's not like Ellie really does anything, anyway. Why do you think I brought that meat loaf over?"

"Because Charles and Poppy must get tired of grilled cheese." Jennifer gives her line of the litany in a singsong. She blows her wispy bangs off her forehead, aping her mother's irritation.

"I guess they must." Madalaine feels drained and falls silent for several minutes as the car passes through aging downtown Maysfield, past Gosset's Drugstore, Lorenz Jewelry and the hundred-twenty-year-old courthouse, into an area still solidly settled in middle class. The homes here aren't new, but they're more substantial, some brick, some aluminum-sided, and there is landscaping. How to keep the house chews at Madalaine's mind. She absolutely does not want to move back into an area like the one she grew up in, a scant step above the white trash, who were a scant step above the blacks in Maysfield. All the boundaries on that miserable west side were blurry, though. There wasn't that much difference in the run-down, patched-roof houses, but the white streets mostly had sidewalks and got electricity back quicker after a lightning storm than the mixed and all-black ones. Her parents' house has a sidewalk in front of it all right, but it's a slatternly place, constructed forty years ago by an unexacting builder and little repaired since.

"Will Brian be home yet?" Jennifer says tentatively, risking a change of subject.

"He should be, honey. Aunt Lydie was going to let Claire have her car this afternoon, and Claire's going to run Brian home after...I don't remember, some meeting at school. That was nice of Claire, don't you think, to say Brian and Christy could double with her and Kevin to the prom? I really didn't want him driving. I know Aunt Lydie suggested it, but, still it was nice of Claire to go along with it."

"You let him drive me," Jennifer observes, a little miffed.

"Oh sweetheart, that's different. I don't have to worry about you trying to sit on his lap to make kissy face while he's driving now, do I? Here, come on, climb over the seat and come up front with me."

Jennifer hesitates a moment but then complies, her colt legs folding and then depositing her sideways into the front seat. Her mother laughs and reaches over to help her right herself, then caresses her hair, as long as Ellie's and Claire's, but downy and flyaway, angel hair on a Christmas tree. Clips meant to hold ponytails slip right out of it because it is so thin. Madalaine is always after her to have it cut short, but Jennifer wants it to be like a cheerleader's. Now Madalaine plays with the strands that have come loose from the rubber band to float beside Jennifer's face and over her neck. She tucks one behind Jennifer's ear, channeled neatly as a little whelk shell, nothing like Brian's, oversize and raw-looking as his hands and feet. Madalaine has always observed the details of her children closely.

"I guess you're getting too big to climb over the seat," Madalaine says, a suppressed smile playing about the corners of her mouth. It's important that Jennifer not think she was laughing at her.

"Mom, could you...I mean, could you, like, I mean, have

another one…a baby?" Jennifer hesitates and lurches through the question.

"Are you wishing for one?"

"Sort of, so Melody won't have anything over us anymore, but, I don't know, 'cause you said being a middle child is awful."

Madalaine breathes in sharply. Her eyes fill and she lets go of the wheel to use a bare wrist to wipe the sudden overflow. She doesn't answer for a moment, then exhales in a long blown-out sigh and rakes the same free hand through her straight hair. Its chin-length darkness shows odd strands of gray here and there all over the top. When she looks in a morning mirror, she is often startled; her hair looks as though she's walked through a faint spider web. It makes her unaccountably angry and she wonders if Lydie is coloring her hair these days. "I don't *want* another baby," she says, fighting to keep her tone light and losing right off. "I've got you, babe…" she sings, her voice wavery.

Madalaine signals left and turns onto the avenue that borders the section of neat crosshatched streets that Jennifer calls her neighborhood. By the time they reach their brick ranch house, with its orderly yellow shutters and doors, three bedrooms and family room with a fireplace, neither has found anything else to say.

CHAPTER 3

Mama's had a spring cold all week and because Ellie feels put upon, she's started talking about Graceland again. She completely ignores what happened when we tried that. I headed there with her almost a year ago, when Bill first left Madalaine, and I had to agree with Ellie that Maddie needed something to take her mind off things. Of course, I knew perfectly well that Maddie didn't give a hoot about Graceland and that when Ellie suggested that I drive the three of us to Memphis, it had a whole lot more to do with Ellie and her ridiculous obsession than our sister's broken heart. Ellie went on about how Elvis's songs could help Maddie if she'd let them, and how we should go during Death Week.

"Death Week? *Death Week?*" I don't usually get sarcastic with Ellie, but honestly. Sometimes it doesn't seem possible that the four of us swam out of the same gene pool, no matter how much we look alike. "Oh yes, I can see how Death Week would cheer her right up." The whole family was at my house. I'd invited them to cook out on the Fourth of July, hoping that the commotion would jolt Maddie out of her zombie state. Ellie and I were in my kitchen. I was making potato salad while Ellie was standing around adjusting her bra straps and smoothing the front of her flowered sundress.

"Don't you know 'Hurt'? That song's exactly what she's going through," she said. "And my chart says the week of August fourteenth is ideal for a trip. The anniversary is the sixteenth, so you can see it's a sign." Ellie reached back and fixed her bow while she acted wounded and indignant at the same time.

I rolled my eyes, but managed not to say anything about her

astrological chart, which is how Ellie justifies every batty notion she gets. "Yes, and Bill is a hound dog who belongs in the jailhouse to sing the blues to that…teenager…he's taken up with, but El, *Death Week*? I'm afraid it will give her ideas…." I tried to make my voice patient and nice while I beat the potato salad into smithereens. I smiled at her, but she wasn't buying it.

"Let's just let Maddie decide, then." She was huffy.

To my disgust, Maddie said, "Yeah, okay, whatever you want," in a spiritless way that made me want to put my hands around her neck and squeeze hard just to make her stand up for herself. Instead, the next month I was stuck driving the three of us seven hours southwest to Memphis. I've always been like this. In my head I'm firm and direct and say no to crazy things, no matter who wants to do them, even me. In real life, though, anyone can leech the will right out of me, and I deliver the goods quietly with despair and a smile.

Except when it came to John. Being with him was my will, and the only time in my life I did exactly what I really wanted. It was like looking into a mirror and seeing a reckless stranger there. What was bizarre was that about a month before John and I met, I'd been to a classmate's baby shower. Sherry, the hostess, had gone and paid a psychic from the Yellow Pages twenty-five dollars to come read our minds and palms and tarot cards. I can remember her exact words, when it was my turn. She first held my hand and sat a minute with her eyes closed. Then she opened them and studied me without a word, still holding my hand. Finally she bent over my palm another throbbing minute.

"I see you have problems with love," she said.

"Not really," I said. "I'm happily married except when I'm picking up his dirty socks." The women around me laughed and stacked up agreement about what slobs their husbands were.

"Any port in a storm," she said with a shrug. "You will love."

"I do love," I corrected.

"My mistake," she said coolly and went on. "I see a child, yes, a daughter, correct?" She traced a branch on my hand with a short unpolished nail. She did not look like a fortune teller. No blood-red lips and nails, no black eye makeup or black-dyed hair. And she was wrong again. That was during the time that I'd been trying for two years to get pregnant. Wayne's sperm count made his shoe size look like a big number, and my friends' baby showers were endurance trials for me. We were talking about adopting, even though Dr. Hays had told him to switch to boxer shorts and think big.

"No, I have no children."

She lifted my palm closer to her face. "This is not the hand of a childless woman," she said. My friends' voices receded into silence.

"Well, your mistake again," I said lightly into the dead quiet of my own aura, and went home to cry in the bathtub that night.

The thing is, within weeks I met John. Okay, so "problems with love," could be said of any woman alive and breathing who doesn't live in a convent. But what about the fact that less than two years later my Anna Claire was born? "Character is fate," my sophomore English teacher kept telling us when we read *Oedipus Rex* and *Antigone*. I don't believe that anymore. After what happened, I think fate is fate.

Sometimes it seems as though my whole real life was compressed into those couple of years, the time I spent with John, and later, when I was actually carrying a baby and felt her quickening, first a butterfly inside, and then like a Mack truck trying to turn around in a closet. In between a pain like an enormous single amaryllis bloomed, so red, so intense it made me want to die, but that too, in retrospect, seems vital and more alive than I was before or after. Maybe when I tried to take Maddie and Ellie to Graceland, silly as it sounds, I hoped that something *would* happen. Nothing like a magical healing for Maddie, or a mystical balm flowing over Ellie's shriveled heart—or mine, for that matter—but that, well, maybe the three of us would have a good time together. I wanted to laugh, to feel connected to my sisters in a way I couldn't lose because they'd always be right near me, unlike Claire who I refuse to keep from having her own life. I should have known better. Sometimes I hardly think I know them at all.

That was the thing with John. When we first started talking, I felt as connected to him as threads woven into a cloth of coherent plaid. I say *when we first started talking,* instead of *when we met,* because that's how it happened. I'd been going to Kathy's Kookin' Kafe for a couple of years, just whenever I hadn't had time in the morning to put a tuna sandwich together, or I had, but then stuck it in the refrigerator at the office to save for the next day because someone died and I had to get out for a while. Kathy's was a little lunch counter downtown that had six booths. If it wasn't busy, I'd take a booth for myself and read while I ate. Other days, I'd have to sit at the counter, but that really didn't bother me. I'd eat quickly and walk the long way back to the office, especially if it was a spectacular autumn and the air tingled with the clarity of burnt orange against blue.

And that's exactly how it happened. On that kind of October day, I got to Kathy's right at noon and, of course, the booths were full. I slid onto a stool and ordered my usual chicken salad on wheat. Kathy set my hot tea in front of me and mixed concern into her smile. "So who died?"

I shook my head. "Dick Bradshaw had a stroke. He's in ICU over at St. Elizabeth's."

"Why there?"

"He was airlifted. They've got a better neurology department than we do, and, you know, Joan insisted."

"I can imagine," Kathy said, with a knowing nod. "I'll hope for the best. He hasn't been in here for weeks. I wonder if he hadn't been feeling well…."

"Excuse me," said the man sitting on my left. "I couldn't help overhearing. Did you say Dick Bradshaw had a stroke?"

The man had dark brown hair, curly and close-cropped except in the front where it dipped purposely over a broad forehead. Straight nose and straighter teeth, the completely perfect ones that say *my parents had the money for braces*. Brown eyes, the kind women call pretty eyes, beneath groomed heavy brows. He was near enough that I smelled his cologne, definitely not Wayne's Old Spice (which he practically showers in when he wants to have sex, after all these years still not remembering that it nearly makes me gag). This man was altogether too good-looking, in a pinstripe suit and subtle maroon tie, not the common Maysfield man in a baseball cap, coveralls and work boots. I was immediately put off. I shouldn't have mentioned a patient's name. I usually told Kathy, but she knew not to spread it around. This was different.

"I'm really not supposed to discuss it. I'm sorry...." I trailed off and looked at my tea.

"It's just that I'm a lawyer, too, and he's a friend, well, not a close friend, but I know him and I'd be sorry if anything happened to him."

I relented a little. "Well..." I began, a beginning indeed. We talked all through lunch. He had a third cup of coffee and Kathy brought me a new pot of hot water, and by the time I left to go back to work, it was way too late to take the long way back.

CHAPTER 4

Madalaine lowers herself into a chair like a much older woman, to put her feet up on the glass coffee table for a few minutes before making dinner. Evening is overtaking the living room from the carpeting up, and she wishes she could just darken into sleep with the furniture. She looks around and allows herself a moment of comfort. This room has always been her favorite because of the brick fireplace and carved wood mantel, where framed pictures of the children are precisely arranged with brass candlesticks holding dusty rose tapers. A wreath of dried roses, eucalyptus and baby's breath hangs above the mantel and it still pleases Madalaine to see how it picks up the soft green and rose and cream of the room, even now, when everything has come down on her at once. She sighs when the back door slams. It takes Brian only seconds to drop his backpack on the kitchen floor and spot his mother through the dining L, in the semidarkness of the next room. He bounds toward her.

"Mom!" Brian is loud, as if she weren't three feet away.

"Brian!" she mimics and then pointedly lowers her voice. "I can hear you and so can the neighbors. What is it?"

He flops on the couch dramatically. "Do you know what a corsage costs?"

"I can't say as I've purchased one of those lately."

"Those little rose things are fourteen dollars and gardenias are sixteen-fifty. Christy wants gardenias."

"Well Christy may have to settle for carnations."

"Mom. No way. Nobody is getting carnations. Christy says they're tacky."

"Maybe Christy should just buy her own corsage. Or maybe

you should get a job so you can get her gardenias and rent your own tuxedo and buy your own tickets." The words are serrated, and she begins thumbing through the TV guide, carefully saved from the Sunday paper, to calm her irritation.

Brian explodes, thrusting a hand forward in accusation. "*You're* the one who said prom should be special. And you're the one who told me it was okay if I ran track again. I don't even have time to get a job and save enough money. That's not fair."

"Life's—"

"God, Mom. Life's not fair. God. Don't you ever get sick of yourself saying that?" Brian hoists himself to his feet, his neck reddening. "I'll ask Dad for money, okay? Will that satisfy you?" The boy lopes from the room without looking back, his arms and legs too long, out of scale with his body.

Madalaine begins to call his name sharply, but sinks back into the upholstery before the second syllable. Brian doesn't hold grudges, one of the qualities that has saved Madalaine too many times lately. Of course his girlfriend wants gardenias for the prom. Hadn't Madalaine herself? And hadn't Bill given them to her? She'll call Claire to ask whether she should order a wrist corsage or a pin-on one. Claire can be relied on in ways Brian can't, to know what will be exactly right.

There are times that Madalaine envies Lydia for having Claire. How can one girl be so nearly perfect—prettier than anyone in the family, no Sams-woman nose, smart, mature, dependable as daylight? Of course, Jennifer may turn into that sort, though at ten Claire already shone in ways Jennifer doesn't. But Brian is just your basic teenage boy, a passable-but-not-excellent student, sports obsessed, who bumbles across his own emotions, tries, and tries to hide his own trying. He will be huge, like Bill, in another couple of years when he finishes growing. Meanwhile, he nearly trips on himself unless he has a ball in his hands, when he turns oddly graceful, a dancing buffalo, she thinks. Not that Madalaine would trade either of her children for anything or anyone in the world. Not at all. They are her life. It's her habit of minute examination and observation of them that leads her to compare them to other children their ages, wanting her own to be perfect enough that the world will not hurt them. When she sees their flaws, she knows they're vulnerable, and doesn't know how she'll protect them.

"You can't protect them," Bill used to say when Madalaine argued with Brian about whether his fall jacket would keep him warm if it rained that day, or whether Jennifer had memorized her spelling words.

"That's my job. I'm supposed to protect them. I'm their mother, in case you hadn't noticed," she would snap back, incensed at his nonchalance.

"They have to learn," he'd say, angling his shoulders so that his enormous body would not face her head-on. His face and ears would redden, making him look foolish, a rough patchwork of pink and white. "Let them take their lumps."

"I'm teaching them how to manage their lives. Kids don't just absorb that from the wallpaper, and they're certainly not going to learn it by imitating you."

That, or a similar retort from Madalaine, usually ended the argument. Bill would withdraw from the room, disgusted and defeated at once, and she would attend to one child or the other or both. She had concluded that Bill didn't, *couldn't*, understand the fierce, visceral connection she had to the children. Madalaine attributed that inability to his being male, until he told her he was leaving the efficiency apartment he'd been in for only a few months to move in with Melody.

"I have an obligation to the baby…and to Melody," he said, looking her in the face righteously, and at that moment Madalaine's fury detonated like a land mine in the terrain between them. He'd lost weight and begun to grow a beard that glowed faintly pink beneath the high ruddiness of his cheeks and his still-blond hair. Both of her children looked like him. He was wearing a sapphire-blue striped shirt Madalaine had never seen, one that brought out the blue of his eyes. They'd always been more gray than hers, but the shirt made them startling, noticeable.

"You can talk about obligation? *You* can talk about obligation? What about your *obligation* to your legitimate children? You can *do* this to *them*?" Her voice rasped hoarsely, emphatic on certain syllables. She gesticulated wildly, her hair bobbing out of place across her forehead and cheeks.

"I haven't left the children," he said pointedly, with a calm that infuriated Madalaine even more as he turned and extended his long reach toward the front door. "Tell them..."

"I'll tell them the *truth*," she said, and intended it as a threat.

"I guess in time they'll figure out the truth for themselves," he said, and left, the door clicking quietly as a period when he closed it.

It made no sense to Madalaine then, and still doesn't. Even in the moments when she is composed, she cannot follow the white thread that should lead from the intentions of her heart to what has become of them. She was a good wife; she *is* a good wife. She had married Bill, and been a good wife. She has hardly spoken to another man in seventeen years. She does not deserve this. *Lydia*, maybe. She could *see* this happening to Lydie. There might be a modicum of fairness in that.

Madalaine sets a plate piled with four pieces of chicken, mashed potatoes, broccoli with cheese sauce and four carrot sticks down with deliberate gentleness on the kitchen table. Across from and next to it, on green place mats neatly set with paper napkins and utensils, she sets two plates with much less food on them. "Brian! Jen! Come on to dinner."

A shuffle of feet sounds in the hall a moment later. Brian and Jennifer are bickering about the television when they reach the kitchen. They pull out chairs noisily and sit, continuing to fuss at each other without real animosity in their tones. Madalaine looks at them without listening as she puts some bread and butter on the table, seeing their sheer, fair coloring, the too-fine, milkweed texture of their hair, their matching blue eyes. Brian has just started to shave, not that he really needs to, and a couple of days' worth of errant hair juts from his chin. Light falls over them in an indistinct circle, and Madalaine feels tears behind her eyes.

"Hey, you two. Let's have a nice dinner, okay? Brian, please get yourself and Jen some milk, and let's talk about exactly what you need for the prom." Madalaine speaks engagingly as she turns off burners on the stove and adjusts the rheostat to lower the intensity of the light from the fixture that hangs by a chain over the kitchen table.

As she knew he would, Brian has forgiven her. "Okay. I need my tux, and Christy wants my tie and cumberbund to match her dress. Hot-pink."

"Gross," Jennifer says. "You'll look like a total dork."

"That's cum*mer*bund, honey," Madalaine puts in.

"Whatever. And I've got to buy the tickets and pay for dinner. Claire and Kevin want to go to Miada's, and Christy says that's cool. I don't care where we go."

"Wow. This is an expensive proposition. And the gardenias, right?"

"Right."

"Okay. Well, I called Claire, and she says a wrist corsage is best."

"Oh. What's that?"

Madalaine smiles warmly and launches into an explanation. There is no way Bill would have thought to check on what kind of corsage the girls were wearing, and Christy doesn't know about the difference or she would have told Brian. They're still children, but this is Madalaine's watch and she'll see that they are cared for.

Ellie is doing the supper dishes again, something she gets stuck with sooner or later every day. They had Maddie's stinking meat loaf two nights in a row, and even though the pan sat in the sink soaking for two more days, blackened residue is bonded to the metal like dried gum to Charles's damn pockets. Leave it to Maddie to bring something that Ellie would have to clean up. Daddy, Mama and Charles are watching *Hard Copy* in the living room with the volume so high that the neighbors must be going deaf. Ellie has a Walkman, not a real *Walkman,* but a little cassette player with headphones that she asked Claire for when Claire got a new, actual *Sony Walkman* for Christmas. It's not that she couldn't afford to buy one, but why spend the money? Claire didn't care. Now Ellie can listen to one of her *Elvis's Greatest Hits* tapes when she wants to shut out her family. Which is a lot of the time. Tonight, for example.

Maddie and Lydie both called today. It would mean something if one of them would *do* something, not just leave her with taking care of Mama and Daddy and Charles. It's ridiculous, like one of Charles's notions, the way Lydie says, "Go ahead, get your own place. All of us can help Mama and Daddy when they need help, you know, you don't have to live there. We'll work it out." Stupid, stupid, stupid. Who would stay with Presley during the day? Not that anyone here really cares, but Presley is terrified of being alone.

Such a fuss all the time about the prom. Of course, Lydie and Maddie both went to their proms, so it doesn't wring them out every time the subject pops up like a dandelion. Ellie didn't get to go to a prom, no, of course not. Lydie and Maddie had already moved out by the time Ellie's senior prom rolled around and word had obviously gotten around school that Ellie had to take care of her mama and daddy and pathetic brother. Why can't her sisters think about how she might feel when they talk about Claire's shoes, or Brian getting some gardenia wrist corsage for his girlfriend?

At night, she sees herself with a man like Elvis on the screen behind her eyes. To "Love Me Tender," Ellie touches herself like the petals of a flower, where a man would. Sometimes, she readies herself first, undressing and releasing her dark hair from its bow slowly, shaking it to fall lushly around her shoulders. She looks at her body in the full-length mirror in her room and sees that her hips are only a little wider than her shoulders, her thighs not so dimpled as either Maddie's or Lydie's. Her breasts are fuller than her sisters', too, though they aren't like Mama's misshapen watermelons, thank God. Sometimes she imagines Elvis watching from behind her mirror. She lifts a breast in each hand and creates a sensuous cleavage, coyly pretending she doesn't know he's there....

She lies down on her double bed in a pink negligee, one strap slipped down to lie against her shoulder and reveal a rich curve of flesh. She closes her eyes to watch herself move through the rooms of Graceland before catching up with herself here, in their bedroom, where she has gradually spread her legs. If he hadn't died, she would have been at a concert somehow, somewhere, and he would have picked her out. He would have known her anywhere. Neither of them would be lonesome tonight.

CHAPTER 5

"I'm so sick of you all going on about the prom. Don't you have anything else to talk about?" That's what I got from Ellie when I told her that the shoe store could dye Claire's blue fabric shoes black after all. When it's not the prom, it's some other avenue that runs to and circles the personal Arc de Triomphe she's erected to prove I'm at fault for her life. I have tried to talk to her, but she is like a reinforced steel door, slammed and locked against any other way of looking at it.

When I agreed to take her and Maddie to Graceland, it was hope that moved my mouth, not reason. I should have known—I *did* know—that it would be a disaster. First of all, there was the whole Death Week nonsense. Ellie packed more white candles than clothes in her suitcase. How much foresight would it have taken to realize that putting that suitcase in the trunk of the car during an August that was melting sidewalks and making the air a choking, wavy yellow color was not a good idea? But that isn't even what went wrong, not at first anyway.

What first went wrong was that Maddie was still moving like a robot and hardly speaking at all. She needed a psychiatrist, maybe electroshock therapy, not to climb in the back seat of my green Ford that couldn't have air-conditioned Alaska in the winter, let alone Death Week. After that trip, I developed a theory that what actually killed Elvis was that he inadvertently opened a window and the Memphis heat overcame and drowned him in his own sweat. We decided to go south to Knoxville and detour through the Great Smoky Mountains. Gatlinburg, a little tourist town there, was a common vacation destination among Ellie's friends at Wal-Mart.

"I've never been anyplace in my life," Ellie complained. "This way I can see the Smokies on the way to Graceland, and the people at work can stop lording it over me."

The driving fell to me. Ellie refused to help because she's convinced that every freeway trucker who gazes down from his cab with a broken-toothed grin is trying to look down her blouse. This forces her to ride with both hands pressing the cloth to her upper chest. I used to explain that if she'd consider driving over thirty-eight miles an hour on the freeway, every truck wouldn't find it necessary to pass her, but I've given up. And Maddie was in no condition to drive. She slumped back right away, her head against the seat, staring at the roof of the car while tears used their familiar stream beds down her face after they squeezed out from beneath her closed eyes. Presley ran back and forth across the back seat over Maddie's lap. Sometimes he'd catch one of his feet between her thighs and struggle a moment to get it free. Even that she didn't notice.

I'd taken three of my ten vacation and/or sick days to tack onto the weekend, loaded my own stuff in the car and gone over to pick up Maddie first, then Ellie. Maddie walked out with just her purse, so I had to go in and pack some underwear, clothes and a toothbrush for her myself. Bill was keeping Brian and Jennifer because Maddie had to let him see them, but Maddie was convinced he would take them over to Melody's. Her attorney had warned her that she *had* to let Bill see the children even if he *was* an adulterous dickhead, which was how Maddie put it to him in a rare flash fire. Unless she could show that Bill or Melody had somehow abused the children, well, then, Bill had the right to see them, the lawyer told her.

"Running around with a slut barely out of her teens who's obviously got the intelligence and morals of an alley cat? Are you telling me that the court says *that's* just fine?"

"No ma'am," he responded with weary gentility. I'd gone with her, and could see in the furrows puckering his eyes and the liver spots on his hands that too many other outraged women shouted those words. "And no doubt he's everything you say he is, including the children's father, and that's the part that gives him the right to see them. Unless you believe he has...molested them? Perhaps, well, your little girl?" The last two sentences were a glittering nugget in the pan of gravel.

I watched Maddie and a shiver passed between us on a frequency only a Sams woman could hear. "Maddie, no," I said.

"Damn," she said to me. "Damn." And huge tears gathered in the wells of her eyes and hovered on the edges. "No," she said to the attorney in his three-piece suit behind his mahogany desk, and the tears tracked a path through her makeup. "But he's certainly screwed me. I take it that doesn't count."

"No, ma'am, unfortunately that doesn't count."

So Madalaine was a wreck when I picked her up to go to Graceland. After the visit to the attorney, she had withdrawn to a place that was desolate and wordless. "Well, she can mourn at Graceland," Ellie had said to me, "that's what people *do* there, you know."

We went on over to Mama and Daddy's. Maddie shook her head in mute refusal of an unspoken question when we pulled up, and waited in the car while I went in for Ellie. Ellie, of course, couldn't begin to carry everything she couldn't live without, and had a separate bag packed for Presley.

"Wait a minute," I said when I saw her putting on Presley's leash. "You're not serious?"

"Whatever is the matter with you Lydie? You know perfectly well that Presley can't stay here with them. It's one thing for them to watch him when I'm at work, but there's no way he wouldn't be scared to death if I weren't with him overnight. I've never been away before. He's only five for heaven's sake."

"We can't bring the dog into a motel. And what will we do with him in the car anyway?"

"People bring their children into motels all the time. And Presley likes the car, it doesn't bother him at all as long as you don't go around curves too fast. So just be careful for once." She thrust a bag of dog food into my arms, which I took in a sort of involuntary reflex, and went on to the car, Presley's leash in one hand and a suitcase in another. Two more bags were packed and set by the kitchen door.

"You'd be best off in the back," Ellie said to Maddie when she reached the car with me in tow. Obviously, Ellie saw this as her show. "I'll throw up if I ride back there, and Presley will cheer you up." Without a word of protest, Maddie just got out and dragged her body to the back seat.

"Turn up the air-conditioning," Ellie demanded.

"It's up all the way."

"It can't be."

"This is an old car. It can only do so much. It must be over a hundred outside."

"Well, it's certainly over a hundred in here." Ellie was going to drive me insane, I knew it. "You need to stop," she said a few minutes later. "I have to go to the bathroom."

"Couldn't you have gone at home? We just left a half hour ago." I was split between just giving in right away to whatever she said, and trying to hang on to some small memory of how reasonable people act.

"Gert says that it's bad for a woman to hold it when she has to go."

"Is Gert a hairdresser or a urologist?" I said, coating my annoyance with a small laugh as I drove past a gas station pretending that she hadn't just asked me to stop.

"She knows a lot about women's bodies," Ellie said, patting the bow on her ponytail. "She's also a spiritual adviser. She could help you, Maddie." Ellie swiveled to look at Maddie in the seat behind her. I watched in the rearview mirror.

"Will she kill someone for me?" Maddie roused herself to speak, but kept her eyes closed.

"You mean like voodoo? Sticking pins into a statue? She

doesn't do anything like that. She helps you know what your soul needs," Ellie said.

"I mean like with a gun." Maddie's eyes flamed open for a brief second before she closed up again.

"Poison might work nicely, too. Let's play alphabet. Every letter has to stand for a way to kill Bill," I tossed in, hoping to inspire Maddie to anything but this terrible defeat, but she didn't bat an eye or answer again.

Ellie stiffened with disapproval. "That's not respectful when we're going to mourn someone who is dead."

I would have dropped it, but irritation stirred Maddie for a moment. "Lighten up, Ellie," she said. "I think it's a hell of an idea. I'll start. Arson."

"Burning," I pushed on.

"That's not really a different way," said Maddie.

"Burning at the stake?"

"Okay. That's different."

"C…C…hmm." I didn't want to waste any momentum when Maddie was even slightly distracted from suffering, but nothing leaped to mind for C.

"Oh come on, it's too easy. Combine. Let a combine run over him," she said. Her voice sounded propped up from the back seat and when I found her in the rearview mirror, she looked slightly bemused. Next to me, Ellie was drawn up in silent, offended judgment, doubtless praying for Elvis to keep her pure.

"Draw and quarter," I went on, trying to spread hope like soft butter.

"Ether, the silent killer."

"Fling him from the top of a mountain." I came up with this after searching a moment.

"No, no, no! Fuck him to death. Let Melody fuck him to death," Maddie broke in, a half shout gurgling into a diabolical laugh. I'd never heard Maddie—still as Baptist as the original when he waded into the river—use the word before, but my nearly dead sister was actually laughing. Maybe Ellie's stupid trip idea wasn't so stupid. I encouraged Maddie with the most mirthful laughter I could conjure.

I wouldn't have believed it if I hadn't been there: Ellie, congenitally lacking a sense of humor, giggled. "Let her gag him with her G-string while she fucks him to death, and it'll take care of two letters." This was even more out of character for Ellie than for Maddie.

"Pretty good, Ellie. I'm proud of you." Maddie leaned forward to pat Ellie's shoulder, chortling with her.

"Heart attack!" I said, figuring it was my turn. "Let him have a heart attack while he's gagged with Melody's G-string and she fucks him right to a heart attack." Maddie and Ellie gave roars of appreciation.

"I…okay, we'll let him live and be both impotent and incontinent for a month before Melody…" Maddie couldn't even repeat the rest of the sentence for boiling-over laughter, which started me laughing again, at Maddie this time, and Ellie was really warming up; I could see her mentally scanning the *J* category.

"I'm torn between jimsen weed and a javelin," she said. "Of course, it would be awfully nice if Melody publicly jilted him first."

"Wow, Ellie. A whole new side of you. I'm impressed," I said, with utter sincerity.

"There you go! Ellie can leave Wal-Mart and become the chief designer of Creative Executions, Inc. You can be her driver and I'll do highly paid hits. Except when some poor woman wants a certified asshole husband knocked off, that will be our pro bono work. It'll even be tax deductable," Maddie shrieked.

"Will you please stop? Now I swear I'm going to pee my pants." Ellie doubled over.

"Sure. Oh, wow, if we go back to *D*, we could drown him in his own pee, that'd be good since we're making him incontinent," I said.

"No good," Ellie said. "Those letters aren't next to each other."

"Who died and made you rule director?" I said. "This is my invention."

"No one…*yet*…however, I am chief designer, remember? Your idea lacks…um…"

"Organization," Maddie put in. "It's unorganized when the letters aren't consecutive." This, and Maddie hasn't even gone to college.

"Thank you very much," Ellie said to Maddie. "That. What she said," Ellie said to me.

"I guess I see your point. I'll do better," I said.

"Good. Now let's get on with it. Get off at the next exit so I can pee and meanwhile, I believe we're at the *Ks*. Your turn, Lydie."

I was ready. "Kebab. We'll cut him up, put the pieces on a skewer, do it up on a grill and serve him to Melody with barbecue sauce."

"Yes! Very nice, good job, very nice." My sisters' voices were a soprano chorus, and we all fell apart again.

I have never had that much fun or felt that close to them before or since. We went on like that through a bathroom stop for Ellie, and an hour later when we stopped for lunch. After the second stop, we lapsed into a comfortable silence, each of us settled into our own thoughts. Maddie napped a little, which I was glad to see. Traffic on I-75 south wasn't bad, and we were in the bluegrass region, soft hills comforting as breasts rising around us as we approached the foothills of the Smoky Mountains. Well before we reached the Tennessee border, though, Ellie's mood crossed a line. As the land became more mountainous, she kept her blouse clamped against her throat with only one hand. The other clutched the padded handle of her car door. Her feet, rigid as wooden carvings, pressed on imaginary dual brakes on the floorboard.

Thinking the heat might be on her nerves, I said, "You know, it may be a little cooler in the mountains. I don't think there'll be much hope for Memphis, though." All of us were cooked by then, the sun pressing relentlessly against the car and into our eyes in the early afternoon, the air an oily heaviness on us when we tried opening windows for the breeze of the moving car.

"Wonderful," Ellie said, her voice saturated with sarcasm as though our earlier hilarity had never happened. "Does it occur to you that some people may be frightened? Perhaps you could think of someone else and slow down?"

"I'm under the limit," I said.

"I don't care what you're under, or on, for that matter, just slow down," Ellie said. In the back seat, Maddie stirred and yawned.

The interstate curved and climbed. It did seem that traffic veered impossibly close to the squat guardrail, which didn't seem as though it would stop a bicycle from flying over the edge. Trucks groaned and downshifted, slowing. When I dared sneak a glance at her, Ellie looked paralyzed except for her breathing, which was too fast. I went as slowly as I dared, which wasn't slowly enough.

"For God's sake, stop," Ellie yelled. Presley barked twice and began pacing back and forth on the back seat, climbing over Maddie, who sat up straight then, but didn't say anything. "Can't you see you're terrifying Presley?" Ellie's voice shrilled toward hysteria.

A shout rose like a wave in my chest. I clenched my teeth to hold it back and tried to stay focused on the road. "If you'll open your eyes instead of your mouth, you'll see that there is no place to stop," I said, as evenly as I could. Of course, I was telling God's own truth. The road had narrowed to four lanes crammed into a niche that had been blasted out of a perpendicular mountainside.

"Stop! Stop! Stop!" Ellie was screaming then, Presley barking and running back and forth behind us. Maddie began crying, moaning, "Bill, Bill, Bill," in a strange counterpoint to Ellie's "Stop, stop, stop." If I could have, I would have stopped just then, to throw the two of them and the damn dog off the mountain. The car rocked with emotion; my ears were clogging up and about to detonate. A semi bore down into my rearview window and its horn blasted twice. Ellie screamed again. The truck moved into the left lane where he lingered alongside me, holding up traffic behind him but apparently unable to generate the speed to pass.

There was no exit for another five or six minutes until we were on the other side. When I realized there was a little valley town, it was nearly upon me and at the last minute I signaled to get off to the right and slowed even more to prepare for the ramp. As I did, the truck that had blasted me earlier apparently decided to move to the right again. Maybe the driver miscalculated how much more I'd dare to slow the car before I actually turned off. All I know is that suddenly, just before I reached the turn, the guardrail was to my right and the truck looming from my left. We vibrated from the sheer nearness of the semi. Ellie and Maddie both screamed, lurching forward from the unexpected forward thrust of the car as I frantically accelerated and turned onto the exit ramp simultaneously.

The din in the car mixed with the semi's steady horn.

I brought the car to a stop as soon as we turned off the exit ramp onto a two-lane highway. Ellie's face was white, her breathing coming in ragged gasps. "You're trying to kill us," she got out finally. On the floor of the back seat Presley whined and barked once more. Maddie was crying.

"God, Ellie, I did not try to kill us. Maddie, are you all right?"

"Bill. I want Bill."

"Are you all right?" She was scaring me, and I reached over the back seat to touch her leg.

"No she's not all right. Neither am I and neither is Presley. Come on, Maddie, we're getting out of here, I have to get out of here, I can't stand that," said Ellie, glancing at the mountains and then quickly turning her face away. "They're going to fall on us. I can't breathe. My heart, oh God, my heart is going too fast."

"What? Where are you going? What are you talking about? Let's find a restaurant and rest a while, wash our faces in cool water and get a cold drink.

"No! Not another inch," Ellie said, drawing her body against the car door in horror.

"Fine. You drive."

"I'm not driving. I can't drive here, I can't stay here. They're falling, it's going to fall." Her words came too fast and ran together, and she gestured up.

"What do you want me to do?" I said, desperation looming like the mountain above us.

"Maddie, you come with me, we're going home," Ellie said, getting out of the car. "Come on, Presley, come to Mommy, sweetheart."

Maddie had apparently lapsed back into her robot state. Still crying, she started to obey.

"Maddie! No!" I said sharply. "This is crazy. Stay here."

Maddie just slumped back into the seat then, great tears coursing down her cheeks. "Bill," she sobbed. "Bill. Take me back to Bill."

We ended up spending the night in a motel in that little town. It wasn't a franchise, predictable and comforting as their sameness can be, but a little roadside place, dingy and poorly lit. Threadbare pink chenille spreads were tucked over a pair of single beds stuck against too-close tan walls. The owner brought in a cot for me and with that addition, there was nowhere to step. The air-conditioning had been installed through the outside wall, and I was almost grateful for its constant wheeze and churning. Maddie had gone on crying—hard, racking sobs from some place she'd not been before—and Ellie refused to speak. She was too afraid, she said, to get Presley's food and dishes and her three bags from the trunk, panting that she couldn't breathe. The mountains were going to fall on her; she'd seen Watch for Falling Rocks signs on the freeway. That night she huddled in a fetal position, her back to us, her breathing shallow and too fast, it seemed. At 4:30 in the morning, Presley whined. Ellie lay there stubborn and unmoving as cement, though I waited nearly ten minutes before I got up and took him out.

The next day, none of us wanted breakfast even though we'd not had dinner the night before. I bought a map at a gas station and used back roads as long as I could before I got on the freeway again. All the way home, no one said a word, necessary or otherwise.

"You back early?" Wayne said when he came in from work that afternoon. The kitchen door slammed against heat that pressed like weights. In the car, I had had rivulets of sweat running beneath my clothes, and Presley had paced and whined intermittently into the silence my radio could not fill.

"A little," I said.

"Oh. Did you have a good time?"

"Great."

"Good. Are we eating soon?" he asked

That wasn't my first, but it was my final attempt to travel with my sisters to the land of grace, so to speak. Since then, I've kept a certain distance, not so they can necessarily tell, but leaving enough room to fit a certain shield. I still do more than my part with Mama and Daddy and Charles, taking them to their doctors and the like, even though it's no easier for me to take off work than for anyone else. The distance is more a matter of hoping for less from Maddie and Ellie than I used to, and that wasn't a whole lot at its peak. Madalaine is stumbling through this thing with Bill and his paramour, and Ellie goes on complaining about Mama and Daddy and Charles. Certain things Madalaine knows about me I wish she didn't, but there's nothing I can do about it.

Claire is sweet to Brian, but that's not something she does for my benefit, it's just her way. I did suggest that she and her boyfriend double with Brian and his girlfriend to the prom, since the laminate on Brian's license is barely dry, but the truth is that the thought had already occurred to Claire. Brian's a young sixteen, not self-possessed, and I know Maddie would have worried herself to death. Everything I've tried to do for my family has pretty much struck back at me like a snake, and I've spent too much time trying to suck the poison out of my own heart.

CHAPTER 6

Madalaine stands behind Brian, who's at the bathroom mirror, adjusting the back of his collar and bow tie, as much as he will let her, anyway. It will be much easier and more fun when it's Jennifer's turn, yet Maddie looks at her son with an unfamiliar admiration, taking pride in his masculinity and even in the way he makes it difficult for her to know what's going on inside him.

Whatever possessed him to agree to a hot pink cummerbund and tie? she wonders. The color is disastrous near his face, where Clearasil has lost the battle against a new, angry flare of acne.

"Are you sure that's how this thing goes? It's killing me," he says, pulling at the tie.

"I know, honey. I mean, men always complain about ties, so I guess they must be really uncomfortable, but yes, that's how it goes," Madalaine answers, though she steps closer to try again. It's then, on an intake of breath, that she realizes that Brian is wearing Bill's cologne. She didn't think he'd left any here, and then it occurs to her that Bill gave it to Brian, or, less likely, he'd bought it himself. The aroma affects her in a wave and she steps back. "Are you nervous?" she says.

"No. I guess. I don't know."

"Well, let's see. Remember you don't just shove the corsage at her and grunt. Tell her, 'This is for you,' and that she looks beautiful, and hand the box to her nicely."

"I can't say that in front of her parents."

"Of course you can. Believe me, they'll notice if you don't. And say something nice to Claire, too. Girls need that, honey."

"Claire's not a girl, she's my cousin. She'd think it was weird if I said she looked good."

"Claire most certainly won't think it's weird, and for heaven's sake, Brian, it's awfully nice of her to take you."

"She's not taking me. We're doubling." He was fooling with the part in his hair now, trying to get it perfectly straight.

"Well, I imagine she could have doubled with other seniors. Do you want me to fix your part?"

"I've got it okay now," he says, as he leans closer to the mirror and does it again.

Madalaine watches him in the mirror, and then her eyes are drawn sideways, to her own reflection where her eyes appear as pale islands set in deep gray ponds. She notices lines between her nose and mouth, and horizontal ones in neat parallels across her neck. The gray webbing in her hair, especially to the right of her side part, looks harsh. Really, her face looks mismatched with itself, still young and too old at the same time, none of the changes blending in a natural or attractive way on the face of the person she used to be in her life with Bill. Even the weight she's unintentionally lost—after so many years of struggle with an extra fifteen pounds—hasn't made her look better, just tired. She wonders what her son sees when he looks at her, and what he sees when he looks at Melody. She catches his eyes on her as she looks at herself, and smiles immediately to distract him.

"So, handsome one, it looks like you're ready. Claire and Kevin should be here now, so it's a good thing. I hope you have a great time," she says, glancing momentarily at her watch and then raising her eyes back to the mirror and speaking to his reflection there. "You shined your shoes, right?"

"Right, Mom." He sighs to communicate that he's sick of her promptings.

"Well, then, I'll be in the kitchen. The camera's all loaded and ready."

"I hate how I look in pictures."

Madalaine understands exactly why, but says automatically, "What do you mean? You look wonderful."

* * *

Claire leads Kevin when Madalaine answers the door. Her niece is in a low-cut, long sheath dress, spaghetti straps crisscrossed three times in a beautiful, intricate pattern against her bare back, the only detail to the dress other than the rich simplicity of the black crepe fabric. Her shoes, black-dyed fabric, have delicate straps crossed over the instep and toes that echo the straps of the dress, and when she sits on the couch, Madalaine sees that she wears sheer stockings. Claire looks the way Madalaine always wished she could look, with her dark long hair curled and caught up to one side and held with gardenias, which she has fastened there instead of on her dress. The effect is original and beautiful, especially against the depth of her hair. Claire's used a flattering coral lipstick, too, one that matches her nail polish, and her eyes are made up with subtlety and flair. Madalaine recognizes Lydia's cultured-pearl earrings, the ones that are set into circles of real gold.

Madalaine has met Claire's boyfriend several times; it's the one thing about Claire that Madalaine finds less-than ideal. What attracted her to this boy who seems arrogant and self-centered? Madalaine doesn't imagine it can be his looks. The boy has ordinary brown hair, small hazel eyes and his head is a little too small for his body. Tonight, though, he looks handsome in his tux, black bow tie and cummerbund. Claire would never have picked a color for herself that would make Kevin look ridiculous, and Madalaine wishes Christy were the type to think of such things.

They make brief small talk while Brian calls to them from the kitchen. He bangs the refrigerator shut and lopes into the living room carrying Christy's corsage.

"Hey," he mumbles, suddenly embarrassed. He looks to Madalaine as if he doesn't know whether to go sit down, shake hands with Kevin or stand on his head.

"You look great," Claire says warmly.

Madalaine waits for Brian to remember to compliment Claire, but he mumbles again and looks down. "Thanks," he gets out finally.

"Claire, you look absolutely beautiful," Madalaine says pointedly, as if she hadn't said it twice already.

"Doesn't she?" Kevin echoes, and Madalaine hates him a little more.

"Okay, you all, you'd better go get Christy. Let her mom get pictures and then stop back here so I can get mine."

"Kevin and I have already been through this at my house and his, you know," Claire says, but her tone is good-natured. "We've actually been dressed and driving around for pictures since yesterday noon."

"I'm sorry, honey...."

"Oh Aunt Maddie, I'm only teasing," Claire interrupts. "It's okay, we don't mind."

"I don't?" Kevin says, and Claire slaps him lightly on the arm.

"No, you don't. Remember? I've told you over and over, you don't mind."

"She thinks I'm just putty in her hands," Kevin says to Madalaine. "Unfortunately, she's right." Madalaine feels the familiar onset of tears when Kevin says this, but she's not even sure what exactly hurts about it.

Forty-five minutes later, Madalaine has finished a roll of twenty-four pictures of her son, her niece and their dates. She's arranged them in couples, girl-girl and boy-boy, as a foursome and as couples again. Just as Brian is fussing that they really want to get going, Madalaine has a thought.

"Claire, honey, take a picture of me, Jen and Brian, will you? Sometimes, a twenty-fifth picture will come out...."

"God, Mom, no. You've taken enough pictures." Predictably, Brian is refusing, and Claire speaks over him.

"You be quiet and get over there. Sure, no problem. Jen, you get here, next to your idiot brother." She propels Brian into place, and he assumes a resigned look and posture.

"Brian, cut that out. Smile and behave yourself, or trust me, you're not going to make it to the prom."

That was the thing about Claire. Madalaine didn't know how she had such a sensitive touch, but she could get Brian to do what his mother wanted, and Madalaine loved her for that, too.

CHAPTER 7

Strange, how moments can play over and over in your mind, like some terrible broken movie. I keep seeing myself in the living room after Claire and Kevin left to pick up Brian and his date. The sun was still well above the treetops; daylight savings had begun, and the shouts of children playing hard before supper came in through the open windows on soft May air. I'd straightened the living room before Kevin came over so I could take pictures, and the first three roses from the yard were in a little vase on the coffee table. I remember looking around, reasonably satisfied that the room was clean and homey. We need new carpet, and yes, the couch has seen better days, but I've stopped looking at those. It's been a choice, and any extra money we've had has gone into Claire, one way or another, whether it was when she was sick, or when she needed braces, violin lessons or ballet classes. Wayne's been good about it, not a word of complaint, really, and how can a woman not appreciate that?

Wayne was watching car racing and I looked at the television pretending to watch it with him, but really I was looking at Claire's senior portrait, the big one I had framed to hang as the focal point of the room. She's wearing a simple black drape—all the senior girls do—and it put me in mind of the dress she's wearing tonight. What a beauty she is, the sweetest gift of my life, the good heart at its center, and given to me twice, both times undeserved. I was thinking about how terrified I'd once been that Claire wouldn't live to grow up like this, go to proms, go to college, have her life. This will sound too dramatic, but I know it's true, in the way a certain knowledge can be wordless in the marrow of your bones: *if she hadn't lived, I couldn't have survived it.* When Claire was little and so sick, I thought about John, the possibility of his comfort. I didn't call him, though. Perhaps I was afraid that he had neatly bricked over the hole in his life where I'd once fit, and the notion someone can utterly disappear was one I refused to allow in my mind.

Anyway, I'd not thought about John in months, nor had I thought of when Claire was sick. Things like that, you can push from your mind if you work at it across time, and I have. That's what makes it feel as if I somehow brought it on, because I'd been thinking about John and about when Claire was sick, and within the hour, the phone rang.

A man cleared his throat to ask if I was Claire Merrill's mother and I said I was, my heart already pounding to escape my chest. He said, "There's been an accident. You're needed at the hospital."

I argued with him, to explain that it was impossible. "She's out to dinner with her boyfriend and her cousin. They wouldn't be at the prom yet."

"Ma'am, I'm sorry, but she's here at St. Francis and you need to come. Is there someone there who can drive you?"

"My husband is here. We'll drive. All right. We'll drive... Is she all right? God, is Claire all right?"

"She's been injured, ma'am, I don't know exactly how serious it is, but she is injured. A car accident. They were brought in by ambulance. She's asking for you. You just come on," he said. Later, I thought that maybe he'd confused me with Madalaine, that he thought it was Claire's mother who would be alone instead of Brian's. It was one of those ridiculous details of no consequence that you focus on, as if in figuring out exactly what happened, the whole insoluble, terrible mystery of how to put your life back together will suddenly appear, clarified and shining.

I didn't even ask about Brian.

I am trapped with my terror, the seat belt pressing it to my chest as Wayne drives like a crazy man, running lights and stop signs on the way to St. Francis. For once I haven't a word to say about his speed. The Saturday-night traffic is dense—it always is—and I am frantic, praying desperately even though I don't believe it will change a thing.

"We've given her a shot, but she's been conscious several times. You can see her," a nurse says. I have run in ahead of Wayne, saying, "Claire Merrill? Claire Merrill?" over and over. Wayne catches up, his soft-soled shoes soundless on the linoleum, while the slapping of my flats echoed my arrival into each curtained-off cubicle, I am sure. The nurse guides me with a light hand on my back, toward the second cubicle. Claire is lying on a cart of some sort, with an IV on one side of her and oxygen tubes into each nostril. There are wires to monitors that flash patterns in neon-green and white. She's draped in white, some of it bloody, and absurdly I wonder where her beautiful dress and shoes are. There are several white-dressed men and women bustling in and out, making adjustments, hooking up another apparatus.

"Claire, Claire, I'm here. Sweetheart, you're going to be all right, I'm here." I touch her hair, then her hand before I notice Wayne, huddled miserably back from the cart, his clothes brushing the cloth divider between Claire's cubicle and the next. I don't have the grace to gesture to him to come up with me, though. I want her all to myself.

"Mrs. Merrill, we need to get a history. We need to talk to you. Her doctors are still stabilizing her. Please come with me, now."

I am crying and shaking my head no, but the woman who's spoken to me is insistent. She puts an arm around me and a hand on my other elbow, the one between us. "She only has one kidney," I babble. "I can't go with you, she only has one kidney."

Even though nobody said he had to, Wayne follows us to a little room, where the nurse sits us both down and picks up a clipboard. "Tell me everything you can," she says, clicking up the point of her pen. Around me, the peach-colored walls are moving forward, squeezing all the air out of the room like lungs that can only exhale.

* * *

I finish giving Claire's history. The one too-small kidney that she was born with, not that we knew it then, and because we didn't know, the bladder infection we didn't catch, how sick she got when the good, the blessed, the normal-sized kidney got infected, too. The care with her diet since, avoiding the enemy potassium, anything that might put undue stress on it. As if from outside myself, I hear my voice bleeding its own chemistry of hurry and begging as I tack on how beautiful Claire is, how talented, how brimming with future.

"All right, Mrs. Merrill. Thank you. Try not to worry. She has wonderful doctors, and she's going to be okay. Try not to worry," says the nurse, whose name and face I never so much as registered. "I'll go see if you and your husband can be with her now. Later, you both might want to be typed and cross-matched in case she needs more blood."

"Yes," I say. "Yes, I want her to have my blood. Please hurry back, I want to see her." Then, as the nurse is leaving, it finally occurs to me. "What about the other kids? Are they all right? What happened?" She comes back in the room and gestures to the seats from which we had just risen. Wayne and I obediently sit back down. The nurse sits in her chair again. I am studying the shades of blue, green and teal in a picture of a sailboat out on the water that hangs on the wall when she says it.

"I'm so sorry. I thought the police had talked with you. There was a fatality. One of the boys was dead at the scene, and the other is critically injured. He was airlifted to Children's Hospital in Cincinnati. Another girl who was in the car seems to be fine. She's already had a cut on her knee stitched up… Your daughter is very lucky…" Her voice continues, but my mind leapfrogs over her.

"The boy who was killed? Which one? *Which one?*"

The nurse consults her clipboard. "Brian Beeson."

CHAPTER 8

Ellie is the last person Madalaine wants, but there's no one else. The police officer who appeared at her door says he has to call someone to come help her. "At least let me get someone to take care of your little girl," he says. "I need to take you to Maysfield General, ma'am. I'd like to have someone meet us there, *at least*." He keeps using that phrase, *at least*. "It's the least I can do," he says when he goes into the bathroom and wets a washcloth for her, and her knowledge begins that she will never be a normal person again.

"No, no, no," Madalaine had sobbed and half screamed when the officer told her. Madalaine gave him Lydie's number without thinking, without putting it together that Lydie would have been receiving her own uniformed visitor. There was no answer, and so she'd fallen back on Ellie to come for Jennifer. As the connection lights in her own mind, she says, "Who else is dead?" and then, when he hesitates, says again, "Who?"

"The other boy has been airlifted over to Children's Hospital," the officer, whose face is too young and raw-shaven for this job, answers. "He's critical, that's really all I know, ma'am. One of the girls is pretty bad, and the other one's just cut on the leg. They're at St. Francis."

"Which girl is hurt? Anna Claire Merrill is my niece."

The policeman can't take any more. Nobody told him the kids were related. They should have dispatched another officer to do this with him. "I really don't have details, ma'am, I'm sorry. I was at the scene, and they sent me to get you," he lies, but she reads his eyes and tone, and knows she will not have Lydia's strength to collapse into.

* * *

Shadows were eating the details of civilization when the policeman escorted her through the hospital emergency entrance. He turned Madalaine and Jennifer over to a nurse who embraced them each before she took in Madalaine's eyes and said, "I can't tell you how sorry I am. Your sister is here for you, she's in the chaplain's area."

"I want to see my son," Madalaine says.

"Of course. We'd like someone to be with you. Would you want that to be your sister, or...his father?"

"Have you reached Bill?"

"I'm sorry, not yet."

"Maybe I should wait for him. No, I want to see Brian. I can't...I don't know. Are you sure it's Brian?"

It was taking root now, the nurse knows, the pit of the terrible knowledge just beginning to erupt and send its long tentacle shoots into Madalaine's being. She has seen it too many times, how unbearably large it grows, crowding out everything and anything else that might have grown in someone the rest of her life.

"Are you sure?" Madalaine's voice is a wail now, and Jennifer is crying into her hands.

"I'm so sorry. Yes, we're sure, the girls gave us the names. But the police need you or a member of your family to make a positive identification, but it's a formality. I can't tell you how sorry I am." While she talks, she applies a gentle pressure to Madalaine's back, drawing Jennifer to her side and working them toward the short hall to the chaplain's office where Ellie is waiting, white-faced and alone.

When Bill comes, Melody toddles alongside him, ready to burst into birth at any hour by her looks, though she's not due for a while yet. Madalaine catches a glimpse when Bill and Melody pass the chaplain's door, strangely unescorted and lost momentarily.

Madalaine shrinks back, furious, humiliated, utterly isolated in the contrast of losses and gains with the other woman. How could she possibly have thought she should go in to Brian with Bill? Bill is crying though, and when he comes in and sees Madalaine, he steps away from Melody and puts his arms out to the mother of his first child. "God, God, God," he rasps, and Madalaine strokes his head even as her own legs weaken underneath her and she weighs into him. They both stagger a little, then balance themselves against one another.

A moment later, they leave Jennifer with Ellie, and the two of them to contend with Melody, while the chaplain on duty accompanies them to the morgue where their son's body lies on a table in an area off to one side. She fingers the stiff neck of her clerical collar and steps back deferentially when she says, "You can be with him as long as you like. I'll wait just outside unless you'd like me to pray with you and him, or just be…in here."

"That's all right," Madalaine says, meaning she's not ready for any prayers addressed to a loving or merciful God right now. She sees her son motionless beneath a sheet that is tucked around him as though he were still her little boy just settled for the night, but she knows he screamed and suffered, and that God did not even have the grace to let him die in his mother's arms. "You can go."

When she and Bill formally identify and claim Brian's body, Bill obsessively asks the policeman exactly what happened. "But what happened? How did it happen? No other car…what happened? Was there any alcohol…or what?"

"No alcohol. Looks like the driver was going a little fast and went off the road just a little on the right. It was out on Route 34, they were taking the back way from the restaurant to the dance. You know, that road's narrow, and where it happened, it has a fair lip on the pavement and no shoulder, just the culvert there. We think he felt the tires hook on the lip, the girl with the cut-up knee said she felt a bump, and he overcorrected, just went right across the road and into the utility pole on the driver's side. The car grazed the pole and flipped at least once, maybe twice. We'll measure, and we'll talk to the kids that made it. "

Madalaine hears him say *the kids that made it*, and feels a quick red hope that Kevin will die. She does not understand how she could want such a thing, and squeezes the notion from her mind.

Bill insists on driving Madalaine and Jennifer home. Ellie, who has huddled miserably over her hands and wept since she arrived, has the sense to offer to take Melody home, and then to come stay with Madalaine, but Madalaine takes her up on only the first part when Ellie adds she'd have to stop home and pick up Presley because he can't be by himself at a time like this.

"You go take care of Presley and Mama and Daddy," Madalaine says gently, though before she spoke a flame had spiked from her brain to her mouth and threatened to leap off her tongue. But Madalaine had doused it, not with compassion, but with the pointlessness of it. Nothing is changeable anymore; she sees that.

Madalaine follows Bill into his former home through the garage door. Neither of them switches on a light. Bill carries Jennifer into her room where he and Madalaine sit on her bed to hold her hands, and rub her back and pale hair, until she falls into a bloodless, tearless sleep. In the darkness, Jennifer's room looks as it did through the nights when the house was new to them, furnished with their hopes and not much else. In the way parents do, Bill and Madalaine know when it is all right to leave Jennifer. They signal and rise at the same time in an old, silent communication. Once they are out in the hall, they still do not say anything. The last of their words are gone, drained out with the first day's tears before they finally left the hospital. Now they just go to their bedroom and lie down on their marriage bed to hold one another until morning.

CHAPTER 9

Ellie has no place anymore. Mama and Daddy have taken over her sadness as though they had been the ones to go to the hospital and be with Maddie. Charles keeps saying, "Brian's dead, Brian's dead," in a cheerful, parrot voice, and she thinks she will lose her mind if she cannot stop him.

"Shut up," she snaps at him like Presley does if you reach toward him when he's eating. "Just shut up." Charles is on the couch surrounded by pieces of yarn. He is latch hooking a small rug. Ellie or Mama match the colors for him when he gets to a new section; other than that part, he can do it pretty well. He has three hung on the walls of his room, their mistakes obvious to anyone but him. Still, Ellie is considering having him do an Elvis rug for her. She could pull out the mistakes and fix them herself. Charles would never know the difference.

"Shut yourself up," Mama says wearily from her recliner. Ellie paces between the kitchen and the living room.

"I just cannot take this another minute," Ellie says, "not another minute. How can you let him go on? I have to get out of here."

"Go," Mama says.

"I mean, it's just so insensitive. None of you were there. You think you're upset, I mean, none of you had to deal with it at the hospital. You didn't even know what was going on. You were just here watching *Hard Copy*, or…well, the point is, *you* were spared. I just can't take any more."

"Go," Mama says.

Ellie picks up her purse from a chair in the kitchen. "Maybe I just will. Maybe I just *will* go."

"Good."

Ellie gets to the back door where, out of sight from Mama and Charles, she stands with her hand on the knob. She opens the door, then, a moment later, slams it in front of herself and tiptoes back into the kitchen. Noiselessly, she sits on the chair where her purse had been. The table is littered with advertising flyers, a few dirty plates and crumbs. The light falls so as to throw into relief the swipes that were last taken over it with a sponge; swirls of greasy residue remain like opaque clouds on a muddy sky. How is she going to get through the funeral? How? She begins to cry but holds the sound of it inside her head and chest.

"Bring a Coke in here to me," Mama calls. Ellie doesn't move a muscle of her body, they just tighten up, like cords binding her in this position to this chair.

"I know you're in there. Bring me a Coke." Now Mama's voice frays all around the edges. "Please, Ellie. I'm hurting all over."

The wake part is the worst. There's Brian, laid out in his basketball warm-up suit, looking like he belongs in a bad wax museum the way they've fixed him up. Madalaine is by the coffin all the time, her face like the papier-mâché masks they used to make in school, white and unmoving. Bill is crying by the other side of the coffin while Melody hunches over her big stomach in a stuffed chair in one corner of the funeral parlor's room, all somber forest-green and mahogany. Ellie is supposed to make sure that everyone signs the book. That had been her job at Madalaine's wedding, too, and the irony isn't lost on Ellie. She thinks Maddie is doing this on purpose.

Mama and Daddy are there, Daddy wearing a tie, which also hasn't happened since Maddie's wedding. Mama is wearing The Dress, the tent that makes her look like a blue polyester blimp, her attire for weddings, baptisms, graduations and funerals. She is crying. Even though her face is pale and waxy, without its usual flush today, Ellie thinks it's for show. Brian had been irritating Mama for a couple of years because he didn't come over much anymore and when he did, he didn't make a big deal of it the way she liked for him to. Teenagers, except for Claire of course, weren't at the top of Mama's all-time favorites. Ellie felt bad for Daddy, though. He looked so out of place, the red wattles of his neck showing up over the collar of his white shirt, and the sports coat, borrowed from Bill, just plain too big. Lydie put in some quick face time, but she's hardly been here at all, which couldn't be sitting too well with Maddie. In fact, Maddie didn't really speak to Lydie when Lydie was here. Ellie tucks that observation away for future examination.

Claire isn't on the critical list anymore, but her good kidney got damaged, along with her spleen. Lydie, crying, said her creatine was twelve point one, and her bun was one-twenty, as if that explained something to Ellie. But they put an emergency shunt in Claire's arm and started hemodialysis, so Ellie doesn't see why Lydie set up camp in Claire's room. Doesn't she know what her sisters are going through? Even Wayne is here, though he's keeping to himself, down-shouldered and miserable-looking. He did say that Lydia was talking with Claire's doctor this afternoon, and that's why she left so early.

Kevin is still in the hospital, like Claire, only he's unconscious. Ellie wonders if he'll be one of those human vegetables people whisper about. Christy is here, dressed to kill and spilling crocodile tears all over Brian, who can't defend himself. Ellie can see Maddie stiffen when Christy touches Brian's hand. Ellie thought for a minute that Christy was going to plant one on Brian's lips, and she would have liked to see how Maddie took that, but evidently, Christy read Maddie's face and managed to restrain herself.

When Ellie actually thinks about Brian, which she tries not to do, she cannot believe that he is really gone. She tries to make her mind bend around that idea, but it is adamant in its refusal. Fortunately, she has the book to keep track of, and Charles to watch. She's hit on how to keep him from singsonging *Brian's dead, Brian's dead:* her purse is crammed with red jawbreakers. Before Charles finishes one, she hands him another which he can't resist stuffing in his mouth in overlapping succession. He couldn't possibly say a word.

Madalaine startles, her attention shocked away from Brian, who sleeps farther and farther away from her in his coffin: across the room, Charles has blood and saliva oozing from his mouth. Ellie is sitting by the visitor registry as if nothing is happening, though Charles is easily in her vision. Madalaine knows she should run to help him, but her feet and legs are paralyzed. There was blood around Brian's mouth when they'd finally taken her to him at St. Francis. She begins to cry, doubling over, and, of all people, it's Melody who heaves herself out of the corner chair and makes it to Madalaine, putting an arm out to support her as she sinks to the floor, calling to some people clustered in muted conversation to come help her. Then Bill's face appears above her.

"Let me get you out of here," he says, an emotion too thick and layered to identify, thorns on the soft flower of his voice. He kneels to get his arms between the floor and her, begins to lift her head. "Did someone say something to you?" Madalaine tries to point toward Charles, but as Bill raises her head and draws it toward his chest, his cologne reaches Madalaine and it is as real and immediate as the scent of her son when she had her arms around him to adjust his pink bow tie. Right now, she sees him in the car, just before the accident, craning his neck, trying to loosen the grip of the tie on his throat. Christy has told him he smells good and he is laughing to cover his equal pleasure and discomfort.

"Hey, Kevin, slow down, huh?" Madalaine hears him say to the driver, the arrogant boy who is so sure of himself. Claire says something, too, but what it is does not come to Madalaine clearly, nor can she tell if Claire is speaking to Brian or Kevin. It is lost in a blur of movement and a sharp intake of breath, disbelieving as the car tilts a little, its wheels lower on one side where they've gone off pavement onto the weeds and gravel. Madalaine senses the moment when Kevin jerks the wheel, too much, too far, and the car rocks again as all four wheels are briefly on the pavement, but crossing it diagonally. Madalaine feels herself scream, the skin around her mouth stretching, her throat aching with the rasp of it, and then the sound of it mingles with the girls' screams and her son's hoarse shout. The car careens wildly and she is dizzy, sick, and then there is a suffocating, jolting crash searing into darkness.

CHAPTER 10

I should be at Brian's wake, I know that, not sitting here watching Claire sleep. She even said, "Mom, I'll be all right, please go for me," but this morning Dr. Douglas said she wanted to talk with me privately, and when I went to the funeral home at the beginning of the calling hours, Maddie hardly spoke to me. I could have sworn she stiffened up and pulled away when I hugged her, but I stayed as long as I could bear it anyway, then slipped out, leaving Charles to Ellie and Wayne to himself, so I could get back here to Claire. My Claire. I don't think I've yet drawn a full breath since the accident; my lungs want to pant in time with my heart's hammering. It's as though it is happening over and over. I'm afraid that if I let go, some nurse will come up to me like doom and say, "Mrs. Merrill, I'm so sorry," like they did to Maddie. Poor Maddie. My poor, poor Maddie. How is she surviving?

I sit in this chair and focus all my energy on keeping Claire alive, even though I know she's not in danger. Not today, I mean. She's going to have to be on dialysis unless she can get a kidney transplant, but Dr. Douglas says transplants are almost routine now, we just need a good match. I was tested yesterday—so was Wayne—but I intend to give her one of mine. It's only right, and it's what I want. She's mine. I think that all the time, although I'd never say it out loud to hurt Wayne, or make Claire feel I thought she was an object I could save in a drawer. But it's the way I think of her, *mine*, and my responsibility and privilege in the end.

This is not a pretty room. Too tiny, and too many machines, a step-down unit from intensive care. They won't let her have the flowers she's gotten, but I've put up some pictures on the wall and brought two of her old stuffed animals from her room, and her radio. I need to get a sun catcher for the window, for the afternoon sun to make a rainbow for her. Her friends have left cards and letters at the nurses' desk. I read them to her and look up too often hoping to catch a smile flickering. Not yet. She's cried so much about Brian, and Kevin, too. I think she cannot tell who or what she's crying over sometimes, her sorrow like patches sewn together into an enormous whole cloth that envelops her body. I feel such pain when she cries, but I am glad for the chance to hang on to her. I weave myself between the tubes and bags and wires, careful not to disturb anything while I work my arms around her so she can put her face into my chest and sob. She is mourning while the dialysis machine keeps my secret, hums its own hymn of praise while it saves her. Claire keeps asking me to call again about Kevin, and I am afraid to. What can I tell her if it's not good news? She cannot take any more. None of us can.

Dr. Douglas sticks her head in the door and gestures to me. I follow her down the hall, catching up as we walk. My heels click on the tile, but Dr. Douglas is soundless as death in the night, a notion that pops into my head to panic me. "She looks better today, don't you think? More color in her face and her eyes not so dull?" I say, demanding the answer I want in the way I put the question. I am always doing that; everyone here must be sick of me.

But Dr. Douglas smiles and says, "Yes, I do think she looks better. She's stabilized nicely." Then she touches my arm. "Is your nephew's funeral today?"

"At 3:00," I answer. "I was there. I just couldn't stay. I'll go back...when it's time."

"I'm so sorry," she says, though she has told me this several times already. "And I'm sorry to have to burden you with anything else to think about right now, but I do need to talk with you." She points toward a small lounge, big enough for just four or five people, but empty now. There's a coffeepot plugged in, with a jar of instant coffee and a box of tea bags next to it. Dr. Douglas puts a tea bag in a paper cup, pours hot water onto it and hands it to me without asking if I'd like any. Then she fixes a cup for herself. "Sit down," she says. "This isn't an easy one."

"Claire? It's not…"

"Nothing I haven't told you about Claire. It's what you haven't told me," she says evenly, but with a thin edgy border between me and her usual kindness. She's been Claire's urologist since we first knew about the kidneys.

"What?" I say, and honestly don't know what she's talking about.

"Lydia," she says, "do you and your husband know that he's not Claire's father?"

I've never prepared for this, and it takes a minute for me to even bring a word into my mouth. "No," I whisper. "Not anymore. I think we've both forgotten that."

After that first lunch with John at Kathy's Kafe, I flew back to work ten minutes late, and tried to concentrate on the billing. I kept thinking about how he'd asked me questions and listened to the answer, as though he were interested. Looking back, it seems so obvious what was in both our hearts, but the truth is that no matter how obvious, I didn't know.

Still, I should have. Since when had I paid particular attention to my clothes, and spent extra time putting my hair in hot rollers in the morning? The next day I wore my red sweater, a white blouse and my black skirt. I put gold earrings on, and a gold bangle bracelet. I have always looked good in red, everyone says so, because my hair is so dark. It had just been a lucky coincidence that I'd worn blue, the color I like best to bring out my eyes, the day before. And since when did I not pack my lunch any day when I had plenty of time to do it? I should have known what I was thinking, but I kept it from myself so I wouldn't have to stop.

Of course, I went back to Kathy's the next day. John did, too, both of us acting as though we had no idea the other would be there. And the truth was that neither of us had mentioned it. We just knew. And for quite a while, that was all there was to it, a bright place like a flower in the middle of each weedy day that made me eager to go to work in the morning, packing anticipation instead of a sandwich.

In January, there was a beautiful first snow, the flakes enormous and heavy, falling with increasing speed. Maysfield people make time out of snow; Kentucky doesn't get much, and the rural areas pretty well shut down. It's not for sport—Maysfield's sports are drinking and suicide, same in winter and summer—but for the novelty of it, the break from gray sheer dreariness. In town, serious business doesn't happen; appointments and events and shops that don't really *need* to be canceled or closed are, so that people can watch it snow, as if the outdoors had become a giant, free drive-in movie. The snow began at about ten in the morning and by noon, when John and I were at Kathy's for lunch, better than an inch had accumulated, and the town was beginning to seal itself in.

"You should see yourself," he said, grinning. "Wow!'

I know I blushed. "A mess, right?" Of course, my hair was full of snow, which meant my careful styling had collapsed.

"Nope. Absolutely gorgeous. Your cheeks are pink and your eyes are the bluest blue I've ever seen. I'll have to think what the word is for that color." He brushed the snow from the top of my head. "Are you cold? We could take a walk after lunch… want to? I am not in the mood to go back to my brief right away. There *is* no precedent that really fits."

"My shoes, though…" I pointed down to my black low-heeled pumps. My feet were cold and wet just from getting to and from the car.

"Yeah. I see. Well, look, you've got to change those shoes anyway. You can't work like that all afternoon. I'll drive you by your house and you can grab your boots along with a dry pair of shoes. Can you be late getting back to work? We could eat fast and get out and enjoy this stuff a little." He gestured to Kathy, mouthed, "What's the soup?" While he wasn't looking, I studied him. I was always doing that, trying to get hold of something. Other than the high, wide forehead broken on one side with a wave of hair—damp now from the snow he'd missed brushing from it—and expensive teeth, no single feature stood out, yet I found him handsome in a way that made me uneasy. I liked his eyes, though, a deep, earthy brown under eyebrows that looked brushed. All of him was groomed, even his fingernails. Not sissified, even though that's what the men at the plant would think.

"We'll have all kinds of cancellations this afternoon," I said. "Donna will kill me if I'm too late, but I could probably get an extra half hour if I call and make nice to her."

"Well, call and make nice, then. How does beef-barley soup sound?"

He'd started to treat me like that, taking charge, but it never made me feel bossed around. I'd always been the one to decide things at home, and I'd fallen into the same role with Wayne. This was different, strange and exciting, and I guarded the feeling like a treasure that nobody knows exists so nobody tries to take it away.

I did get my boots from our house, a little embarrassed because it's so small and unremarkable, while John waited in the idling car. My secret life briefly intersected with my life with Wayne and I was conscious of it. Why guilt didn't tarnish my pleasure in John's company, I have no idea. It was much later that guilt's infection came to a head; that day, we went to the park and set off into woods that had turned magical when the wet weight on branches lowered them into a canopy over the unbroken path. The grace of the land unhid itself, roots to trunk to branches, and it seemed we were being blessed. When John took my hand, I did not take it back.

It was one of the loveliest hours of my life. When he kissed me, I kissed him back, and there it was, the dime on which my life turned.

CHAPTER 11

Chaos is erupting at the wake, and Ellie has no idea what to do. Bill is carrying Maddie out of the room, following the oily funeral director who asks people to stay calm and wait where they are. Ellie waits a moment, but then follows like a lost child. She crosses the room, weaving through stunned, whispering mourners, but then remembers Charles and turns around to collect him. She ignores Mama and Daddy, who don't seem to know what's going on, and in a run stretched into a slow-motion caricature by Charles, whom she drags by the hand like an anchor, takes the way the director and Bill turned when they left the room.

By the time she finds them, Madalaine has been laid out on a table ordinarily used for a coffin in one of the rooms for smaller funerals. Ellie feels what she takes for a physical blow, that sharp is the shock and the sensation that she will never get her breath. The funeral director is bending over Maddie, and Bill is just stepping back. Ellie recoils and jerks her hand from Charles. Unrestrained, and the last jawbreaker shrinking as he works it down, Charles takes two lumbering steps, uncertain and disoriented as a bear about which way to go. "*Maddie's dead, Maddie's dead, Maddie's dead,*" he begins. Hearing this, Ellie expels the first air she's been able to gather into a long scream.

Bill jerks to consciousness and heads toward her in long strides, gesturing with palms-down hands to keep it down. "Ellie! Eleanor! Stop it. She's fainted is all, or she's had some kind of seizure, I can't tell. Go get Lydia."

Ellie stops, and Charles does, too, momentarily. "Lydia's not here. She went to the hospital. She's supposed to come back for the service." Ellie forces the words out.

"Jesus. Is Wayne with her?"

"No, he's here."

"Then go get Wayne. And take Charles with you. No, leave Charles here." Charles has begun his chant again.

Ellie obeys.

A moment later, Ellie and Wayne both hang at the doorway.

An edge of desperation is in Bill's voice. He looks at Wayne. "Can you get hold of Lydia, get her here to take over? I've got to get a doctor or something, Maddie's collapsed, I don't know. Should I take her to the hospital?"

Wayne is not a take-charge man. "I'll get Lydia," he says, and has no answer for anything else.

"Look, could you…I mean please, take Ellie and Charles with you," Bill says, his face reddening, as he runs his hand across the top of his ashy and thinning hair. "I can't…"

"Right," Wayne says. "Come on, Ellie, bring Charles. We'll go get Lydie."

Ellie goes into the hospital while Wayne double-parks and keeps Charles in the car. She has been to see Claire once since the accident, but she was with Wayne, and paid no attention to the labyrinthine floors and corridors. She's not good with directions, even when they've been repeated, and is frustrated just looking for the elevators.

Finally, a candy striper accompanies her to Claire's floor, where a nurse tells her that Mrs. Merrill is in conference with Dr. Douglas in the small lounge. Through the glass panel in the door, she sees Lydia on a two-person couch, crying. The doctor is seated next to Lydia, her shoulders inclined toward her in concern, her hand over Lydia's two, which appear to be clenched together. Ellie assumes there is bad news of Claire, and she jerks to one side and flattens her back against the hospital wall, afraid to either enter the room or leave.

Perhaps five minutes pass, during which Ellie peeks in intermittently. Finally, the doctor gets up to leave. Lydia is still crying.

The doctor gives her a last pat on the shoulder and opens the door. "Oh, were you waiting to get in here?" she says when she sees Ellie.

"I need to see my sister, Lydia Merrill. Is Claire…?" Ellie says.

"You can go on in," the doctor says. "We're finished. It's okay."

Ellie opens the door, but hesitates in the doorway. Lydia looks up from where she is still seated, startled.

"Ellie! What is it? Why aren't…"

"You need to come to the funeral home," Ellie says. "Bill sent us to get you. Something's happened to Maddie."

"What? Is she all right?" Lydia bolts from the couch and hurries toward Ellie.

"I don't know. She collapsed or something. Bill said for you to take over. I think he was going to get a doctor or something."

"But Claire…" Lydia shook her head as if trying to clear it. "Yes, all right, let me tell Claire's nurse so she can tell her why I'm gone when she wakes up, and I'll come." Lydia walks in the direction of the nurses' station as she talks. Ellie trails by a step.

"Wayne and Charles are down in the car. You'd better hurry up. I've been here forever. What was the doctor saying?"

"Nothing," Lydia answers, and Ellie knows it is a lie.

Lydia heads straight for the room where Ellie had left Madalaine with Bill and the funeral director. Madalaine is sitting up now; a friend of hers trained long ago as a nurse is beside her, holding a wet paper towel to Maddie's forehead and another to the back of her neck. Madalaine is holding a paper cup of water and nodding her head.

Bill steps up to Lydia. "She's okay now, she fainted. Please, go out and be next to Brian for her," he says. "She can't do it anymore."

"I do not want her next to Brian," Madalaine interrupts loudly.

"What? This is Lydie, Maddie, it's Lydie. I asked her to come, she can…" Bill thinks that Madalaine sees Ellie instead of Lydia.

"She shouldn't be next to Brian. She doesn't deserve to be. She has no right. I followed all the rules, and my husband's gone and my son is gone, and she's broken every one but she has everything."

Lydia thinks that Madalaine is blaming Claire through her. "Maddie," she says, taking a few steps closer and putting her arms out. "Claire is devastated. You can't blame her, really, do you?"

Madalaine flies into a rage of tears that blur into hysteria. "Not Claire, you. You. Why does everything work out for you? I didn't do anything wrong but my child is the one who's dead. Claire's only my half niece, anyway, or doesn't it work that way?"

Lydia realizes the road Madalaine is barreling down, drunk on memory, rage, jealousy and grief, altogether shredding reason and coherence. Even facts are garbled, coming as facts do, from sources as unreliable and biased as her own eyes and ears.

CHAPTER 12

Every part of me goes hot and icy when Maddie accuses me. The whole life I've constructed out of will and work and love is collapsing around my feet. I have to keep Claire out of this—that's all I can think right now. I have to put Dr. Douglas with her impossible questions out of my mind, and just deal with this part, here and now.

I gesture to Bill and the nurse, who are the closest to us. "Please, just let me talk to her alone." Their faces wrinkle up, but they step back toward the door, though no one actually leaves the room except the nurse. Even Charles huddles silently behind Ellie, who is still blocking the doorway out into the hall. I do the best I can to get my voice directly and only to her. "Maddie. Maddie. This is a terrible thing that's happened. The worst thing anyone can ever have to endure. You can blame me if you need to, but I want to be here for you. I'm your sister, you know I love you, and you know I loved Brian," I say. This is only partly true. I don't want to be here. I want to be anywhere but here, anywhere I can wrap myself around my daughter and keep all this from touching her.

Maddie seems to come to a little, and I can see her back up inside herself. She crumbles into a softer, wordless crying.

"I know I don't deserve what I have." I cross the last few steps between us, sit and put my arms around her, and whisper this into her hair. "I know. I know. Please, I'm begging you, don't hurt Claire."

"That's all you care about," she says back bitterly, but privately, quietly, and I can tell she is getting her impulse under control.

"I know you love her, too," I say, "not for me, but for herself,

I mean. Take out whatever you want on me, but please, find a way not to destroy her world."

"I'm going out to be with Brian," is all Maddie says. She stands up unsteadily. Bill advances toward us and I step aside for him to help her, though there was a time when Maddie would have turned her back on Bill to lean on me. Isolation settles over me like a bell jar set down by the enormous hand of God.

Ashamed and embarrassed, I stay behind. Ellie and Charles follow Maddie. Wayne waits, shifting his weight from foot to foot, an awkward distance from me.

"Well," he says. "Well. I guess the cat's out of the bag. I guess it was all along."

"Wayne, please," I say, "not now. Dr. Douglas told me that my kidney isn't right for Claire because there are antibodies in my blood from my gall-bladder operation, when I had that transfusion. You're not a match either, we knew that was a long shot. She asked me point-blank who Claire's father is." My body feels as though I'm trembling, but I cannot see the shaking.

"I am," Wayne says, his face a rigid mask.

"I know you are. Wayne, I'm sorry, I'm so sorry. I know I promised, but I'm going to have to try. You understand, don't you? You don't want her on dialysis any longer than she has to be, do you? I have to find him and ask—"

"No," Wayne says. "Absolutely not."

There is a whole funeral service I have to get through, with Wayne's words pounding against the inside of my head. The one hymn is slow and mournful, the minister's words comfortless, at least for me. Wayne is one of the pallbearers, and so is Daddy. Bill actually sits next to Maddie, leaving Melody three or four rows behind him. Both sides of Brian's family ignore her, and for the first time, my heart goes out to her. How frightened and wounded she must be by this picture of Bill and his wife. Her being here requires courage, and I respect that she has not tried to hide anything. Not the smallest thing, and certainly not something as big as life itself. It's very warm outside, and the windows are thrown open for the May breeze instead of air-conditioning, which would have made sense. Melody sits fanning herself with the little program and memorial card the funeral home has made up, her beach-ball stomach resting on her lap for the whole world to see. She leans her head back, and the soft hollow of her throat, below the vulnerability of her Adam's apple, is right there for people to hurt, and of course, they do, they will.

Brian's coffin is left beside the deep hole in the ground that has been hidden with AstroTurf, as if we didn't know that as soon as we all clear the cemetery, he'll be lowered into it and buried forever. Even at the grave, I am not concentrating on Brian or even Maddie. My mind is racing, darting down blind alleys, trying to find a way out. I wish I were more like Melody.

I imagine myself picking up the phone tomorrow. "John? This is Lydia," I'll say. "I hope I'm not calling at a bad time." No, I involuntarily shake my head. That's all wrong. Weaving themselves between the words in my head is the minister's. "Yea…through the valley of the shadow of…" and I bury my face in my hands so I can use my thumbs to cover my ears, sliding them beneath my hair so no one will see. I cannot think about the shadow of death. I will think about how to call John.

It is so rare that I allow myself to think of John that now, when I must, I am quickly confused. I don't know what I believe anymore, as though the type inside a book changes to read something different every time I open it. Once, to me, he was perfect, then he changed—or the lens through which I saw him did. And then, over time, it all seemed to change again, and I remember him softly now, wrapping him with the silver benefit of every doubt.

CHAPTER 13

Bill has actually done it again, left Melody to fend for herself while he takes Madalaine home from the funeral. Jennifer is with Emily, her best friend, whose mother offered to keep Jennifer with them as long as might be necessary after Madalaine collapsed at the wake. Even though the refrigerator is crammed with meat and cheese trays, and soft rolls are stacked on the counter along with coffee cups, napkins and plates of cookies, word passed at the burial service not to go back to Madalaine's house afterward, and the driveway is mercifully empty when they pull up.

The burial of her son nearly killed Madalaine, and Bill wasn't far behind. The late afternoon had been sunny, the cemetery in full, late-spring bloom on the kind of day Brian would have spent ignoring homework and shooting hoops. Now his father's car is parked beneath Brian's basketball net, and Brian will not be asking if he can move it.

They have not spoken since leaving the cemetery, driving out from beneath a canopy of new leaves, but the silence is as replete with empathy as if the last months—and indeed, the year before those—had been deleted from their lives. Bill's hand is on the back of Madalaine's black dress as they go in through the garage door.

Madalaine is in one of what she calls her amnesia periods, when her attention turns to some minutiae of living and, for a few moments it is as though she is in her old life. It is doubly disorienting when she is with Bill now because she may forget that he has left her, forget that Brian is dead, or both, until either memory is jolted awake and despair washes over her again.

"Look at all this stuff," she says, clicking on the kitchen light to dispel the shadows. "Where will we put it?"

"Honey...who cares?" It comes out as nearly a moan. He has slipped and called her *honey* again, though it escapes his own notice, and, at the moment, Madalaine knows Brian is gone, but has forgotten that in his way, Bill is, too.

Madalaine glances at him and sees the dark smudges like bruises around his eyes. "You look exhausted," she says, and rubs his back. "Do you want to lie down awhile?"

"You're the one who needs to lie down," he says. "Has the dizziness come back?"

"No, I'm...okay. It was the red stuff on Charles' mouth, you know? I didn't know... It was like...Brian, and I thought I saw Brian again. I don't know."

"You just couldn't take any more," Bill offers. "It's so...unreal, isn't it? I keep forgetting. Not forgetting, really, just not believing, I guess."

"Yes, that's exactly it. You feel normal, and then suddenly you know nothing's normal." Madalaine puts her arms around him and rests her head on his chest. "Yes," she says then. "I guess I do need to lie down."

This is how it's been since the night it happened when Bill brought Madalaine home from the hospital after they had seen Brian's body. They'd alternated falling apart; when one did, the other pulled himself or herself together just enough to drag the two of them to the next hurdle. Bill welcomes Madalaine's need; it gives him something he can do. And when he is overcome, well, Madalaine's hands are as knowing and kind as he'd seen them when she bathed the children, back when the children were small and the four of them were a family.

They make their way down the hall to the bedroom. Without a thought, Madalaine pulls her dress over her head and hangs it in the closet after kicking off her low-heeled shoes. She peels off her slip and black panty hose and then stands in front of her bureau.

"I have no idea what to put on," she says. "How can I just put on shorts, I mean, it doesn't seem right. Nothing will ever be right again." Tears refill her eyes, and her body begins to sag. Bill thinks she may be about to faint again and quickly crosses to her from the bed, on which he had been sitting, letting his body crumple into itself.

He puts his arms around Madalaine, easing her toward the bed where he arranges her limp body. He climbs over her on his knees and lies alongside her, working one arm underneath her so he can gather her up close to him. For the second time in three days, Bill and Madalaine lie on the bed they shared for years to hold each other while they cry.

For perhaps twenty minutes, they comfort each other with their hands and the wordless history that passes back and forth between them. "Is it too late for us to have another baby? Let's have another one, please?" Madalaine whispers. "I am…so empty, so empty. I need…inside me, I need…"

Bill doesn't answer, but his mouth is on Madalaine's so that she cannot say any more. Madalaine unbuckles his belt and opens his pants while Bill undoes his shirt and her bra. There is desperation in their movement; the first gentleness of their comfort gives way to fierceness, though they are more tender with one another than they'd been for years before Bill left.

Afterward, Madalaine gets up and pulls on a T-shirt and shorts. She roots through a bottom drawer and pulls out a pair of athletic shorts that had been Bill's in their old life. She tosses them to him, along with an extra-large T-shirt of his that she had long ago taken to wearing as a nightshirt. "Let's get something to eat," she says. "I'm actually a little hungry."

"Yeah," he says. "Listen, I…"

"Don't say it," she orders, and for a moment Bill thinks that she is as she was when he left, but she says, softly, "please," begging him with her eyes, not a trace of anger in them, and he thinks that everything is, indeed, different.

They make sandwiches, and sit together at the kitchen table.

Bill gets himself a beer. "Want one?" Bill asks rhetorically, and does a double take when Madalaine says yes. That's the thing, he realizes, their past and this loss—beyond the grasp of anyone who isn't Brian's parent—make them the only person each of them can turn to, yet they are discovering each other as if they were strangers. After they eat, Bill gets them each another beer and, still at the kitchen table, they go through seven of the eight picture albums that Madalaine has kept since they were married, the ones with pictures of Brian.

The baby pictures are nearly indistinguishable from the ones of Bill that his mother sent Madalaine when Brian was born. Hairless, squinty and mottled, a day-old Brian in the hospital nursery gazes back at Madalaine, and she strokes the picture as though it were the skin of her newborn. She and Bill turn the pages of his infancy. "Do you remember when he rolled off the changing table? There it is, safety buckle and all," she says.

"Oh, God, how could I forget? I thought I'd killed him," Bill answered and when he hears himself his eyes fill again.

"It wasn't really your fault," Madalaine says for the first time.

"Yes, it was," comes the answer, another first.

"You were a good father."

"Not good enough. Look at what I put him through. He was so upset, when I left, you know…" Bill stands up to cover his emotion. He opens the refrigerator and stands looking into it vacantly. He closes the door without touching anything.

"No, listen to me. That wasn't about Brian and he knew that. You were a good father to him, even though I got in the way."

"I appreciate that, Maddie." Bill turns around and looks at her, still seated with the toddler album in her lap. "I'm sorry."

"I'm sorry, too."

"I ought to be going," Bill says, running his hand over the top of his head. "I'll change out of your clothes."

"What do you mean, my clothes? They're yours, and I thought

you might stay tonight. I don't want to be…I mean, Jennifer's not even here and…"

"I didn't know if you'd want me to…with the situation, I mean." Bill is flustered and his hands gesture meaninglessly as he stands leaning against the kitchen sink for support. It is the closest either will come to mentioning Melody, and Madalaine takes it as a reference to Brian.

"I meant what I said. You were a good dad to him. You always loved him. Just because we didn't always agree about how to be parents, I'd never pretend that your loss isn't as great as mine. It's our loss. I'm sorry for things I've said that sounded like… that." She trails off, looking down into her lap where her hands hold the album of Brian's preschool and early elementary school. She is caressing the dark green cover, which is cool and smooth as his cheeks at that age.

Bill shakes his head, as though in disagreement, but stops and says, simply, "Okay."

"Do you want to look at the rest of these pictures?" Madalaine says.

"Yeah, actually, I do," Bill answers.

"Hold on a minute," Madalaine says, and leaves the room. When she comes back, she is wearing one of Brian's long-sleeved shirts over her T-shirt. "I was a little chilly," she says as she sits back down. "He wore this to church last Sunday. I'm so glad I hadn't washed it." Madalaine holds out her arm toward him. "Smell—he must have poured on that cologne."

Bill obediently sniffs the sleeve she proffers as he comes to the table to sit down with her. He recognizes his own scent, and flashes to himself giving Brian a new bottle of it the week before the prom. He doubles at the waist and puts his head in Madalaine's lap, where she strokes the back of his head. His hair there is the color and texture of Brian's.

A half hour later while they sit in the twilight leaning closer to one another and to the pages of the album at hand, the phone rings. "Let the machine get it," Madalaine says as Bill begins to rise automatically.

"But it may be..." Bill begins.

Madalaine misses his meaning again and interrupts. "I told Jennifer we'd call her. It's probably Lydia and I don't want to talk to her." Bill sits back down. He is not a man who can attend to more than one thing at a time.

CHAPTER 14

My mind aches from darting from problem to problem, each one alone too much to encompass, and all together enough to blot the smallest particle of light from the future.

I put the phone down thinking that Maddie knows it's me and just won't answer, even though I know that is ridiculous. She wouldn't just not answer the phone, knowing how worried everyone is about her. There must have been twenty people who told her she shouldn't be alone when she refused to let me go with her. You can only do so much; you can't force someone to accept what you have to give. She wanted no part of the funeral limousine, and left with Bill. Poor Melody stood there trying to look dignified, and I did, too, embarrassed and ashamed, wondering who had heard what at the funeral parlor, and desperate to get back to Claire.

When I go into the hospital room, I am alone, and I think Claire wonders where Wayne is, but doesn't ask. She is awake, just staring at the wall, not watching television or even trying to read, too still. I gather a smile and show it to her. It must seem a bizarre grimace; I can feel it fail.

"Tell me about the funeral," she says. "I should have been there, I should have..." Claire's eyes are making new tears, and suddenly I think that I myself may never cry again I am so numb, so far from tears now.

"Oh, sweetheart. I don't know what to say. It was very sad. Brian was in his basketball uniform, the warm-ups I mean, and well, there were the calling hours and then a simple service. Here, I brought you this little program they gave out, and a memorial card." I have already decided I won't tell her about Madalaine collapsing.

"He loved basketball so much," Claire says. "I just don't understand it, how could God let this happen? Nothing was Brian's fault." Now she is sobbing. "It was more my fault. I was the one who said he could come with us." Claire pulls the sheet up and buries her face in it.

"It is *not* your fault," I say, a certain hard defensiveness to my voice. I try to soften and stretch it out, like pulling too-stiff taffy. "It was not your fault, honey, not at all. You were doing something loving and generous, and it was an accident. Do you want to talk about what—how—it happened?"

"No. I don't know. We were having a great time. Kevin had been really nice about all the pictures, but we were running late. We took the back way, you know, to the restaurant and to the prom. Maybe he was going a little fast, but it wasn't that bad, Mom, or I would have been scared. I did ask him to slow down once...then..." I can see the drama replaying itself across her face, so much that I think she may scream at the moment of impact in her mind. I put my hand out and try to pull her away from the memory, desperate as I am to pull her from that car myself.

"It's okay, honey, it's okay, you don't need to." The truth is maybe that I can't bear it, but I hope it is her I'm trying to spare.

"I had to tell the police about it," she says dully. "Is Kevin going to get in trouble?"

"I don't know, honey," I say softly, and begin adjusting the sheet that is crumpled over her chest to take my eyes off hers. "I don't know. Do you think you could sleep a bit now?"

"I can't sleep. Kevin's mother said she'd call me with any news. Anyway, I have to get plugged in pretty soon...." Claire juts an elbow toward the housing of the dialysis machine. "What's going to happen to me? Dr. Douglas said I can be evaluated for a transplant, but meanwhile I have to stay on dialysis. I hate this thing in my arm. She said there's a way I can do dialysis myself, peritoneal, I think. They're going to talk to me about it."

"Honey, it was an emergency, the shunt, and you'll just be on dialysis awhile. I'm sure you'll be a good candidate for a transplant."

"If somebody dies..."

I flinch. "No, not necessarily. I've been tested, and so has Dad, and we're hoping a relative can donate a kidney." I cannot meet her eyes so I get out of the chair and go adjust the venetian blind that slices the light like an onion. My eyes sting. I cannot tell her that I'm not a match. Not yet.

"I can't let you do that, Mom."

"It would be the only thing I'd want to do for the rest of my life, Anna Claire. Look at me. That's the truth. There's nothing I wouldn't do for you."

I leave Claire's room and just do it. I cannot *not* do it, no matter what Wayne says. In the hospital lobby there are some phone booths that are little rooms with a chair, a phone book and a pay phone on the wall. Complete privacy, except for the little glass window through which people peek to see if someone is using the phone. These are the places where people make the calls of bad news; I know that as surely as if there's a neon sign over them, because there are other, out-in-the-open pay phones, near the reception desk where ladies with blue-tinted hair wearing pink jackets and name tags that say Volunteer give room numbers and directions. Those phones are so that joyous news can reverberate relief down the halls. *Don't be afraid*, those open phones say. *See? Everything works out for the best.*

My footsteps are muffled; the reception area is newly carpeted and painted in shades of muted rose. Hope. You can tell it's meant that way.

I pick one of the little private rooms with its own phone and shut the door. I dig around in my purse for my wallet, and from my wallet, from its hiding place behind a collection of updated pictures of Claire, I fish out the folded slip of paper with seven numbers written without a hyphen and backward. I haven't figured out what to do if I don't recognize his voice, or if someone else answers, but it turns out not to matter. Three rings is all it takes, long enough for seasons to change. I have to think to breathe, to have the air to get the word out. "John?" I say. "This is Lydia."

Wayne is asleep in his recliner in front of the television when I get home. It's been completely dark outside for quite a while, though I've lost track of the exact time. Maybe he'd been waiting up for me, but on the other hand, the lamppost and the porch lights were both off when I drove in, so I guess he wasn't. I move through the kitchen and put on only the light over the sink. I don't want to flood any place with light just now. My living room, with its dated green carpeting, and green-and-gold flowered couch and chairs, looks cozy, especially in semidarkness. I've made it as homey as I can with pictures and brass lamps, but it's not nearly as nice as Maddie's, which is over in a subdivision where teachers and managers live. I used to envy her that. Imagine.

"Wayne. Wayne, it's me. I'm home." I shake his shoulder gently. By the light that makes it this far from the kitchen, I see how old his face has grown. Did this happen in the last week, or was it coming on for months or even years? I realize how long it's been since I really looked at him. Deep creases fan out from the corners of his eyes, a watery blue when they're open, and now the hollows around them look nearly black, skeletal, and I know I am seeing bruises from the fist of suffering. He loves Claire; from a silent distance, like an invisible red rose he guards inside himself, he loves her.

He startles a little and opens his eyes. "It's me," I repeat, seeing he is confused. "I just got home from the hospital. I'm sorry I'm so late. Did you get anything to eat?"

"No," he says.

"Do you want me to fix you something?"

"No." He lowers the footrest and begins to unfold his body from the chair.

"Maybe you should stay there a minute. I…need to talk to you."

"Is Claire…?" he asks.

"No. Not Claire. No change, but she's okay. The funeral hit her hard. Hit us all, I guess, but she's…" I realize I am letting myself sidetrack, and switch back to where I must make myself go. I pause and then just plain force myself. Like I'm water being driven against my own current, that's how much I don't want to go where I must. "I have to tell you. I did it. I called John."

"No," he says. "No way." And his refusal is as emphatic as anything I've ever heard him say, even to a small gesture with his hand. The movement distracts me, and when I look down, I see it hard and balled.

This next sounds as if it can't be anything but a story, like someone saying that when she and her new husband came out of church on their wedding day, a perfect rainbow arched right in front of them. But it's true, one of those times when it seems like the earth conspires with God to warn you. As I gather myself up to tell him, a shift in the weather that may or may not have been forecast—I hadn't listened to the news for days—rumbles toward us on distant thunder.

"Yes," I say, while my heart sounds too fast, too loud inside me. I sit down on the chair nearest his, not all that close.

"You promised. You said never. You can't do this to me. You can't do this to Claire. No. No way." His voice is some strange new metal.

"It's too late, Wayne. I've done it. But there's no choice, don't you understand? I have to…" I cannot even finish. While I am speaking, his face closes down entirely, like an impenetrable vault door. Maybe, no matter what he ever said, I didn't believe he wouldn't see this was what I had to do in the end. But it doesn't matter. I really mean it. Whatever will give her back her normal life. Whatever. I am strong and destroyed at the same time when Wayne gets up and stares me out of his way. I just sit there without moving, looking at how the stuffed arms of his recliner have darkened like a permanent shadow from the oil of his skin after so long.

CHAPTER 15

Neither one of her sisters cares about her in the least. Ellie hasn't gone to work in a full week, she is too upset. Presley senses tragedy, animals always do, and she's not wanted to leave him. Of course, Daddy just walks the yard pointlessly rearranging the fenders and tires he keeps out back by the shed and seeing to the withered tomato plants Mama wants, even though every year they get choked out by weeds. Weeds fringe the house like an old woman's shawl. There's some Queen Anne's Lace that's pretty, though. Ellie picked some last night and put them in a jelly jar on the kitchen table.

Charles has been driving her flat crazy with his wide, mindless grin and his slurry parroting. Nobody understands, really, that's the thing. She needs a man to talk to and a place of her own. It's not as if anyone will leave her alone when she goes in her room, locks the door and plays Elvis's songs, especially "Hurt," and the others that are filled with the loneliness of his soul. Every time, though, not ten minutes goes by before Charles is pounding on the door, or Mama is calling her to fetch some fool thing. Mama is crying a lot, too, lodged in her chair like a rock in a river. Ellie will give her that, though she could show some consideration for Ellie's grief.

Brian was like a son to Ellie, it's just like she has lost a son. She knows she is taking it every bit as hard as Maddie, though of course, no one recognizes it. When did Maddie or Lydie ever recognize anything about their sister? As usual, they're both just thinking of themselves, leaving her to take care of Mama and Daddy and Charles.

At five o'clock, she prepares their soup. Chicken with Rice

tonight, because Ellie is feeling uneasy at the stomach. She has some trays of meat and cheese, and some rolls that Maddie had Bill bring over, when nobody went back to their house after the funeral. No one comes to the table anymore, not that Ellie cares. She puts the food out and they can get what they want when they want it. Except she takes it in to Mama because it's hard for Mama to get out of the chair. She needs to lose weight, and a lot of it, but there's a lost cause if ever there was one.

Ellie is swiping at the dishes dispiritedly when Wayne, of all people, knocks at the back door. She can see him through the screen, haggard and poorly looking, his face pasty behind his beard, which looks in need of a brushing at the very least. Ellie never has understood why a man would want all that hair on his face mixing into his food.

"Hey, Ellie," he mutters, glancing past her and craning his neck toward the living room where Mama and Charles are watching *A Current Affair*.

"Hey, Wayne. Lydie's not here."

"Yeah."

"Well, what're you looking for, then?"

"Nothin'..." The silence expands with the heat of the room.

"So, um, have you had supper?"

"No."

"Do you want something to eat?"

"No." Wayne is shifting his weight foot to foot. His raw-looking hands hang too far below his sleeves and he is altogether a picture of unkempt awkwardness, like an aged adolescent.

"So what do you want?" Ellie is staring him down, now. Her sisters have married strange men, nothing like the one she'll be with if she ever makes it out of here.

Wayne opens his mouth and shuts it again. A hand goes into a pants pocket and comes back out with a handkerchief he uses to wipe his mouth and then the back of his neck. “Lydia’s not here. Madalaine here?”

“I told you, Lydia’s not here. Madalaine’s not here either. I have no idea where either one of them is. What do you want, Wayne?”

Wayne looks around again, which Ellie takes to mean he doesn’t believe her.

“She’s not here, I told you. What’s going on?” Ellie is irritated now, with a little insult mixed in. She sets the kitchen rag down with unnecessary emphasis and puts her hand on her hip.

“She been here?”

“Who? Lydia? No. And no, Madalaine hasn’t been here either. You don’t think either one of them would come see how we’re doing, do you?”

Wayne’s neck flushes. “Sorry. Bad idea…shouldn’t of…” he mutters and abruptly leaves, letting the screen door slap shut behind him.

Ellie is not about to be treated like that. “Wayne,” she calls, following him to the door and through it. “Wayne,” she calls to his back. “You can at least talk to me a few minutes and tell me how Claire is.”

Wayne doesn’t even turn around. “No change.” He raises his voice enough for her to hear it over the sound of the car door opening and letting its slam provide the period for the terse response.

CHAPTER 16

It's Madalaine who finally gets up and goes to the front door. She and Bill and Jennifer have been sitting in early twilight at the kitchen table finishing the lasagna that Evelyn, the next-door neighbor, brought over.

In this singular light, the walls, counters, and appliances appear nearly a pewter-gray, like an old mirror that has lost its spirit and purpose. The kitchen still isn't back to its normal pristine clarity. Pyrex dishes and silver trays list in stacks on the counter, ready to be returned when someone is willing to venture out.

They have been talking about Jennifer going back to school tomorrow, her concern that she'll be either fussed over or ignored. Madalaine understands all too well. She's ducked as many phone calls as she can and dreads going back to the office, whenever that comes about. She feels utterly unlike anyone she knows, as though Mother of the Dead Boy is stenciled across her chest. It's altogether too easy to sense the relief of another woman that this happened to Madalaine's child, not hers, as sympathy is dished up along with the gifts of casseroles and cakes. A certain bitterness sometimes creeps into Madalaine's thanks.

When they hear the knocking, all of them freeze a little, and they look at one another without voicing the question: *Should we ignore it?* The garage door is closed and they've not yet turned on any lights. Perhaps whoever it is will leave their offering on the step and go away. Thank goodness the flowers and plants have trickled off. There were enough to stock a greenhouse. Yesterday, Bill loaded the car with some of the more ostentatious ones and took them to a nursing home. At least, that's what he told Madalaine he'd do, though he'd also said that they made him a little crazy with anger and he had a mind to drop them in the trash.

It occurs to Madalaine as she crosses the living room toward the door that it might be Melody. As far as she knows, Bill hasn't even called Melody. How like Bill. Even though she's been on the other side of an unringing phone, she takes a small, secret pleasure in what she can guess is the other woman's distress. Yes, Madalaine's been there, done that. Would Melody dare to come to Madalaine's home to grab Bill by the scruff of the neck and drag him back to their apartment while they await their baby? Madalaine knows how a woman can be impelled to do the unthinkable. She herself showed up at Melody's one evening to create a scene that makes her cringe when she recollects it.

The thought slows her pace and she reconsiders the notion of just not answering. Surely they can just not answer the door for at least a few days. Maybe then she'd begin to feel ready. Lord knows she's not now. She can't give Bill up. He and Jennifer are lines mooring her, however loosely, to reality's dock. It's a fair trade, she thinks, you get a baby and lose the man, I lose the baby and get the man back. She has wild, bitchy thoughts like this one off and on, feels ashamed and then gets right back to them.

I've got to be a better person or I might lose Jennifer. Madalaine feels sick and clammy again as she does whenever she sees that particular fear crouching in a dark, unvisited corner of her house, clogged with gray webs that trap and kill small lives. That thought, because it's the one that coincides with the front door knob being in front of her, is the one she acts on. When she opens the door a scant eight inches, Wayne is standing outside, his baseball cap folded lengthwise in one hand and promptly shifted to the other. His short-sleeved shirt is dirty, coming untucked again.

"It's Wayne," Madalaine calls over her shoulder as she opens the door the rest of the way and pushes on the screen latch.

"Come on in." Of the possible people to be on her front stoop, Madalaine considers Wayne the most innocuous.

"Lydia here?" he asks without ceremony as he steps into the little entryway that quickly becomes living room when a guest steps off a small square area of hardwood flooring onto plush off-white carpet.

"No, why?" Madalaine says with a degree of caution in her voice. She wants nothing to do with Lydia.

"Maddie, look, I don't know…I mean, it's a bad time, but I've got to talk to you. You've got to stop her."

"Stop her from what?"

"I think she's gone back to him."

Madalaine's forehead wrinkles. "Him? Who? Claire?"

"Lydia. The guy. The guy she…you know." The two of them are standing on the edge of the carpet as though it were a cliff. Wayne feels a flush rise to a burn on his face and neck.

"What?"

Bill appears in the hallway. "Hey, Wayne," he says, and after hesitating a moment, crosses the living room in five long steps, hand extended.

Wayne's eyes dart to Madalaine and, back on Bill, narrow almost imperceptibly. "How're ya doin'," he mutters, not a question, and returns the handshake with something like reluctance.

"Now, what's this?" Madalaine says to Wayne. Confusion and curiosity have won. "Lydie went to who?"

When it comes right down to it, Wayne doesn't exactly know how much Madalaine knows, but he's guessing it's the most part of the truth. His shoulders sag at the thought of trying to explain it if he's wrong. Still, he's got to have someone's help, and there's no one else he can think of. He hates every part of this. "John," he finally answers and, unaccountably, his eyes fill with tears. "I know you know about it," he says and his voice has a ragged edge of pleading.

Madalaine knows all right, not that Lydia had confided in her.

No, she had to stumble on the dirty little secret and discover what her sister was about all by herself. "Oh, I know all right," she says. "I just doubt that you do."

Bill catches the tone in Maddie's voice. "Maddie," he says, as though her name were an order.

She wheels. "Don't you Maddie me," she snaps. "Nobody saved my child."

Bill has no idea what she's talking about, but he recognizes this side of Madalaine, the one that always put him in mind of a snarling dog. He tries to speak to the other Maddie, the new one who's willing to see which way he wants to go before taking off around her own block. "Hon, let's be careful here," is as far as he gets.

"I will not be careful. She wasn't careful, not that you'd know anything about that. I'm sick of being careful. Listen, Wayne, Lydie isn't here and if she were, I'd tell her to get out anyway. Don't you think it's about time you woke up? If John'll have her, that's where she'll be. Did you ever even figure out where your precious Claire came from?" Madalaine's eyes are like a desert glare now, the light in them a killing one.

Wayne's jaw visibly tenses and a small muscle jumps coincidentally below one eye. He doesn't answer. Bill takes a step backward, elongating the triangle the three of them had formed. "I'll not listen to this. If you're going to be like this, I'm leaving."

"Oh, that'll be a big change, won't it?" Even as she spits the words, though, Madalaine knows she's gone too far. Heat spreads from her neck up into her cheeks as if she'd stuck her head too close over an open oven. "Oh, God, I'm sorry, I didn't mean that," she says. "I'm sorry, I'm so sorry."

"I need to get going anyway," Bill says, the words wooden as his body.

"Please. Please, I'm sorry. You're right," Madalaine says, taking a step toward him to close the gap again.

Wayne stands awkwardly in the same place, apparently forgotten by the other two. It is as hard for him as anything he's ever done in his life to push his way back between them. "You can't be talkin' like that. Claire's my girl, no one else's."

"Of course she is," Bill says. "Come on, I'll walk you to the truck. You're probably blocking me in."

"No, I'm out on the street. I've got to talk to Maddie," Wayne says. He hands his cap off to the top of a chair, as if to make it plain he intends to stay.

"Have it your way, then," Bill says, shaking his head in an involuntary negative gesture, as if to say this is not a smart thing to do.

"Don't leave, please don't go." Maddie is crying now. "You're just doing this to punish me. I said you were right."

"It's time I got going, anyway. I'll go talk to Jen and go out through the garage." He turns to Wayne and says, "Thanks for your help at the service." Maddie takes a couple of steps toward him, opening her mouth, but Bill holds his hand up, palm to her, as if to make a stop sign of it. Then he leaves the room.

"Okay," Wayne answers.

Maddie makes her way to the closest chair, the wingback one that Wayne has set his cap on, and lowers herself into it while tears course soundlessly down her face.

As Bill heads for the kitchen, Wayne avoids his sister-in-law and crosses the room to the couch, a distance from which he could not possibly comfort her.

A flair of fresh anger ignites in Madalaine when she sees Wayne plunk himself down to demand something of her at the same time Bill is walking out on her for telling the truth, but it is a dud, fizzling quickly and falling out of the black sky inside her. She shakes her head as if in disbelief.

"What do you want?" she finally says.

"I don't want you to say that again."

Madalaine knows what he is talking about, but she's wary. "What?"

"About Claire."

"What about Claire?" They are dancing around each other now, both of them unsure by a hair exactly what the other knows. "Please, this isn't a good time, you can see..." The sound of the door from the family room into the garage closing reaches them.

"About Lydie...and Rutledge. Claire." It is as much as Wayne will put into words.

"Did you...know before?"

"Yeah. I always knew. Lydie told me," he answers.

Madalaine is surprised. "Well, I wasn't a hundred percent sure myself, even though it seemed...well, pretty obvious, given the problem you two..." She breaks off, aware that Wayne's neck is blotchy red. "Bill doesn't know anything," she adds, surmising that Wayne assumes he does and is embarrassed.

"And you don't think he'll figure it out now?" Wayne is angry, she sees, and also that his is the quiet sort of anger that simmers invisibly.

"Well, he's gone now. He may think about it or not, but he won't say anything, anyway. It's not his way." Madalaine feels a wave hit her again, and tells herself that Bill would have left even if she hadn't unloaded onto Wayne. She never should have allowed herself hope. Outside, she hears Bill's car door open and shut, his engine turn over in instant metallic cooperation with his will, equally hard and mechanical. She wants Wayne gone so she can go ahead and cry. "I told you, Lydia's not here."

"Claire's goin' to need a transplant."

"I know."

"I'm not a match and neither is Lydie. She called him."

"Him...John?"

"I'm trying to stop her."

Madalaine holds up a hand, palm out, as if to slow him down. "She wants...?"

"She wants him to get tested, wants to ask him to give a kidney to my daughter."

"Well..." Madalaine is stalling, trying to sort out the ramifications. "Maybe that's best...a relative...a parent... is usually the best match, right?"

Wayne sits mutely, staring at her, waiting for her to get it.

"Oh...you don't want anyone... Oh, you don't want Claire to know."

"I don't want Claire to know." There is something in his voice that might be a trace of mockery, Madalaine can't tell. "It's not...right, anyway. She's not any part of him," he says.

It wouldn't be like Wayne to be sarcastic, Madalaine decides. "What do you want me to do?" she says, when she's finished the weighing.

"Make her stop."

"Make Lydia stop?"

"Make Lydia stop." Again that faint trace of something that riles her in his voice. She's beginning to feel like she's in a three stooges non-conversation, always lagging a step. She sits forward in the sofa, signaling that she's about to stand.

"Look, Wayne, I'm sorry you've got trouble with Lydia. To tell you the truth, I'm sick to death of Lydia. It's not so much I blame Claire for what happened...but, I mean, Lydia, well, it was Lydia's idea that Brian double with Claire. Claire must have known that Kevin drives too fast. Lydia should know that kind of thing if she's any kind of mother."

This is beyond Wayne's ken, these subtleties of old and new angers, these assignments of nuances of blame. He goes back to what he knows.

"Make Lydie stop," he says. "She won't listen to me."

"And you think she'll listen to me?" Madalaine snorts and waves a hand in dismissal, bumping it, as she does, into an arrangement of late yellow tulips that came three days ago. A little shower of large, edge-withered petals falls onto the dusty end table.

Jennifer appears from the kitchen. "Hi Uncle Wayne," she

says, then addresses her mother. "Why are you two sitting here in the dark?"

Neither Madalaine nor Wayne have noticed how much the light has drained from the room. They have little real connection one to the other, but share the long custom of seeing what they expect to see. Jennifer points at a light with upraised eyebrows, and when Madalaine nods, the girl reaches under the shade and switches on a lamp.

"Thanks, honey. Now, please let Uncle Wayne and Mom finish up. I'll be just a minute longer." As she speaks, Madalaine gets up and switches on two more lamps. The room comes alive with its evening colors, alive but muted from what they are in daylight. While this is going on, Madalaine's mind is trying to wrap around the dilemma Wayne has brought instead of a casserole or a plant.

"I suppose all this is your idea of expressing sympathy," she says when she thinks Jennifer is well out of earshot.

"I know this isn't the time to come askin' favors."

"You're right about that… Look, I don't know. I've lost my son, my husband just left again because of something to do with Lydia. I'm just too tired, Wayne, I just don't think I can help you." She tries to put closure into her voice, and remains standing. Madalaine knows she is telling only part of the truth. The rest is that she's not sure Lydia is wrong. Who cares what Wayne or any other man wants when it comes to doing what your child needs? Really, just who the hell cares?

Wayne doesn't budge from his seat, just sits ramrod straight and leans toward her a little. "You want me to beg? This isn't for Lydia, it's for Claire. I was going to ask Ellie," he tacks on as an afterthought, picking up his cap and fiddling with it.

"That's right. That's exactly my point." Now Madalaine has said more than she intended. She doesn't know exactly what her point is, and she is too tired and drained to figure it out. "I don't know, Wayne, I just don't know."

Then Wayne takes her totally aback. "Can I stay here?" he says.

"What? Stay here?" If she keeps repeating what he says she'll sound like Charles, but she couldn't grasp what he wanted.

"I need a place to stay."

"You're not going home? I mean...what about Lydia?" This is too much. Madalaine sits back down into the plush cream upholstery of the chair.

"I don't want to be around her, if she's talking to him."

"Oh."

"So, can I stay here?"

Madalaine shakes her head in disbelief. Then she shrugs. "I guess," she says. "Tonight, anyway." She gets up abruptly and heads for the kitchen, where she can hear Jennifer opening cabinet doors. "I don't want you in Brian's room, but you can sleep in the family room if you want." A moment after she's left, Wayne still sitting in the living room, she pops her head back around the corner. He hasn't even stood up yet. "You were going to ask Ellie? Wayne, you are dumb as cement. Ellie! Good grief."

CHAPTER 17

Wayne hasn't been home or called in over twenty-four hours, but I cannot think about what threat he means for me to glean from it. And I can't think about what to say to Claire when she asks where her father is if he doesn't go to the hospital again today. Of course I admit I'm breaking my promise. I told him that, and that I knew I was bringing him pain greater than the one I tried to wrap in silver paper when I told him about John, and that I was pregnant. My promise, his pain, so what? Nothing matters except Claire, and she is all I will think about.

I've not seen or talked to John in seventeen years and seven months. Once I saw him driving down Main Street. In a panic, I turned my head to Anna Claire, when we still called her that all the time, in a pink snowsuit in her car seat beside me. I don't count that as really seeing him, but even if you do, it's been seventeen years. Maybe he got a new car, or moved away. I wouldn't have known. It's not as if lawyers and secretaries run in the same circles. I never allowed myself the tiniest gesture—like looking under Attorneys in the Yellow Pages—to find out. Sometimes, if the phone rang and someone hung up, I used to wonder, but even that passed. I was glad when Kathy sold the Kafe, and the building was renovated and expanded into a McDonald's. I never eat there, though.

He's there before me, which I didn't want to happen, positioned with his back to the wall in a far corner in the nonsmoking section. A cup is in front of him, and another one opposite him, as though someone else were sitting in the booth. He stands up when he sees me, his old politeness training that I'd found so charming, the remnant of a rich or cultured childhood, one, or, I was guessing, both. Neither of us says anything at first. He leans to kiss me on the cheek, and though I want to let him and even to hug him, I pull back as if I didn't know what he was going to do, and slide into the seat across from him. Then I see that the extra cup has a piece of lemon and a tea bag neatly laid on its plastic top, and I know it's his way of saying he remembers everything.

"This is as far away as I could get from the smoking section," he says. I used to complain about the smoke in Kathy's. He catches me looking, and runs the palm of his hand over his head ruefully. "Not so much, huh?"

"Thank you for meeting me," I say. I cannot do this, exchange pleasantries as if this were another kind of reunion. I am undone, seeing Claire's rich deep eyes on John's face. I've come to think of them as Claire's, instead of John's, as though a trait that distinctive could be a genetic accident.

"I saw your nephew's obituary in the paper. I'm so sorry," he says, and I realize that he thinks Brian is why I called him. Did he see the write-up of the accident, too?

"I didn't know you even knew Maddie's name."

"I knew *Madalaine*," he says. "It's an unusual spelling."

"It makes Maddie so mad," I say. "Mama just didn't know how to spell."

"Do you—or she—need help with something?" For some utterly unfair reason, it makes me angry to hear him imply that I'd called him for some professional service. John picked up his coffee and gestured at the tea he'd bought me. "That's for you. Is that still what you like?"

"Yes. Thank you. You didn't have to do that…." I sound stiff, too formal. In spite of the too-high air-conditioning, my face burns beneath my skin. I fidget with the lid of the cup, then with the tea-bag string.

"Lydia. It's a cup of tea. Please. What is it? You don't need to be so…polite. It's me, you know, just less hair. Is it Charles, then, or Ellie?" He reaches across the table and touches my hand, but when I don't move a muscle, he withdraws it as if he'd planned to all along.

I cannot believe that he has brought up my dead nephew, my retarded brother and my crazy sister, but not what should have been the first thing on his mind and out of his mouth.

"I'm sorry I had to call you," I begin formally. "If there were any other way…"

"You haven't forgiven me." His tone sounds like he wants to say, *I knew it.* "I've wanted to call you hundreds of times, but I couldn't convince myself that it was fair. Please don't be sorry you called."

"If there were any other way," I begin again. He starts to protest, but I hold my hand up. "Please. Just let me talk. I'll never get it out if…" I feel tears stir behind my eyes, and will them to stillness. He is so much the same, still smooth and tailored like no man I've known except Dr. Hays. His voice, a rich, warm baritone, is exactly the same. He's aged in small ways; it's mostly that the wave over his forehead is diminished, falling higher, thinner and lightened by a little gray, but not much. Not much. I've changed much more than he has; I must be seven or eight pounds heavier, and anyone can see the lines that fan out from my eyes above the deeper ones that run like a set of parentheses between my nose and mouth. Here it is, the old magnetic pull of him so that even while I'm burning with fear, worry and the irritation he's added like a dash of pepper to the mix, I'm feeling the old draw, the desire.

John has caught the tears or something else, though. Within an instant, he switches channels in a way that Wayne never once has, and gets it right: something terrible has brought us to this, something about which he has absolutely no notion. "Lydia. Lydie." He repeats my name the way he used to, to order me to look at him. "Tell me, now," he says, in a voice I wholly recognize as having existed between us alone. Suddenly time has lifted enormous wings and flown off our shoulders, and we are as we were.

"*Tell me now*," he ordered. We were at a motel we'd been to several times, a good hour from Maysfield, a nice one where we went when we'd squirreled a half day instead of an hour or two. The colors of the room were a soft blue and green, pleasing, elegant and warm at once, and I could imagine the room as one in a home we'd have. Early afternoon sun streamed through the window. We'd not pulled the drapes yet; we were still sitting in chairs, John drinking coffee and I tea, both of us working on the last of the morning's doughnuts from the coffee shop next door. John had taken off his sports coat and loosened his tie that had been tucked neatly under a vest. He slid his hand across the little round table and picked up mine with a solid pressure. "Come on. I won't have you keeping something from me. What's the matter?"

I was fidgeting. "Nothing, honey. Well, actually, I mean, I'm… late. Very."

"I thought we had all afternoon," he said, his brow furrowing in confusion but not irritation.

"No. I mean, it is late, *I* am late. It should have been two weeks ago."

A silence white and blank settled between us while he figured out what I was talking about.

"We've used…caution," he finally said, looking at his coffee instead of me.

"I know. Of course we have. It's probably nothing. I…I bought one of those new do-it-yourself tests, I thought we could…"

"You really think…?"

"I really think," I answered, and I remembered that I smiled and waited for his joy to blossom. "I really think that we are really and truly joined forever."

Joined was the word I used for it almost twenty years ago, in the long era of loving John. Of course it was about making love, but the strange thing was that the physical joining was separate from what I felt. What I felt resembled recognition more than discovery. John and I were wooden jigsaw pieces sliding into spaces that had been stamped Reserved but left unoccupied all our lives. We fit each other. That's the only way to say it. Once we'd taken our places in one another's lives, it was unthinkable that we'd not stay there.

"I love you," I used to say, lying naked in his arms in a motel in some little town east, west, north or south of Maysfield.

"I know," was what he would answer, and hold me so tightly that the cells of our skin couldn't have told themselves apart. "*I know. It's the same for me.*" That was it. We did know, and we knew we knew. That much I'm sure of.

We'd discussed the marriage we'd have, gazing skyward instead of at the structures and shadows of two existing marriages that marred the horizon if we looked straight out. We dreamed on and invented life together, as if there really were a life other than the lives we'd already created of our own free and ignorant wills.

"It says to test the first time you go in the morning, but I can't do that. Not at home, I mean I couldn't do the test, but I...brought it, and I thought I'd just do it here in the bathroom. I got the little bottle from the office...." I was babbling, looking to John to tell me it was okay, that this might accelerate our plans, but it certainly wouldn't change them. I actually opened my purse then and took out a little urine specimen container, which I'd carefully filled at six-thirty that morning behind a locked bathroom door.

"Lydie, I *have* two children, I mean, I have to..." is what he said instead, as if I didn't know it, and he was still looking at his coffee instead of at me when he spoke. His left hand was around the cardboard cup, his wedding ring, heavy, faceted gold, apparently weighing it down there instead of allowing him to reach across the table to touch me.

"I'm aware of that," I said, scrupulous not to allow a tinge of sarcasm to tint the edge of the words. I'd worn what I thought was a beautiful outfit, a dress with pastel spring flowers for the season, but I saw then, in the untimely way I have of noticing unrelated things, that it was all wrong. The day was colder than had been predicted. John had worn a light tan vest of what must have been cashmere under his sports coat.

And that was the end of it. Oh, of course, it wasn't that simple, not at all. It's just that when I look back, I see that it could have been. Really, from the time I answered that first *tell me now*, and took in his reaction, I should have known and let go. I didn't. I clung to what I knew was true between us instead of seeing that people aren't always as brave as their visions.

"Tell me now," he says, and I feel as if a too-big piece of ice is shivering its way through my body toward my two useless kidneys. The words make me light-headed with fear.

"I had a girl," I begin. "I mean I *have* a daughter." I had intended to say *we have a daughter*, but I am so rattled by the double meaning of the past tense that I only correct the one word.

"Did you think I didn't know that?" he says.

"Well, you've not mentioned it yet, so yes, I guess I thought you didn't know that," I say. I am taken aback, but try not to show it.

"Then you didn't know me very well."

"No," I say quietly. "I discovered that." I am immediately ashamed that I've taken this shot at him, but worse, I am afraid of angering him.

But he sits back in the booth and takes it in. "I deserved that," he observes and looks down. "I'm sorry. Just so you know, I kept checking the birth records at the courthouse. October 20. Five pounds four ounces. Seventeen and a quarter inches. Anna Claire. Thank you for the Anna—I can't tell you how much that would have meant to my mother. How much it meant to me. I sort of took it as a sign...that you...um, understood. Was something wrong that she was so early?"

"She goes by Claire now. Is your mother still living?" I can't bring myself to satisfy his curiosity just then. I want to tell him only the thinnest, pencil edges of Claire's and my life, nothing of what is inside, at the same time I want to erase every line that has ever divided the three of us.

"No. Eight years ago the twenty-ninth of last month."

"I'm sorry." I am postponing it. I take a swallow of tea. "And how are your boys?" My voice sounds like Emily Post.

"They're fine. Both married. Mark went to law school. They had a rough time of it for a while. Barb and I divorced six years ago. But they've come through it. Nathan actually became an elementary school teacher, fourth grade. Mark is working in the prosecutor's office over in Cincinnati."

How was it that this can hurt so much, this glimpse of his family, the life he's lived without me? I find no satisfaction in his divorce except that it removes an obstacle. I do what I so often do then, just push myself over the cliff. My heart thumps like something caged, wild, icy, burning.

I do it on one long exhalation. "Claire was in the accident that killed my nephew. Maybe you saw it in the paper? She's on dialysis now, she needs a kidney transplant and I'm not a match. I had a transfusion when I had my gallbladder out and there are some antibodies. I want you to be tested and if you match, I want you to give her a kidney."

CHAPTER 18

"I'll talk to her, Wayne." Madalaine is sitting across from him at the kitchen table, a cup of cold coffee dregs in front of each. Leaf shadows dance on the shaft of sunlight that enters on a diagonal above the brass rod for the white café curtains. Jennifer is within eye- and earshot, in front of the television in the family room. They'd planned for her to return to school today, but she's not ready for it yet, she says. Madalaine is thinking that Bill's leaving last night set her back. It set Madalaine back, too. Last night in bed she felt his absence as palpably as she felt his presence the night before. On the other hand, maybe Jen's just caught the obvious wind that there's something up with Wayne and Lydia and didn't want to miss out on a different disaster than the one she's living with. Madalaine amazes herself with the cynicism that pops up like an internal jack-in-the-box since Brian died. She sighs and looks directly at Wayne to make eye contact and draw a precise, small box around a precise small promise. "That's all I can say. I'll talk to her," she says and sighs again. He has been at her all morning. "Where is she?"

"Don't know. But she won't miss a day at the hospital. They might send Claire home, with portable dialysis, something where she puts stuff into her stomach and then drains it out again. They were going to teach her and Lydia how to do it."

"Aren't you going to learn it, too?"

"I was, but..."

Madalaine tenses for another round. The problem is that she is of entirely two minds about this. Lydia does not deserve anything she has, that much Madalaine is sure of, but nothing else. She gets up and begins clearing their few dishes to the sink. "So are you going to work today, or what?" Wayne is in his denim coveralls, his cap with the plant logo on the table next to him. "Aren't you going to be late?"

"I called in before you got up," he says. "Thought I should wait to see if you get anywhere with Lydie."

Madalaine doesn't like this at all. Somehow this is falling to her and she doesn't even know what she really thinks. Last night, she stared at the ceiling in the dark and weighed it out: her own anger at Lydia, what Lydia does and doesn't deserve, against saving Claire. On a spreadsheet like that, it came out clearly enough, but damn, she could see Wayne's point anyway.

"Don't count on anything," she tells Wayne. "Lydie and I aren't on the best of terms. Don't put this on me."

In the shower, she cries the first of her daily mourning for Brian, and now, again, for Bill. The running water absorbs her sobs, mixes her tears into itself. When she towels herself dry, she thinks she has lost weight and steps on the scale. Down seven pounds. There was a time when this would have made her very happy. In spite of the gray in her hair, she's still a sleek woman, her flesh unmottled and shapely. Bill has left a few things in the bathroom—the soap he likes, a kind that dries out Madalaine's skin too much, a stick of deodorant, a straight razor. She arranges them neatly in the medicine cabinet, refusing to allow herself any interpretation of the gesture. No hoping, that is her rule.

What is she going to do with Wayne? He's sticking like peanut butter on the roof of her mouth. As she dresses in a denim skirt and black scoop-necked shirt, she contemplates what to say to Lydia, if, indeed, anything. She tosses the wet towel on her unmade bed, exactly something that she'd have fussed mightily about, back in another lifetime.

Heat has intensified as the day blooms toward noon. By mid-June, there will be days well into the nineties; what will keep the dust down and the vegetation by the roadsides green until well into July is the rain. July and August so often bring drought that people don't complain much about the rain in June, not that it's excessive, but enough. Madalaine begins the drive to the hospital with the driver's window down, letting the wind whip her hair back and forth until it resembles her mission, whatever it is. Maybe she won't have to say anything, she thinks, maybe Lydie won't be there and she'll just visit Claire, which she ought to do anyway. She'd as soon keep the upper hand, not give anyone reason to criticize her. But why hadn't she just said no to Wayne? He can hardly expect her to drive all over town and county looking for Lydia, whom she really has no desire to see.

But Wayne was right. Lydie is in Claire's room, fussing with the pink carnations and sweetheart roses on her nightstand. She looks terrible, Madalaine notices, her face grayish, lipstick already mostly eaten off, white cotton blouse wrinkled.

"Hello, Lydia. Hello, Claire. How're you feeling?" Madalaine says, too formally, a strange bile wetting the words against her will.

"Maddie!" Lydia says and comes at her with arms extending into a hug.

It is a moment before Lydia senses that Madalaine is not going to hug her back, and retreats from the one-sided embrace. "How are you doing? You've been on my mind all the time."

"Really." A flat statement, no question to it, extra emphasis on the first syllable, tone like unbuttered cold toast, a direct stare into Lydia's eyes, but then it's Madalaine who averts hers first.

"Really. I've felt so torn, like I need to be here with Claire, and I need to be with you at the same time."

"I'm doing all right."

"Come, sit," Lydia says, drawing her into the small room, which is additionally crowded by a recliner-type chair and various machinery, at the same time Claire chimes in, her voice innocent as choir bells. Even Madalaine can feel that much.

"Aunt Maddie, I'm so, so sorry I couldn't be at Brian's funeral. They wouldn't let me out, even though I thought I could do it, in a wheelchair, but Dr. Douglas said no, it was too soon, with whatever…starting dialysis and all, I guess. I'm so sorry."

Madalaine sets her purse on a chair, then sits on the edge in front of it. "It's quite all right, please, don't worry about it." The words are too distinct, as if she'd snipped each one off her tongue with nail clippers, but Madalaine doesn't know how to fix it.

Lydia goes back to the head of Claire's bed, as if for support. "We're just waiting for the dialysis nurse and technician to come. And Ellie's coming. We're going to be trained how to do peritoneal dialysis at home, until Claire gets a transplant, that is. Right, honey?" She directs the rhetorical question to Claire, who nods assent, but looks a little embarrassed.

"Ellie?" is all Madalaine says.

"They, uh, they recommend that two people be trained to help with it, because, well, if I were sick or held up somehow, or something, it's good to have a backup. Mostly, Claire can do it by herself. We wanted to ask you, but…I…wasn't sure, well, I didn't want to add anything that you'd have to think about."

"What about Wayne?" Madalaine says, surprised at her own maliciousness.

"Oh, well, you know, he's at work, and they said it's a good idea to have someone who doesn't live with us, just in case." Lydia brushed her hand across her forehead as if to tame a nonexistent unruly clump of hair, a dead giveaway to her sister.

"Really," Madalaine answers. Again, she emphasizes the first syllable. It's her new favorite word, she guesses. "Well…everything Ellie knows about machinery could be scratched on the head of a pin and still leave room for an encyclopedia. Any news about a transplant?"

"Oh, there's really no machinery. Bags and clamps and an IV pole. Well, Wayne and I have been tested, but we don't know yet. It'll work out. Claire will get a kidney, won't you, honey?"

More lies.

Claire is huddling—it is perceptible to Madalaine—into

her pillows, trying to make herself smaller. Her mother is embarrassing her.

"I'd think the results would be back by now," Madalaine says, a deliberate torment.

"I don't know. These things take time. How is Jen doing? I've been thinking about her—people tend to forget siblings," Lydia says.

That's right, Lydie, change the subject. I guess you're hoping that'll work, Madalaine thinks, and in spite of a quick sear of shame that precedes the words, she says, "But you all must be pestering the doctor night and day. Waiting for these kinds of results is so hard. When does she say you'll know?"

"I'm not sure. Listen, I've been fighting a headache all morning. I think a couple of aspirin and a shot of caffeine might work. You want to come to the coffee shop with me? Claire, honey, if the nurse comes, have me paged in the coffee shop. Is that okay?"

"Sure," Claire answers, and picks up a fat paperback from the nightstand.

"You might think about catching up on some of your calculus instead of reading that," Lydia says, keeping her disapproval mild but evident.

"Mom…" Claire gives an eye roll so familiar to Madalaine as a teenage gesture that it is like a blow to her solar plexus. Brian used to annoy her with that on a daily basis.

"Come on, Maddie, keep me company. Please." Lydia stands at the door waiting.

Madalaine briefly considers pushing Lydia's panic button by saying no, I'd rather not, I'll stay here and talk with Claire. After all, she is Mother of the Dead Boy. She can pretty much defy anyone she wants. But she's curious to see how Lydia will try to shut her up about the tests and what she'll say about John and Wayne, so instead she sighs and gets up slowly, to enact the artifice of reluctance.

* * *

Their steps are not in unison so there is a strange tat...tat tat...tat syncopated rhythm to the sisters' progress down the square tiles of the hallway. A black custodian in blue coveralls, like Wayne's, swirls a rag mop wetly up one side, where a sign cautions them to be careful. Madalaine sidesteps the watery area by moving closer to Lydia, but as soon as the sisters have passed it, she moves back to her right, increasing the distance between them again. Madalaine expected her to talk as they walked, a breathy exhortation, but Lydia is silent and Madalaine follows suit.

In the coffee shop, which is virtually empty, Lydia orders iced tea and Madalaine refuses anything. Lydia waits for it to come by digging around in her purse for change, but as soon as it does, she takes a deep breath and forces herself off the diving board headfirst. "Maddie, I'm asking for your help."

"Seems that's the current trend." Madalaine stares her straight in the eyes. She, for one, has nothing to be ashamed of.

"What?"

"Never mind. So what favor do you have in mind?"

"Maddie, what's going on? What have I done? Please, I need to know." Lydia leans over her iced tea, which has already formed condensation all over the outside of the glass.

"I thought you wanted a favor." Madalaine leans her back against the booth, neutralizing Lydia's lean forward.

"Well, I do, it's just that the...vibes are terrible, as Claire would say. You're angry at me. I know this is a nightmare time for you. I don't want to...involve you, but I have to. First, though, I need to be able to talk with you."

"Talk away."

Lydia sighs, and her shoulders slump. "Maddie. Maddie. I'm so sorry...for however you find me guilty of contributing to Brian's death. Please, you remember, you have to remember, I loved him, too. I'd have never done anything to hurt him."

"No, of course not. You'd just live your life in careless ways, draw other people into your carelessness and get away with it, while people who play by the rules get everything taken away from them." Madalaine hadn't intended for any of that to spill out, nor the tears that came so quickly she couldn't fumble in her purse for tissue before they were rolling down her face. "Damn," she says, and takes the napkin Lydia hands to her.

"I understand," Lydia says. "You're right. What can I say? You're right. What do you want me to do? It's not Claire's fault. Do you want me to stick a sign on my chest?"

"I really don't care what you do," Madalaine says, even though she's ignoring what Wayne's sent her for. Lydia will get to that soon enough, she figures.

"You're my sister. I need your help. Can't we—"

"I doubt it," Madalaine says, cutting her off.

Now Lydia's eyes become teary. "Maddie, please. Wayne didn't come home last night...he's furious because I...I called John."

"Really." That wonderful little emphasis on the first syllable when the word is said slowly, so that it comes out as if she's said, *Oh, tell me more.* Too bad she only just learned how to do it; it would have been useful when Bill was cheating on her with Melody and lying about it like a member of the Olympic Prevarication Team. Too late, she remembers that Lydia coined that phrase, taught her the word *prevarication.* Well, of course, Lydia would know about prevarication.

"Look. You were right all along. I'm sorry I tried to lie to you. I did tell Wayne the truth, though, I mean back then, that John is Claire's father. I can't really say it's why I lied to you after...that day. I did it...well, I just did it, and after that, after I told Wayne, he was adamant that no one ever know and of course, I agreed. I mean, he wanted the baby. But now, everything's different. The thing is, the test results are back. I can't give Claire a kidney because of antibodies in my blood. Of course Wayne's not a match—there was no reason to think he would be, but we had him tested anyway. Can you see what I'm saying? What would you do?"

Madalaine is somewhat disarmed. She's not expected this nakedness from Lydia, the brittle bones of her life exposed this way. She gestures at Lydia's tea, and Lydia nods. Madalaine picks it up and takes a sip, mainly to buy herself a moment.

"What does Wayne want you to do?"

"Wait for a cadaver, I guess. The discussion didn't…get that far."

"How far did it get?"

"Nowhere. I couldn't wait. No, it's not that, it's…no matter what Wayne thinks, I can't listen to that. Can you understand? That's why I called John."

"Why is that?" Madalaine says, knowing perfectly well.

"To ask him to be tested. He's a parent, a parent or a sibling, that's the best chance for a match usually."

"And?"

"He needed time to think. There are…ramifications, but frankly, I can't see how any of them have the least importance compared to Claire."

Lydia's elbows are on the table, her fingertips closed and pressing together as if in an unconscious posture of prayer.

Madalaine idly looks at her own hands. Her fingers are woven together but there's a big gap between her palms. They might be the arches of her ribs, sheltering the empty place where her heart should be.

"You think you have the right to do this to Wayne?" Madalaine can't quite hold her eyes to Lydia's. She hates that she does know how Lydia feels.

"No. But I think that nothing is as important as Claire and I'll do whatever…anything." Lydia's voice doesn't even waver.

Lydia's so damn sure of herself. Madalaine would almost like to see Lydia up against something as immovable as death. A degree of shame expands in Madalaine, the way darkness soaks the land at night, slowly. She switches on the light of justice, that notion that tells her who deserves what.

"I've got to get going," she says.

"Maddie, please. Just…can you understand?" Lydia is almost pleading for some sort of absolution. "I don't know what Wayne's going to do, I don't even know where he is. I need someone… just on my side."

"No. You'll probably do exactly what you want. You always do, but I guess you'll have to live with it this time." Madalaine slides out of the booth as abruptly as that movement can be accomplished, dragging her purse alongside her. "I'll see you sometime," she says. "Tell Claire I'm sorry I couldn't stay."

CHAPTER 19

The Ohio River unfurls itself in slow dancer's curves along the northern edge of Maysfield, dividing Kentucky from its northern relative with whom it differs in the insistent, vociferous way of siblings who generally resemble each other as much as not. It's an ordinary, good-sized town, much like the ones across the river if you ignore the silly and sad rantings of longtime residents who need to call themselves Confederates and pop "the South will rise again," into conversation whether it fits or not. Even as a child, I wanted to be in some different, exotic place—not just "across the river" to Cincinnati's outer reaches, or even into that real city itself, the biggest move most Maysfield people made. The river was a knowing, secret friend, one whose back I could climb on to hitch a free ride all the way to the sea someday when I had to.

Of course, like my other fantasies, and sooner rather than later, I confided it to John. He took the notion, and blew his own breath into it like a life preserver big enough for two. We talked about it, not seriously at first, but, with time, the idea of our simply running away together gathering momentum. We told each other, we really didn't *have* to deal with my husband, his wife, even his children, sad as it would be for him to leave them. The children would...well, of course, he'd eventually make contact and they would forgive him and understand. They would someday get to know and love me, and would tell us that it had all been for the best after all.

In good weather, John and I used to meet in a spot just above the riverbank. It wasn't one of the parks, naturally, we were more circumspect than that. One day we'd just gone looking for a private place with enough space that we could park not far from the water, and sit on the sandy, pebbled and wood-strewn edge to talk, and, yes, to kiss and hold each other without fear of someone coming upon us.

Ironically, that's where someone did come upon us, and it was Maddie.

She had gone to Dr. Hays's office at noon, her own bologna sandwich bag in hand, under the impression that I still brought my lunch and ate in the staff room, intending to eat with me—which we'd not done for quite a while—and remind me that I'd said I'd get off work early that day to take Charles to the dentist. Dr. Hays certainly never minded if she came, and she knew the other office help well enough. Donna, I came later to understand, told her that I'd been eating at Kathy's usually, but that day, she knew I'd brought my lunch. "She said she had a headache and wanted some fresh air and a walk," Donna had filled Maddie in. "She's done it a couple of times since the weather's been so pretty. I think she goes along the river because last week her shoes were a mess and she said that was why. She had to take them off and practically wash them with a paper towel."

I wondered if it was some inborn instinct, a blood knowledge of me, that made Maddie decide to go on down to the river area and take her own walk. She said she'd thought to surprise me by joining my picnic, and, she pointed out, she wanted to make sure I was planning to take Charles. But it wasn't like her, not Maddie, who would practically drive to her next-door neighbor's house to avoid a two-minute walk to borrow an egg. I just never believed that she didn't know there was more to it, and was determined to get something on me.

But I don't think she reckoned to get what she did. I never did know exactly how much she saw, how long she'd been standing up on the weedy ridge above the river, where I'd pulled off the dead-end pavement and parked next to John's car. She could have driven up any number of blocks to stop and scan for my car, or me, for that matter, and I have no idea whether she looked long and meticulously, a secret determination, grim and bitter, impelling her from block to block, or whether she simply got lucky fast. I never could talk to her about it. Never. The judgment on her face, not shock, mind you, judgment, closed the subject thoroughly. Maddie's face was chiseled granite, staring, and then she turned her back and walked away without a word. I called her name, but she would not answer. I heard the door of her car slam and the sound of the engine, the wheels on the pavement, all too fast and churning their own message. When I frantically called her later from the office, she said, her voice without a single loophole through which I might have crawled, "If it's what you're worried about, I don't plan to broadcast this."

"I'd like to explain," I remember I said.

"Oh goodness me, Lydie, it's quite self-explanatory."

"Please," I began, but she hung up.

Of course it didn't stay that way, not entirely. Maddie slowly seemed to come around. The line between us kept, from that moment on, a honed edge, even if it was more or less wrapped in padding at any given time. It was never really the same, although I don't believe anyone but she or I would have known it. I knew she carried a concealed weapon; for her part, I believe she thought she knew the truth about me, and because of that, she was already the winner of any present or future comparison of us, of our lives.

Much later, I dropped over to her house one afternoon after work and told her that Dr. Hays had done a test for me, and that Wayne and I were finally, really, actually going to have a baby.

"Right," she said. "Sure you are." We were at Maddie and Bill's first tiny apartment. The television flickered and droned like a swarm of insects stirred by Bill as he provoked it from channel to channel. "Tell it to Wayne."

"Well I already did, of course. He's thrilled. So am I, Maddie. We've wanted this for so long."

"Strange it took so long, isn't it, after all those tests you had and all." Maddie's hair was long then, and she lifted it off her neck and piled it on top of her head before shaking it out again, and I remember that shaking of her head, as though to say no, no, no, no.

"It's not what you think."

"What is his name?"

"Who?"

"The man."

"I'm not seeing him anymore." A pause while I considered. "His name was John."

"Does Wayne know about your…John?" The pause she put before his name was replete with ironic suggestion.

"Please, it's over, it's been over for a long time. There was nothing to it."

"You are such a liar," Maddie said, disgusted and unapproachable. "Such a liar."

"I know I was wrong," I said. "I *know* it. I just hope you'll find a way to…"

"Not in this lifetime," my sister interrupted, her final word on the subject until she erupted at Brian's funeral, and then yesterday, in the hospital coffee shop, where she toyed with me as if I were a monkey in a cage.

John asked me to meet him at the river, to, as he put it, discuss the options about Claire. I wonder if he's done this deliberately, to pull up the file of the terrible time Maddie saw us here, and then I think, no, that didn't have the impact on him that it did on me. Once he knew she wasn't going to tell anyone, he exhaled, went on and told me to do the same. Still, I don't know. Could it be to evoke what was between us, and to signal to me that he won't let me—us—down again? Lately, I've done nothing but this: search everyone's every word, every gesture, every nuance of expression, even the weather, even the silly horoscopes printed in the *Maysfield Citizen* for a sign. Perhaps I really believe God will tell me something; perhaps I really am pacing on the slippery peel that underlines sanity.

I have dressed several times for this, alternating between trying to look sexy, impressive, anything to make him want to please me, and then that seeming absurd, going to the other extreme, to look as pathetic and wrung-out as I feel, to push the guilt button, if he has one. There's that slippery peel again. Finally, I shake my head, not in decision but because I can't think what to do, and put on a khaki skirt and a scoop-necked white cotton shirt. I brush my hair, which I washed when I was going to try to look good, and slip a sheen of lipstick across my mouth. Then, something occurs to me and I do get manipulative after all, though not enough to paint my nails with Revlon's Rose Julep, which he used to say made my hands look like I was a highborn lady of the old South, before work and worry left their map. I open my jewelry box and take out the two real pearls surrounded by circles of real gold, set into earrings that John gave me, before it all happened, before I knew that what I had given all my faith to wasn't what I'd believed it would be. But I remember what he said when he gave them to me. *Since it can't be a ring quite yet, these are for the meantime. Wear them as a token of my constant faith, abiding love*. Actually that was a line of the ring ceremony from the Episcopal wedding service he'd read to me, the one he wanted us to use. Then he said that the next time he said those words, it would be as he slid a gold band onto my left hand.

A man would think that this kind of failure could only happen because I'd been manipulated into bed; a man would think I'm a naive, delusional woman if he heard that I still believe John meant it. Only a woman might understand how I can think that maybe John loved me exactly as he said he did, the most deeply and truly he had loved anything or anyone in his life. He simply did not have the character to be true to the self he'd found with me. He did not have the courage. All the strength I'd thought I saw in him, like that trait of issuing loving orders— "Tell me now."—well, *the strength* was the illusion, not the love. He wanted to be more than he was.

I pray he's grown up since then, because the big test is coming. I guess I'll find out what John meant by *abiding love*.

At the river, I can tell he saw me first; his face is expectant, alive, though not with the joyousness I once knew to be there when his eyes found me. He opens his arms and like a ninny, I walk right into them and put my head on his chest as I did so many times so long ago. Contrary to all plans, I break into tears.

"Lydie. Lydie. Shh, I'm so sorry, Lydie...sweetheart." The last word is almost a whisper, tentative but real.

"I can't lose her. You don't understand, I can't lose her."

"Shh. Shh. It's okay. It's okay. I'm here."

Now here comes the utterly irrational part. John, Claire's father, the man who loved me and I loved, who wasn't there for five minutes that counted when it counted; he says *I'm here*, and I melt like chocolate on this flame of words.

I know I can't give in to it, not for myself, not now.

"Do you mean you'll do it?"

"Well...can we talk about it? About the implications, I mean."

"I thought you wanted to think those through on your own. You said, you said, let me think about the ramifications and then we'll talk." I step back from him. A sudden anger like a black thread surfaces in the neutral fabric of my voice and I try to compose my face, do nothing to put him off. I look down at my feet to get control and then look up, directly at him. When I do, I see him notice the earrings and I know I've hit home. Behind him, the sun glints on the river, the light fragmenting into a strew of diamonds across the top. There was a time when something beautiful like that mattered to me. Not now, not anymore, not unless it's a sign.

"I did. Now I want to talk to you about them."

"It seems simple enough to me. She's in the hospital, on emergency hemodialysis. A machine is keeping her alive. I'll bring her home and she'll do peritoneal dialysis every four hours. I don't even know yet all the things that can go wrong. She was going to go to Wessel in the fall, she got scholarships and we saved money. She can't go now, don't you see? How hard is this to understand?"

John reaches and takes my hand from its clenched position at my side. "Come on, let's walk a little," he says, pulling slightly, and I yield. My foot slips, awkward on the slope where gravel and uncut weeds are ragged, above the bank, which is muddy and now, brief and steep. John tightens his grip and catches me up. The river level is still high; later in the summer, it will diminish in generosity like a desperate heart. A barge heads toward us.

John leads me a little lower where the footing is better but out of the shade. I squint in the glare and almost immediately begin to feel too hot.

"Lydie, Lydie. Can we get to know each other again?"

"Not if you're going to say no." I am wary.

"I don't know what I'm going to say."

"What does getting to know each other have to do with giving Claire a kidney?"

"Well, maybe a lot. You know, my mother's death hit me very hard."

"Of course. I'm sorry I didn't know...."

"I thought you might have seen it in the paper."

"No, really, I didn't know. And I *am* sorry." I feel guilty because I'm less sorry than I should be, not wanting him to digress away from the subject of Claire.

But John continues. When he starts, I counsel myself to breathe slowly, practice patience. Think of it as labor. "You know, she drove me crazy for years. After Dad died, I felt like I had to take care of her for him, but it wasn't something that came...easily, you know, something you do because you want to. I don't think I realized how close I was to her while she was living. Anyway, that's not the point. The point is, I guess, that I wanted to call you. You were the person who came to mind, you were the person I felt I needed, even though, well, I was surrounded with people, and ones who loved me, knew her and loved her, the kids, Barb, the whole ball of wax. But it was you I wanted."

I look at him, but he keeps looking ahead at the approaching barge. "Why?"

"Why indeed. I decided it was because I really loved you, differently and more than I understood when we were together. Anyway, I wanted to call you then."

"But you didn't." I am sweating now, the sun magnified by the river, the humidity of the day mounting. I pull my hand from his to push my hair off my face, wipe my forehead with the back of my wrist.

"No, I didn't."

"Because?"

"It wouldn't have been fair to you."

I shake my head no, glad he doesn't have my hand at the moment. This isn't smart, it flashes to me, but I blurt it out anyway. "I doubt it. I'd guess that you didn't call because you didn't have the guts."

I expect him to respond defensively, but he seems to consider this notion, turning it around in his mind like a found object—an interesting leaf, or rock, or shell. He shakes his head no, but responds with a yes.

"Maybe that's exactly right. I guess so. Doesn't say much for me, does it?"

Then I want to put my arms around him and say it's all right, even after all these years, it's all right. Right then, I know that I love him. It makes no sense, but I do. At the same time, I'm thinking, it's not all right, it's not all right, but you have a chance to make it right. A chance to redeem yourself.

"I know I didn't have the guts when it counted." John speaks more slowly than he used to. "Back then, whatever I said about my obligations, maybe I thought it was true. I hope I thought it was true. But really, you're quite right, I didn't have the courage, and I didn't have the faith."

"Faith in me?" In spite of myself, I am being drawn into his stream.

"That too. But first, not enough faith in myself, that I might know what I was doing even if it was...radical, unacceptable socially, whatever." He pauses, a silence I don't fill. "And I didn't...believe, or understand maybe, that that kind of love really is that important. I thought I could get along without it, I guess, because it was a whole lot easier and less messy."

"I guess you thought it was easy for me."

"Before you were pregnant, yes, I guess I did. No children, and all."

The barge is almost to us. I swear I will not let it pass before I force him back to the tests that he needs to have. I'm determined to tell him about the IVP, the renal arteriogram, the MHC complex on human chromosome six. I have what the initials stand for and a little explanation of each one all neatly written out in my pocket. John dips a little as he walks, sidestepping a hole in the ground, and as he straightens, he picks up my hand again. A breeze ruffles the leaves slightly and cools my face some. Just breathe, take your time, but do it, I counsel myself.

John tightens his grip on my hand and stops us, faces me square on and says, "I'm sorry. I'm so sorry. I was wrong...you got it a lot quicker than I did, the love part, didn't you?" It's a rhetorical question.

Two, three, four seconds. Five, six, nine, ten. I make myself. "Please, we have to talk about Claire. She's on dialysis, she needs a transplant. I have a list of tests...."

"Lydie, I *am* talking about Claire, don't you see that? Is there any chance for us to try again?"

"Then once, live it. If you love me, do this for me. If you won't do it for your daughter, do it for me." I pull my hand loose; the gesture feels angry.

John is very quiet. I am giving him nothing, I know that, and I know that no matter what I feel, that I'll give him anything I have to to get the best chance for Claire. But I'm trying to give him nothing, because…I'm not sure. And what about Wayne? All these years of loving Claire, of claiming her, of protecting her from history? I have no idea what anyone's rights are now. Claire's life, that's all I'll think about now.

"Fair enough. Fair enough," he says. "I see your point. Why would you believe me?"

"So you'll…?" I can't take a chance that I am only hearing what I want to.

"Yes. I'll be tested. How do I go about it?"

The moment is an eggshell, blown and painted by hand in twenty-four-karat gold, sky-blue and green, that fragile, that precious. I pull Dr. Douglas's card out of my skirt pocket and hand it to him.

"This is Anna Claire's doctor. She knows…about you. She'll make the arrangements at the hospital. Here's the tests, I've got it all here…." While I'm unfolding my list, I do that much for John. I give him Claire's real name, which, like the size and color of her rich, earthy eyes, comes from his side of our lost family.

CHAPTER 20

"The whole thing works on gravity, see? Really, you'll be amazed at how efficient it is. It's like you're a car getting your oil changed four times a day every day."

Ellie is looking at Claire instead of watching the nurse the way she's supposed to, so she sees Claire roll her eyes. Lydia is intent on the nurse's most minute gesture, and interrupts every three sentences to ask another question.

"Now watch this, carefully. Remember from the video, the first thing is to set the IV pole up, you should be able to just have a place at home where you keep it in place. Here's the Y set, see, you connect one of these tubes into your catheter and one into the bag of solution...." The nurse runs on and on, her manner as cheery as a television commercial.

It's their third training session, and supposed to be a review. Ellie feels sick when the nurse is demonstrating again how the titanium iodine cap twists onto the tube that snakes out of Claire's abdomen, "...to kill any bacteria on the outside. Sanitation is essential, you know, we've talked about that."

"I've taken baths all my life," Claire says, "once a week whether I need it or not. Does this mean I'll have to kick it up to twice?" She laughs, just a little, but Ellie thinks the nurse, whatever her name is, might be getting on Claire's nerves as much as on her own. Either that, or Claire doesn't want to do this. Ellie's never been one to know what goes on in someone else's mind.

They're on the dialysis unit in the hospital. Big, modern-style paintings of geometric shapes in bright blue, yellow and green decorate the walls. When Lydie first complimented the nurse on how attractive they'd made the unit, Claire said she likes paintings of oceans and mountains better, and the nurse said, "Well, at home, you can look at whatever you want while you do your exchanges." A tube has been surgically inserted so she can do peritoneal dialysis at home and won't have to come into the clinic three times a week.

How can Lydie just get her face right in there that way, studying what an occluded tube looks like? The catheter looks like it just pokes straight into Claire's flesh. It has to hurt; it's not possible that it doesn't. This almost seems like the opposite of when Claire was on hemodialysis after the accident, with all her blood draining out of her as if the machine were a giant metallic leech. Now, the image in Ellie's mind is of all that solution pouring into Claire, and how Claire would have it inside her—the world's most serious premenstrual bloating is all Ellie can imagine—and then drain it back out into another plastic bag that would itself get drained into the toilet.

"We can handle this, we've got it now," Lydie says to the nurse, "don't we, honey?" The last part to Claire.

"Of course you do," says the nurse, who looks grandmotherly, in her bright manner. "Can you see all right, Eleanor? Have you got this part?"

What Ellie sees is that the nurse's gold-blond hair is dyed that way. A half inch of gray is visible at the roots when she puts her head way down. "I'm fine, yes," Ellie lies. "I get it," she adds before the nurse has a chance to question her.

"Remember, the most important thing we have to avoid is peritonitis." The nurse's name tag says Joann McCalley, R.N., Training Director, but she's not wearing nurse clothes. Who's this *we*, Kemo Sabe? Ellie thinks, and reminds herself that it's definitely not her problem. Lydia's the Tonto to Claire's Lone Ranger act here. "It's very, very important that the diallite solution is never heated higher than ninety-eight point six, and that your body doesn't get overheated by something like a swimming pool. Hot tubs are out, for example."

"Damn. And I was just about to have my Jacuzzi moved to my dorm room," Claire says. Ellie sees Lydie's head swing to check Claire's face, but she doesn't say anything.

"Peritonitis is the main danger, and it can and will make you very, very sick. And don't miss any exchanges. There won't be any symptoms initially, but remember that poison is accumulating in your system."

"She won't miss any, but can you run through the symptoms of peritonitis again?" Lydie asks, her forehead furrowed, but her voice calm and factual. Lydie's always calm and factual, Ellie thinks.

"Two different things, remember. But peritonitis? She'll know. Your temperature goes way up, you can't move, well, the whole body malfunctions. Patients say it feels like the worst grippe you've ever had. It's very important to get to the hospital right away, any symptoms."

When Ellie tunes in again, Joann is reviewing diet. "...and no bananas, either. Lean red meat is good—emphasize protein, remember that. I gave you the list of sodium and potassium levels in foods, right? It's best to keep a careful watch on processed foods, especially. No fast food... Watch for your ankles and feet swelling."

Ellie thinks she remembers that swollen ankles are a symptom of pregnancy.

"Could you explain the nephritis symptoms again?" Lydie asks a minute later. Ellie pats her bangs and the white bow at the top of her head. The humidity from the rain this morning made her hair flat, in spite of extra hair spray. She smoothes her skirt, a blue Vista fabric that just refuses to wrinkle, over her thighs. It's from a line the store is pushing and Ellie gets a nice employee discount, fifteen percent. When Elvis did the Hawaiian concert it must have been really humid. How would she have fixed her hair there?

"So there's no cure for that except a transplant," Lydie is saying, and Joann says, "Unfortunately, no. But don't worry about that. I can't imagine that Claire won't be a good candidate for transplant. I know they've been doing the workup on you, honey. You've talked with the social worker, right?" When Claire nods assent, Joann goes on. "Well, see? That's one of the last things we do. You'll be on the UNOS—did I already tell you? That's the United Network for Organ Sharing—waiting list. The social worker went over all of that with you, didn't she?"

Ellie glances at Lydie and sees there are tears in her eyes.

"He asked me about my sex life," Claire says, and there's no telling from her voice what she thought of that. "I'm going away to college pretty soon," she says then. At the moment, Ellie doubts it big-time, what with that tube thingie and all the rules. She doesn't get the connection to the sex life question either. *What sex life?* she wants to know. Does this have some connection to the swollen ankles? She doesn't dare ask.

"Well," Joann starts to answer Claire, but hesitates. Then she starts up again and says, "It's a lot easier to monitor diet and rest and fluid intake when you live at home. Your urologist will probably tell you—"

"No," Claire says. "I want my life back."

"I know it would be a disappointment…" Joann begins again, but seeing Claire's face, stops and leaves it to her doctor to go into that. Ellie notices that Lydie's face looks like it's carved out of granite while she listens to Joann and Claire and says nothing.

CHAPTER 21

Madalaine blows out a sigh as she gives herself over to the air-conditioning. She tosses her purse on a kitchen chair and opens the refrigerator to see if Jennifer has left any iced tea in the pitcher. An inch sloshes on the bottom. Madalaine sighs again and as she turns to the cabinet for a glass, she jumps in fright. Wayne stands like a specter on the other side of the refrigerator. It seems impossible that she didn't see him before, yet his body has the posture and quietude of someone who has long been right where he is.

"Wayne! God, don't do that. You scared me to death."

"Didn't mean to. What'd she say?"

"Hi to you, too." Madalaine sets the glass she's taken out down on the counter with more force than necessary. "You want some tea? I can make up more. Jennifer always puts the damn thing back empty so she won't have to wash it. Brian always did that, and…" She breaks off there, fighting tears that surface like an underground stream whenever and wherever they want.

"No. What'd she say?"

Another sigh from Madalaine. "Will you stop badgering me? Are you just worried that I don't have enough on my mind?" She deliberately turns her back to pour the inch of tea from the pitcher; it becomes two inches in the bottom of a tall glass.

"Sorry," he mutters, yet doesn't move a fraction to relieve the relentlessness of his gaze. It is sheepish, but a demand all the same.

"Look, I couldn't stop her."

"That's it? What'd she say?"

"Do I look like a damn tape recorder? She just said no, she's going to do what she's going to do."

"What'd you say to her?"

"Oh, God, I don't remember. Told her you deserved better, that it would all work out with Claire if she'd just back off, there'll be a cadaver. Just ask me, hey, there's cadavers all over when you least expect them. And Wayne, before you jump off that rock onto my back, yes, Brian had been gone too long before they knew Claire's kidney was damaged."

"I wasn't going to say that."

"Oh, so now you're Mr. Sensitivity suddenly? When'd you get religion?"

Madalaine sits down at the kitchen table. This is how she used to talk to Bill, anger rising over any decent impulse she had, like tolerance or forgiveness. It took her over, was what it did. Just took her over. It's worse now, too, since Bill left again. "I do not want to think about that," she says aloud, meaning Bill.

"No, really, I wasn't. Appreciate your..."

Madalaine knows she's switched on Wayne's guilt, finally. Good, let him stew in it. Let him and Lydie and even precious, perfect Claire stew in it. Her satisfaction isn't unmixed when he turns and walks to the bathroom. She does feel a little sorry for him, too. It's really Lydie she wants to hurt the way she hurts, though Madalaine couldn't say why in a sentence or paragraph. Right away she hears water running full force in the bathroom, too quickly. She goes to the end of the hall and then, her footfalls absorbed by the carpeting, stands until she can hear his rough sobs.

Madalaine hasn't wasted much time feeling bad, and it's a good thing. She'd thought Wayne would be done with her, but no, he comes back into the kitchen while she's still at the table trying to call up the energy to make more tea for the refrigerator. All the morning's momentum has dissipated, flying off in every direction like dust motes and then disappearing the way they do when the sun goes behind a cloud, and a room chills and darkens at once.

"That's it," he says, as though twenty minutes hadn't elapsed.

"What's it?" Madalaine says, brow furrowed as much in irritation as confusion.

"I won't be party to it. Can I stay here?"

"Slow down, will you? Won't be party to what?" she asks, angling for time to think. She's pretty sure she knows exactly what he's talking about.

Such weariness she feels, and no thought emerges with enough clarity to trust.

"What Lydie's doing. I can't have it. It's not right."

"Well, I worry about what she's going to tell Claire. Will the doctor let her just lie and say they found a match from the cadaver pool whose family said yes?" Madalaine is being clever. What does he mean, *Can I stay here?* For what? For how much longer? This afternoon? Six years? She is wary, wanting to know how to maneuver. She doesn't want Wayne in her house, not Wayne or anyone else except maybe Bill, in her house, but wouldn't Lydie just have a fit? Not that Lydie would admit it. Not now, not to the Mother of the Dead Boy.

"I dunno."

"You *dunno* which?"

"Either one. I don't want to know it, anyway."

"Well, Wayne, for heaven's sake, she's your *daughter*."

"Not mine, his now."

Madalaine wonders if she's gone too far. She shrugs invisibly, fatigued at the whole mess, and then the stream rises again and she knows to go to the bedroom to cry awhile for Brian.

It's late afternoon when she emerges from her room again, to answer the front doorbell. Two late arrangements of longer-lasting flowers, some kind of nasty-smelling mums in the dining room, are finally exhaling their last. She hasn't watered them in days, which has, doubtless, helped them toward premature death. Bill stands outside on the step up to the door, though only a day ago he was coming in whenever he liked, not even shouting out a hello of warning. "Wayne here?" are the first words out of his mouth, and he gestures toward Wayne's truck, still on the street in front of the house. Then he remembers his manners, and says somewhat formally, "How're you doing? I came to pick up Jenny for dinner, did you remember?"

Of course she hadn't. "I was sleeping," Madalaine says. "I guess she's in the family room, or the yard…Jen?" On the last she raises her voice, and when there's no answer, calls again. "Outside, I guess. Check the back."

Bill returns to it. "That Wayne's truck?"

"I guess. Like I said, I was sleeping." Madalaine had hoped Wayne would be gone when she came out, that the question *Can I stay here?* would have disappeared like a stillborn problem.

Bill takes a step deeper into the living room. "Wayne?"

"Yeah," comes back the answer from the family room where the local news has just started on the television.

"Hey, how're you doing?" Bill calls again.

Wayne's answer, an inaudible blur, gradually separates into distinct words as he walks through the kitchen to respond.

"Hey, how're you doing?" Bill repeats it, sticking out his hand to shake Wayne's. "What's up? I thought you'd still be at work."

"Didn't go," Wayne answers, which is true, although he's dressed in his coveralls.

"How's Claire and Lydie?"

"Don't know."

Bill is confused, shoots a look at Madalaine then turns back to Wayne.

"What do you mean you don't know? Is Claire worse?"

Wayne hesitates a moment, dreading the number of words he'll have to string together if he really answers, and decides he's not up to it. "I dunno. I haven't been up there."

"What? I mean, why not? What's going on?"

Wayne sighs. "Me and Lydie have a difference and I asked Maddie if I can stay here awhile."

Bill shoots Madalaine a look that says, *Jesus Christ, what have you done now?* at which she instantly takes offense, even knowing she's had some hand in it. He has no right accusing her.

Bill runs his hand across his head, his fingers leaving rake tracks in his dark blond hair. "Jeez, man, I'm sorry to hear that, but isn't this sort of a time that a family ought to stick together? I mean, what with Claire's dialysis and all…"

Madalaine snorts and says softly, "Yes, Wayne, take it from Bill. A family ought to stick together."

Bill ignores her. "Can't you and Lydie work out…whatever it is? I mean, this just isn't the time to be…doing this."

"Bill, there is just so amazingly much you don't know about this family that you would, if you'd taken your own advice for five minutes. As I told you, Wayne, you're quite welcome here."

Wayne sees the look on Bill's face and mutters, "No reason anymore not to tell Bill."

"Tell me what?" Bill wheels to Madalaine. "What's going on?"

"Look, Bill, if you want to be part of this family and know our business, then tell Melody goodbye and come home. Otherwise, our family will keep it to ourselves, thank you." Madalaine knows this makes no sense, that Bill's connection to the family is, if anything, stronger than Wayne's, there being a biological child connecting him. And, of course, Wayne is, in his way, doing exactly what Bill did. It all just makes her too tired to sort out. She hates both of them standing there uselessly as men do. She just plain hates them, and now she's stuck herself with Wayne for at least another night.

"I'll go find Jennifer," she says, before Bill starts picking at the holes in her gauzy logic. She doesn't want to talk to him anymore.

The two men stand, both looking at the floor and air space Madalaine just left empty.

Moments pass, and Madalaine comes back with Jennifer behind her. "Hey, Daddy," she says with an open smile and picks up speed to get around her mother, across the room to Bill, who lifts her off her feet in a bear hug.

"Hey, yourself, princess. Where you want to eat?"

Madalaine realizes that Bill is telling her he won't take Jennifer to Melody's apartment for dinner, and a small flare of gratitude lights and then subsides like a match.

"McDonald's!" the girl cries.

"Yuck," he answers. "Well, I suppose. Did you ever hear of vegetables, young lady?"

Since when had he been able to identify a vegetable, let alone care who ate one? Madalaine feels the presence of another woman in Bill, and the gratitude extinguishes.

"I'll have her back by nine," Bill says, opening the door and guiding Jennifer out with one hand on her back. "After we eat, we'll get ice cream and maybe go over to school, shoot a few hoops? Or..."

"I'll get the basketball," Jennifer says, pleased that he'd play ball with her, something he used to do with Brian.

Madalaine closes the door behind them a good deal more loudly than necessary, but stops short of slamming it for Jennifer's sake. She turns to Wayne. "You can stay here tonight, and maybe another night if you need to, but after this, you'd better find your own place."

"Yeah," Wayne answers. "Yeah."

Three days later, Wayne is still there. He's gone to Lydie's and gotten some shirts, socks and underwear, the razor he uses to shave above and below his beard and a few more items of that sort. He sat around for another day, but then got up and went to work, as though homes and lives were interchangeable without the occupant having to much notice. But he's silent most of the time. While he's watching television in the same room with Jennifer the second night, a memory of Wayne's mother comes to Madalaine. "He's ate up," Madalaine had heard Mildred say one Christmas at Lydie's, referring to someone who was angry or brooding or both. "Just ate up."

CHAPTER 22

I am bringing Claire home. No working spleen, which is no big deal, and no working kidney, which is a very big deal, and half the basement filled with a one-month supply of her Y sets, povidone iodine caps and forty boxes of bagged dialysis solution. Claire's IV pole is already set up next to Wayne's recliner so that she can watch television or read while she does her exchanges. John was tested yesterday and I can almost believe that he will be a match. I caution myself; God's made me no promises. No one has except Wayne, and I believe he's breaking his now, though with good cause, he'd say.

Years ago I wanted to believe in John and I did. Too much. How much of what I saw in him did I paint there, with the hues of the palette I carried, and with my own brushes? I find myself slipping back to that place—seeing what I need in him, seeing what I long for. Of course, then I wanted something for myself and now it's for Claire, but perhaps that's not so different and I haven't learned a thing after all.

He wants something from me, that's for sure. There's a price. The pull is there, strong as the moon on tides, and I know he knows it. Maybe he believes that I still cannot say *no* to him, even though *no* has shot out of his mouth to me as easy as spitting ice a couple of feet, more than once and when it's been about more than a casual question. Perhaps he's right and I still can't. Of course, it's all too confused now, with Claire's life on one side of the balance scale, as light and tenuous as soul. I know I'll put whatever I have to, whatever I can find from wherever I find it to lower the platform that holds her up there like someone all ready for God to take, back toward this grounded life here, here with me.

* * *

This morning, I got in the shower before I went to pick up Claire. I've not told her that Wayne isn't here. It's twice occurred to me that he might be at Maddie's, but only because she's made herself so scarce and I'd think she'd want all the support she can get, but I remind myself that Bill's been with her and he's doubtless more comfort than she'd consider me.

That brings me back to Wayne, though, and where he is. Not why, of course, that's not really a question. I know the answer to that. What I don't know is what he means to do. I don't let myself have feelings about his being gone, except for Claire's sake. But I don't even know if Wayne's been to see her in the past two days and asking her could only provoke questions I don't want to answer. My mind chases its tail around the presence of the IV pole and the absence of Wayne, but I made myself put on cheerful colors, fixed my hair and put on makeup, so Claire wouldn't guess how frightened I am.

"Mrs. Ellis is going to come over after she sees Kevin today, Mom, is that okay?"

"I guess." Really, I wanted Claire to myself today, but like a ninny, I can't say no to her, not now. And I've not asked about Kevin the way I know Claire wants me to. I try to correct my lapse, infuse hearty concern into my voice. "How is he doing? Still no change, I guess, or you'd know."

"No," Claire says and her eyes fill. Kevin is still unconscious—she avoids the word *coma*—and the longer it lasts, she understands, the worse his chances. Beth Ellis, his mother, has stayed in contact with Claire by phone, and wants to see her. This much I understand. Claire must feel like a link to her son, to the last time Kevin was himself, awake, vital, possessed of a certain future. I do understand. I know that by tomorrow Claire will be badgering me to take her to see him.

We're in the living room, Claire on the couch with a sheet

underneath and then folded over her as if she's the filling for a cotton taco. Her schoolbooks are piled on the coffee table, with a pitcher of water, a glass, tissues, the TV guide from the paper and a pink rose in a bud vase, surrounded by baby's breath. She's thin, but she's here, she's alive. She's brushed her hair and pulled it back into a barrette, which makes the hollows under her eyes stand out. I find myself touching her in every little way I can, smoothing her hair, squeezing her shoulder when I pass alongside the couch, sitting beside her and stroking her hand. It's too much, I know. Before she shoos me away, I try to lighten up on my own.

"Did you believe Ellie? She'd pass out if she ever had to actually help you hook up," I say with a laugh.

She grins. "Presley would be more help. I was pretty impressed when she said she understood everything, especially since she kept her eyes closed when the nurse was showing her how to connect the catheter to the Y set. I think she actually did lose consciousness when they were showing us how to give me the Epogen shot," she laughs. "Actually, I couldn't believe she even agreed to show up."

I'd stepped widely around why it wasn't Wayne being trained by saying what I'd told Maddie, that the hospital suggested one person who didn't live in the same house be trained...patent nonsense, but credible enough. "Yes, well it *was* like nailing Jell-O to a tree, pinning her down to come. We probably would have been better off with Presley...or Charles."

We smile at each other and roll our eyes. Then, she turns suddenly serious. "Mom, is Dad mad at me about something?"

I pause, too long. I'd hoped to open the subject myself so Claire wouldn't think I've been hiding it from her. Which, of course, I have. "Of course not, sweetheart." My heart feels like a rock in an avalanche, pounding and falling, pounding and falling. I sit on the edge of the couch, but between her feet and her knees, where I can touch her but not up by her waist where eye contact would be requisite.

"Where is he? I mean, not right now, I know he's at work, but he didn't come to see me with you…"

"He's angry at me, not you." Let this cup pass from me.

"What?" This isn't something Claire is accustomed to. Wayne and I rarely argue, and certainly not in front of Claire. She doesn't realize that we don't have enough in common to argue, that's how separately the currents of our lives run, though on the surface we're as unrippled as the river on a windless night.

"He's angry at me, not you."

"What do you mean he's mad at you? Why?"

"We disagree about…how to go about getting you a kidney."

"What's there to disagree about? I'm on the list, aren't I? I mean, I had the interviews, I had the tests, what else is there?"

"Yes. Yes, you're on the list, I mean. But…usually a relative, they call it a first-degree relative, is the best match." This has to be the hardest thing I've done in my life. "The chance of rejection is less if the donor is a first-degree relative, I mean it's a better match, more of the tissue matches…you remember about the antigens." I'm stammering, sounding like Charles, the way I'm repeating myself. I can see the confusion gathering on Claire's face.

"But you and Dad were already…"

"Honey, there's no easy way to say this. Dad's your Dad and he loves you more than anything in the world. He's not your biological father, and—"

"What?" Claire cuts me off. It's a disbelieving gasp.

"He's not your biological father. That doesn't change how he loves you, or how much he wishes he were, and, see, I'd promised him that I'd never… Claire, I'm so sorry. I can't stand that I have to tell you this, but I have to. Your dad isn't here because I contacted your real, I mean your biological father, to ask him to be tested. I'd promised your dad that I'd never let the man know anything about you or me, but, can you see, I…" I stop, seeing the shock on Claire's face, a deadly white replacing the hospital pallor she'd worn home.

"Are you telling me I'm adopted?" She is trying to sit up, but the angle is awkward. Maybe she's sore from where they inserted the tube.

"Not exactly, but I guess that's kind of it, I mean with Dad."

"Was I born to you?"

"Oh yes, sweetheart, yes. I didn't mean…yes, you were born to me."

"But Dad's not my father? Do you mean you were married before? I thought you and Dad were married way before I was born."

Forcing the words out is like physical labor. My hands and face are clammy with shame. "We were, honey."

"So you…?"

"Yes, I did. I hope you'll try to understand, I'll try to explain it. Your father is…"

But Claire doesn't want my nice, fuzzy explanation with the watercolor wash that would run right and wrong into a coherent picture together. She is crying, but interrupts, making her voice clear as words newly etched on a marble tombstone. "My father is Dad, and I don't want to hear anything else. I don't want anything from whoever you're talking about, especially not his kidney. I'd rather die. And I don't want anything from you, either. Could you please leave me alone now?"

Nothing she could say would be worse than what she's said. *Leave me alone.* I plead with my eyes and put my hand on her leg. "Claire, please let me ex…" But there's no point in going on. She's turned her head toward the couch back and closed her eyes, like Ellie yesterday, keeping themselves from the bloody, the ugly side of life where I, sister and mother, live now.

Claire lies like that, unmoving for better than an hour. Twice I tiptoe to the end of the couch and start to open my mouth, wanting to beg. Twice I close it and slink away, because there's nothing to say. The doorbell rings, and Beth Ellis, a tiny woman, is on the porch, dwarfed behind a bouquet of red roses all arranged with greenery and baby's breath in a clear glass vase. There must be at least a dozen, maybe more. She had sent flowers to the hospital, too, signing Kevin's name to the card with a sweet note. I've never liked Kevin all that much, but maybe I'd not think anyone was good enough for Claire. He's not really objectionable; he's okay, that's all, okay. Claire could do a lot better; probably she could do worse, too. I've never seen what she sees in him. Hoping Claire hasn't heard the bell, I keep my voice low when I greet her.

"Oh, Beth, come in." I widen the door and then my arms for what I intended as a brief hug, but Beth clings to me. I've only met her on two or three occasions. I can smell hair spray and some other light scent, overlaying a faint sweaty odor. How exhausted she must be, how despairing. I need to remember I'm not the only mother suffering, but it is I who finally pull back a little and gesture at the roses. "Those are so beautiful. All of us have thought about Kevin so much, and you know, I hope, that we are praying for him. How are you—how is he today?" What a liar I am; he's hardly a shadow in my mind. Scum-sucking bottom dweller: isn't that what Brian used to call people he considered low? Of course my daughter has closed her eyes and turns her back to me. I am defensive and offensive at once, of course, beneath a suffocating quilt of hopelessness.

Her eyes fill and my shame expands like a sponge soaking in her tears. "No change. I'm hoping you'll let Claire come as soon as possible. Different voices, you know, maybe..." Beth says.

"Actually, she's asleep right now. Could I have her call..." I begin, but Claire's voice comes, an arrow shooting down the hall at me.

"I'm awake, please, come in Mrs. Ellis. I'm in here, in the living room," she says, as if I wouldn't show Beth the way.

"Oh good, she's up. I know she wanted to see you very much," I say. "Let me take you to her."

Claire has worked herself to a sitting position and is hurriedly jamming some pillows behind herself. I quicken my pace to help her, but she says, "I've got it." Then she slides herself over, making extra space by her on the couch, and opens her arms for Beth to come sit next to her, to hug and be hugged. The vibrant rose bouquet Beth sets on the coffee table mocks the pale, half-open bud I bought her. I stand awkwardly off to one side, watching.

Politely, Claire does something she never would have before. "Mom, would you mind? Mrs. Ellis and I might like to talk in private."

"Of course," I answer as naturally as if I weren't being banished and humiliated. "I'll bring you something to drink."

In the kitchen, I get out ice and tall glasses and meticulously make up some powdered iced-tea mix for them. I do everything as quietly as possible, trying to hear what they are saying, but their voices are low and exclude me.

CHAPTER 23

Madalaine sighs, a nonresponse. Sometimes Jennifer will drop a subject when Madalaine sighs, getting the message not to pursue it. No such luck now.

"So can we, Mom?" Jennifer repeats the question, which is about going to see Claire.

Madalaine sighs again, involuntarily this time, trying to gather and arrange the words that will keep this exchange short and definitive. They are eating an early supper at the kitchen table, another pasta casserole from someone at church. The freezer is dangerous to open, a ghetto of stacked foil-wrapped packages and Tupperware with people's names neatly taped to the bottom, which means she's got to use the stuff up within a reasonable amount of time so the dish can be returned with a little note of thanks in her precise backhand. Unnecessarily, Madalaine uses a knife to cut some of her salad to give herself another couple of seconds to think. The utensil scrapes on stoneware, a sound hollow and grating at once.

"I think not, honey."

"Why?" The inevitable question, complete with Jennifer's whiny tone.

"Because Mommy is having a hard time thinking about Claire right now."

"But she's going to be okay, right, she's not going, she's not like…?"

"No, she's not like Brian, she's not going to die. She's on dialysis, that's when you have to use some special solution to do the work of a kidney to clean your blood. She can live like that until they find a kidney that will work in her."

"Can she sit up and watch television or stuff like that?"

"Sure she can. She's just getting her strength back. Ellie told me that she may even be strong enough to go ahead and graduate with her class. She can't have the real diploma until she takes her finals, but if the doctor says it's okay, she may get to do the ceremony."

"So why can't we go see her if she's not going to die?"

"I told you, I'm just having a hard time, I can't. I get too upset."

"But you said she's not going to…"

Madalaine sighs again. Nothing is easy. "It's not that, honey, it's that, well, maybe I feel like it's a little bit her fault because her boyfriend…"

"It's not Claire's fault. I don't see how you can think that."

"Well, sweetheart, maybe I just get too jealous because she'll be okay and Brian died, you know?"

"But that's not fair. It wasn't Claire's fault. She's nice, Mom, she wouldn't, she wouldn't…" Jennifer sputters indignation and Madalaine begins to regret her comparative honesty. She should have just said that Claire wasn't allowed visitors. Actually, for all Madalaine knows, she's not. Her informant is Ellie, and Presley would be more likely than Ellie to get a story straight.

"I'm sorry, Jen. I really am. I'd just prefer we keep to ourselves right now." Madalaine tries to look Jennifer in the eyes without shame and without letting her sense any weakness. Her daughter knows all too well how to work her over since Bill left. Used to be, Madalaine was the one who knew how to hold the line, but it's gone slack, abandoned to lie on some forgotten deck while Madalaine tries to remain in her skin. "Can you try to understand?"

Jennifer bangs her fork down on her plate, splattering a bit of sauce onto the place mat, already a week in need of washing. "You're mean," she says, and starts to push her chair back.

"Hey, where are you going? Don't talk to me like that. Finish your dinner."

"I'm not hungry. I'm going to my room."

"Can you finish your dinner? You need to eat your salad at

least. Come on, princess." Even Madalaine hears the wheedling that's crept into her voice.

"Don't call me princess. I don't want it. I want to go." Jennifer's eyes are glittering, and Madalaine realizes how little Jen has cried since that night at the hospital when she covered her face with her open palms and sobbed against them.

"Honey, I'm sorry..." she begins, but Jen averts her face and leaves the table, heading through the kitchen toward the bedroom hallway.

It's been a bad day, another one. This morning, Madalaine picked up the roll of pictures she took on prom night. She'd dropped them off at the Rexall in town yesterday, somehow not expecting the next-day service that's been standard for five years at least. But she's not opened the envelope. She needs the pictures to be good, to show happiness on Brian's unsuspecting face. They are the last news she will ever have of him. If she never opens them, there will always be something of him that can still be discovered.

She is still sitting at the table in settling darkness, half-eaten food on dirty plates at Jennifer's place and her own when Wayne comes in. Jennifer's made no appearance or sound since their words earlier. The house feels empty even though Madalaine knows it's not. All the will is leached out of her again; the will to get out of the chair and clear the table, the will to try to talk with Jennifer, the will to drag air into her lungs, the will to push it back out again.

"Hey," Wayne says after a moment of silence. He is standing just inside the house, the door shut behind him.

"Hey yourself," she says irritably. "What do you want?"

"Nothin'," he says.

Madalaine knows exactly what he wants. Permission to cross the kitchen, go into the family room, turn on the television, doze in front of a couple of hours of inane crap, then use her bathroom for a while and sack out on the couch in the family room. She guesses he's keeping his clothes in his truck; she rarely sees anything of his around the house. Who's doing his laundry? What a weird bird he is. Really, he's not bothering her, it's just stupid, that's all, stupid that he can go on not deciding anything.

"What do you mean, nothing? Why are you standing there?"

"Okay if I look at vour television a while?"

"And then?"

"I'll sleep on your couch if it's okay."

Madalaine shrugs. "Look, it doesn't bother me, but what are your plans?"

"Sleep on the couch.' Wayne is obviously confused because he's already said this.

Can anyone alive really be this dumb? "You sound like Charles. I *mean* after tonight again. What are you going to *do*? Tomorrow or the next day, or the next? You know, you've got to do *something*."

Wayne shrugs, as if to say, *How should I know*, but what he says is, "Go to work."

Brian used to call it going ballistic when she did it: raise her voice and let her irritation bounce from wall to wall. "For God's sake, Wayne, do you know what a wumpf bird is? It's a hairy-feathered wingless bird that flies in ever-decreasing concentric circles until, wumpf, it flies up its own ass. That's you, Wayne. You're driving me insane. I don't care what you do, just do something. See, you're not like me. There're things you *can* do."

Wayne is still trying to figure out the wumpf bird. He's distracted by Madalaine having said the word *ass*.

Madalaine says, "Oh, come here. Sit down. Have you eaten? I can stick some of this casserole in the microwave for you." She gestures at Jennifer's chair, and pulls Jennifer's plate back from the edge.

"I ate at McDonald's."

"Another gourmet meal, huh?"

"It was all right."

Madalaine is roused enough to stand up anyway and pivot two or three times to put the dirty dishes over on the kitchen counter. She flips on the light over the sink, opens the refrigerator and pours two glasses of iced tea from the pitcher. Then, though, she thinks better of it, pours the tea back in, and when she replaces the pitcher, takes two beers from the refrigerator. She puts one at Jennifer's place and points at it. "Sit," she orders.

Wayne apparently can't help staring as Madalaine takes a sip from her can, and then another. She sits back down, her chair back from the table and at an angle now.

"It's no big deal, Wayne," she says, something like defiance in her tone. "I can drink a beer if I want."

"Yeah," he says. "I guess." And sits.

"Look. You can't go on like this…like Casper the Ghost, gliding in and out of McDonald's, my couch and your truck. It's just not a workable plan, it's too…you've got to…"

Wayne looks miserable. "You said it wasn't bothering you."

"That's not the point. You need to do something about Lydia…and Claire, for that matter. What do you think Claire thinks? I mean, have you talked to her?"

"Whatever Lydie told her."

"Don't you think *you* should tell her something? You know, nothing's changed, Wayne. For God's sake, you raised her, you're the only father she knows. None of this is news to you, you said that yourself, so nothing's changed. This isn't between you and Claire, it's between you and Lydia." Madalaine is surprising herself, and what she's saying seems inconsistent with what she said to Jennifer until she remembers that she has an entirely separate reason for her feelings about Claire. Really, it's just all too much to keep straight, and she's suddenly exhausted by even trying. She takes another drink, and then just sits, slouched in the chair. Neither of them say anything and they do not look at each other. When Madalaine's can is two-thirds empty, she's gathered enough effort into one place to get up and walk toward her bedroom.

Wayne finishes his beer, and then finishes Madalaine's. He gets up and goes out into the twilight through the same door he came in.

CHAPTER 24

I am convinced that John has refused permission to Dr. Douglas to release his test results to me. There's not a reason on the planet that she couldn't have just told me on the phone, instead of my sitting here in her waiting room with John for her to tell us in person, and the two of us together. I'm in no position to argue with him, so, of course, I just agreed to meet him here at ten o'clock, as he said.

Several plants stand in corners looking extraordinarily healthy and one hangs from the ceiling nearing the one, large window, trailing greenery like it expects to go on forever. Gert, Ellie's hairdresser, would definitely call these flourishing vines and leaves a sign, and I even remind myself that the Norfolk pine could also be called an evergreen. That's got to be as good a category as any could be. When my horoscope says something good in the morning paper, I suck hope through it like it's a straw stuck into lemonade. This morning, though, it said, "A new moon in your birth sign means new beginnings. But first there are still loose ends that need to be tied up on the work or money fronts. Don't let anyone persuade you that you are anything other than capable, competent and entirely committed to the cause." I like the first sentence, but what do I do with the rest? I toy with the idea that I can just cross out whatever doesn't apply, and I'm sitting here working that idea around to see if that's a fair use, when a nurse opens a door and says, "Mrs. Merrill? You and…you can come in now." She suppressed a double take when she looked up from her clipboard and had to modify the sentence she had ready in her mouth. As I'm walking ahead of John, I touch the leaf of a beautiful schefflera for luck and discover it's silk. I immediately think that's bad, that beautiful things die here and they've replaced real plants with artificial ones to fool people into thinking that anything will come out all right.

The nurse shows us back to Dr. Douglas's office, the official one with the big wooden desk, framed diplomas and prints on the wall. There's a small aquarium and the four tropical fish within it all look healthy, their amber and yellow strips and wide filmy tails vigorous and busy. I take that as a good sign to cancel out the silk plant, and dare a look at John.

He's in a charcoal business suit with a striped shirt—muted red, green, blue and gray stripes on a white background—and wears a tie that has the exact colors of the shirt in them like a miracle. I know he's been trying to get me to look at him, and now, when I do, he holds his hand out wanting me to put mine in it. When I do, more than half because I don't want to offend him, it's my left hand and my slim white-gold wedding band and matching engagement ring get briefly covered by his thumb. I have to shut Wayne out of my mind. If John is a match, no matter what Claire or Wayne says now, I'll know I was right, I did the right thing. Last night Wayne still had his ring on, but I know him too well to think that means anything. It wouldn't occur to him to take it off, no matter what his intentions. He just wouldn't think of it one way or another.

I, on the other hand, have so many thoughts they're aerobic, each jumping around to different, private music. Such chaos, though I cling to one central notion: Claire. Claire. Claire. Claire.

As I hear footsteps approach, I pull my hand from John's and set it alone in my lap. I tried to fix myself up today, not for John's sake, but so I'd look as if it weren't the sort of day on which I'd receive bad news. I smooth my cotton skirt and resettle my hands, as if I were calm.

"Hi, Lydia. Mr. Rutledge, nice to see you again…" Dr. Douglas smiles her professional greeting but doesn't look directly at me or John as she lifts a manila file and sits behind her desk. She's a middle-aged woman, pretty but naturally so, not one who appears to spend hours of her time on it. Dark-blondish straight hair falls from an off-center part and curves under her jawbone. Now she tucks one side of it behind an ear and puts on a pair of glasses to read a computer printout that's in the folder. She knows it by heart, I'm sure. She's stalling a little, sorting words into some order that she thinks won't make me suicidal. She's wrong.

"Mr. Rutledge, have you thought about discussing this with Lydia yourself?"

What does she mean? Does John already know? I look at him, but he is fixed on the doctor's face.

"No, I'd prefer you just tell us your findings, as we discussed."

Dr. Douglas gives a little shake of her head and a tiny, almost imperceptible shrug. "Lydia," she says, now looking at me and ignoring him. "I'm sorry to have to tell you this, but Mr. Rutledge is not a potential donor for Claire. I can only imagine what a blow this is to you, but I don't want you—or Claire—to be too discouraged...." She goes on about tissue matching and typing, antigens, the odds of finding a cadaver donor, and the like. She reminds me that people can live indefinitely on dialysis, as long as they're scrupulous about their diet and hygiene, avoid peritonitis, watch their blood pressure, fluid intake...I'm not really listening anymore.

"There has to be some mistake, doesn't there? I thought parents were always the best match? Can't you run the tests again?"

Dr. Douglas studies the open folder, though I know she just doesn't want to look at me. She blows a little puff of hair up onto her face, as if the room were extraordinarily hot. I'm clutching my own arms now to suppress shivering. "Yes, well, that's usually the case," she says carefully. "Sometimes, there are other factors, like the antibodies you have, or hereditary ones...." Dr. Douglas finally glances up, but at John, and there's the slightest hint of a raised pitch as her answer trails off, like a little hill leading toward a question. But, of course, neither of us have an answer.

"Well," she says. "Well, we'll just keep our fingers crossed...." Dr. Douglas stands, and comes around her desk to put her arm around me as I rise. Much more formally, she shakes John's hand. "This can't be easy..." she says to him, and then, to me, "I'll be in touch about the dialysis." I, however, am still stuck on *We'll just keep our fingers crossed.* I'm trying to figure out how it took her all this medical training to learn to cross her fingers, and how that's better than reading my horoscope and crossing out anything that's not pertinent. I'm thinking I'll just take Claire directly to Gert to let her get her hair cut and a side dish of spiritual healing when I start to cry.

John puts his arm around my shoulder and helps me toward the door. We cross the waiting room like an old married couple who have just received bad news, and right then, it feels like that's just what we are. I can almost hate him for this, that after these years of denial, regret, neglect, I can still slip into this connectedness as if it were a silk slip instantly, perfectly fitting even the revised contours of my body. I love him without reason. In defiance of my best interest, I love him.

That, however, doesn't mean I'll make the same mistake twice. Now there's something else that matters, not he, not I. Something that really matters.

"So what's the next step?" John says.

I'm getting myself under control. By the time we were in the parking lot, the crying I'd begun in Dr. Douglas's office was bunching into sobs and my legs weakened. I tried to pull free of John's arm to head for my car, but he steered me to his, opened the door and literally put me into it. He dug his handkerchief from his pants pocket and handed it to me when he got in the driver's side.

Early June sunshine is breaking into shards on the water when I focus on where he's driven us. The car is pulled into a little parking area above the river, one of the places we used to meet. Neither of us has spoken during the ride. I glanced over at him once, embarrassed that I'd fallen apart so badly, and saw him wipe his cheek with the back of his hand. I put my hand on his leg, and then he wrapped his around it, and the two of them rested on his leg for the rest of the ride. The back of his hand was still moist; my thumb pressed into the residue of his tears.

When he asks, it all overwhelms me again. "I don't…there's nothing, I don't know what…the dialysis…and Thursday is graduation, but she's too weak and now she's talked to Wayne and she left…"

"Whoa," John says. "I'm lost. Slow down, what's going on? Is this about a transplant?"

Of course it's not. And then I can't help it, the tears start all over again. Last night and this morning have been too much. The news about John is devastating and anticlimactic at once. I can't sort it all out.

"I told Claire about you. I had to. Wayne's left, I don't know where he's been, because I called you. I had to call you, can you understand that?" I hear it in my voice: I am begging for something.

"What did she say?" John looks out the car window, away from me when he asks.

"She was, I don't know, furious, disgusted. She wouldn't let me explain, then her boyfriend's mother came to see her—Kevin, the boy who was driving, he's in a coma and it doesn't look good. And then I couldn't tell if she was sleeping or pretending to, but Dr. Douglas told me a dozen times that she needs a lot of rest. I was going to try again to talk to her when she woke up and then Wayne showed up."

John shakes his head and looks out the window again. "God," he says. "God." He's still not looking at me when he goes on. "So what did he want?"

"He knocked on the door. Isn't that bizarre? He never told me he was leaving me, but he knocked on the door like he doesn't live there. He just said, 'I'm here to see Claire,' when I opened it. She wouldn't let me stay in the room, I tried to hear what they were saying, but… I've made such a mess of things. I don't know what I should have done."

John shifts in the driver's seat so he can see me. "It'll work out, try not to worry. I thought I'd lost my kids, I mean the divorce was really hard on them and there was enough anger in that house to blow out the plumbing."

I'm sure he means well, but right now I would like to kill this man who I once thought walked on water. I would like to put cement boots on him, set him down in the middle of the river and let him walk.

Bile mixes itself into my tears. "That's very nice, John, but I think you miss the point. You *did* lose one of your kids, or didn't you ever even think of her that way? Now I'm losing her, too, even though I've been there for her every minute of her life, when her own father turned his back on me and her. Now *I'm* losing her because of *you*. And you're not even a match. The one thing you ever could have done that would have counted now, and, no, of course not. No help from John." Yes, I recognize that the last part is wildly irrational, but I don't care anymore. I just don't care.

"What do you mean?" John ignores most of what I've said. "You can't assume you're going to lose her. I know it's not as good, but there's no reason to believe there won't be a cadaver donor."

"There's more than one way to lose someone, John. I'd have thought you'd have figured that much out by now. She's gone. She went with Wayne."

"What? What about…"

"Yes, the IV pole, the Y sets, the iodine caps, and I don't know how many of the boxes of solution, he made a bunch of trips."

"Where…?"

"I don't know." And it's the truth. I don't. Claire took four T-shirts, two pairs of shorts, a bra, a couple of pairs of underpants, her toothbrush, her hairbrush, some rubber bands, her schoolbooks, Kevin's senior picture, the dialysis equipment, and left with Wayne. She leaned on him going down the two steps off our porch, and then again, when he helped her into his truck. I am as bitter as I've been in my life. "See how easy it is to lose?" I say to John. "Isn't it just amazing how many ways there are to lose someone?"

CHAPTER 25

Things have plain spun out of control. Lydia flat out promised Ellie that she wouldn't have to actually *do* anything that involved dialysis, and now Madalaine has just called and said Ellie has to get over to her house now.

"I'm on my way to work," Ellie told her. "I can come over tonight if you want."

"Wal-Mart is going to have to let retail sales slide today, Ellie, because somebody that knows something has to be around. Claire's shaky. Call in sick, or, just tell them the truth. Whatever."

"Where's Lydia? What are you talking about?" Ellie had been completely confused. "I thought you said to come to your house."

"I did. And I suppose Lydia's at home." Some crazed, elated flame had ignited Madalaine's voice. Ellie checked out the kitchen window to see if the world looked normal. Across the street, the Henkel kids were straggling from their yard toward school. Belle, the Daltons' ugly pug, crossed the street in front of the Sams' house, squatting to pee in their yard in her leisurely fashion, driving Presley to his morning frenzy. Charles's cartoons chased across the television screen. Ellie had closed her eyes and turned her back to the window to try again with her sister.

"What's Claire… Claire's at your house?"

"And to think people have said you're not bright. You got it, El."

"Why?"

"Ours is not to reason why… Look, just call in to work and come over here."

Ellie wonders if Madalaine could be drunk. She doesn't even believe that Claire is at Maddie's. Maddie has been spacey since

Brian died, not mean and not teasing Ellie about Elvis the way she always has. Ellie's not been herself, either, of course; how could anyone be? But Maddie's stayed away more than usual and when Mama calls her on the phone, Maddie gets off fast. Daddy's not had a word to say about it, nothing unusual in that anymore, but something seems off to Ellie. Maybe Maddie has gone and lost it. That's most likely it. Lydie will have to do something. Obviously Ellie can't deal with this. Mama and Daddy and Charles are on her list, she has to go to work and Presley's needing attention. He's snappish and it's obvious that he feels the weight of the house—the attic floor is practically sagging over their heads with just the feelings Ellie has personally stashed there.

And it's even worse when Ellie does get to Madalaine's, a good hour and a half later. Lydie had been no help whatsoever on the phone. Ellie had asked, just to confirm for herself that Madalaine was drunk or off the deep end, "Is Claire there?"

Lydia had said, "No, I'm sorry, Claire's not here," just as if Ellie were one of Claire's friends calling about going to the movies.

"What do you mean?" Ellie had been confounded, stammering out, "How can she...I mean, why isn't she, where...?"

But Lydia had said in a wooden sort of way, "I'm sorry, Ellie, she's gone out with Wayne and I don't know where she is. Did you want me to take a message?"

This wasn't Lydie at all. Lydie was always telling Ellie that she wasn't making sense, and here she was making absolutely no sense herself. Lydia, of all people.

"What's going on? I just got—" Ellie was about to go on and tell Lydia about Madalaine's call, but Lydia cut in.

"Excuse me, Ellie, but I've got to go. I have an appointment with Dr. Douglas in a little bit and I've got to...it's urgent. Please give my love to Mama and Daddy and Charles." And then she'd actually just hung up on Ellie.

Ellie had paced between the kitchen and living room,

working on a ragged cuticle on her thumb with her forefinger and then her teeth, until she tore off a big hunk of skin and it bled. She talked to Presley and then directly to Elvis, because there have been times when she's been pretty sure she could feel his spirit guiding her. She thought it might have been Elvis who gave her the idea to call Gert.

Gert had a customer in the chair with a perm half-wrapped, but was nice enough to listen and say, "Ellie, it sounds like you'd best go to your sister's house. Honey, you know, when people are so hurting, they don't hardly know what comes out their mouth. You'd best go see what you can do for her."

Well, it had sounded right when Gert said it, but now Ellie has half a mind just to get out while she can. Maddie opens the front door and sort of leers and laughs at the same time. "Oh yes, you must be the nice lady from Lobotomies-R-Us come to do my free in-home demonstration. Well, come right on in." This Maddie says to Ellie, and steps back with a grand sweeping hand gesture. Then she bows and offers her arm to Ellie, like she's some kind of escort.

"You'll have to excuse the commotion here," Maddie goes on in a confidential, lunatic's whisper. "I'm having a home-decorating consultation today, too. The interior designers here like the neo-IV pole and plastic-bag look, but I'm leaning in favor of some delightful, very, very soft rubberized wallpaper in a soft gray. It has the added attraction of being easy to clean if some extra liquid happens to spatter around."

Maddie sort of half pulls Ellie through the kitchen—the table has dirty dishes and the rinds of toast in disarray on it, very un-Maddie-like—and to the threshold of the family room. There sit Claire, looking frightened and determined at once if that's possible, as well as looking very thin and very white, and Wayne, huddled miserably, and looking as if he has no idea in the world what to do. Which he doesn't; Ellie gets that much immediately, and begins to panic herself.

"What's going on?" Ellie aims the question at Claire, who usually can be counted on have a clear head.

"Aunt Maddie and…Dad don't want me to start dialysis without you here because they think I'll pass out or something and they won't know what to do." Claire sounds pinched, an unidentifiable something in her voice.

"You'll pass out?" Ellie is horrified. No one has mentioned that to her. She feels light-headed.

"No, I won't pass out. I'll be fine. They're just worried. All you have to do is sit down and watch television. I don't need anybody's help. I've done it before. I'm just pretty late now, I mean, this was supposed to be done already."

"I…I'm not good at…I mean, where's Lydie?"

"Nobody is accusing you of being good at anything, Ellie." Maddie interjects this with a giggle.

"I assume Mom is at home," Claire says evenly, but does not look at Ellie.

Ellie feels like she is in a Three Stooges skit, everyone deliberately misunderstanding each time she asks where someone is.

"I know she's at home. Why are *you* here, and if you're here, why isn't *she* here, too?" Ellie spits the questions, as precisely as she can phrase them.

No one answers. No one says a word.

Madalaine pops a beer even if it is barely afternoon. Well, actually, it's only eleven in the morning, if you're insisting on precision, but since she's been up since five, it should be afternoon. Another cosmic mistake, she snorts to herself. God is really slipping these days. She needs to calm down and think this through. Both Claire and Ellie had obviously been counting on Lydia to actually know what to do. Ellie was flat useless, but Maddie should have expected that: if an intelligent thought managed to be born in Ellie's head, it would soon die of loneliness. "Look, El, you go on to work and get those M&M's alphabetized or whatever you Wal-martians do," Maddie finally snapped in exasperation. Of course, Ellie immediately went off in a huff. "Aren't there...instructions, I mean some sort of review sheet of the steps, maybe a diagram?" Madalaine asked Claire after Ellie left.

"That's what Ellie was looking for. I have enough instructions and diagrams to paper a room," Claire said, miserably. "I was getting some clothes together." Madalaine noted how Claire dropped the *Aunt* before Ellie's name once Ellie was gone. The girl looked alarmingly frail to Madalaine. They were in way over their heads.

"Maybe you ought to go over and see if they won't train you at the hospital," Madalaine said to Wayne.

"No," Claire interjected quickly. "No, I've got to get it myself, and I'd be more...comfortable if it were Ellie or you. Dad, I'm sure you need to get on to work. I'll just call the hospital and go over this with one of the dialysis nurses. It's really not hard at all. I've got to talk with Aunt Maddie, anyway."

Ah, Madalaine thought. *Here it comes in all its glory.*

Wayne looked as if he'd lost two inches of height and twenty pounds during Ellie and Claire's fumbles with the long, clear tube that extended from Claire's abdomen and the bag they hung from the pole. "See, it's okay, it all works by gravity," Claire said. "I'm pretty sure this is right."

Madalaine would have sworn that there was actually a tail tucked between his legs as he slunk toward the door between the family room and the garage.

"Well, then, I guess...I'll see you later," Wayne mumbled, and was gone.

Then it was just Maddie and Claire. Madalaine had to admire how Claire sat right there at Madalaines's kitchen table, sucked in and tackled it head-on.

"Aunt Maddie, I need to tell you how sorry I am about Brian. I know I've told you before, but I don't think I can ever say it enough."

"I know," Madalaine answered, and meant it, not that it would make an actual difference.

"I've had the feeling off and on that maybe you partially blame me. Not that you've said or done anything, but maybe just because I haven't seen you too much." A questioning, apologetic tone crept into Claire's voice, and Madalaine knew that her niece hoped to hear a convincing denial.

Well, too bad. We just don't always get what we want, now do we? Madalaine thought, but tried, unsuccessfully, to moderate the harshness when she answered. "I think you could have seen to Kevin's driving…" she said. It was the obvious understatement, what she doesn't add that is most devastating.

Instantly, Claire's eyes filled. "I know. I know. I did ask him to slow down once. We were late, you know, from all the pictures."

Maddie's back stiffened. Was Claire trying to drop it back into her lap? She looked intently at Claire, though, and saw no trace of malice or even awareness on the girl's face.

"Would it have been such a big deal to be ten minutes late? Was it worth my son's life?"

"No, no, Aunt Maddie, I didn't mean it like that. I'm so sorry. I just meant that Kevin is usually a good driver, he doesn't…" She trailed off, recognizing that it was the wrong thing to say. "I should have made him stop. It's my fault that he's…where he is, and that Brian's gone."

Silence filled the kitchen like something palpable, the noon sun flooding the window as it moved around for a clear overhead shot, the angle from which a tennis ball is served. Madalaine used to play tennis, back when she was alive.

Claire broke into the quiet, her voice low, although there was no one else in the house. Jennifer wasn't even due home from school for three hours, and if Maddie remembered right, Bill was taking Jen out to dinner tonight, unless, of course, Melody went into labor early, as Jennifer had gratuitously reminded her mother.

"Aunt Maddie, I wanted to ask you if I could possibly stay with you. I mean, I was going to ask, but now, I'm not sure if it's even okay to ask, because...of how you feel toward me. I can't stay with my mother. Dad told me you know about it...and my dad, I can't stay with him either, it's not fair, he's not...not really...I don't know who else to ask, except someone in my mother's family."

"I'll need some time to think about it," Madalaine answered, not that she'd really consider saying yes, but wanting it to appear as if she'd at least struggled with the request. Now that she thought about it, she realized that Lydie would end up modeling straightjackets if her husband and daughter were both here. A *nice touch*, she thought, *and I don't have to do a thing except respond to their requests out of the kindness of my heart. I get to be Saintly Mother of the Dead Boy, an extra adjective.*

Now, though, with Claire asleep on Jennifer's bed, and the first three swallows gone from Madalaine's beer, it's not so simple. All this should be beneath her, she knows, but a thornbush grows now in the space in her chest left empty when her heart was ripped out. Madalaine is still sitting at the kitchen table, statue-like except for the small movement of her fingers on the Coors can, when she hears and ignores a knock on the door. She whites out a second episode of knocking by allowing the roar in her ears to approximate the ocean, but then Ellie appears in the doorway, anyway.

"Where's Claire?" Ellie demands, glancing at the beer, then up at Madalaine's face. "Madalaine, do you really think—"

"Don't *Madalaine* me, Eleanor. Yes I really think, and Claire's asleep. What do you want?"

Ellie flounces her hair, in a blue-and-white polka-dot bow that would have matched the blue of her Wal-Mart smock if she had ever put it on today. She waves a sheaf of white papers at Madalaine. "I went to Lydia's but there's no one there, so I went to the hospital, and Joann, she's the head of the dialysis training team, went over it again with me, and I've got the papers. See, it's peritoneal dialysis. You can learn it in about four hours."

Ellie says *Joann* in a important tone, lording it over Madalaine, as if Joann were the president of the damn country, or the nurse's first name were a state secret, and Madalaine is monumentally irritated. At the same time, she's impressed against her will; this is not vintage Ellie, this business of doing something on her own.

Ellie goes on. "We need to go ahead and get this done, while I remember."

"Claire says it's no big deal, she can be late. She wanted to rest and she was going to ask Wayne to get the review diagrams and stuff from Lydia's."

"Well it is a big deal, Joann told me the schedule is important. It's four times a day and at night. Did she do it last night? Will you please tell me what's going on? Why isn't Claire home with Lydia? Lydia memorized every word Joann said while we were with her. Lydia could *write* the damn manual. I never heard anyone think of so many questions." Ellie pulls out a chair facing Madalaine across the kitchen table and sits. For once in her life, Ellie just sits and waits for someone else to speak. Madalaine wonders if she's on something.

"Well, as far as I know, Lydia doesn't know Claire's here, or I'm sure she'd ride right in here and let her horse shit all over my floor while she took care of her precious Claire. Just because Brian's dead and Claire helped him get that way, well, we certainly wouldn't want anything to happen to Claire."

Ellie's mouth literally falls open. She blinks, then again. "What?"

"You heard me."

Everything seems utterly and forever lost to Madalaine. There's no hope because there *is* no hope. Even hurting doesn't raise a spark in her flinty soul. "Listen, ask Lydia or Claire or Wayne. Don't ask me. And tell Claire not to ask me any more if she can stay here. Wayne can stay, I don't care about that."

Ellie's jaw may never close again. She's shocked, genuinely so, and trying to fit the jigsaw together but coming up with a picture of a three-headed woman with an eye in the middle of her forehead. She trashes the pieces and tries again.

"Wayne's been staying here?"

"You hear good, El."

"He's not with Lydia?"

"Both ears work, I see. I'm too tired, I'm going in to sleep now. Do what you want, the dialysis thing, whatever, but get her out of here." And with that, Madalaine stands, picks up the beer and walks—steadily enough it seems—toward the hallway that leads past Brian's bedroom to the one she and Bill used to share.

A half hour later, when Claire makes her slow way out of Jennifer's bedroom and down the hall to the kitchen, she finds Ellie sitting at the table staring at four sheets of paper spread in order on the kitchen table. Her aunt is crying, her face bleary and red-splotched, like a mirror of Claire's own.

Claire walks to Ellie and puts her arms around her, lets Ellie's face rest against her chest while she stands there. Her own tears start, and run down her face as if to mix with Ellie's tears until aunt and niece are borne along together in a great, unstoppable river. "Shh, shh," she says. "It'll be all right."

"Will you please just tell me what's going on?" Ellie pleads, not really expecting an answer. "Maddie won't, Lydia's disappeared somewhere, not at home… It's the same old thing, no one has the least consideration. What am I supposed to do?"

Claire smoothes Ellie's hair. She's hesitant, knowing Ellie, how everyone always goes around her. "I'll tell you, if you're sure you want to know. Sometimes it's better not to. I found that myself."

Ellie blows her nose into a crumpled tissue she's fished out of her skirt pocket. "Tell me," she says, and almost imperceptibly, the river begins a bend.

CHAPTER 26

I can barely come up for air, sobbing in his car while the river runs alongside John and me, behind and ahead of us and through me. My eyes and nose are running, I am drowning in this river of grief, while the bones of hope, washed ashore, bleach and grow brittle. He has put his arms around me and I have let him, though I imagine it is like pressing a wet, dead fish to your chest.

I have never hated John as much as I do now.

What time is it? I straighten up, I check my watch and see that it is past time for still another dialysis. I bargain for her safety: she can never have anything to do with me again, I tell God, if only You will keep her safe. Suddenly, I am desperate to get home. What if she's come back, wanting help? Suppose she's forgotten something and wants me to explain it to her? The two times we did it at home she was tired and I did most of the steps of the exchange.

"Take me back," I tell John. "I need to get back."

"I don't think you should be alone," he says, and doesn't budge.

I reach over and turn the keys in the ignition. Even though his foot isn't on the gas, the car answers right away as expensive cars do. "I need to get back. You don't understand. She's not done it alone before, I don't know what she did last night and this morning. Maybe she's called me for help."

John shifts the car into gear. "Okay," he says.

We're in downtown Maysfield before he says anything else. He clears his throat and I look at him. The wet spots on his white shirt are fading but still visible and I see a little of my makeup has come off on him, too. "Lydie," he tries. "Lydie, I'm so sorry. I want you to know I would have done it."

I only half believe him. What has he got to lose telling me that?

"Thanks," I say, the bitterness crimping the edge of the word.

"You probably don't believe me, I understand that. I know I've never acted like it, but she's my daughter, too, and I do love her."

He is turning into the parking lot at Dr. Douglas's where I left my car after we got the test results. "Save it," I say, and get out, closing the door harder than is necessary.

By the time I reach home, I have at least collected myself into a coherent bundle. My heart leaps when I notice a yellow stick-up note perched like a bird on my front door, but it's from Ellie, saying to call her. I crush it and drop it in the kitchen trash once I am inside. Ellie is the last person I can talk to.

I should go on in to work. I only said I needed the morning off, and now it's well into my lunch hour. Pacing doesn't help, wringing my hands doesn't help. Wouldn't Claire think to call the office if she wanted me?

I walk through the house; there's no sign Wayne has been here either, though I don't think I really expected one. In the bathroom, I wash my face, rinse it in cold water. My eyes stare back at me, red-rimmed and empty-looking. I comb my hair, apply eye shadow, liner, mascara, blush, pink-lilies lipstick. What have I done? The enormity of the pain I, Lydia, have caused... What have I done? I try to argue with myself a little. If I hadn't had an affair, Claire wouldn't exist. How can I say that whatever brought Claire into this world isn't a good thing? But now I stumble on this: maybe Wayne was right after all, and I should never have contacted John, never have told Claire the truth. Hindsight, all hindsight. And what if John had been a match?

I put a note on the door reminding anyone who might care that I'm at work and he or she can call me there. At the office, I feel like a leper who's the object of conscious kindness, everyone careful not to ask me to do anything, careful of each word that I hear or might overhear. They are relentlessly cheerful, especially Donna, who gives me sympathetic looks periodically but doesn't ask any questions. And they don't even know what's really happening; all they know is that Wayne and I aren't a match, and, of course, that my nephew is dead. I guess that's enough.

I leave work fifteen minutes early. Not a call on our answering machine. Not so much as a hang-up. And I begin to feel angry. Surely Claire knows I'm frantic by now. Surely Wayne knows the same. How can they do this to me? After all I've… After all, I'm her mother.

I pace, flip through magazines, fold a load of laundry that's been in the dryer for days. At seven-thirty, I can't stand it. My nail beds are white, bloodless from the pressure with which I push the telephone's buttons when I call John. My intention is only to distract myself, tell someone—anyone, I think—that I can't bear this any longer. I would call Maddie, except that it seems so unfair to ask anything of her, now of all times.

On the phone, at least I do not cry. I just tell him that I've still heard nothing from Claire or Wayne. The strange thing is that I want to be mad and stay mad at him for leaving me in this mess eighteen years ago, but when I hear his warm baritone say, "Lydie, Lydie, are you all right?" the anger shrinks down to the size of something that can be set toward the back of a deep shelf.

"I…I'm… No, I'm not all right, I'm a wreck. I don't have anybody else to call. Maddie, well, I can't, not with what she's going through with losing Brian, and Bill's gone, of course, and Ellie doesn't seem…"

"I remember about Ellie. Does she still have to get her passport stamped every morning to leave Elvisville for Wal-Mart?"

I laugh. And then I remember how John used to make me laugh. He hears me laugh, and he starts laughing, and I keep laughing, as if I were sighting an island from the splintered rafters of a wrecked ship, it's that welcome.

"She still works at Wal-Mart, but it's turned out pretty well, because now they carry a lovely new line of dresses with extra-extra-long sleeves that can be tied in a real pretty bow. In back."

A beat passes while he digests that. When he gets the picture, he chuckles. "Well, then, I guess that employee discount comes in right handy," he says.

"Yeah," I say. "Do you maybe want to come over?" Not a well-thought-out plan, I suddenly realize.

But John is on top of that. "Have you eaten?" he asks. "I bet not. Let me take you out and get a decent meal in you."

"I'd like that. Yes. That'd be nice. Thank you," I say, meaning it.

"I'll pick you up within a half hour." He lives in a fancy apartment, way the opposite side of town. "If I'm late, it just means traffic," he says. "Hang on, sweetie."

Sweetie. When has someone called me sweetie, or any other endearment? I have no idea, but what balm it is. What a sucker I am for balm like that.

CHAPTER 27

"I don't think we did so bad," Ellie says to Claire, though she's been shaky for hours, quelling nausea and light-headedness. The thought of that stuff draining out of Claire and then a whole bag of new stuff going in gives her the willies. Now that it's over, the tubing put away, and the bag of used stuff set up behind the closed bathroom door to drain into the toilet, Ellie's feeling pretty good. She didn't faint and she read a paragraph out loud to Claire when Claire couldn't remember a sequence of connections.

"Aunt Eleanor, you were superb."

Ellie can tell Claire means it, because she gives her the respect of her real name. If there's anyone in the family who ever remembers Ellie's wishes, it's Claire. Ellie's always asked people not to call her that—*Ellie*. She'd really rather the full Eleanor Ann, which she's sure Elvis would like, especially since he named his daughter Lisa Marie, and married a woman people called Priscilla, not Prissy. She absolutely surprises herself when she says to Claire, "Oh, honey, that's okay, you can call me Ellie. Everyone else does...."

"Well, whatever you want to be called, I'll call you that, and I mean it, I can't thank you enough."

"You're welcome. Really, it wasn't as bad as I thought. I can probably handle it again...if your Mom has to be away or something."

Claire puts her hand on her forehead as if she has a headache. She's wearing cutoff denim shorts and a T-shirt, and looks like very breakable porcelain, but her voice is resolute and adult. "I meant it, I'm not going home. I can't forgive what she did to Dad, and I can't believe she's lied to me all these years. She brought me up with standards, and to believe in certain things, and just because she broke every one of them doesn't mean that they're not still what I believe. Or does that make any sense? I may not be saying it right because I'm tired, but I don't want to even see her. And don't worry. I can do the exchanges by myself. Dr. Douglas said. It's just a safety thing to have someone else trained, in case I have a problem. I'll get real efficient with it. I think I was just still upset this morning."

Ellie leans forward from one of the upholstered chairs in Madalaine's family room toward the other, where Claire sits. She opens her mouth and then, realizing that she has no idea what to say, shuts it and leans back against the cushion. "Claire..."

"My mind is made up. I'm staying here." Claire's tone is like a red warning.

"Maddie says you *can't* stay here." Ellie's capacity for tact has been stretched to the limit recently. She makes the statement flatly, without any softening.

"But Dad's been..."

"I know." Ellie could happily shoot Madalaine right between the eyes this minute for leaving the house and not coming back all afternoon, sticking her with telling this to Claire.

"Oh...she doesn't want me here..." Claire trails off and covers her face with her hands. She is rocked, Ellie can tell.

"I think she just can't..." Ellie tries, but can't come up with anything to explain her sister. "See why you have to go home? You've got to have a place to be, you know, for your treatments and all those boxes of stuff in your dad's truck. What if it rains? Besides, you still have the operation and all when they find a donor."

But Claire isn't listening. She's uncovered her face and is looking around the room, not seeing the wood stove, the tweedy neutral family room carpeting, the console television, the sliding glass doors out to the patio, even the half-mature trees that Bill planted ten years ago. What she sees are the number of framed pictures of Brian and Jennifer on the paneled walls, in the bookcases, on the end tables. She doesn't say anything when she's finished looking, only buries her head back into her hands. Her shoulders begin to shake and she lowers her head almost to her lap, but there is no sound in the room.

Ellie hesitates a moment, then gets up and takes the three steps to Claire's chair. Awkwardly, she balances herself on the arm and just as awkwardly lays an arm on Claire's back. It lies there useless as an untied rope. She looks at it a moment as if it doesn't belong to her. Claire's back is still shaking, which makes Ellie's arm shake, and as much to stop that as anything else, Ellie applies a little pressure and curves her wrist and hand down around Claire's upper arm. When the shaking still doesn't stop, she pulls Claire toward herself and cradles Claire's head with her other hand.

Ellie strokes Claire's hair, lifting and twisting the ponytail and smoothing it down. Claire does not pull away. They stay together that way for what seems a long time, and the shaking subsides.

When Wayne shows up, Claire and Ellie are rooting in Madalaine's refrigerator and wondering if Madalaine picked Jennifer up from school to keep from having to be at the house. "Maddie said Bill was taking Jennifer tonight, I think," Ellie is saying, "but who knows what's going on?"

"Hey," Wayne says, appearing in the kitchen doorway in his ghostlike way.

Ellie claps a hand to her chest. "My Lord, you scared a year off my life. Don't ever do that again."

Claire laughs. "He does that all the time. He doesn't even do it on purpose, do you Dad?"

"Nope." Wayne just looks at them and stands there, as though he could last all night in that one spot, and he's standing right on Ellie's last nerve.

"Will you sit down or something? You all have some decisions to make. Claire, how about I leave you two alone?"

"No, that's okay. Stay." Claire's found two containers of strawberry yogurt and hands one to Ellie. "I'm sorry, I don't mean to be rude, but I've got to eat something." She peels off the foil top and stirs up the fruit from the bottom. Everything's being stirred up off the bottom it seems.

"You eat, honey." Ellie tries the endearment and seems to get away with it. "Wayne," she goes on, swiveling her neck and letting her shoulders follow, to face him instead of Claire. "Maddie's said that Claire can't stay here."

"What?" he says, like he hadn't heard her perfectly well.

"I said, *Maddie's* said that *Claire* can't stay here." She places a heavy emphasis on the names as if trying to penetrate an invisible barrier.

Wayne's expression doesn't change perceptibly.

"Don't you have anything to say?" Ellie demands. She'd never realized how irritating Wayne can be.

"Not really."

"Dad, what are your plans?" Claire's looking concerned, Ellie sees.

"Don't really have any." Wayne looks down. "I can take you back to your mother's."

"I told you, I explained to you, I'm not going back there. But I guess I'm not really your responsibility, am I?" Claire leaves a pause in what she says, looking at Wayne to read where she stands. He's illegible.

Wayne keeps staring at his boots. The steel-reinforced toes are scuffed and display their wear like a union card. "...I don't know all that much...about girls, your mother's...she's always seen to..."

Ellie is watching Claire's face, and sees an entire drama play out. Claire had been hoping for a vehement assertion from Wayne that she's his daughter, that that fact hadn't changed, wouldn't and couldn't change.

Wayne does look up, now. "It's not…that," he gets out, but Ellie doesn't trust him. Maybe he is going to say what Claire needs to hear and maybe he'd even say it because it's true, but good grief, what if he doesn't? What if he comes up with another page of lame nonsense? She jumps in. "Claire, I think you and I better stay together. It's probably best if you're not alone during the day, at least until you're strong enough to be back in school. I have so much vacation time coming that Wal-Mart won't give me any more until I take some."

"Use it or lose it, the plant's the same way, and I'm up to five weeks a year," Wayne mumbles, nodding. Was there relief on his face, or is she just imagining it? He's taken a few steps, so he can stand leaning against the refrigerator, as if it's an oversize back support.

"Yeah. It makes me mad, but what can you do?" Ellie says. It wasn't, strictly speaking, true. After this year, she'd have the maximum amount of time she could accrue. She's not there yet. Still, what's the difference? It's not as if she has anywhere to go. "So, Claire, I'll take some vacation time, and we'll do this thing together. What has your doctor said about school?" If she'd had time to think, Ellie would have been surprised at herself. As it is, she pulls out a kitchen chair and sits down at an angle to the table. Then she thinks again, gets up and pulls out another chair and gestures to Claire. "Get off your feet," she says, and then hearing herself, goes on to soften it with, "You're supposed to rest, honey." She doesn't want to sound as if she's talking to Mama or Charles or Daddy. "Wait a minute!" she almost shouts. "You're not supposed to eat dairy."

Claire sighs and puts her carton of mainly eaten yogurt in the trash and then does come back and sit down. "I was hungry. I'm supposed to graduate next Thursday night." Anger leaves a wispy trail in Claire's voice, or maybe it's a smoke of regret. "I don't have to go back, I have the last work that I have to turn in. I'll just need someone to take it to school for me."

"Don't you have to…take exams, or…?" Wayne looks surprised.

"Seniors who have a B or better in any course don't have to take the final."

"And you…" he begins the question, surely one he should have known the answer to.

"Had all As and one B, but now, because of the accident and missing school, I'll probably get a couple more Bs. But I still won't have to take exams, actually, the teachers already told…said that." Claire twirls a piece of her ponytail, knotting it into her fingers.

"Oh," he says, remembering that Lydia had gone to get Claire's assignments and talk to her teachers. He doesn't remember her telling him that Claire didn't have to take any exams, but maybe she did.

"That's wonderful, honey," Ellie speaks up, surprised that Wayne doesn't have more to say, surprised at herself that she does. Of course, it was always Lydie who said things like this. "I'm so proud of you, with all you've been through and all. Did the doctor say you could go to graduation?"

"She said, *we'll see*," Claire answers. "I hate it when someone says that. But I'm going. I'm determined."

Ellie lets this pass, not knowing the right response. She switches the subject. "We need to figure out what to do. I mean, there's not really space at Mama and Daddy's, well, I guess we could manage for a while, but the other thing is, we can't trust Charles around the equipment…and lord, where can we put those boxes, the ones with all the full bags?"

A long moment. No one knows what to say. Ellie hesitates even after she thinks of it, then internally shrugs. Somebody's got to do something. She swivels in her chair enough to look straight at Wayne and waits until he looks back at her, and then she holds him that way with her eyes. "Wayne, can you get me and Claire a room at a hotel? It's got to be a decent place, like with a really clean bathroom. We'll need two beds. And floor space, you know, a place for the equipment. Oh, and a good chair, for Claire, for when she's doing her exchanges." She just gives it to him as she thinks of each thing, not lowering her eyes.

Wayne can only take so much. Before Ellie gets to the end of her list, he has to look away. "Yeah, okay...where?"

"Good grief, Wayne. Do I have to do everything?"

Apparently the answer is yes, because Wayne doesn't answer.

"I'll figure out a list from the phone book, but you'll need to go look at them to make sure the room is big enough and has what we need. And you'll need to help with the dialysis stuff, getting it there and all."

"Okay."

"Aunt Eleanor, are you sure? I mean, I don't feel right about putting you to this trouble. What about Maw Maw and Charles...and Presley?" Claire tacks the dog on as an afterthought, startling to the recognition that, for Ellie's sake, she should have mentioned Presley first.

"Well, it'll just have to be a place that takes pets. I guess your mother can go check on Maw Maw and Charles. I don't know, we'll just have to figure things out as we go along."

"Are you sure?" Claire is hesitant and grateful, all mixed together. "I really appreciate this. I don't have any money and...well, actually, I do have a couple of hundred dollars in my savings account—" Claire breaks off, glancing at Wayne. Her hands flutter like two small, nervous birds between her denim lap and Maddie's kitchen table. It's not like her, and seeing it, Ellie quiets her own hands that have started rearranging dirty dishes resting on the counter.

"Well, I know your mother will just sign her paycheck over to the hotel if she needs to." Ellie says this pointedly, a shot at Wayne, still propped against the refrigerator like a permanent part of the closed door.

"I don't want her to do any..."

"Okay, well, we'll figure it out." Ellie interrupts and stands up, takes two spoons over to put them in the sink, in order to get out of the way of the real issue, let it pass by untouched again. She's got a lot of figuring to do.

CHAPTER 28

It's been four days since I've seen my daughter, and more since I've seen Wayne. I know someone's been here because there are things missing from Claire's room, and a few more of Wayne's things are gone. The most obvious sign is the disappearance of boxes of her dialysis solution from the basement. I wonder if Wayne brought someone to help him from the plant. The boxes weigh better than thirty pounds each and there were thirty-five of them down there when all this started. Shame is what's preventing me from pasting up picture posters of Claire like those terrible ones on milk cartons that plead Have You Seen Me?

Three days ago I called Wayne at work. "Yes, it's an emergency," I had to say to the switchboard operator so she'd page him.

"Hullo," he said when he finally answered, his voice flat and unperturbed.

"Wayne, it's me, Lydia. Is Claire all right? Where is she? What's going on?"

"She's all right."

"Is she getting her treatments? I don't think you understand how complicated this is, she has to do everything exactly right or…"

"I told you, she's all right."

"But where is she?"

"It's taken care of."

"I'm begging you, don't do this. I have a right to know where my daughter is. I have a right to talk to her."

"She don't want to talk to you," he said, and hung up.

John's called me every day, and, each night, like it's a brand-new idea, he says, "I bet you haven't eaten. How about I come get you and put some food into you?" I've done it out of…well, gratitude, I guess, or maybe it's that I know in my heart that we are guilty together. My mind bumps back and forth from Claire to John to Wayne, switching directions like a cumbersome houseboat on the river, heading across the wake of faster, larger traffic trying to avoid collisions and jouncing heavily into the wave troughs. That's just what it's like, and I'm struggling to stay afloat.

I had decided to accept John's offer to hire a private investigator to find Wayne and Claire if one of them didn't call today. He knows about these things, he said, from the seamy side of being a lawyer, and know that an investigator can find them and just let me know where they are, whether Claire's really all right. How can they not know I'm wild with worry? Or maybe that's exactly what they intend. Just exactly what they intend.

Naturally, though, it's also John who came up with another possibility. "Try the dialysis unit at the hospital," he said tonight while I toyed with beef-and-noodle casserole at the little Frisch's west of town.

"I've *called* the hospital every day to make sure she hasn't been readmitted," I said, trying to keep annoyance weeded out of my voice. He should have remembered that that's my first call every morning.

"Down, girl," he said, but it was gentle, undefensive. "I mean, how about checking personally with the dialysis nurse or director or whoever trained you and her, the one from the outpatient clinic. If she'd had problems and wouldn't come to you, who else would she call?"

"Well, supposedly, Ellie. That's why they make you have a second person."

"Have you checked with Ellie?"

"She wouldn't call Ellie. Neither of us thought for a minute that Ellie would really learn the stuff, or really be a backup."

"Then why…?"

"Because she was ready to be released and Wayne was upset about my calling you, and it somehow seemed, just, well, not right to ask Maddie. We, I, never thought we'd really need a second person. It's just a precaution, they said." How could I have been so careless while I thought I was doing everything, anything, to keep my daughter alive and safe? "I intended to train Maddie later, and Wayne, if..."

"I know," he said, "I know," and reached across the table to put his hand over mine for a moment. Moist, warm. I looked up at his face and saw a light sheen of sweat on his forehead; myself, I'd been chilly since we sat down. "But back to the dialysis unit. Wouldn't she...?"

When I actually bent my mind around to his point, it was absolutely logical. "How can I...what can I say?"

"Lydie, who cares? Just ask. Call Dr. Douglas, have her ask. She already knows the whole thing. Whatever." He set his fork down too hard and I could tell he thought I was being ridiculous.

My own fork clattered on the table, anger for anger. "Isn't it strange how *now* you don't care what people think? It must be wonderful to be so brave with other people's lives, when it doesn't count for you anymore." In the booth behind John, the conversation quieted and the man glanced over his shoulder at me. I averted my eyes. I hate scenes. Usually, I am the one trying to stop Ellie or Maddie from carrying on.

I'd stung him, but he didn't sting back. He just sat and stared me down and when he could tell I was finished, spoke quietly. "The point here is finding Claire and making sure she's okay. How about I call Dr. Douglas and ask her to check it out."

"No. It's my job. Of course you're right. I'll call her. It's a good idea."

Dr. Douglas's voice comes through the receiver as if from a great distance. My ears roar their blood and I can feel my hand shake as I press the phone against my ear.

"Look, we can't have this," she says. "I'll have to get Children's Services to put her in a medically qualified foster home, Lydia. She's got a whole regimen and...how many days has it been? You should have called me right away."

"She's with her...with Wayne," I say.

"Is he trained?"

"No," I whisper.

"Don't you know she could become dizzy? It's not unheard of to faint during dialysis if her blood pressure's a problem. Once she's used to it all, being by herself will be all right, but..." An indictment.

"Yes." Guilty.

She hesitates, then backs off a little. "Well, all right then, I'll check with the staff. They'll be a record of it if she's called or come in. I'll let you know. Lydia...hang in there," she says, and when I hang up, I am crying.

Ten minutes later the phone rings. I stub my toe hard on the foot of the couch as I run to the kitchen to pick it up before the second ring. The pain momentarily distracts me from the impact. "Ellie Sams has been in once and called once about her niece's peritoneal dialysis, according to Joann. Joann thought you'd sent her because you'd misplaced the review material," Dr. Douglas says.

I can't process the news. "No, I...didn't," is all I get out.

"How do you want to handle this? I've got to know that her exchanges are occurring. When is she scheduled to see me?"

"Tomorrow." I am nauseated, flopping like a just-hooked fish, trying to reject what Dr. Douglas is saying. "Ellie? Ellie went in? Was she...was Claire...? I mean, is Claire all right?"

"Joann didn't see Claire, so she really doesn't know. She asked, and your sister said she was all right. Joann didn't pursue it because she assumed Claire was with you."

"Oh...God..." I fold at the hips into a kitchen chair, my legs giving out.

"Lydia, are you okay? Look, there's no need to presume any

disaster. Your sister did get a review sheet and go over the procedure with Joann. Joann said she seemed to be paying attention this time."

"Yes," I say. "Yes." Words won't form in my brain.

"Give me a call when you've talked to your sister, and seen Claire. Check to see if she's missed any exchanges, or is having any problems." Dr. Douglas's voice has grown kinder. Obviously she feels sorry for me.

"Yes. Thank you."

I have to stand up to replace the phone in the hook. My foot won't support its share of weight, so I brace myself against the kitchen counter and run the cold water. Filling the cup of my two hands, I stick my face into them to quell the nausea. I am light-headed, tears hot beneath my skin.

"Maddie? Maddie? Answer the door, Maddie. It's me. I know you're there. Answer the door," I shout, pounding on the door with the heel of my fist between demands. I looked through the back door into the garage when she didn't answer; her car was there, so I went back to the front and leaned on the bell again before I began this banging.

The dead bolt turns and Maddie's face appears in a slot of open door.

"Will you be quiet? What do you want?"

"What do you think I want? Let me see Claire." I push on the door, but Maddie blocks it with her foot.

"She's not here."

"Don't tell me that. I was just out home, and Mama said that Ellie was staying here with you. I know Claire's with Ellie. How could you do this? I've been frantic. Let me in." With that, I push hard enough that Maddie's foot slides back and I force my way into her living room.

"Claire's not here and neither is Ellie."

"I don't believe you," I say, and head for her family room.

Nobody there. I am nearly running, bumping into things as I make my way back through the kitchen to the bedroom hallway. The bedrooms are innocent, Jennifer's bed neatly made and Maddie's a rumpled tangle, but both empty. I glance in the open bathroom door, being thorough, looking for an IV pole or any other trace.

I wheel on her and start to advance, backing her into the kitchen. She puts out a hand as if to stop an assault. "You tell me. What's going on?" But even as I shout this, I see for myself. The laundry-room door is open and I see it all, clear as day and twice as real on top of her dryer: a roughly folded pile of underwear and denim, topped by Wayne's green plaid shirt, next to a plastic glass with Wayne's toothbrush and razor sticking up above the rim. His deodorant—same brand as always—lies on top of the clothes. "My God, Maddie. Wayne's here, too? You didn't tell me? You let him do this to me? *You* did this to me? You got Ellie to *help* you do this to me?"

Maddie's face is white, but her eyes, bloodshot and widened in fright when I tore through the house, have narrowed back down. The web of gray on the top of her head looks more dense, less lacy than it used to, but this can't be. It's only, what?—three weeks?—since the accident.

"Well, excuse me," she spits. "Maybe you'd rather I'd just let your child die, like you did mine. Next time I'll be sure to get it right."

CHAPTER 29

Madalaine knows perfectly well that Lydia's assumption was on the mark. She had taken in first Wayne and then—if only briefly—Claire, intending Lydia's suffering, but she can make herself forget it when she needs to. When Lydia first burst into the house, Madalaine had been frightened and sputtered out a denial, but then anger, wild and inevitable, had chosen weapon and target at once, and unrecallable words had been shot like bullets.

In fact, Madalaine happens to know exactly where Claire and Ellie are. Ellie had asked for a hotel room, but once they started looking around at the slim pickings in town that had two beds, an easy chair, enough space for two people, space for medical supplies, a microwave to heat the solution *and* would allow a dog, well, it had come down to a double at the Maysfield Manor downtown, for a hundred and forty-five dollars a night not including the damage deposit for Presley. So Ellie and Wayne, who knew which one of them, had somehow come up with a two-bedroom furnished apartment rentable on a month-to-month basis, and Wayne had paid for a month.

Madalaine hadn't let on to Lydia that she knew, though. She'd not bothered to contradict that Wayne was staying there after Lydia saw his stuff, but the house hadn't given up a clue about Ellie or Claire, and she hadn't either. Push Madalaine hard enough and she'll push back harder without even thinking about it. Now she's popped a beer and paces in the kitchen, trying to figure out what to do. The sun is still around on the back side of the house, so the kitchen holds last night's cool even without the air-conditioning on. The comparative darkness and the beer are calming, even as she rehearses her grievances and justifications and finds them satisfactory. What's nagging at her is what an idiot Ellie is and a certain concern about whether Ellie and Claire are actually getting the dialysis right. She can't quite convince herself that she doesn't care if Claire dies. Oh, she can say it all right. She just can't quite make it stick in place.

"All right, all right," she says out loud to the emptiness. She picks up the phone. "Can you page Wayne Merrill?" she says after it's been answered on the other end. Then the wildness gets loose again. "Yes, goddammit, this is an emergency."

Ellie and Claire both startle when a knock sounds. Presley begins his frenzied barking, charging the door and then throwing himself at it. Ellie freezes, whispering, "Presley! Presley!" ineffectively, but Claire glances at her watch, shrugs and gets up.

"It's got to be Dad," she says. "It's past four."

Wayne, in his work coveralls, is standing several feet back, as if he'd knocked and then retreated. Presley sniffs him and retreats in disappointment.

"Come on in," Claire says. She gestures behind her at the small living room furnished in neutral, nondescript furniture. The only personal touches are Claire's schoolbooks splayed on the Formica coffee table and Presley's water and food dishes on the kitchenette floor. "See? We've even unpacked. Did you see it when you rented it, or just Ellie?"

Wayne doesn't glance around nor come in. "Your mother knows you're with Ellie. Maddie called me at the plant and said she knows and that she's flippin' out. You better call her."

Claire starts to shake her head no, and opens her mouth to say something, but Ellie appears beside her. "What did Lydia say?"

"Maddie just said she was wrecked. I dunno anything else."

"Well, how'd she find out?"

"I dunno. Maddie didn't say."

"Can you call her? Lydie, I mean?" Ellie asks Wayne.

"No, Claire ought to call her."

Claire takes a step forward and inserts herself. "And I'm not calling her, either."

Wayne shrugs. "I won't say nothing, but if she comes and asks me flat out, I'll tell her. Just so you know." He pauses a moment, then looks in Claire's direction. "You okay?"

"Yes. I'm fine. Thanks."

"Okay, then, I'll be going," Wayne says, shifting his weight.

"Don't you want to come in awhile?

"Naw, that's okay. I'll see you."

Disappointment washes across Claire's face. "Okay, bye," she says. "Thanks for getting this place."

"Yeah," Wayne calls, his back already turned, but his voice isn't cold.

When Claire shuts the door after watching Wayne walk away, Ellie starts up.

"Claire, I think you should phone your mother. She's just going to get more and more upset."

It's not like Claire to be defiant, but she looks Ellie square in the eye and says, "No." Claire heads for the larger bedroom she shares with nearly a month's supply of dialysis solution, povidone iodine caps and bag sets now, and shuts that door behind her. Ellie picks Presley up and sinks onto the couch. When the dog squirms and jumps back to the floor, Ellie buries her face in her hands. She stays that way for a few minutes, then leans back and stares into space for another fifteen. Presley jumps back onto the couch and curls up beside her, where she strokes his head again and again.

Claire couldn't have canned soup because it has too much potassium and sodium in it, so Ellie fixed scrambled eggs because Claire says they have protein, and toast (dry, because Ellie had forgotten to get margarine) for supper. They ate watching *Jeopardy!* on the television, Ellie astounded at how many of the answers Claire knows.

"I don't mind cooking," Claire says as she carries both their plastic plates to the sink. "How about I give you a list of some basic stuff to get. I'll figure out some meals we can have."

Ellie starts to protest, then stops. "Okay. Good. You make the list and I'll run to the store."

"Oh, I didn't mean this minute," Claire laughs. She scrapes a runny clot of egg into a paper bag-lined garbage pail under the sink. "We'll need some plastic garbage bags," she adds.

"I'd just as soon go now," Ellie says. "I could do with some fresh air, especially now that it's cooler."

"Oh, Ellie, you already went once today. It can wait…or maybe you're feeling a little cooped up with me? I'm sorry, you're so nice to do this."

The plastic glasses are battered, the color leached out of them. Claire puts them in the sink as Ellie hands them to her. "It's not that," Ellie says hurriedly, afraid she's given the wrong impression. "Really, I just need a little exercise. I like to get out in the evening when it stays light. Will you be okay alone for a little while?" Already she is heading across matted, fatigue-colored carpeting to her purse.

"Sure. But don't you need a list?"

"Oh, yes, of course. Please, do make one. I'm not a good shopper. I always get sort of confused about what I should buy, if I need it or not."

"A list helps," Claire says without a trace of sarcasm.

"I'll try it."

Ellie watches *Hard Copy* while Claire sits at the table and works on two pieces of notebook paper. Within fifteen minutes, she gets up and hands Ellie one of them.

"I've done up meal plans to take us through the rest of the week, so the weird things on the list are an ingredient for one thing or another. Is that okay?"

Ellie reads the shopping list. "Sure it's okay. I may be a while. I don't know where to find a lot of this stuff." She is in awe that

Claire knows how to make different dishes, and from memory knows what goes in them. "What's the barley for?"

"Mainly for a change from rice, since I can't have potatoes. You can cook it in broth and it takes on a nice flavor. I'll use the broth from the chicken—see, the chicken will be stewed the day before for chicken salad. That's what I need the celery for. I'm supposed to have red meat, too, so I put down two small steaks, if that's okay."

"Oh."

"Unless you don't like those things. Here, read the meal plans...." Claire crosses to the table to get the other sheet.

"No, no, I like them fine. I've just never...I mean, that will be fine." She stands, picks up her purse and bends to pat Presley. The basset raises his chin so she scratches beneath it. "Presley, you take care of Claire. Mommy will be back soon. Be good."

Claire, sweet Claire, doesn't even laugh when Ellie says this, the way everyone else in the family does. She just says, "Don't worry. We'll be just fine." And Ellie believes her.

At Thriftway, Ellie goes up and down every aisle and goes to the deli three or four times to ask the worker behind the high glass display case where something is. It takes her a long time to get everything, partially because she passes some items three or four times and has to backtrack when she comes to it on the list. There's more to it, though. She's distracted by what made her in such a hurry to get out to do the shopping tonight to begin with. Her initial impulse, which had blazed like a comet, has passed beyond discernment and now she's less sure. She's chewed her bottom lip all the while she's shopped, anxious from the stress of looking for things on the maze of shelves and trying to search the sky of her own mind for a sign.

Once she's paid and the bagged groceries are in the cart, she has to decide once and for all. She fishes a quarter out of her purse and pushes the cart to the pay phone mounted on the wall of Thriftway's entrance.

"Lydie?" she says when the phone is answered at the other end of the line. "It's me."

CHAPTER 30

Graduation. To think that I spent so much time alternately swelling up and deflating myself like a tree frog, so proud of Claire and so worried about how I'd manage when she left for college, when what I should have been worrying about was something that would have been unendurable to imagine. But I never did imagine it.

I never thought I'd go into the auditorium alone on the night of June sixth. It never occurred to me that the dusk would be scented by a lovely flowering tree planted to the left of the school entrance in memory of some poor, lost student. *What that girl's mother must have been through, must go through every day*, I think. *Really, I'm lucky. Mine is still alive.* A small, bronze plaque propped at its base has white, fallen petals around it like so many snowflakes, that cold comfort.

I expected to cry when Claire received her diploma, but I never thought I would cry in a stall in the girls' room before the time came to find a seat. I didn't think I'd sit alone, surrounded by strangers, in the back section where they stick "other guests," as opposed to immediate families. From my seat I try to see over heads and through bright movement and waving programs to where Wayne must be, but I can't. Is Ellie there with him, in my place?

When Ellie called from the grocery store, I was equally inclined to melt into a puddle of gratitude and take off after her with a crowbar. I think she told me the truth, at least mostly, but she resisted certain questions like a birch that gives in the wind but doesn't snap. "El," I said desperately, "you can't do this to me. This is my daughter, she needs me, I need her, we have to work this out. I know she's angry at me, I know. But you've got to let me see her. You don't know the first thing about this, and it's my job, not yours."

She'd been a little apologetic until then, and I thought she understood. I thought she was on my side. I never thought I'd be pleading with and threatening either of my sisters, let alone both, for my child.

"Well, Claire seems to think I'm doing the job just fine," she said. "I shouldn't have called you. I didn't want you to be all scared and hurt. I can't believe you're yelling at me." There was a scratchiness in her voice that sounded as if the words were pebbles rolling over the flint of her tongue. A fire was about to be started.

"God, Ellie. I'm not scared and hurt, I'm terrified and crushed. Can't you—" I broke off, afraid that she might hang up on me. I tried what used to work all the time, lowering my voice but trying not to wheedle. "Don't you think Elvis would insist on seeing Lisa Marie? Wouldn't he do whatever he had to—to be by his daughter's side? I'm sure they had tough times when he and Priscilla split up, and maybe Lisa Marie was really mad at him, but I think he still got to see her." The strange thing was I really felt it. I think I know what everyone who has ever been separated from his child, her child, feels. *Don't let this happen*, I want to pray for us all.

"Are you and Wayne splitting up?" Her voice came pitched over the wire, a high line drive, the kind that breaks the pitcher's nose.

I lost it then, which made her neat sidestep work. "How the hell should *I* know?" I was nearly shouting. "He's not said a word to me since he walked out. I just discovered that Maddie—my *sister*—has been hiding him and that you, my *other* sister, has been helping her. I should ask *you*—are Wayne and I splitting up?"

She completely ignored that. I wondered if the phone line had snapped, stretched too taut between us.

"Ellie? Are you still there?"

"I've got to get going. I don't want to leave Claire alone too long," she finally said. She'd switched to fencing. Parry and thrust. She must have known how that long blade would hit home.

"*Wait*. Wait. What about her graduation? Can she go? Has she seen Dr. Douglas? I guess the dialysis is going all right, she'd not be with you if it weren't, she'd be in the hospital, but…do you know all the signs of peritonitis? Is she taking her Norvasc—that's the one for blood pressure, and how about the Epogen shots? She can't forget those—" I was babbling. Ellie cut me off.

"She doesn't want you."

"At her graduation? Claire wouldn't do that to me. I can't believe it, Ellie, she knows how much I love her. She couldn't do that…."

"Look, I'll send you the guest ticket you sent me. Try not to let her see you. I've really got to go."

I stood there listening to the unwavering dial tone for a couple of minutes, the flatline sound from the machine hooked up to my heart.

The boys are in black robes and mortarboards, the girls in white ones, and they progress slowly, in boy-girl twosomes down two aisles simultaneously. "Pomp and Circumstance" is being played, beautifully, with dignity, by a trumpet soloist accompanied by the band director on a small organ. The students are moving in a slow, practiced cadence, the music swaying through their bodies. Just above the necklines of the boys' robes, white shirts and ties emerge; their black dress shoes are freshly shined. The girls are in white two-inch heels, and no one's dress hangs below the robe. They are transformed into shiny new adults, at least for these few hours, ready to march on into fresh futures. Maysfield High School does only a few things with magnificence and perfection, but the graduation ceremony is one of them, and I cannot find my daughter.

I look at the students in one aisle, then swivel my head to the other side, knowing I'm missing a glimpse of at least two faces on either side at any time. Finally the class all stand in place in front of their seats. Their backs are to the audience, and it is too late.

The band, minus its graduating seniors, plays the national anthem and the alma mater. Then on stage, flanked by flags, speakers begin to step to the podium. Nine or ten awards are announced. "For Excellence in French Five, the Mark Mortine Award goes to Anna Claire Merrill," the principal says over the loudspeaker. "This award carries a five-hundred-dollar scholarship for further study of the language," the principal intones, and I am taken completely off guard. I had no idea this was coming. But then maybe Claire didn't either. Then I see her. She stands from the very front row and climbs the six steps up to the stage. Claire has worn her dark hair loose—and it cascades just onto the shoulders of her robe, a striking image against the rich, deep red stage curtain. She's had it cut a couple of inches since I've seen her, which makes it more curly than wavy. She wears a gold medal around her neck: the honor accorded to the top five percent of each graduating class. She made it. My baby made it.

Ms. Seeley, tall, dark-haired and dimpled, doesn't fit a single stereotype of a principal. Instead of shaking Claire's hand, she steps from behind the podium and gives Claire a hug. Then she leans back to the microphone and says, "How's this young woman for a profile in courage? Your school and, I know, your family, are so proud of you, Claire. It is a privilege to present this award. I only wish the school had one for bravery and determination." Then she begins to applaud and the audience takes it up, and every senior stands up for Claire. They stand and applaud her all the way off the stage and back to her seat.

Two more awards are given out and then the roll call begins for each senior to cross the stage and accept a diploma. The top honor graduates are first, then the rest of the class, in alphabetical order, carefully seated to insure a slow, orderly flow of handshakes across the stage. When Kevin's name is called, his parents mount the steps and take his diploma for him, his mother with tears coursing down her cheeks, his father carrying himself with the bearing of an ex-marine. The senior class all stand and applaud again for a good twenty seconds before taking their seats. These are good young people, I think. They care. Even though I'm locked outside of that circle, for Claire's sake I'm grateful that it exists. *Go ahead, surround her. Love her and encourage her. Please. Keep her safe.* I beg with no idea now who I'm addressing—something inside or above that circle of the undamned, someone who can do what I can't.

The father of one of the senior girls, a minister, gives "A Parting Word," because they can't call it a benediction anymore. "Go with God," he says at the end, hope and admonition at once, and it is over. The class processes out to a trumpet voluntary, and parents crush behind the last of them to find their children and gather them up in great hugs and congratulations.

As I walk up one aisle, I see him standing just inside the door open to the other aisle. John. John came to see his daughter. He either sneaked in—nearly impossible, I've heard—or used some lawyer connection to get an "other guest" ticket. I have to cut across several people and find an empty row that I can use to cross the seats. Then, even when I am in the right aisle, I have to angle myself sideways and crowd between people. "Excuse me. I'm sorry. Excuse me," I say over and over, trying to outswim the current.

I approach John. He sticks the handkerchief in his left hand into his pocket. His eyes are red-rimmed, like a rabbit's. He stands still and I hesitate. But we see the evidence of each other's tears, and when I take another step, one that brings me close enough, he puts his arms around me. "Beautiful," he whispers. "She is so beautiful." I feel his shoulders shake and his weight increases on my shoulder.

"I know," I whisper back. "It's okay. I know. I never thought it would be like this, either."

CHAPTER 31

"I'm going. Period. Full stop. I don't care what Dr. Douglas says or doesn't say," Claire says.

There's a steely side to her niece that Ellie is just discovering, though it's not been directed at Ellie. The quality (always popping up like a jack-in-the-box out of Maddie, and Lydie) has seemed as if it represented a whole genetic code unreplicated in Ellie. Of course, she's never let either of them know there's an iota of admiration mixed into her jealousy and frustration. With Claire, though, it's somehow different. Ellie's been watching her.

The soft side of Claire is the one Ellie generally sees, though Claire certainly doesn't laugh as much as she used to, nor spend a lot of time on girlish things, probably because she has nephritis in her feet bothering her now. It used to be Claire who would sit and listen to old Elvis concerts on tape with Ellie, and compare him unfavorably to other stars, but now she's immersed in books and spends a lot of time writing. Once, while Claire showered, Ellie flipped open the notebook Claire keeps with her, all the time it seems. *Kevin, my love*, was on the top line beneath *May 20*, which was five days after the accident that had killed Brian. Claire's steady, unadorned script covered page after page. Ellie thought her heart would break, though she only got as far as *June 2*, when the bathroom door opened abruptly and Claire appeared with a turban-style towel on her head. Ellie thought she had reacted quickly enough, sliding the notebook to her side and shifting her torso to hide it while she pretended to adjust the two throw pillows on the couch. Claire did not appear to notice, but after that, the notebook disappeared.

You won't believe my aunt Ellie, Claire had written. *She went to the hospital by herself to get the dialysis review, and even though it's obvious that she can hardly bear it, and it's really unnecessary, she stays with me when I do an exchange. Four times a day and again at night—it's like having an umbilical cord all over again. I hate it. I just want my old, normal life and your old, normal life back.*

"You're damn right I can hardly stand it," Ellie had whispered, but then she allowed herself a little secret smile.

Ellie understands Claire writing to Kevin all too well. She's written to Elvis so many times, inking pages with her frustrations, angers, fears and longings. But she never thought he would wake from the dead and answer her—that's the difference between Ellie and Claire. Claire still has hope.

Ellie hasn't written anything in a while. There just hasn't been time. Claire had noticed—not the absence of Ellie's notebook, of course, nobody even knew about that—but she'd mentioned something else in the notebook of letters to Kevin: *She's actually not mentioning Elvis in every other sentence.*

At first, when Ellie read that she felt guilty. She hadn't meant to be unfaithful in her remembering of Elvis. Finally, she had shrugged. She was doing the best she could, and Elvis was the kind of man who would understand that. Even if there had been time, Ellie's book to Elvis is still stuffed between the mattress and the box spring back at Mama and Daddy's house. Strange how little they've called her, even since the phone's been turned on here, compliments, again, of Wayne. Two days ago, Mama said they'd had Kraft Macaroni and Cheese for supper and she'd opened canned peaches for desert.

"Charles doesn't like peaches," Ellie objected.

"I told him they were big grapes and he scarfed them right down," Mama answered with an edge of pride that cut Ellie.

"I guess I can come tomorrow in the afternoon after I help Claire with her exchange, that's what it's called when she does her dialysis," Ellie countered on the phone. "It'll be late, though—it's pretty complicated."

"No need. We got plenty groceries in the house. Daddy took me. You take care of yourself…and Claire."

Ellie turned the conversation over and over like a rare rock in her mind's eye, searching out its clues to the history of how her world had formed, how and where it would end.

Once, a bird had been trapped in the one-car garage at the house and had batted itself frantically against the walls. Ellie had taken an upturned broom to try to encourage it toward the open door. The bird, a sparrow, she thought, plain and brown, had gone everywhere but out. Ellie feels like that same bird is inside her, banging itself against the walls of her body, reminding her that she has no idea of what she's doing when she gets into these conversations with Claire about college.

"I told you. I'm going," Claire says. "How about I make us chicken fajitas tonight? Low potassium, no salt. Salt's not good for you, either, you know."

"Dr. Douglas said probably not first quarter, anyway, you know, till we know everything's working okay."

"College is on semesters, not quarters. You're thinking of high school. See, that makes a big difference, because it's the whole first half." How can Ellie argue with that?

"Dr. Douglas said that you could stay here and take classes at the NKU branch."

"That's where my mother goes," Claire answers flatly, then, after a pause, continues in her unassailable way, as if Ellie has spoken, which she hasn't. "That's not the point. I'm going to Louisville. I wonder when I'll hear about my dorm assignment."

"But…"

"Look," Claire says, sweetly, swiveling to pick something off the kitchenette counter so that her back is momentarily to Ellie. "Did you see this catalog that came from Penney's? I saw a dress in here that would look so good on you. Have you ordered from the catalog before, or do you usually go to the downtown store?"

Ellie remembers Lydie telling her how Claire had loved Wessel, an old, well-endowed private college, the third school she'd looked at. It was beautiful, Lydie said, with old, brick buildings connected by winding paths beneath canopies of high branches. The students were friendly, the academic standards top-notch and yes, she *could* get certified to teach French if she decided to go in that direction, although they strongly encouraged their students to go straight on to graduate school. "We'll see...if you get enough financial aid..." Lydie said she'd told Claire, and Claire had set out to get it.

And had. Just the way Claire had declared that hell and high water could *both* come, while Dr. Douglas stood on her head and spit wooden nickels; it wasn't going to stop her from graduating with her class. "And I did, didn't I?" she'd reminded Ellie during one of these go-rounds a couple of days ago.

"Well, yes, but that's..." Ellie picks at loose skin around her thumb. It comes loose with a little snap and she drops it onto the rough tweedy blue sofa. Presley, curled by her side, flicks an ear. A prick of blood appears, and Ellie quickly wipes it off. It reappears immediately, over and over.

"You see? I know what I can do. Peritoneal dialysis is no big deal. Please don't worry, Eleanor, I'll be fine." Claire had taken to dropping the *aunt* during these discussions, and calling her Eleanor. Ellie had to admit it: the girl was good. But Ellie is getting better. She knows she can keep Claire in one place during her dialysis, so every day or two she braces herself and brings it up. Not that she is making any headway, but she's trying to introduce the notion of Claire *not* going away without specific mention of the images of a kidney transplant in her own head: glass and steel and small blinking lights, masked doctors, the flash of a scalpel, blood. More than enough to leave Ellie quite light-headed.

"I'm so tired tonight," Claire says. She pours herself a small glass of orange juice from the refrigerator. "Do you mind if I turn in early?" She raises her voice over the television. Ellie is watching the CBS Sunday Night Movie, something about a woman sleeping with her best friend's son, based on a true story. Ellie could tell a true story if she wanted to.

"Of course not. Are you feeling okay? Did you count that juice into your allotment?" Ellie's voice squeaks a little. The dialysis nurse had told her to watch for fatigue, nausea, poor appetite, swelling feet and ankles, the flush of fever or rising blood pressure, any flu-like symptoms, which could mean peritonitis. Ellie thinks rising blood pressure might squeeze the soul right out of the body when it gets too tight in there and the thought scares her. Elvis had had high blood pressure.

"Here's the pencil, here's the paper," Claire says lightly, gesturing to the running total of her daily liquid intake.

Ellie sleeps lightly, listens for Claire among the too-close neighbor night noises, and she does hear her when she vomits, as quiet as Claire tries to be. This after Claire hardly touched her own fajita. No matter what Claire says, Ellie is going to call Dr. Douglas in the morning.

CHAPTER 32

I never did catch so much as a glimpse of Claire after the ceremony. John and I slipped into the crowd of families pushing after the seniors. I could see them bunched together looking like a flock of penguins headed for the lobby, some waving their hats and craning their necks, or even walking backward, trying to spot someone. Of course, the families were calling their names and trying to see over the throng, a grand, joyous melee. I turned into the hall that led away from the lobby, past empty classrooms to another exit. John walked beside me but we kept more than two arm lengths between us.

Night had overtaken the school and parking lot. John and I didn't say anything, but he stayed nearby as I headed for my car, and I assumed he was seeing me to it safely. When I reached it, though, he said, "Please let me take you home. I don't think you should be alone right now, and I know I don't care to be."

His face, illuminated faintly by one street lamp, looked youthful, much the way I remembered him eighteen years ago. He'd gotten his hair cut, and dressed in a dark suit and red patterned tie, like a proud parent. I didn't know if Wayne had bothered to wear a coat and tie. It was always I who told him when an occasion required it. Not all of the fathers had, but the ones who hadn't stood out. Claire and I had bought her graduation dress and shoes almost a month before the accident, and I was glad of it. I knew she had what she needed. Wayne must have taken them out of her closet when he took the supplies out of the basement.

"All right," was all I said to John, and handed him the keys to my Ford. When he got in the driver's seat, he let the seat back all the way and changed the rearview mirror. Then he reached out and changed the side mirror, too. The details that fit me all switched around to accommodate him. Wayne used to do that, too, and never put anything back, like the way he'd leave cherry pits on the end table in the living room and I'd find them, sticky and wizened, the next day. In the mornings, now, the end tables are clean when I go out to turn the coffeepot on, and I pull my nightgown off over my head on my way back toward the bathroom. I can walk through my house wearing nothing but my bare breasts, an old pair of Claire's bikini underpants with frayed elastic and a certain…well, freedom.

After we'd traveled a block or two, I startled. "What about your car?"

"We'll come back and pick it up later," he said. "I'm parked out on the street, anyway."

I'd assumed that by "take you home," John had meant my home, but I realized shortly that we were heading the wrong way. "We can go to my place," he said. "I put a bottle of champagne in the refrigerator, hoping we could…"

"That was nice of you," I said. "I appreciate…"

"Listen, Lydie. I think I have some idea of what you put into being a mother to Anna Claire. It kills me that you're being cheated out of celebrating with her. It's so unfair…"

Maybe it was just that I couldn't bear to talk about what I was missing. "I imagine you've got some feelings yourself, tonight," I said.

"Yeah. I do. But I've *got* what *I* deserve." His voice grated over his throat.

I looked over at him then, his eyes glittery. I touched his shoulder, and when he reached out his hand, I held it. "I'm sorry," he said. "I've no right to this. None at all. I want to help you, that's the point, not me."

"Thanks," I said, all I could manage, and except for a brief word here or there, we rode in silence the rest of the way.

* * *

I'd not been to John's before: a condo, large-roomed and airy, with big windows and creamy walls. Traditional furniture in neutral colors. A brick fireplace with a carved wooden mantel, something like Maddie's, and prints—mainly landscapes—hung low over tables with small sculptures carefully placed. A potted Norfolk pine and a tall ficus tree are spotlit from the floor; a reading lamp is adjusted to the side of a leather recliner by the one wall of floor-to-ceiling bookshelves; the living room says *sink into me and rest*.

John took off his suit jacket and loosened his tie. "Take your shoes off, Lydie, get comfortable," he said, gesturing toward the sofa. "I'll get the champagne." I heard him in the kitchen, opening the refrigerator, then opening cabinet doors. A moment later, he emerged with a towel and green bottle. "Moet," he said. "Good stuff." The cork popped perfectly into the towel and he set the bottle down in front of me. *He's done this many times before*, I thought, but dismissed it, too tired to fuss inside myself. *So what? He's had his life to deal with, I've had mine*.

He disappeared into the kitchen again and came back with two crystal champagne flutes, a plate of shrimp and a little dish of cocktail sauce, and a plate of cheese and crackers on a tray. When he put the tray down, I saw that he'd also bought little party napkins with mortarboards, balloons and *Congratulations* on them. They matched the invitations I'd bought for Claire's graduation party, though, of course, John couldn't have known that.

John brought two white tapered candles in sterling candlesticks from the dining-room table and put them on either side of the bottle of champagne. "Busy, busy, busy," he teased, pretending to wipe sweat off his forehead with one of the napkins. "Just one more thing, then I'll join you." He disappeared into the kitchen again and I heard the refrigerator door open and close. He came back with a vase of pink roses surrounded by greenery and baby's breath. "These are for you, to thank you."

He poured two glasses of champagne and handed one to me. "A toast," he said. "To Anna Claire and her mother."

We finished the bottle over the next two hours. John asked questions about Claire. I fed him answers like fresh green grapes, pulling them off the stem one at a time and raising them to his open mouth. Her Girl Scout cooking badge with the crêpes suzette masterpiece. Falling off the balance beam in gymnastics, and how she'd played "Twinkle Twinkle Little Star" over and over on the violin until I thought my last brain cell would commit suicide when she was in the fourth grade. How she'd started her periods in December of the year she was twelve, exactly like me. Her first boyfriend, the one in serious need of a personality; her second boyfriend, the one from Zit City; and, now, Kevin. "When I taught her to drive," I said, "it was so funny, she refused to back up." He laughed with me, long and deliciously, the way parents share moments.

Then I told him more about when she had the first infection, how we'd thought she was just in a bedwetting phase from bad dreams, and the damage that had been done to the big kidney by the time we knew what was wrong. "I felt like the little wheel was turning all the time, but the mouse was dead. You know? I was so afraid all the time that I shut out everything but Claire. I couldn't get out of the crisis mode. I felt like an enormous elephant had just stepped out of thin air and onto us—then, later, the elephant disappeared back into the air, and I couldn't get up from being flattened. Finally, I sort of forced myself back to life—that's when I started taking classes at NKU, to distract myself as much as anything else. I was…hovering, you know, couldn't let her out of my sight. I just got better at hiding it, I guess."

"I have something I have to tell you," he said, looking away, across the room. "The elephant didn't step out of thin air. My father had it, and so did one of his sisters. There *is* a family history. When Dr. Douglas told you I wasn't a match...look, that wasn't the whole truth. I have it, too, the one undersized kidney, I mean. It's a hereditary trait. From my father's side. He had it. I should have told you back then, though I can't say I really thought of it, honestly—but, there's no excuse, I should have told you when you first called me about being tested. Gutless. See, no one's had anything happen to the good kidney, no one's had to be on dialysis, or needed a transplant, let alone died." John finally looked at me. "I don't think I realized the full implications of having it, though we always knew it *could* be serious. There's no excuse, I don't claim one. When you called, I just couldn't... I'm sorry, Lydie. So sorry. I should have told you."

I was sure that I was missing a piece. Maybe he was telling me that there was another source. "What about the boys?"

"Both the boys have it, Mark the worst. Nathan's little kidney does function moderately, but Mark's not so much. We've been so...lucky. Their good kidneys haven't been stressed, no infection, no injury, it's been...okay."

"So you knew you couldn't donate, and you let me get my hopes up...you let me believe? You didn't *tell* me this could happen when you knew I was pregnant? Maybe I could have done something, maybe there was a way not to have her good kidney have to work so hard. You knew? You got Dr. Douglas to *lie* to me?" I was shouting at him by the end, incredulous and outraged, some taut wire in the center of my body vibrating unbearably.

"She didn't lie. She just told you I wasn't a match. I wouldn't give her permission to disclose information, she would have had to have my written consent. I did go see her, when you thought I was being tested, I mean. I wanted to give Claire my kidney and go on dialysis myself. I'd wait for the cadaver donor."

That slowed me down. That, and that I could see his shame. Maybe I'd had too much to drink, or maybe I've just become so tired of feelings I couldn't hold on to any of them anymore. Maybe I needed someone as base and alone as me.

Forgive us our trespasses as we forgive those who have trespassed against us. I used to pray it. I'd like to give myself that fine an intent. John is not a strong man. Surely I'd known that for long enough. The truth is, though, it was my old weakness that rose in me, my need. I touched his cheek, then nudged his face up and around until he looked me in the eye. In the semidarkness, I couldn't tell the pupil of his eye from the iris, they looked that black. "It might not have changed anything for me to know," I lied.

Tears, for the second time that night, came to his eyes. I leaned toward him, next to me on the couch in this room of soft shadows, and opened my arms. He moved toward me and at first I was holding him, then he was holding me; the weight of us shifted back and forth between our bodies and then combined until we were holding each other equally.

Is it surprising or shameful or both that I spent the night? Well, I did. The truth is that I don't care so much anymore. I'm all cared out. Except for Claire, I just don't really care what I should or shouldn't do, what anyone might think. I hadn't the slightest reason to think Claire might call me the night of her graduation, and I plain didn't want to be alone. Who else should I have spent the night with? Her father and I, exiles from our daughter's life, he by his choice, I against my will: why shouldn't we comfort one another?

It was I who had moved closer to John on his plush sofa so that we could lean on one another. His cheek against mine was utterly soft, like an old woman's. I stroked it with my thumb. "You shaved tonight?" I said. I remembered how John hated to shave. He used a straight razor.

"Our daughter's graduation. Of course I shaved again."

When one of his hands dropped from the center of my back to my waist, the signal that would have been required to tell him no would have been infinitesimal, the smallest shift of my body.

Instead I drew him closer. And when he pulled his head back to look me in the eyes, I saw the question there. He would not have risked anything he thought could possibly be wrong for me. It was I who answered, *Yes. Yes. I need you, too.* I unbuttoned his shirt looking straight at him all the while, so he would know that I was sure.

He was still being cautious when I unzipped my dress, and made no move to help me. I stood to step out of it, and then pulled the skirt of my slip over my shoulders. As I did, he stood, too, and finished lifting the slip over my head in one sweet, brief motion. He unhooked my bra; I peeled off stockings and underpants, but slowly, stopping to unbuckle his belt and unzip his pants, and all the while keeping my eyes on his.

"Lydie, oh Lydie, you've not changed. You're the same, beautiful Lydie. Those periwinkle eyes," he said, breaking away to look at me frankly.

"Did you just come up with that or did you remember?" I asked it lightly, to hide how it affected me that he remembered the word he'd used.

"Of course I remember…I remember everything. The snow?"

"The first time we kissed," I answered quietly.

"And it's the same. It's all the same," he said, his hands sliding down my hips and leaving their feel the way cream leaves itself on the side of a pitcher.

"Flatterer. You're the one time forgot," I told him. The hair on his chest was half-grayed, like November bluegrass; other than that, it seemed the same body. This was a man who'd worked at staying in shape.

"Well, I'm glad if you're pleased, I thought I'd changed a lot since we were…since we were." There wasn't a right word that he could find for it. He put his arms around me and caressed my back a few moments, but then just held me to him as if he were trying to press a flower between the pages of himself. I put my head on his chest and took in the scent of him. A couple of times

I've sprayed a sample of it on my wrist, when the department store had it on display, but it was never right, never precisely the same. I could tell that much—just that it wasn't the same. That night, I breathed John in and the scent of him, as much as the feel of his arms and mouth on me, was the way I remembered it when the two of us first found each other.

Afterward, one of his shirts was my nightgown and I slept, spooned against him in his king-size bed, straight through, not even waking to go to the bathroom. It didn't matter, either. When I got home early the next morning, there were no messages on my machine. No one in my family had missed me at all. No one.

I showered and got ready for work. Friday. Always, the phones thrum with calls, patients wanting to get in or get a prescription renewed before the weekend when the office shutters down. I was shifting gears, thinking about the drug rep who'd bring in chocolates along with his boxes of samples, until I looked in the mirror to put on makeup. My face didn't have its own natural roundness, but hollowed out under my eyes and cheekbones. My hair jutted wrongly, out of control. I couldn't quite take my own direct gaze. "The son of a bitch didn't tell you, and you still did it again," I said aloud.

CHAPTER 33

Madalaine's footsteps—she has always struck hard with her heels—sound in the hospital hall a good ten seconds before they reach Claire's room, and she pauses too long when the scuffing of her flats stops just outside the door. By the time she opens it, both Claire and Ellie have their eyes fixed there. Madalaine sticks her head in, sees their expectant looks and laughs self-consciously. "Oh," she says. "You are here."

"I told you that on the phone," Ellie ticks, emphasizing the *told*. "But we were going to get together at eleven." She looks at her watch to point out that it's nearly eleven-thirty.

"Well, this isn't so bad. At least it's a cheery room… It's so beastly hot outside, be glad you're not missing anything out there." Madalaine gestures unsteadily at nothing in particular.

"Hi, Aunt Maddie." Claire looks small against the white pillow.

"Have you been out to see Mama and Daddy lately?" Madalaine directs this to Ellie.

"I talked to them a day or so ago. I've been pretty busy with…other things. I thought you'd be looking in on them."

"When I can," Madalaine says, keeping her voice casual. "Of course, last time I went by I didn't stop because the grass was too high to find the house. What, did Gert advise against mowing this year? Or did Charles plant trees again?" She's referring to Charles's attempt to grow gum trees a couple of years ago, when he saved up all the gum Lydie brought him, and placed chewed pieces all around the yard when Ellie thought he was looking for four-leaf clovers. Ellie is still bitter because Daddy made her clean the mower blades and it was disgusting. Madalaine knows where her sister's buttons are, with exactly what pressure to push them.

"How is Jennifer doing?" Claire interrupts. Her voice is shadowy, not quite right. A machine thing is a couple of feet from her bed, but Madalaine can't see that she's hooked up to anything right at the moment, though there's one of those pole things beside the bed. She looks faintly yellow, her hair a limp, dark bedraggle fallen back from her face onto the white pillow that props her. Madalaine wonders if since she can't make pee right, it backs up into the body and turns the skin that color. Then the sight of her sister's violently ruffled blouse and oversize pink hair bow briefly focuses Madalaine's irritation, and she ignores Claire.

"So what's up?" Maddie says to her sister, her voice like glass underfoot.

"Well…I mean Claire's in here and you know, well…family… and Dr. Douglas said we should…" Ellie glances meaningfully at Claire for her sister's benefit and then gives Maddie a look meant to wither flowers.

Madalaine moves a half stop, reducing the distance between herself and the door, though she doesn't turn around. If Ellie thinks she's going to back her into keeping Claire company, she'd better start consulting Gert about the future more often. Maddie has Jennifer to think about at home, especially now, when Bill is so unreliable, hovering over Melody who's well past her due date. From the brief glimpse Maddie had of her on Wednesday when she and Bill picked Jennifer up for dinner, Melody looks like she's going to deliver a full-size outhouse, or something equally deserved.

"Why don't we run down to the cafeteria and get an iced tea, since it's so hot outside?" Ellie says to Maddie. Then, to Claire, "I'm sorry, honey."

"No problem," Claire answers her. "I'm tired of it, but used to it."

"Honey, I don't mean to make you feel bad."

"It doesn't, really, it's not…what anyone else does."

Maddie is almost spun around with Ellie grabbing her arm as she heads for the door. "Want me to bring you a Coke or something?" she tosses over her shoulder at Claire on the way out.

"Six of 'em," Claire calls back.

The heavy door to Claire's room is still swooshing shut in Ellie's hand when she says, sharply, "Don't do that."

"Do what?"

"She can only have sixteen ounces of liquid a day now. Don't torment her offering Coke. And she's got this terrible diet she has to stay on. Has to do with potassium."

"How was I supposed to know?"

"I guess you're supposed to know because you're her aunt and she needs us. I can't do everything, even though you've always expected me to."

"God, Ellie, don't start."

"Dr. Douglas wants to talk with the family. I'm sure she's down waiting for us. Lydie's probably there."

"I don't want to talk to Lydie."

"You have to. We've got to do something."

Maddie stops short and plants her feet squarely. "Don't tell me what I have to do," she says. "Don't even go there." She braces herself for a fight, but it doesn't come. Instead, Ellie stops too, and studies her, her head slightly tilted.

"Have you been… No, never mind," Ellie says. "I didn't mean it that way. You know, since Wayne is staying with you…you could at least, sort of…represent him. I don't know. I mean, Dr. Douglas wanted him in on it, but…"

Immediately Wayne's ghostlike presence in her house conjures itself in Madalaine's mind and adds another layer to the fog of aggravation enveloping her. She shakes her head as if to say no, but she's trying to clear it.

"He's not there?"

Of course Ellie would misunderstand. Sometimes Madalaine is convinced that Ellie's dumb on purpose. It's far more irritating than Charles's...what, dumbnitude? She can't think of the word, and giggles for a second at *dumbnitude*.

"Yes, he's there," she finally gets out. "Not right now, now he's at work, I guess." What's the subject, anyway? Maddie's lost the thread. Ellie has, without Maddie noticing, gotten her moving toward the elevator. Gliding, actually. She doesn't think she is moving her feet, so it's a mystery how she can hear her flats on the cool hospital tile. "I can't stand to come here," she says as Ellie shepherds, a hand on Madalaine's upper back. "I can't stand it."

"I know, I'm sorry. I'm so sorry," Ellie says and touches Maddie's hair as if she's a child. She doesn't sound like Ellie at all, but like...Lydie. That's it. Maddie is satisfied that one thing is cleared up.

The elevator leaves Maddie's stomach on the third floor while it descends. She studies her hands to be able to put her head down without Ellie knowing she's nauseated. They're not really Maddie's hands, though. She never would have had these stubby, uneven nails, with old-looking ridges and a little hint of grayish dirt under a couple of them and bloody little holes where she's pulled the cuticles. She used to use an undercoat of ridge filler and polish them sweet peach or that gorgeous brownish wild-berry, and change her lipstick to make everything coordinate, just to go to the office. Maybe not every day, but most, except when she was letting her nails rest. Then they were filed and buffed to bring up natural shine. Even though she was back to work at the phone company, Maddie knows she's not really Maddie, but some stranger, with a sketchy set of instructions, who's come to take over her body, put it through the motions. Maddie would never wear this same old denim skirt day after day, just putting on whatever shirt was more or less clean, and not even bother to turn the ends of her hair under with a curling iron. "Maybe it's the invasion of the body snatchers," she says to Ellie.

"What?" Ellie says.

It turns out that they aren't even going to the cafeteria. Ellie pulls her off the elevator at the first floor instead of going to the basement. Something about Dr. Douglas and Lydie that sounded faintly familiar, but there's a humming that's started in Maddie's head.

"This isn't going to work," Ellie says to Dr. Douglas when she and Maddie reach the cubbyhole office where the doctor talks to patients' families. "Somebody needs to take her home."

"But we need to…" Lydie is sitting there all wrought up, and looking helplessly at Dr. Douglas.

"Mrs. Beeson..? I'm Sarah Douglas," the doctor says, standing and putting out her hand to Madalaine. A hank of her blond pageboy falls forward as she tilts her head, assessing. Her glasses are open on her desk, on top of an array of pink and green papers and yellow crinkly papers that put Madalaine in mind of party streamers.

"Is the caterer here?" Madalaine asks the doctor.

"I'm afraid I don't understand."

"Maddie," Lydia breaks in, using her warning voice. Damn her. Definitely, right to hell.

"Really, this isn't going to—" Ellie says.

"Maybe we could all just sit down a minute. Is Claire's father coming?" The doctor comes from behind the desk and pulls the two empty chairs up next to Lydia's. "Please, have a seat."

"Which one?" Maddie breaks up.

"Oh, either one will do."

Maddie's laughing harder now. "I suppose they are interchangeable," she chortles.

Dr. Douglas looks at Ellie, then says to Maddie, "I'm sorry Mrs. Beeson. Just take whichever seat you'd like."

"Oh, I thought I could take whichever man I wanted. Lydie did, you know, and so did Melody, come to think of it. If Ellie can have Elvis's ghost in addition to Presley, I don't see why I can't have a couple—"

"Sweet Jesus, Maddie, shut the hell up," says Ellie.

That stuns them all into momentary silence. Dr. Douglas clears her throat. "Maybe you're right, Ellie, perhaps this isn't the time."

Lydia moves forward in her chair until she is barely perched on the edge of it and her hands flutter like a distressed bird. "Wait. Please, this is about Claire. You said…we have to do this, to see if there are any options."

"Well, I'm out of here," Madalaine says, pushing the chair Dr. Douglas pulled out for her back into the corner to clear her way to the door. The burning weight of her own shoulders is too much; that and the fuzz around her eyes and mouth.

"One of you better go with her," the doctor undertones.

"I don't need one of them, thank you," Madalaine says, huffy, pulling the door open. It gives with less resistance than she expected, and she loses her balance, banging her thigh on the hard molded arm of the chair she's moved. Her feet scuffle with each other like small squabbling animals. Finally, it's Lydia's quick reach that steadies her. "Damn. Damn," Maddie says, as the bruising ripples out on her leg. "Damn." Then she's gone, favoring the injured part of herself, and slowed by it, but gone all the same and glad of it. Her flats pound the hall until she reaches the tweed berber of the lobby area, which mutes and sobers them in an instant.

It's Lydie who catches up to her there. "Maddie. Maddie. What's going on? Are you all right?" Madalaine can hear her scurrying along on the tile, and then the abrupt change when Lydie reaches the carpeted area. The modulated voice of an operator pages a doctor with a long, foreign-sounding name. Lydia's hand touches her arm.

"Right. Sure. Never better in my life." Sarcasm drives Lydie up the wall. Good place for her.

Lydia angles herself in front of Madalaine, not quite but almost blocking her forward movement. Madalaine slows, but continues walking. "Maddie, this isn't you. I know how terrible everything's been for you, but please, just talk to me. We're supposed to be upstairs talking about Claire."

The universe is utterly clear to Madalaine. She can see her lost Brian tumbling over and over in black space between planets and stars, and she must anchor him firmly in everyone's consciousness for him to be at rest, in a fixed spot where she can go to be with him. She hears her own voice, which sounds strangely like she is screaming, although she's sure she's not. She's calm and deliberate. "I do not want to hear another word about Claire. Do you understand me? I am busy trying to save Brian. Leave me alone. Let go of me." She jerks her arm free, giving her heavy purse the momentum that makes it thud heavily against Lydia's side.

Lydia stumbles and before she can right herself, Madalaine is headed for the automatic doors that lead from the lobby to the parking lot. She looks back only once. Lydia looks positively comical, with her mouth hanging open and two strangers approaching her with wrinkled-up foreheads and outstretched hands.

She has no real memory of driving home, but obviously she did because here's the steering wheel between her hands and her own garage looming open the way she left it this morning. The front door seems to fling itself open, and here comes Jennifer, positively dancing down the walk toward the car, a yellow flower in a happy wind.

"Mommy, Mommy. You're home. I'm glad, I'm glad you're home."

Madalaine's mouth stretches into a smile. Jennifer will help her. Jennifer will be able to see Brian with her, and help her hold him still. She opens the car door and puts her arm out to gather Jennifer in a hug. Jennifer bounces to her, and actually bumps the top of her head against Madalaine's chin.

Tears spring to Madalaine's eyes from the sting of her bitten tongue but she reins in her reaction. Jennifer doesn't notice, in the oblivious way of children.

"Whoa, sweetheart. Who wound you up? Did we win the lottery or what?"

Jennifer giggles and pirouettes in a little dance of joy. "Melody's finally having her baby, and Daddy wants me to come to the hospital with him. It's like three and a half weeks late and the doctor is inducting it."

"Inducing."

"Daddy says I can come and maybe even watch it get born. She's having it at Maysfield General, she could'a gone to St. Francis, but… He says I can be in the birthing room and everything. I just have to stay way out of the way, but he'll be in there, too. "

Madalaine is fighting for control. "Daddy says that, does he? When did he call?"

"About ten-thirty. He went to the doctor with her and the doctor said daddy's too old to worry like this, and they're going to induct the baby. So he's going to come pick me up at one o'clock."

"Induce."

"So can we get a present for the baby?"

Madalaine closes the car door heavily and avoids her daughter's hands and feet, flitting around her like a little flock of butterflies. So much yellow and pink, her daughter in motion. "We'll have to see. Daddy didn't talk to me about this."

"But I can go, can't I?" Jennifer is stricken to stillness, in her dramatic way.

"I don't know, Jen. This is Melody's baby, you know. I thought you were all upset that Melody was having a baby, and that Daddy left us to be with her."

"But I'm happy about it now. Daddy wants the baby to have a big sister, and I want a little brother or sister. I hope it's a sister."

"Brian's your brother. You have a brother," Madalaine lashes, walking toward the front door now. "I don't want you there. You belong here with me."

"I don't want to be here with you," Jennifer shouts. "All you care about is Brian 'cause he's dead."

Madalaine wheels and without a thought, without any conscious decision to it, her open hand flies through the air. A slap resounds across Jennifer's cheek and Madalaine has just enough time to see the red-and-white print of her palm before Jennifer gets her own hand up across the mark.

"I hate you," Jennifer half chokes, half shouts, and runs down the walk, across the asphalt driveway and around the side of her house beyond Madalaine's sight.

CHAPTER 34

"She didn't used to be like this," Ellie says into the ragged silence after Lydia follows Maddie out of the doctor's cramped room.

"I'm sure. It's quite understandable, but is she getting any help?"

"Well, I'm pretty busy with Claire, but Wayne, well, he's around...." Ellie trails off in embarrassment, not wanting to say that Lydie's husband was living with Maddie.

"No, I meant professional help...a psychologist or psychiatrist, maybe."

"Oh. No." This is definitely the first time anyone has suggested that someone other than Ellie needs a shrink. Part of her sucks the moment like a cherry Life Saver, while another weighs the doctor's notion. "Our family isn't the sort to do that."

"You might want to suggest it to her," the doctor says. Her voice is kind enough, but Ellie suspects she feels safe and superior. Probably doesn't have children.

"Do you have children?" Ellie lobs this to her without having planned it.

"No, not yet."

"A dog?"

Sarah Douglas smiles in a way Ellie recognizes instantly. "That I do. I always had a dog growing up, so I can't stand not having one," the doctor says. "Now I've got a sheltie mix that I rescued from the pound. Toby. Why? Do you?"

"Oh my, yes. Presley. He's a hound."

Dr. Douglas smiles appreciatively, but doesn't laugh. "What a great name."

Ellie leans forward and speaks in a confidential tone. "See, I don't think Maddie's lost her mind. When Claire was over there, when we were first doing the dialysis, Maddie was drinking beer. I saw her. She wouldn't let Claire stay, either."

Dr. Douglas waits, but Ellie's told the whole secret. When nothing more comes, the doctor speaks conversationally but seriously.

"Yes, I understand what you mean, but sometimes we find that drinking goes on because someone can't cope. Not always, of course, so you may be right, but the drinking could be a symptom instead of the cause of how she's acting. A professional might be able to help her grieve and cope without the alcohol. I can recommend someone, give you names and phone numbers."

"I don't know. Maybe Lydie." Ellie feels her bangs. The curls are safe, sprayed in place. She licks her lips.

"You seem to be doing a fine job with Claire," the doctor says warmly, and Ellie can't tell if the suggestion and comment are connected in some way.

"Lydia may have trouble getting through to family members right now. I was wondering if you might be able to help her with that, in fact. This is pretty tough, you know. I don't have to tell you how she feels about Claire."

"Claire's being cared for. It's my job now." A vein of silver in the mine of her attachment to her niece. Lately Ellie thinks about having a daughter.

Dr. Douglas looks briefly perplexed. She fiddles with a pencil, shifts in her seat, swipes at a nonexistent hair that may have strayed onto her forehead. "Yes," she says. Then again, looking up at Ellie. "Yes. Tell me. Have you considered the possibility of being tested yourself—to see if you might be able to give Claire a kidney?"

Ellie can't fathom what she's saying.

"There are a lot of tests, of course, but there's the possibility that you might be compatible, might be a match for her, that is. Is that something you'd consider looking into? Do you have high blood pressure, or any other condition?"

Ellie is still silent, so the doctor plunges on. "Maybe I can explain this. I'd hoped to talk about this in a family meeting, so everyone would understand, but since it seems that won't be possible, maybe I can…give it to you?" Her voice rises, looking for assent, but Ellie might as well be a little cement statue of a goose, like the one that used to be out in their front yard. Sarah Douglas breathes in and exhales the basics. "The best situation is always an identical twin, their kidney, I mean. Then a fraternal twin or any sibling. Obviously, all those are out, since Claire's an only child. After that, we look to parents as the best possibilities. Well, we strike out again there." In response to Ellie's slightly raised eyebrows, the first indicator that Ellie's hearing anything, she adds, "Yes, they've…*both* been, um, examined. He was willing, but it's not an option. Anyway, well, not all doctors will, but I do look for the possibility of a willing blood relative who's young and healthy and a good tissue match. Barring that, then, of course, we're left with cadaver donors."

"The dead people," Ellie mutters, a small shudder in her upper body.

"Yes. See, we tissue-type. A six is the best possible match. Without a four or a three, then if necessary, in an emergency we can look at a two-point match, but they only give us a forty-percent chance of success."

"Forty percent? That's all?" The walls of the room, no farther apart than those of a decent-sized walk-in closet like the ones in Graceland, are painted a sickly white, a dead white. Ellie wants off this hard chair, out of this room. Someone has sucked all the air out of this room.

"That's all for a two-point match. So what do you think? I don't mean to push you on this because the peritonitis is under control. I'm concerned though, because we're seeing higher potassium, higher electrolytes, higher blood pressure, some swelling. A transplant is definitely in her best interest. And she's a good candidate—even her dental work was already all up to date. You know, maybe she was having some problems before the accident even. We really don't know if the kidney was stressed before it was damaged."

"But she's not going to die. You can save her, right? I thought the dialysis was enough, that it did what she needs."

"It is. And many patients live for years on dialysis. You mustn't feel pressure, but it's my job to inform you." Dr. Douglas keeps her body unmoving and holds her eyes directly on Ellie's blue ones that have widened perceptibly, until the irises look like marbles on a white floor.

Ellie tries to fight off the knowledge born of Dr. Douglas's deliberate, undeviating gaze. She studies her hands, the nails polished pink by Claire three days ago, now a little chipped in a couple of places. Claire says Ellie has pretty hands, and in her heart of hearts, Ellie's always thought so, too. That's why rings are a special weakness of hers when they come up on the Home Shopping Network. Today she has on the rose-colored cubic zirconium, which is a perfect match for both her nails and the bow in her hair. Claire rather thinks she should do something different with her hair, and Ellie's been thinking about it.

"Ellie? Are you with me? Is there some part of this you don't understand?"

"I...don't know... No, I think I understand."

"Is this something you might consider? The testing?"

"I'm not a person who can take needles," Ellie says, shifting her weight uncomfortably from one hip to another in the hard chair. The thought of having a part of her body cut out, and an actual needle and thread stitching her skin together the way Mama used to patch the rends in Daddy's coveralls is just horrifying. Horrifying.

"Well, I understand about that, and certainly a lot of people feel that way, but remember that before you began all this, you thought you weren't a person who could even look at the exit site or the catheter, either. But see how you've taken it up, and really taken over when you were needed. You have a lot to be proud of. It seems you and Claire have become quite close."

Ellie flashes the doctor a quick, pleased smile.

Sarah Douglas smiles back. "You've really been serving as a second mother," she muses. "You know, in medical law and ethics class we used to talk about someone who could act *in loco parentis*—that's Latin for in the place of a parent. Maybe you want to think about taking what you've been doing one step further…."

"*In loco parentis?*" Ellie tries the pronunciation.

"That's it," the doctor says, her neat blond pageboy bobbing with the animation of her nod. "That's exactly it."

CHAPTER 35

The door to Claire's room is closed. I stand in the wide, tiled hallway staring at what I guess is her chart, stuck in a clear plastic holder on the wall to the right. There are copies of test orders, half-size pastel sheets attached, but the melange of letters and numbers is indecipherable.

I am trying to suck courage out of parched air. My throat is stuck, not a drop to lubricate the right words even if I knew them. Still, what more do I have to lose?

The door gives with a cross between a squeak and a moan. Claire opens her eyes. When she sees it's me, she averts her head.

"Please leave."

"Claire, sweetheart, please, just talk to me."

"There's really nothing to say. You taught me right from wrong."

My daughter's hair is spread in plumes on the pillow. The color of her face is somehow unearthly, and I think wildly, I am losing her, she is slipping toward God. "You don't need to say anything," I jump in. "Would you listen for a minute? Didn't I teach you that, too? Did I ever not listen to you?"

Claire sighs. "Go ahead."

Now I have no idea what to say, although I've rehearsed this a thousand times, like some neophyte with a too-large part in a local production of a Eugene O'Neill play.

"I...I want you to know how sorry I am. I hope you'll be able to understand my side of this. I did the best I could at the time. Your father and I..." I realize that the word *father* no longer has a clear reference. "Wayne and I decided together, I mean, I didn't deceive him. I don't know what he's told you, but we thought it was the best decision at the time. We'd wanted a child for so long, and—"

Claire snaps off an interruption, the way she used to snap fresh beans in her resolute hands. "That's not the point. What about me? You deceived me, and you're the one who taught me that deceit is wrong. And besides, what you did, being with *him*, is wrong. Do you expect me to just ignore it? Just pretend…just do as I say, not as I do? I'm not like that. I'm sorry, too, it's just the way I am, the way you taught me to be."

For a moment, I am lost in admiration of such confidence, such innocent, absolute clarity. Whatever part of me was ever at all like Claire was muddied up long ago, and I am sad for the loss.

"I know it's easy to judge someone else, and I know I taught you about honesty, but I thought I taught you to be tolerant, too. How can you just turn your back like this? Do you care what this is like for me?" As I talk, anger is overtaking sadness. She's come first every day of my life. There's one bouquet of cut summer flowers, daylilies mainly, on her table, and I have to stand here like a stranger who happened into the wrong room and wonder who knew she was in the hospital before her own mother did and brought flowers here.

Not a modicum of softening. She is granite. I go on anyway, taking a breath first and lowering my voice. "I'm going to be retested, there's not much chance because of those antibodies, but we're doing…"

"I don't want anything from you," she shouts, her voice a hoarse sob. "Don't you understand? I don't want anything, I'd rather die."

Behind me, I hear the door. I'd rather be shot than interrupted now, when we're at least talking—or shouting, it doesn't matter, just getting a start. This is my baby here. I gave her life and I'll give it to her over and over.

"You're not going to die, honey," says Ellie. She strides into the room, pink bow flouncing past me to Claire's head, my place, where I am unwelcome. She takes one of Claire's hands, and with the other plucks a tissue from the tray table and hands it to her. "Calm down. This isn't good for you. I'm going to give you my kidney."

CHAPTER 36

Well, she's done it now. Ellie just opened her mouth and out the words flew like bats out of hell, as they say, though these idiot bats were more likely flying right into it. And she'd just got done telling Dr. Douglas that she just didn't know if she could stand up to the needle sticking to find out if her kidney was even a match. As far as she knew, Elvis's kidneys hadn't been donated to save anyone's life, although Dr. Douglas had specifically asked her if she used any drugs, so they'd probably explain away that decision with the lie about Elvis being an addict. Ellie needs to talk to Gert.

What had come over her? What indeed? Before she'd even opened the door, she'd heard Claire crying and shouting at once and realized that Lydia must have taken the opportunity to sneak in, entirely against Claire's wishes. And then Ellie saw Claire's face, like a drained canned pear there on the pillow—an awful color, really—and the anguish, and it was just instinct. Ellie had to protect her and, at the moment, it hadn't mattered how. It was all instinct, and, at the time, worth it, too. Lydia shut up for a good minute, gaping at her with a whole movie's worth of feeling playing across her face. "May I talk to you privately?" she finally got out.

"Leave her alone," Claire shouted to Lydie, still crying. "Just leave us both alone." None of this was in the least like Claire: it was like a whole new person had been born nearly full-grown but helpless and needing Ellie. That was the miracle of this birth. Claire needed her, *Ellie*, to live. Ellie's reticent heart—and now her kidney, too—had turned into the womb and breasts capable of sustaining life.

"Claire needs me right now," Ellie responded, the strength still coursing through her. "I think it would be best if you leave. If you want, I'll meet you in the coffee shop or the lounge after I've taken care of her." She enjoyed saying it and the enjoyment made her ashamed until the look flashed across Lydia's face—fierce, angry, barely controlled, and then Ellie was glad.

Lydia is waiting in the coffee shop, even though it's taken Ellie a good half hour to get there. Claire didn't want her to leave, afraid, Ellie could tell, that she'd get into it (Claire's words) with Lydia, and not even mentioning the kidney. Lydia had managed to steal Ellie's thunder; she always did. Kevin's mother had already been in with a bouquet of flowers she'd cut from her own garden, Claire said, and Claire tried to get Ellie busy adjusting the arrangement and adding water. Ellie noted the daylilies as a motherly gesture, and filed it with the list of new behaviors she was working on.

"I appreciate your coming," Lydia says to her, letting Ellie know she'd gotten herself under control. Well, Lydie always was a lady, anyway, Ellie had to give her that much. But that's all.

Ellie smoothes her skirt under her thighs and slides into the vinyl booth. After she shifts her weight back and forth a little to settle herself and nestles her purse next to her thigh, she looks at Lydie. Her sister's face is thinner. Actually, Ellie notices, the whole upper part of her body, the part above the tabletop, is thinner. Her skin isn't quite right, though certainly not the awful color of Claire's. Ellie thinks she must be mistaken, but she'd almost swear that more gray strands are scattered into Lydie's dark curls. Maybe that's what's making her face sallow, but her eyes look dull, too, gray-blue instead of that clear, startling color people always remark on. Her hair has grown past where she needed a haircut to keep her curls from getting unruly, and they spill almost to her shoulders. She's dressed in her usual, overly simple way, in a green print skirt with a green blouse that matches. Maybe she'd gone to work this morning before she came to the hospital for the abortive meeting. Really, anymore, Ellie knows almost nothing about her sister's life, the way Lydie had known nothing of Ellie's, not really, when it was Lydie who'd been absorbed in a child.

"How's Claire? I mean, is she still upset?" A furrow is leaving a permanent track across Lydie's forehead.

"She's settled down some. You can't do this anymore. Her blood pressure goes up. I'd appreciate it if you would—"

Lydia obviously can't bear to hear it. "I know," she interrupts. "But you've got to remember, she's my daughter, I have to—"

"Well, it just can't be. Not now, not anymore." Ellie can't quite look Lydie in the eye as she says it, despite the fact that it's utterly true.

Lydia takes a breath, holds it for several seconds and lets it out in a cross between a sigh and the puffing noise an athlete makes at the beginning of exertion. "I can't tell you how much I appreciate your taking care of her. But she is my daughter. I have to be the one who makes decisions about her care. I've tried to stay back and let her get her feet on the ground...about Wayne and me...and John, and no matter how I felt, that was okay while she was doing fine and on the dialysis, nothing was immediately *pressing*. But this is different. Can't you see, El? She's *my* daughter. You can't just cut me out."

Ellie hesitates only a couple of seconds before letting loose. Lydia's missing the whole point. "Look. In the first place, she asked me. She's over eighteen, in case you've forgotten, so she doesn't need your permission, and she's the one who says she doesn't want anything else from you. In the second place, I'm going to give her my kidney, and I don't need your permission, either." There they were again, those words, right out of her as if they have a mind of their own.

"You were serious? Have you talked to Dr. Douglas about this? You haven't been tested, have you? She would have told me..."

A waitress approaches with menus, but backs off, seeing another family argument has recessed to her domain.

"Yes, I was serious. I am serious." Even as she says it, prideful and defiant, Ellie can feel fear turn again in her stomach. "I've discussed it with Dr. Douglas, and she's arranging the testing." An outright lie. Ellie'd said she'd think about it.

"I...I thought you were, well, I don't know what I thought, but not that you... Ellie, is there a chance it could work? I mean, thank you, thank you so much. I can't believe you would do this."

"Why not?" Something in what Lydia said is insulting.

Lydia looks down. "You're usually afraid of blood and hospitals. But I'm really glad you're not anymore."

Ellie surprises herself with her answer. "Well now I have Claire to take care of." She can see Lydia struggle with herself, wanting to fight about who is Claire's mother, and watches herself win on her sister's face.

The waitress sees a lull in the action and approaches again, menus in hand. Ellie notices her and reaches for a menu. "I don't know about you," she says, "but I'm starved."

Of course, it had gone on some. Lydia tried to wheedle information, and Ellie kept her hand close to her chest. "Will you let me know about the testing right away? When will she check for a tissue match? Will she take it to the committee if it's a two-point match, or only if it's a three or four? ...Probably it'd have to be three or four, from what she said."

Ellie looked around the coffee shop, renovated by the hospital auxiliary a couple of years ago in warm yellows and greens with some nice plants hanging by macramé in brass containers, the plants silk, doubtless, but nice all the same. The seats were still sticky if you came in hot from the outdoors, but once the hospital's well-modulated temperature cooled a body down, the vinyl was all right. She saw everything differently, because everything *was* different in spite of the fact that nothing had changed. Ellie had seen the paradox at once. She'd always been the one to take care of Mama and Daddy and Charles after Lydie and Maddie had made their escapes, but nobody thought that was important. Nobody gave her any respect for that. Now she had Claire to take care of, and weren't people ever starting to sit up and take notice?

CHAPTER 37

Whatever progress I'd made has been swirled away as surely as if a giant invisible hand had pushed the flush handle. I left the hospital after Ellie ordered and ate a patty melt, fries and coleslaw, just as though nothing out of the ordinary were happening. She didn't even bang the ketchup bottle on the table to hurry it. I tried to talk to her, but I was no more than a piece of fluff caught in her eyelash when she opened her eyes one morning, that easily brushed aside. The thought crossed my mind that she was enjoying having me like a bug in the shadow of her raised foot, but I tried to shut it out as unworthy.

I've been keeping myself intently distracted, building a little shelter of activity and telling myself that I needed to make a life of my own anyway. John's been a part of many evenings but I've been careful, hoarding the little flame of separateness that's been taking hold, not letting the presence of anyone get close enough to smother it. He doesn't like this, but I say, *Too bad*, to myself, and go on. I've never been the least like this before, and it doesn't feel natural, but I simply can't let myself care. *You'll be all alone if you go on like this*, I sometimes whisper to myself, and then I answer, *You are already all alone*, *or have you missed that fact?* It goes to show what happens when you've put all your eggs in the basket love recklessly dangles off its arm, even the love a mother has for her only child, love that expands your soul to the full size of joy before it crushes it in equal measure.

And I was doing it—not well, maybe, but doing it, keeping myself intact, that is. Now, though, I've plain lost my footing. "You don't understand," I said to John last night on the phone.

"*You* have as much relationship with Claire as I do now." I didn't mean this as a compliment, but he still didn't seem to get it.

"You've got to hang with it," he said. "She needs you, and Ellie does, too, whether she knows it or not."

I pondered this for a while, the thinking like a physical effort as I twisted a lock of hair between my finger and thumb. I was lying on my bed in the dark. Since she left, I've been sleeping in Claire's room, redone last year from her junior-high obsession with shades of purple into the sleek neutral colors she called *très chic*, on the sheets she last slept in, which I've not changed, but last night the room itself seemed to say *unwelcome*, so I returned to the room I shared so many years with Wayne and tried to fight off a different ghost.

"I really don't know about that. Ellie's different. She's spent years complaining that Maddie and I supposedly left her to take care of our parents and Charles, not that it's a bit true, but here she is slamming the door in my face when I want to do the job that *is* mine."

"All I'm saying is that you can't just lay down and die. Keep trying with Claire, keep calling the doctors, keep talking to Ellie. You'll get through." His voice faded a little in the phone. A storm is rolling in from the west. Lightning had crackled our connection once already. I was just too tired, the air too heavy for me to carry on my body anymore.

"Okay," I said, and hung up a minute later. That's what I mean, that sinking abdication into a lie. I wouldn't have done that before. I would have tried to explain myself, as long as it took for him to understand and love me still.

How insubstantial the men I've known are: Daddy, Wayne, John, standing on such different rungs of life's ladder, but each of them in his own way ready to cut and run when things are bad. You can't really count Charles, except to say that in his way, Charles is the most reliable of all of them, and I appreciate that. I know exactly what to expect and there's ease in the knowledge.

He loves me, too, loves everyone if truth be told, so I don't see any reflection of myself in it.

Of course, John says he's different now, and maybe he is. What he doesn't understand is that I'm different, too.

I looked in the mirror this morning. Really looked, rather than just putting on blush and eyeliner, a dash of mascara, a slash of lipstick with the practiced, unseeing skill of a blind woman. I look different: my skin is uneven, too tightly drawn over the bones, stretched like a drum top over the hollows, yet bunched around my eyes and drooping beneath my mouth. I'm nearly transparent beneath the makeup, my eyes altered to a nondescript dullness. Telltale signs of change are everywhere. A stain on my blouse. I need a haircut; my nails are ragged. Inside and out, I'm different.

"Our house," I correct automatically, in spite of how I've come to feel, as a matter of respect. "I would appreciate it if you'd meet me somewhere, then. Obviously, I'm not comfortable coming to Maddie's." I'd called Maddie's looking for Wayne, and he answered the phone. Until right now, he's been more successful at avoiding me than at anything he's ever done. Maybe his heart has been more in it. He says right off that he doesn't want to come to our house. "*Your* house," he calls it.

A long pause, very Wayne-like. "Look, Wayne," I say, to help him out. "Wouldn't it be less awkward to meet here than in some restaurant? This is your house, you know. I didn't ask you to leave it."

"What do you want?" he asks in the voice he used to use with telephone solicitors, superficially polite with a curt undertone, distant, gruff.

"I'd like to talk about Claire."

"What about Claire? She's with Ellie."

"She's in the hospital. Did you think I didn't know? Look, we need to communicate with each other, about Ellie being tested, about—"

"Ellie being tested?" There's genuine surprise in his voice. He'd not been able to suppress it in time.

"You didn't know? See what I mean? Please, we need to talk." While I wait for him to drag an answer out of himself, I run a finger through the dust that's accumulated on the kitchen windowsill. A dirty teacup and one plate are in the sink, a half-dried tea bag next to them ringed by its own brown stain. An unwashed fry pan is on the stove.

"All right," he finally gets out.

"Will you come over tonight?"

"Tonight?"

I force my voice through the sieve of my teeth. "I don't think we should let this go."

"Yeah. All right."

"Can you come now, or in a little while, then?"

"All right."

He sits uncomfortably upright in the wingback chair, ignoring the one that faces the television with hollows the exact contour of his body. The living room holds accumulated heat of the day too great for the air-conditioning to conquer. Wayne has left his truck on the street, as if ready for a quick escape that will require no reversals, and come into the house that is his as much as mine like a stranger, gesturing to a chair wordlessly for permission to sit in it. Claire's portrait oversees the living room where two months of a weekly magazine are stacked. It's like the rest of my life: tidy to a quick glance, but utterly unlike me.

"I can't see how this involves me," he says, speaking first. It's not like him to start any conversation. He's not even taken off his blue baseball cap with the plant logo. In another lifetime I would have cared that he's wearing an undershirt with yellow stains under the arms. Who's doing his laundry? I wonder. Maddie?

"I know you better. You can't mean that. You're paying for

the apartment. You didn't find out anything you didn't know for all these years. None of this was news to you." I'm jumbling two things together the way people who have been married a long time will.

"You made her not mine." I can't read the look in his eyes when he says this, not hate, I think, but something close that comes and passes.

"So what...you'd have let her die so you wouldn't be embarrassed?"

"She doesn't care about me anymore."

"Charles would know better than that." It's the ultimate insult a member of the Sams family can speak, something I get angry when I hear, but now I throw it at Wayne and serrate its edge with sarcasm. "If the way she treats you has changed, and I'd be the last to know if it has—but *if* it has, it's because you changed first. Or you didn't let her know that it didn't make a lick of difference to you." I have no restraint anymore. "Did you tell her it didn't make any difference? Did you say anything? Did you even *try* to help her understand? Where are your priorities? Your pride is more important than her life?"

"Wasn't my place. Didn't do no good anyway. A dead man would've been more use."

"Oh for God's sake, Wayne. Your pride was hurt. That's plain and simple all there is to it. You're free to leave me, and you obviously have, but no one's free to just break a commitment to a child. Can't you work with me? You've got access to her that I don't. And now there's this whole new thing—about Ellie, I mean."

I know that to get anywhere with Wayne, I have to leave him a way to save face, so I back off the mountain of anger I've climbed. "Ellie says she told Dr. Douglas that she'd be tested—that if she's a match, she'll give her a kidney."

In spite of himself, Wayne is piqued. His hand goes up to his beard. "Do you think she's for real?" he says.

"I didn't take her seriously at first, but she got mad, and said yes, she meant it. Have you been to see Claire?"

"No," he says, but some of the defiance is out of his tone, and he looks down, as though he's not proud of it.

"I wish you would. I'm begging you, Wayne. She needs a parent, she needs one of us. She'll accept you better right now. I'm not asking you to do this for me. You two can sit there and talk about what a shit I am if you want, just sit with her." This gets his attention. The expression on his face says that I am someone he doesn't know. I don't talk that way. It just came out of my mouth like another change in the mirror.

"I don't know," he says. "I've got to be going," he adds and stands, tall, remote, unreachable.

"I'm sorry," I say. I could leave it at that. It even comes to me that if I go on, it will be I who effectively finishes our marriage. "I know your feelings were—are—hurt, and I know it turned out to be for nothing. And I'm so sorry. That was never what I wanted, and you didn't deserve it. But I'd do the same thing again, Wayne. There was a chance, and I'd do it again in a heartbeat."

CHAPTER 38

Against her will, Claire is at Mama's while Ellie goes to the hospital for the first test, the basic tissue-matching process.

Claire insisted she is fine alone, and wanted to know who Ellie thought was going to babysit her when she went to college at the end of next month. Ellie, backtracking, told her then that her Maw Maw needed some company, that Maddie wasn't helping out near as much as she should. "Let my former mother do it, then," Claire said. *My former mother?*...Ellie wondered who Claire's mother was now, and the thought bolstered her resolve about the tests.

The whole college business was another matter. Ellie doesn't say anything as Claire goes about filling out papers from the college and reading the two books assigned to incoming freshmen for summer reading, but Claire's certainty confounds her. Yes, they'd gotten through the last immediate crisis back to their little apartment and dialysis, and yes, Claire is meticulous about her diet—low potassium, high protein and strictly measured fluid intake—but Dr. Douglas has told Ellie that a transplant is Claire's best option. Then, of course, there's the possibility of rejection. Ellie turned off the volume in her head when the doctor talked about it, and skipped that section in one of the green photocopied patient information sheets about transplant procedures that Dr. Douglas has given them. A straggling pile of them curl like the dropped leaves of a flower vased too long on the coffee table. Ellie is struggling through them one at a time. Claire read them all in an afternoon, of course. Ellie marvels at how smart she is. Most of the questions that seem too difficult to figure out how to ask—why, Claire can not only tell her what she's trying to ask, but what the answer is. The idea of rejection, though, that's more than Ellie can bear.

Whether or not Claire can be by herself, which she insists she can, isn't really at issue. Ellie thinks it's possible she'll not come back out of the hospital, and then Claire should be with someone. Mama's not a good choice, but there isn't anyone else. Maddie is out of the question, not that she'd do it anyway, and Wayne hesitated a couple of beats but said he had to work. And Lydia—Lydia, who would have cheerfully exchanged years of her life to be asked to stay with Claire—well, Ellie knew better than to suggest to Claire that her *former* mother come keep her company. Not that Ellie wanted to ask her sister, anyway. She was fussing about it all to Mama on the phone, when Mama just said right out, "Bring her over here. I'll watch out for her."

"But you don't know what she needs," Ellie protested. "Anything could—"

"I know how to dial 911," Mama said, "and I raised you, didn't I?" The universal argument of grandparents, unassailable no matter how absurd.

In the car, Ellie reasoned with herself: *there's no cause to think I won't come back. This is just a test.* She felt better until another thought occurred to her. *If I pass out, will they just take out a knife and cut my kidney out?* Dr. Douglas said "as soon as possible," after Ellie has a very complete physical, and that they'd begin giving Claire transfusions of Ellie's blood in preparation right away, but Ellie doesn't know what "as soon as possible" means. What if she dies from the operation? That thought has occurred to her, too. It's been known to happen. Her mind muddles in heat like this, sticky and smothering. She said nothing to Claire, who lapsed into a private silence, staring out the passenger-side window at the patches of burned grass languishing beneath hardy still-green weeds. Before they left the apartment, though, Claire stood at the door blocking it when Ellie said, "Let's go," until Ellie repeated it and looked at Claire with a question on her face.

"Thank you, Aunt Eleanor, thank you so much," Claire said simply, and Ellie put her arms around her niece and whispered, "My treat," with a little laugh. That's not something you can back down from, even if you want to. Realizing that, she patted Claire's back as she held her, and said, "I love you," and meant it, regardless of Lydia, Wayne or John, if that was his real name.

Ellie hasn't been to Mama's in nearly two weeks, by far the longest she's ever been away in her life. She expected to find Charles slobbering over the junk food he naturally favored, a heap of unwashed laundry next to the washer, and the kitchen piled with unwashed dishes, even dirty paper plates. When she and Claire and Presley arrived, though, there were only breakfast dishes in the sink, and she'd left Claire and Mama sitting on the back porch with some iced tea Mama had Ellie get out of the refrigerator. Someone, Ellie didn't ask who, had planted a triangle patch of red, white and blue petunias by the step, and the cement porch looked swept. When Ellie opened the door of the old Frigidaire to get the tea, it was obvious that Daddy or someone had gotten groceries, because the date on the milk was for early next week. It should have made Ellie happy.

The bedroom she'd made like a picture of Lisa Marie's at Graceland because it was so ruffled and pink, and she couldn't begin to do the one Elvis had shared with Priscilla anyway, held heat like an oven and smelled dank when she opened the door. "Mama," Ellie complained, stalking out with a withered brown philodendron and an African violet. "Couldn't you have watered my plants? Do I have to do everything? Look, they're completely dead. Charles, put these in the trash. I need to get going." She felt unaccountably better then.

And now it's over. She's off the hook, or probably, anyway. She's a two-point match, only a forty-percent chance of success, Dr. Douglas says. "Not enough," she says. "Just not good enough. I'm sorry." Ellie sits in the same little meeting room alone with the doctor again, the usual fan of papers and files spread on the desk. How does the doctor keep them straight? What if she's confused two sets of test results and is really reading numbers that belong to some entirely different person? The air-conditioning is cranked way up, and Ellie thinks she feels goose bumps on her arms, but she feels hot, flushed beneath her skin, and wants to lie down.

"If it's critical and we have to buy time, that's when to go ahead with a two-point and hope for the best. For now, though, we're better off staying with the dialysis and pray for a three- or four-point cadaver match. Just watch her very carefully. We're still not sure what brought on the peritonitis."

It frightens Ellie to hear a doctor talk about praying. Maybe it was just a turn of phrase, but she isn't looking at Ellie much. She reminds Ellie a little of Lydie with her simple clothes. Dr. Douglas's shell-pink short-sleeved sweater with pearl necklace and earrings are just what would appeal to Lydia, who tries to look and sound upper class, Ellie thinks. Where has it gotten her? Where has anything gotten any of them? Everything that anyone in her family has ever really wanted has floated elusively out of reach—a feather wafting on a teasing breeze. She thinks of the tatters of Lydie's life, Maddie's, even envisions her mother holding her firstborn, her only son, with the wide, flat space between his eyes. She thinks of her love for Elvis and sees herself as pathetic, even ridiculous, as exposed as an aging starlet in a boa and false eyelashes.

"But..." Ellie falters. "But...it's not...she won't..."

"We'll do the best we can. The best we can."

She has felt suffocated for a good hour, but it still feels to Ellie like she cannot draw an unweighted breath. There's nothing to do now but stop driving around and go pick Claire up. She passes the Schlicter house, observing the missing red shutter and the height of the Queen Anne's lace, cornflowers and dandelions that have taken over the front, and puts the turn signal on for her family's short driveway, once gravel but now mainly weeds. At the last second, though, she corrects the wheel she's already turned, and passes the little house again.

Two more times around the block and Ellie makes herself do it. Actually, she's consulted her secret mental guidebook, the one she dislikes to name even silently, and looked up what Lydie and Maddie would do in this situation.

Before she's even out of the car, Claire appears at the screen door. Ellie knows Claire will search her face, and she checks for a memory of how to smile.

"Aunt Ellie? Ellie, what happened? When will we know?" The slam of the door is muffled by the whooshing in Ellie's ears that sounds like a white river, or perhaps it's just the amount of humidity in the unyielding air. Ellie can no longer tell what causes anything, just that there is always another leaden, dimensionless fact that she must watch as it falls from the sky to flatten her.

"Hi, honey," Ellie says brightly.

"Oh, God. You already know, don't you? You're not a match, are you?"

Claire's eyes glint like pebbles at the bottom of a sunlit stream, before she turns and covers her face with her hands. Ellie is beside her in two or three quick, long strides and from behind, puts her hands on her niece's shoulders. Claire leans forward, rejecting the gesture it seems at first, but then Ellie sees the girl's legs are buckling. Ellie catches her around the waist, pulls her back up, and maneuvers to brace the girl against her own body. Once their balance is stabilized, Ellie strokes the waves of Claire's hair that put her in mind of the smallest ripples on a night beach, like the ones she saw the time Lydia took her with them to Lake Cumberland for a week, when Claire was five or six. The memory shames her. If truth be told, it's not the only time Lydie was good to her, either.

* * *

Ellie has to try. A night's sleep hadn't altered the impulse. She knows from Maddie—not from either Lydia or Wayne—that Lydia begged Wayne to visit Claire. He must have refused because Ellie hasn't seen a hair of his beard, although the landlord has assured her that the rent is paid a month in advance on their apartment. The point, though, is what Lydia did, going to him for Claire even though Wayne might as well as have spit on her. There is only one more blood relative that Ellie has a shot at. She has to try.

After Claire has finished her exchange and settled back in with one of the books on her freshman reading list, Ellie says, carefully casual in her tone, "I'm going on in to work early, honey. I'm not supposed to start until eleven, but we're taking inventory next week, and my department is sort of a mess. Nobody does what they're supposed to, you know? I need to get into the stock and straighten it out before we start counting. Stuff is all mixed up...." She falters, realizing that she's saying too much, but Claire's not really listening, anyway. How guileless the girl is; even after all that's come into the glare of daylight, it wouldn't occur to her that Ellie is lying.

"Whatever," Claire says, but not unpleasantly. "Will you be home for lunch?"

"Not today, but you—"

"Don't worry, I'll measure every drop."

Ellie smiles, waves, blows a kiss, straightens her bow and heads out into the rising heat of the day.

At Madalaine's, she can see that no one is up, although it's past nine. Maddie's bedroom drapes are drawn. Still, Ellie parks in the driveway and knocks firmly on the door, though she knows Maddie will be ticked off at being awakened. A minute or so later, she repeats the knock and calls, "Maddie? Maddie! It's me, Ellie. I have to talk to you."

It's Jennifer who opens the door, though, rumpled and thick

with unfinished sleep. "Hi, Aunt Ellie. Um…" She looks behind her uncertainly, as if looking for a cue as to what to say or do next.

"Is your mom up?" Ellie asks rhetorically.

"No, not yet. She had a bad headache last night, she said to let her sleep."

"You don't usually sleep this late, do you?" Ellie demands, still on the doorstep.

"Um…I was up late last night. We got pizza and watched a movie in Mom's bed. Mom fell asleep, but I watched the whole thing. It was rated R, but Mom said it shouldn't be, it wasn't that bad."

Ellie is suddenly suspicious. "What was the movie?" she asks as she takes a step into the house, letting the screen door press against her back.

Jennifer catches on, though. "Something about *Fear* something, I don't remember."

"Not *Cape Fear*?"

"I don't know," Jennifer says, but Ellie sees the recognition on her face.

"Well, I have to get your mom up, I have to talk to her about Claire."

"That's not so good, I mean, she won't like it," Jennifer says, backing up deeper into the living room and looking anxiously in the direction of the bedroom hall.

Ellie is all the way in now, and closes the front door behind her. "I know it's hot outside but this is ridiculous. It's freezing in here. Where's the thermostat?"

"Mom says it's too hot."

"Jen, come here. Come talk to me," Ellie says, drawing the girl toward her by cupping her hand on the pale fluff on her head. Static electricity makes flyaway strands cling to her palm like a handful of dandelion fluff. "What's going on? You can tell me. Is your mom sick? Is she drinking a lot of beer or something else?"

Jennifer's eyes fill with tears. "I tell her not to." She yields to the pressure of Ellie's hand, which has slid down to her shoulder, and sits beside Ellie on the couch.

"I know, honey. It's not your fault. Are you cold? Let's get you some clothes and turn down the thermostat. Or turn it up, I mean. I can never get that straight. Maw Maw and Daddy don't have air-conditioning, you know, and it gets so bad there. Are you hungry?"

Jennifer nods her head yes. "A little."

"Has Uncle Wayne been here?"

"Sometimes," she says.

"Like when?"

"He comes sometimes after I'm asleep, I think. I see his truck in the morning sometimes. Mom said he's working shifts, extra shifts I mean."

It occurs to Ellie that the apartment money is coming from somewhere. Who's paying Lydie's mortgage? Does Lydie make enough? It's not Ellie's habit to think of things like this. She has no head for it, really.

"Run and get yourself into some clothes. We'll turn the air-conditioning off for a half hour and open some windows. That'll warm it up quick."

"Mom'll get mad..." Jennifer warns.

"It'll be okay. We'll get you some breakfast and then turn the air-conditioning back on, only higher. I mean lower. You know, so it's not so cold in here. It's sweltering outside."

"I know, but I get to go to the pool."

Ellie had started to stand, but slumps back down against the hard back of the pale green couch. There's no give to it. She glances around, noticing that several of the plants look desert-parched. "Does Mommy take you?"

"She drops me off. Emily's mom is there, usually."

"Like on her way to work she drops you off?"

"Sometimes."

"Is she going to work?"

"Sometimes." Jennifer shifts her slight weight from foot to foot. She's not sure what the right answer is. "Did you know about my little brother?"

"Yes, honey. Maw Maw told me. I guess your mommy told her. Are you happy about having him?"

Jennifer's voice drops to a whisper. "Yes," she says. "He's so cute."

Her eyes are wide and blue; she looks so much like Bill that Ellie wonders how Maddie stands it. That hair, too. It needs to be brushed out and plastered in place with some good gel. "He looks like me," Jennifer adds.

"Well, then, he's a very handsome boy," Ellie says warmly.

Jennifer looks at her intently and then sidles over on the couch, closer. "I'm glad you came over," she says, and Ellie knows that Jennifer has never said anything like that to her before.

"Wake up, Maddie." Ellie has already sent Jennifer, fed and dressed, over to a friend's house, and opened the drapes in Maddie's room. Maddie squints and moans.

"Go away. How'd you get in here?"

"Jennifer let me in. What would you do if the house were on fire? You wouldn't hear a thing. You're passed out, that's what."

"Am not. Go away." Maddie covers her eyes with one hand and turns away from the light. The temperature is chilly, but she has only a sheet over her, the blue-and-green leaf-print quilt that coordinates with the drapes rumpled on the floor at the foot of the bed.

"Here. I've made you some coffee. I'm putting it here on the nightstand. Where are your shorts and stuff?"

"Leave me alone." Madalaine turns again and pulls the second pillow over toward her so as to partly cover her face.

"You're getting up." Ellie is pulling out bureau drawers one by one. She triumphantly pulls out a bra and a pair of underpants. Next she locates a pair of khaki shorts, limp and wrinkled as the wings of a dead moth. She tosses clothes onto the bed as she finds them. "I've got to talk with you and you need to get up. Now come on!" She wonders at herself, yelling at Maddie the way she used to yell at Charles, and Maddie used to yell at her. She hardly recognizes any of them—herself included—anymore. Ellie marches into the master bath and returns with a wet washcloth. "Here," she orders. "Wash your face with this. Do you need a couple aspirin?"

"Yeah," Maddie mutters, surprising Ellie.

"Okay, then," she answers and goes back to the bathroom. When she comes back, Maddie is half propped up holding the washcloth over her face like a white bandage. She puts it down to take the aspirin and water that Ellie brings from the bathroom.

"You'd better have an incredibly good reason for busting in here," she says, her voice managing anger and great fatigue at once. She yawns.

"Have some coffee. Get dressed. I've got some breakfast made for you."

"What do you know about cooking?"

"I made Jennifer and you some eggs and toast. Yours is on the stove. I'll fix you a plate. I always could make eggs, but I've been cooking for Claire, in case you didn't know."

"More likely Claire's been cooking for you," Madalaine shoots back.

"Excuse me, but what would you know about anything in the family these days?" Ellie's hands are on her hips now and she's bossy.

"Well, excuse me, but I've been a little busy burying my son."

"Do you think I don't know that?" Then, Ellie's voice softens. "We all loved him, Maddie. But other things are happening, too. I need your help."

"What?"

"You get up, drink coffee, pull yourself together. I'll get your breakfast on the table."

"Ugh. I couldn't eat anything."

"You've got to eat something, come on." With that last

command, Ellie leaves the room, knowing she's shot her wad on giving orders and that if Maddie doesn't get up now, Ellie's probably lost already.

But Madalaine does get up, and appears in the kitchen within five minutes, blinking against the morning sun flooding from the sliding glass door that goes out to the patio, and clutching the mug of coffee that Ellie brought her.

"So what do you want?"

"Aren't you going to even ask where Jennifer is?"

"She's in bed."

"No, she's at Jessica Wample's house. Should she really be watching *Cape Fear* after midnight?"

"Well aren't you just the new sergeant? Who died and made you God?" Madalaine says sarcastically.

"Brian, I guess." Ellie says it very softly, with the directness of a simple truth, knowing she's taking a risk.

Madalaine's eyes immediately fill with tears. "Don't you dare!" she shouts. "Don't even say it…and don't you dare try to make me feel guilty about Jennifer. I take good care of her."

Ellie's overshot the mark. She tries to regroup, turning to the fry pan on the stove in which scrambled eggs kept warm too long have turned hard and lumpish. *I'm not any good at all this*, she thinks. Whatever happened to her old life, when she dreamed of Elvis and knew she had been meant for him? "I'm sorry, Maddie. I didn't mean to upset you. Do you want these eggs I made you? They got a little overcooked from sitting here. The toast is all ready. I put strawberry jelly on it, Jen said that's what you like."

Madalaine pulls out a kitchen chair and sits with an audible thud. A little coffee sloshes out of the mug when she sets it down too heavily on the table. Ellie picks up the sponge and wipes it up, pours some hot coffee over the liquid cooling in Madalaine's mug.

"Just the coffee. No, okay, I'll try the toast," she says, but her voice is flat.

Ellie brings the toast to the table and sits down opposite her sister. "I have to talk to you. I wouldn't ask you if it weren't a matter of life or death."

Madalaine laughs bitterly. "Oh, I think I've had my quota of life and death for this year, thanks."

"Maddie, listen to me. Claire has to have a kidney. I don't know, the doctors explained it. She had bad peritonitis. A blood relative is the best chance, otherwise we have to wait for a dead person who's a match. Lydie's got antibodies in her blood from when she had her gallbladder out, and John only has one kidney. He was born that way and that's hereditary, that's why Claire… are you listening?"

"What does any of this have to do with me?"

"I got tested, to see if I could give her one of mine. I'm only a two-point match, and the doctor says there's too high rejection with a two-point match. She's looking for a four-point, I don't get what the points are, but anyway, will you please be tested? You can get along fine with one kidney, you don't need two, the doctor says. There's a little risk, I mean, but…" Ellie is breathless now, afraid she's saying it wrong, but plunging forward like a hula hoop careening on a downhill.

Madalaine stares at her. "No way. Absolutely no way. This all is Lydia's fault to begin with…."

"But it's not Claire's fault…." Ellie argues.

"I don't care. Lydia will have to deal with it. It's not *your* problem, anyway, El."

"You don't know what's happened. You don't know it all. Can't you just try? Wouldn't you want us to save Brian if we could?"

"But nobody did, did they? Nobody did. I'm not talking about this anymore."

Ellie looks down and smoothes the wrinkles from the lap of her yellow pastel skirt. Her tan flats are exactly side by side, neatly lined up. She feels the back of her head for her bow, to tell whether it's straight. She has no idea what to do now. "Will you think…" she begins, not knowing where she'll take it, but it doesn't matter. Madalaine doesn't let her get beyond the first three words.

"No, I will not think."

CHAPTER 39

I've been digging around the yard when I come home from work in the afternoon. Dr. Hays lets us go early on afternoons when the patient load has been light and we're not booked up to and beyond the last appointment, the way we always are during flu season. I tried studying when I came home, but I need a break from mental work and there's no family I need to fix a supper for.

I try to rest my mind and concentrate on the soil and the little bits of squirmy life in it while I work. Even though it's way past planting season, I found some more flats of leggy, anemic flowers for seventy percent off at Thriftway, and bought them out of pity and for the sake of saving something I could save. I've stuck marigolds and petunias everywhere, and wished I had another good shady spot for some sad impatiens I didn't buy for lack of room. The geraniums, ageratum and ivy in containers on my porch shout their bright health, and so does my favorite, the bed of dahlias spilling color in spite of the leaching sun. I've mulched them to within an inch of their lives and warned them well. Nothing in my yard would dare die this year. The loamy chocolate smell of the dark mulch is what I give my attention to. I don't think about how it's the color of Claire's eyes, how they're the replica of her father's, how one thing leads to another and another past curves in the road that leave you no better than blind. Completely blind. As I weed between the plants, itchy streams run through my scalp while others wind down my back and legs, as though my body is doing the crying while my mind goes briefly numb and blank.

But evening falls. When I go in, the thoughts begin again.

John calls, and I do see him many nights when I don't have class. I even love him. I can't recapture the thrall, but I do love him, in spite of myself, in spite of whether or not he deserves it. I park my six-year-old Ford in the street and he pulls his swanky late model into our one-car garage to keep the neighbors from having me for breakfast when they go out to fetch their morning paper. It's his idea. I care less and less what anyone says. When he comes over, sometimes we sit out on the porch to watch the stars, like risen fireflies moving in swirling patterns around the sweetness of a lemon-sherbet moon for an hour before the welcome drowning of sex.

But always the past rubs into the present until the present is threadbare. I remember the end of our trip to Graceland and I hear Ellie's prophecy again. When I brought her home, she jerked Presley's and her luggage out of the trunk, and I said something like, "I'm sorry it didn't work out. Maybe we can try to get to Graceland another time." Kindness is what I intended, in spite of how she'd acted. I knew how much stock she put in the trip, the Death Week pilgrimage, the candlelight vigil. Before they melted all over the inside of her suitcase, she must have had twenty-five white votive candles ready for the watch.

"You'll get yours, Lydia. When you're least expecting it, you'll get yours." I want to know how she could see around those blind curves when I couldn't. The look in Ellie's eyes was venomous, the look of a body possessed if you believe in such a thing, which I never have. I've never forgotten it, although things soon enough smoothed over on the surface the way sometimes a wind will brush the surface of water smooth while turbulence goes on churning below the surface. I've learned this much from John and my sisters: what is fractured may heal and the scar may be invisible, but it is never the same again. I've heard that business about a bone being stronger for having been broken, but you couldn't prove it by me.

Today I was home at three because Dr. Hays was called to

Maysfield General for a delivery that proved complicated. He's one of the last general practitioners around here who will still pull out a baby, as he puts it. Donna and I called the rest of the afternoon patients to tell them he'd see them tomorrow unless they felt it couldn't wait and then they'd need to go on into the emergency room, then she and I closed up shop. It's more than just as well because I certainly wasn't concentrating on the insurance claims. Ellie's not a match, Dr. Douglas said. When she called me at work yesterday, I was certain it was with good news. I was actually lighthearted when Donna whispered, "Sarah Douglas on line two for you," convinced that good news was overdue. Ellie saying she'd donate was such a miracle that it seemed a sign from God: *Be faithful, believe, it will be all right now.* How could such hope be given and then taken away? When I heard, *Just a two-point, we'll wait for better,* I might as well have been a boxer who'd taken too many blows to the head and can't process what he hears anymore.

I didn't go to class last night, and, though I'd first thought I couldn't bear to be in anyone else's presence, when John called I said, *Yes, okay, come.* He wears a gold chain around his neck and the clasp tangled in my hair while he held me as if I were made of handblown glass, that carefully, and let me rant and cry. "Shh," he said, not extricating the chain but lying next to me in the dark on Claire's narrow bed and holding my head so my hair wouldn't be pulled. "Shh. Sleep. Tomorrow we'll figure out what to try next."

But we didn't, we haven't, and neither has the *I* of that breakable *we*. Instead, my mind is dredging in the distant past. While I cultivated around the miniature roses today, a remote, strange memory from my childhood, one that makes me squirm with shame, involving some elderly neighbors back when our house had no other neighbors because the sprawl of the town had not begun. I had had rose fever, Mama called it, all summer, sneezing sometimes twenty or thirty times in a row while my eyes sank in perpetually streaming pools. Mama finally made Daddy tear out the red climbing roses that had trellised themselves right up the house like an accidental amazement after Aggie and Zeke, the neighbors, gave Mama the bush for some reason I can't recall.

I loved those roses. They were the only flowers in our yard and I loved them as only a six- or seven-year-old who spends too much time watching out for an older brother who's not right in the head and two younger sisters can irrationally take a shine to something and claim it. When Daddy put on extra-heavy gloves and set to work pulling up every root of my rosebush, I cried and begged and promised not to sneeze anymore, but of course, it did no good at all. Mama was never one to have a soft spot for flowers or feelings. "They just makes you wheeze," she said. "I never gave 'em much account anyways. We only planted the thing so's Aggie wouldn't be put out."

The crude extraction of the rosebush and my misery about it must have been linked to what came next, because I remember it all together. Perhaps to distract me, Mama gave me the leftover from a roll of white crinoline material, a stiff and gauzy fabric she used when she made my school dresses, to make the skirt puff out around me the way it was supposed to. She told me I could make myself a fairy princess costume, and cut out a crown from heavy paper Daddy could "borrow" from the plant. By the next day, my outfit was constructed: a baffling drape job held together with many silver safety pins, and a taped-together crown with points so jagged and staggering it must have looked like it came from the jaw of a prehistoric creature. I crayoned the crown heavily with the still-pristine silver from my Christmas box of sixty-four Crayolas.

I wish I'd stopped there, while I was beautiful and magical and never discovered the secret self who will go too far to get what she wants. "Can I go show Aggie and Zeke?" I asked Mama.

"Don't make yourself a pest," Mama said. "Come right back. Take Maddie and Ellie with you."

I liked to walk across the unused field dotted with saplings to Aggie and Zeke's. They were old and they fussed over me, and often gave me a dime or at least a handful of cookies. "I don't want to take them," I shrieked, wanting the limelight to myself, especially since Aggie and Zeke were scrupulous about fairness.

The late-afternoon light poured an anointing gleam over the crown, straight up on my head, and my last inspiration, a scepter, fashioned out of the cardboard tube around which the crinoline had been wound and a large five-point star I'd made by superimposing right-side-up and upside-down triangles as I'd learned in first grade. The star was the same waxy silver as my crown. I must have cut a majestic figure, four feet tall with a headful of black curls emerging above and below the crown, as my sneakers tripped over dragging gauze. No matter. I have never again felt as beautiful.

Zeke and Aggie were home and provided the audience I wanted. They praised my beauty and ingenuity at such length it may have occurred to me to wonder about their sincerity, but it was completely gratifying all the same. What's next is the part that bothers me. I wanted more, something I hadn't been given freely. I don't remember consciously calculating, but I obviously did and more to the point, there wasn't an iota of truth in what I said.

"Mama said you might like my costume so much that you'd give me some change, maybe a quarter."

"She did? You bet, little missy. You come see us again, now, hear?" Zeke said digging into his pants pocket and handing me thirty-five cents, by far the most he'd ever given me at once. I know perfectly well that I thanked him, and that the whole exchange most likely meant nothing to him or Aggie. Even then, I doubt thirty-five cents was enough to trouble their slim, pension-controlled budget.

But the magic was sullied. Stumbling my way back home with the coins buried in my fist, I felt hot, clumsy and unlovely, much as I feel now, flashing back as I am to the moment when I—

without the words for it, of course—knew that I'd gotten what I wanted by manipulating someone else. "Be careful what you want, because you'll get it," someone at the office laughingly quoted an anonymous pundit to me once regarding something as unimportant as what sandwich I'd ordered. What I've really wanted and gotten in my life has turned around to bring suffering to us all. That first time I lied, I spent away my innocence and more, the ability to see myself as innocent. Maybe the river of my life as it has flowed over Wayne, John, Claire, my sisters, all came from that small spring. For all I've escaped, it's been by swimming in that same water.

CHAPTER 40

Three beers and no help from them. Bill is to pick up Jennifer any time now, and Madalaine can't bear the sight of him, especially since he's told Jennifer yes, he'll bring the baby in the car with him, the new son he's had the unspeakable temerity to name Brian William. Whether or not they call him *Will*, as Jenny says, the blood spills on from the fresh wound in Madalaine. How could he? Jenny says that the baby looks like her own baby pictures. Even a ten-year-old knew enough not to say he looks just like Brian, which amounted to the same description, but wasn't so much an assault on her heart.

She is trying. Trying not to cry, trying not to hate, not so much anyway, trying not to mention Brian all the time around Jenny, trying to get to sleep at night, trying to put one foot in front of the other and drag herself through the days. Madalaine pops a fourth beer and pours this one into a tall green plastic glass. She gets three ice cubes from the freezer, plops them in and settles herself back on the couch to wait. In the family room, the television is blaring the *Oprah Winfrey Show*. Jennifer has taken to watching the talk shows lately. Maybe it makes her feel less like a freak, seeing other families try to kill each other off. At least hers wasn't on national television, although who knows? Maybe Melody is negotiating this very minute to do a show on Women Who Seduce and Reproduce. Better yet, Second Wives Who Steal Dead Boys' Names. Melody would be the lead-off story for that one. *Let's have a big round of applause for our first guest...*

During the commercial, Jennifer comes into the living room to check out the front window. "He's late," she complains. Madalaine sees her daughter has changed into the new denim-shorts outfit she bought her the day before yesterday. Red gingham borders the pockets to match the short-sleeved shirt that Jenny left unbuttoned so she could tie the tails across her waist to make a modified halter. A narrow band of skin, one to give Madalaine a fresh headache, shows itself between the blouse and shorts: pale, unspeakably vulnerable.

"He usually is." Madalaine tries too late to correct her tone. "He'll be here, honey."

Jennifer looks at her appraisingly. "Mom, you're not?"

"Ginger ale," Madalaine says and holds up the glass in such a way as to make the ice clink.

"Good. I'm sorry, I thought… Call me when you hear the car, okay?" Jennifer's overnight bag is already positioned by the front door. It's been there since this morning. She takes less and less with her; now she's accumulated basics like a toothbrush, hairbrush, some spare underwear and socks at her father's, and a T-shirt or two. Madalaine has resisted, but Jennifer leaves them "on accident," or Melody buys extras for her to keep there.

"Yup, will do."

When Jennifer goes back to Oprah, Madalaine fishes the ice out of her glass and lays it beneath the leaves of the nearest plant to melt in peace, something she'd not mind doing herself. Not at all.

It's not another five minutes until she hears the car door. "Jenny! Jennifer! Hurry up, he's here," she shouts. Madalaine dreads that Bill may ring the doorbell.

Jenny does scurry in. She plants a kiss on Madalaine's cheek and squeezes her. "Bye, Mommy. I'll see you Sunday." She hoists the small bag to her shoulder by its red strap.

"Okay, honey. Have fun. Better run."

However quick it was, though, it was too slow. Bill is halfway up the sidewalk, though he's left the motor running and the driver's-side door wide open. Madalaine can see him out the picture window. She steps to the side so a drape will obscure her view of Bill, and vice versa.

"Daddy!" Jenny's out the door. Madalaine closes it quickly behind her and leans against it with a ragged sigh. She stands there letting the door bear her weight.

A minute later, Madalaine is thrown off balance by the door abruptly pushing open. "Mom!" Jenny bursts into the room. "Mom!"

The door bangs her hip as Madalaine tries to correct her balance using the wall. "Ow," she says, pushing back. "For heaven's sake, what's the matter?"

"What're you doing back there?" Jenny says, but rushes on without waiting. "Will spit up all over the place. It's all over his car seat and everything. Daddy needs a towel."

"A kamikaze pilot needs a helmet, too," Madalaine says. Of course, Jennifer doesn't get it, just looks confused and waits for her mother to say it in English.

"Oh, go get him one. Get one of the old ones, hear? Those green ones on the linen closet floor." She calls the last part to Jennifer as the girl runs down the hall.

But Jenny only makes it back as far as the steps between the front door and walk, after smacking Madalaine loudly on the cheek again and, so excited she shouts, a breathless, "Thanks, Mom." Bill emerges butt first from the back seat of the car with a sodden, squalling infant in his hands. He jostles awkwardly, trying to keep from holding the baby against his shirt, but can't figure out how to support the flopping head without using his own chest. He gives up, presses the baby to him and looks helplessly toward the house.

Jennifer looks at each of her parents in turn, the dilemma written on her face. "Mommy. Please." It's not much above a whisper.

"Jenny, I..." I can't do this. How dare you even ask me? Responses of this sort race, wild horses beating their way through her mind at once. She simply can't hold on to the shield of her anger with her daughter's face—anxious and pleading—trained to hers. Madalaine sighs. A hot wind whips her hair across her face and into her mouth just as she opens it, calling, "You look like you need some help," to Bill.

"Here Daddy, I can help." Jennifer is skittering back down the sidewalk. "We can clean him in the house. I'll get his stuff." She disappears into Bill's blue Mazda and reappears with a diaper bag.

Bill hesitates, looking at Madalaine with a question on his face.

"Come on," she says with resignation, and turns back into her house. Bill follows, the baby screeching himself cherry with rage.

Madalaine stops in the living room. Her room…their old bedroom? No. Brian's room? Out of the question. Jenny's…possible—bring a basin in. The kitchen, maybe. She sidesteps to the linen closet in the hallway and grabs another old towel and runs smack into Bill and the baby, who followed her. "No, the kitchen. Put him on this towel folded up, next to the sink. You've got a change of clothes?"

"I dunno," he stammers. "…Melody…I didn't pack the bag, I mean."

He steps back against the wall to let Madalaine lead.

In the kitchen, Madalaine folds the oversize towel three times to make a soft pad. Bill lays the his son down and fumbles with the gooey snaps on his suit. Madalaine sees his hands are shaking a little. Jennifer is doing a little dance to the side of him, trying to help and getting in the way. The baby's screams reverberate against Madalaine's eardrums, and mix into the throb that had started before Bill came. The odor of vomit is strong.

"Come on, Will, come on now, it's okay," Bill says. The baby, arms and legs flailing, seems to quiet for a couple of seconds, but begins coughing and another round of curdled milk shoots out of his mouth. The smell is strong, nauseating. A gurgled scream comes from the baby and then a fit of choking. Madalaine shoves Bill aside with her hip as she puts her hands into the mess.

"He'll choke to death, for God's sake," she says sharply. "Get him on his side, at least. Jenny, go get a washcloth." Jenny runs toward the hall. "Here, let's get this off," Madalaine says in the general direction of the baby, who gasps for air between coughs and screams. She pulls on the top snap of the light blue terry-cloth sleeper, and all of them pop apart in succession as if by magic. "You never were much for undressing them, were you?" she says to Bill. "Or dressing. Or anything else, for that matter... What do you call a man with half a brain?"

"I don't know," Bill says, confused as to where she's headed.

"Gifted." Madalaine chuckles a little. "You pretty much stink, Bill." Jennifer looks horrified and Madalaine laughs at her. "Why don't you take that yucky shirt off? Roll it up with the throw-up on the *inside*."

Bill blushes and pulls the shirt over his head, leaving a milky wet trail on his face, which he hastily swipes with his hand. Then he grimaces and sticks his hand under the faucet. It's as easy to embarrass him as ever.

"Gross, Dad," Jennifer says.

The infant is still crying, but it is a quieter cry, as Madalaine gets the suit and diaper off. "Here," she says giving Bill the suit. "Roll that up inside your shirt." She braces the baby with one hand while she turns on the water, sticks an elbow under the stream to test it and then wets the washcloth in tepid water. She sponges Will gently, beginning with his head and lifting it expertly to clean the vomit out of the folds of his neck. His head is downy in her hand, his hair so pale and fine that it looks as if he doesn't have any. "Has he been sick?" she asks Bill, working her way to the baby's chest and down the rest of his body. "Have you got a pacifier?"

"No, I mean he wasn't until in the car. Yes, a pacifier, I think so. Jen? In the bag?"

"He feels hot, but he's worked himself up pretty good."

"Is he sick, Mommy?"

"I doubt it. Too hot, maybe in the car with the sun on him and that sleeper. And maybe too much to eat. Sometimes they just want to suck, they don't need more milk. Anyway, they throw up all the time when they're little. At least you and…*you* did."

"Gross. I did not."

"Okay. He's done. Hand me that other towel," Madalaine says. Jenny, who's been clutching the towel she got out of the linen closet first off, hands it to Madalaine, who dries the baby off. "Got a pacifier in there?" she repeats. "He's exhausted." Indeed, the baby, still whimpering, has his eyes at half-mast. She inserts the pacifier Jennifer hands her into the baby's mouth and he seizes it eagerly. "Good boy," she says. "Now, let's have a diaper and a clean outfit," she instructs.

It's Jennifer who responds again, rooting through the bag while Bill stands with his hands, ridiculously large and useless, splayed at his sides. "I can't find anything but diapers and…baby powder, and shampoo…a giant jar of Vaseline, oh wait, here's… no, it's a blanket."

"Wonderful. A blanket. It's a hundred and six in the shade, and we have a *blanket*. Oh, but it's okay, because we've got shampoo, the *important* thing. Genius at work. Well, you certainly can't put that back on him," Madalaine says, gesturing to the vomit-soaked sleeper while she fastens the tape on a disposable diaper. "So, you want to take him like this or what?" she says to Bill.

"What should I do?" he asks. "I didn't realize, I mean, I see I should have checked what was in the bag. Melody, this is her first, see."

"And *your* excuse is…?" It is said sarcastically.

"I had you," Bill answers, and his honesty and simplicity disarm her.

"I guess you did. Here, c'mere." Madalaine picks up the baby, who quiets again in her arms. She carries him into the family room with Bill and Jennifer in tow. "Sit," she says. "Look, put your hands here and here. If you hold him like this, see it's too flat. Angle him a little, you remember that much, don't you? Hold him on your left side, they like to hear your heartbeat. Now just hum a little. I'll be right back."

Madalaine goes back through the kitchen, past the dining and living rooms and down the hall, leaving Bill with Will and Jennifer. Halfway down the hall, she pauses, turns and goes back to retrieve the plastic glass she left in the living room. She takes a long drink out of it, wincing at the taste, warm and watered down, but swallowing and quickly taking another. She carries the glass with her down the hall.

"Help me," she whispers aloud. "Help me."

She goes into Brian's room. Posters of Michael Jordan and Shaquille O'Neal are still on the walls, and the basketball-hoop laundry basket she'd hung on his closet door in vain hope. Madalaine directs a puff of air upward, levitating the few straggling bangs there, and steels herself to open the closet door. On the far back part of the top shelf, there's a cardboard box that she can barely reach on tiptoes. She inches it forward and then tips it off the shelf into her hands. She holds it with trepidation, as gingerly as Bill holds his new son.

Inside is white tissue paper that crinkles softly when she touches it. She unfolds it as delicately as an origami bird. Inside is a little white short-sleeved shirt and a pair of shorts sized to fit over a newborn's diaper. There is a bit of pastel-blue-and-white embroidery on the shirt and a white, lace-edged receiving blanket with matching embroidery. She opens it and holds the soft cotton to her cheek a moment. Then, Madalaine refolds the receiving blanket and puts it back in the box, puts the box back on the shelf. She carries the shorts and top out to Bill and Jennifer. Bill is relentlessly humming, as tuneless as ever. It occurs to Madalaine that she's done the baby no favor by suggesting that Bill do anything remotely musical.

"Here. Lay him on the couch. Let's see if we can't do this without waking him up. Here, you do it. I'll talk you through it."

"I recognize this…didn't your mother…?"

"Brian's baptism," Madalaine says softly. "Come on, first just thread his hand through this sleeve, then lift his back with your left hand while you scoot the shirt behind him with your right."

"I can't take this…"

"You're right. It would look stupid on you. How about you put it on the baby?"

"I'll send it back to you with Jennifer…"

"Brian would want to give him a gift. It's from Brian, not me. Brian."

"You're a good person, Maddie," Bill says. "I'm sorry I couldn't…"

"Dress the baby," Madalaine interrupts.

Bill fumbles through dressing Will after Madalaine shows him how to put powder in his hand and rub it under the baby's arms and around his neck to prevent prickly heat. All the air seems to have been sucked out of the family room. Jennifer is breathless, attentive, and gets in there twice to help him while Madalaine keeps her hands out of it. When Bill has the shorts on, he looks at Madalaine. She is looking at the baby lying on the fabric—worn, tweedy, neutral—of her couch, big-eared and raw-looking, with goosedown hair and ruddy skin. She has seen him before and on that very couch.

"Just let me hold him a minute, will you?" she asks Bill.

"Are you sure?" he answers, seeing what she does.

"Just for a minute." Madalaine picks up the bundle of Bill's son and cradles him against her breast, his head nestling into the hollow between her collarbone and neck like a puzzle piece that had been missing. She kisses the top of his head and then rubs her cheek on it. She breathes in the baby's scent. Helpless tears spring to her eyes. "Damn," she whispers. "Damn. You have a good life, have a happy, good life." She hands the shapeless, sleeping infant to the man who'd been her husband. "Take care of him, hear?" she says. "Not that you didn't…"

"I will," Bill says. "Thank you. This was really good of you. You didn't have to do this."

"No," she says. "I didn't." But she smiles, speaks to Jennifer. "Come here, baby, give me a hug."

"Maybe you want Jen to just stay with you tonight? I can run over and pick her up tomorrow."

"I'll stay with you, Mom, if you want," Jennifer inserts, though her tone belies her and her eyes are on the baby.

"No, it's okay. Jenny's been wanting to spend time with Will. I have someplace to go."

"You've been there enough, I suspect," Bill says.

But after Bill leaves with Jenny and the baby, Madalaine doesn't visit the cemetery after all. She goes to her room and takes an envelope out of her underwear drawer, where she's tucked it beneath her two white slips for safekeeping. Sitting on the bed, she breaks the seal for the first time and carefully, as if they're dried flowers, removes the pictures she took the night of the prom.

CHAPTER 41

What's left? I am a hooked fish, flailing and flapping, slamming myself against a wooden dock with weakening hope for mercy. There's no one to turn to except Maddie, who blames me for her son's death. I even understand that. How can we bear the unbearable if there's nothing and no one to blame? If there's fault, then we can believe that we can stand guard—that we can even know which gates need a guard posted—and save our children, if not ourselves.

I didn't know why I started going to see Kevin at first, though after the first two times, even I could guess what I was looking for. I always call Beth, his mother, first to make sure I don't run into Claire. I know she'd assume that I'd done it on purpose, that pursuing her was my reason for coming. It's not, though, as I said, I'm not sure what is. Kevin's been moved to a rehabilitation hospital. I confess I don't see any progress. Tied into a wheelchair, a feeding tube is in his stomach, a catheter in his bladder, his only movements are random and spastic. His fingers splay rigidly from bony wrists. He's shrunken, of course, from the loss of weight and muscle tone, as though he's lost years of his age, too. The bruising is gone from his face and his hair has grown back over where they put the shunt in his brain to drain the accumulated fluid, but when his eyes are open, they're uninhabited, a ghost town. Except for the close shave he's given daily, and the hair on his arms and legs, you'd think you were looking at a twelve-year-old. Beth and her husband Nate hope on, though. They talk about *when* he's well, not as if they're referring to an unlikely miracle, but with conviction, as if they knew something.

It's their conviction that draws me there. I need to see if the mountain moves. If they find a way to do it, I will find a way to pack more guilt—along with gratitude—into my bag.

Beth hugs me each time I come, as if it's I whose child is comatose. I have no idea what Claire's told her, but tiny, dun-colored, mousy Beth is big-hearted enough not to mention it. I see that Claire has taped up notes and little marker-drawings where Kevin would see them if he could see anything, and likewise, I don't mention those. Beth darts about Kevin, straightening his head, drawing the cotton blanket higher or lower depending on the temperature of his room, and noting every word that's said by someone in a hospital uniform in a spiral-bound notebook. She and Ben take shifts; he comes to relieve her after work in the evenings. On Saturday and Sunday, they are there together, the whole of their real lives now enacted on this enclosed stage, cramped with machinery and white draping, in a state of suspended animation, the oxymoron of chronic crisis. Here's the strange and shameful secret I keep: sometimes I envy Beth.

This morning, a Sunday, I carried in a vase of dahlias and zinnias, intense, primary colors to dispel the grayish cast of Kevin's room that persists through relentless sunshine.

"How lovely," Beth murmured. "Wherever did you find these? They're enormous."

"In my garden," I said, embarrassed that I'd had the time to spend hours outdoors.

I sat down next to Kevin in his wheelchair. "Hi, Kevin," I said. "It's good to see you. I brought some flowers, I didn't know what kind you like, I've got most everything this year, anyway, I just picked the brightest ones."

Kevin had a long, thin line of drool between his mouth and the towel that Beth keeps draped around his shoulders, and when Beth turned toward us and spotted it, she immediately wiped it away. I went on a while more about the garden: the aphids, the fungus that had sprung up on top of some mulch, the lack of rain, the heat. Beth's told me the doctors can't tell her for sure whether or not anything is registering in Kevin's brain, so she's decided it is, and some of the technicians have encouraged her with stories of patients waking from semiconscious states able to repeat what's been said by visitors. She asks people to talk to Kevin as if he were still himself, still there, the essential spark of himself still lit and aware. So I do. And I do it for a good ten minutes before Beth excuses herself—she usually takes advantage of someone else being there to monitor Kevin and slips out to buy a sandwich or stretch her short legs with a walk around the parking lot, even in this wilting, killing heat.

"While you're here, would you mind if I run to the cafeteria?" she asked softly, while I was rambling on about how ladybugs combat Japanese beetles.

"Of course not, you know that. Take your time. I'll call a nurse if I see the slightest thing amiss."

When the door shut behind her, I slid forward in my chair, leaned a little closer to Kevin. "If you can hear me," I whispered. "Please. Please, when Claire comes, help her understand." I went on, as I have before, explaining myself to this once-arrogant, fallen boy I never even particularly liked. I might as well be praying to a totem, I understand, but somehow I can talk to this flawed boy who's brought all his suffering on himself by errors at once innocent and fatal. I can ask him for help and there's the slimmest chance that he may give it to me. God is way too far out of my reach.

Sometimes, I do it all at once, visit Kevin and then Brian's grave, I mean, one right after the other like the stations of the cross. That's what I did today. Sometimes I talk to Brian the way I do Kevin, ridiculously asking for help, when I know the only help to be had for me is whatever I make for myself, and I've plain run out of ingredients. I usually bring some flowers—maybe a duplicate of the bouquet I brought Kevin, as I did today. I never know what I'll find on the polished marble base of his headstone. Sometimes a weighted bunch of helium balloons, like enormous simplified replicas of my flowers, sometimes a note, sometimes a miniature basketball. Once, a single metal key. I never know who leaves these things. School friends, I've guessed. Probably Maddie, and maybe Claire, too, when she's able.

Today there was a little framed picture of Brian as an infant propped up. He was in the christening outfit Mama embroidered for him, back when she did things like that. I was his godmother; I held him in that suit and I know these little blue flowers, and that there are raised white ones, too, that have receded into the shadows of the picture. Mama made long white dresses with pink flowers for Claire and Jennifer, and this little shorts outfit for Brian. It "wasn't right to put a dress on a boy, it could make him turn pervert," she said. I squatted to look closely, thinking Maddie had put it there, unwilling to disturb it by the smallest touch.

Brian is buried under the spread arms of an old maple in an area overlooking a steep, unused decline to a wide creek. The cemetery is hilly and well-kept, except for some of the oldest sections, which are mowed by the keepers but rarely pruned and planted the way many of the newer graves are. You can pick out the graves of children without reading a word on the stones. They're like shrines, dotted with mementos. Teddy bears nap, toys rust gently if too quickly. Once I saw people arrive with a birthday cake. I cannot say how wrenching they are, these places of terror neutralized by having done its worst, leaving nothing more it can take that matters.

"Brian, if you're there, if you can hear me...please. She loves you, and I know you love her," I whispered, setting the flowers next to the picture. I stayed just a few minutes more, letting one knee go forward to rest on the baked earth to balance me. That's all I said. There was nothing more. Then, I just stood up to leave.

I can't imagine how I didn't sense someone approach, but I

didn't, so when I turned and saw there was someone not eight feet behind me, I gasped. A little squeak of startle and fear got out before I realized it was Maddie.

"What are you doing here?" she said.

I've not seen her in weeks. I don't call her anymore, because she won't return my calls. If Jennifer answers the phone, Maddie tells her to say she's not able to come to the phone and will call back. But she doesn't.

She looked terrible. Haggard, her hair stringy and the gray webbing whiter and more extensive to my eye, at least, but maybe it just looked that way because she wasn't wearing any makeup. Her eyes were ringed, and the fullness through the cheeks that all we Sams women have has hollowed out, giving her the gaunt look of a survivor.

"Maddie, Maddie." All I could get out was her name. I took a step toward her and began to open my arms but she backed up a little and I knew immediately that she'd rebuff me. "I'm sorry," I said. "I didn't mean to intrude. I just brought these." I gestured toward the garden flowers, suddenly garish.

Maddie looked past my pointing hand. I followed her eyes and saw what she saw. "Oh, not that picture of Brian. That was here. But I guess you must have put it there yourself..." I didn't finish the sentence because it was obvious something was wrong.

"That's not Brian," she said flatly.

"Yes, sure it is. I didn't touch it, but I got down and looked closely. It's from when he was christened. It could be Jen, except it's the outfit Mama made him, too. I'd know him anywhere."

Maddie brushed past me and leaned to pick the picture up. She looked at it briefly and said, "No, this isn't Brian." My sister crumpled then. At first I thought she'd fainted again, but when I knelt I could feel her shaking, dry sobs beginning to surface like lava from her center.

"He'd thrown up all over, and he was screaming, just screaming, and I gave him a sponge bath and changed him and got him dressed in that…that Mama made. His hair was, like it was transparent, practically invisible, because of the color, and his ears were big and stuck. I told him to have a good, happy life. He was so beautiful and I held him and I didn't want to put him down or give him to anyone else to hold."

"I remember," I said. And I did. I didn't remember Brian throwing up or Maddie giving him a bath, but I remembered that hair, and his ears.

"No, the baby. This baby. They named him Brian William. I held him…."

It took me a good minute—that's how much the baby is Brian to the eye—to realize that Bill's new son had been born. "Oh, God, Maddie, oh my God, I'm so sorry. I'm sorry, I'm sorry for everything." On the ground beside her, I pulled the upper half of her body onto my lap and stroked her hair. Then we were both crying, but I was crying with her, *for* her, those first minutes. That one time had no artifice, nothing disingenuous in it, nothing for myself, and neither prayer nor gratitude for Claire. I was with Maddie.

I try to remember that—that one moment that it was real and I loved her and tried to help her. I try to remember that because it didn't last very long, and then I was crying for myself again, and for my Anna Claire, and as I felt Maddie let go and let herself need me, I knew she was vulnerable and that I'd ask her, not directly, of course. I waited, still stroking her hair and saying, "I know, I know," until the heaving quieted and she'd lapsed into more shallow, normal breaths. I let myself cry on, though, even as I thought through what to say.

"I feel what you're going through. I know you haven't thought so, but Maddie, this is me, this is Lydie. I'm Brian's godmother. You know how much I love him. I'm so sorry, so sorry—sorry about the prom, sorry I asked Claire to watch out for him. I know you can't forgive me, I understand. I can't forgive myself either."

No answer came, but Maddie unearthed the arm that was curled beneath her on my lap and extended it around my waist.

No breeze cooled the sweat on my face; I wiped my forehead on my free forearm. My legs, which I'd bent around on the ground to make a graduated lap for Maddie's head and shoulders, were beginning to cramp and ache from her weight on top of their unfamiliar position, but I wasn't going to risk the smallest disruption. She was reaching for me, she was holding on to me. Something was present but wordless, like the exact moment the tide turns from ebb to flow, the exact fulcrum of balance, of power.

Her voice was ragged with the sobs. I thought I smelled alcohol faintly, but it didn't seem that she was drunk. "It really wasn't your fault, or Claire's. It just felt like, you know, like it didn't have to happen, and I can't understand why it did. How all those stupid unnecessary things can coincide—it's so accidental, so…"

"Random?" I offered.

"Yes, that's it. Why? Why didn't something else random happen that would have ended up with them at the prom? Brian was so up for that dance…."

"I don't know," I said, softly, truthfully, still stroking her hair, lifting and smoothing the grayest strands, almost wiry between my fingers. Her bra strap, once white, now yellowish-gray in need of a good wash and bleaching, had slipped down her shoulder, and I eased it up and tucked it under her sleeveless blue shirt. "I think about that all the time. Brian was innocent and so were you. There was no reason to it. He was such a great kid, such a wonderful boy. I would give anything if I—if *anyone*—could have saved him, made it come out right, you know? Made it come out some way that made sense. We ought to be able to do that. I'm so sorry, Maddie." It's not that I said anything I didn't mean. Everything I said then or later was how I really felt, really feel. It's that I know the impurity of *why* I said it. I know what I really wanted.

Maddie spoke through renewed tears, went right where I wanted her to go. "How is Claire? I heard—I guess Mama told me—that Ellie was being tested."

I let myself spill over again. "She was. She's not a match, well she's a two-point match, which they'll only try as a last resort. We have to wait for a cadaver donor. I know it's not the same as Brian, I'm not comparing it, I know it's my fault that I don't have Claire with me anymore…but this dialysis, I can't make any sense of the world anymore, not with what's happened to Brian and…this. I feel like I just have to find something I can *do*, you know? Something…to strike back, to say no, there has to be *reason* in life, there has to be *something* we can control." I thought about Kevin, too, the waste—but I thought better of mentioning him. I was too close.

I could see it on her face. I watched her struggle and remember, and I did nothing to unhook her. Then, I could see that I had won. I had bottomed out and achieved the top at once.

"Maybe…I could be tested," Maddie said, hesitating.

"I couldn't ask you to do that. You've been through too much, you can't take on anyone else's problems." I could hardly get the words out, to see this thing through.

"You're not asking me. Actually, Ellie asked me, but I couldn't… It's something *I* can *do*. Remember when they were little? I was so crazy about Claire, of course she was the first, and then I got all your maternity clothes, and I was so scared when Brian was born. You gave him his first bath at home. His cord was black and I was afraid to touch it."

"I remember. I was the one who told you his ears were *not* too big."

"Yeah. You liar." Maddie laughed a little, not bitterly, and blew her nose into a tissue she fished out of her skirt pocket. "So what do we have to do? To get tested, I mean? You'll keep Jennifer, won't you?"

"I'll keep Jennifer anytime. Anytime. You know that. The house is…empty, a lot. I miss Claire so much," I said. "It would be good to have Jennifer around. I'll take off work…."

Birds were chirping softly, randomly hopping through the

heat-waved air toward full bellies or a pouncing cat or an eventual collision with a plate-glass window. I felt dizzy, as if I could feel the very movement of the earth, and how tilted it is on its axis.

CHAPTER 42

"Maddie's on the phone for you, honey," Ellie calls to Claire. She arches her eyebrows to indicate that she has no idea what's prompted this. Claire dog-ears the page she's on and pads barefoot across the worn apartment carpeting to the phone.

"Hi, Aunt Maddie." Claire is a little wary. "How are you?"

"More to the point, how are you?"

"I'm okay."

"Good. How'd you like to be better?"

Claire shrugs in Ellie's direction to indicate that the call is still a mystery. Ellie answers with a worried look. It makes her nervous when one of the family calls for Claire. They have their routines settled and she doesn't like to see Claire upset. Claire's been cranky lately, like Presley when he's out in the heat and snaps if a stranger leans over to pat him. Her blood pressure has been high, Ellie knows that much from Dr. Douglas, who increased her dose of Norvasc, and her feet and ankles are swollen. On the other hand, Claire's horoscope hasn't contained anything ominous for over a week, and the moon is moving into Capricorn, which is a good thing considering Claire's birth sign. Claire says horoscopes aren't a reliable way to plan your life, and Ellie's come to think that what happens to Claire will pretty much be the ultimate test of that.

"Well, I'm doing okay. I'm getting ready to go to school, you know. Only a few weeks. Aunt Ellie's all worried, but there's an infirmary, not that I intend to use it, and I can do my exchanges in my room. I've contacted them."

"Ellie tells me the doctor has said no, about going away right now, I mean."

"Not really. She's just worried about my picking up infections, or my blood pressure or whatever, but I just tell her I don't plan to breathe around any strangers." Claire maneuvers the phone so that she can pull the plastic dishes out of the drying rack and shelve them. Then she makes herself stop. It's exactly what her mother does when she's nervous, some mindless housework task to keep her hands busy.

"Are you busy a week from Wednesday?"

"Not between exchanges. Why?"

"How'd you like to go get a new kidney?"

"What?" Claire can't make the words connect with an idea. She turns to Ellie for a cue, but of course, Ellie doesn't know what Claire's heard.

She's across the living room in the stuffed chair, patting her head to feel her hair. Claire talked her into getting it cut, and the ends, softly layered and turned under, feel very short to Ellie. Gert said, "I've been wanting to do this for twelve years, so let me at it, honey." No bow anymore, and here she has a whole drawerful and can match any outfit she wears—and practically any she might ever want to buy. Claire says she looks sophisticated, though, and the women at work have raved. She's even gotten compliments from some of the men.

Claire motions frantically for Ellie to come over. She angles the receiver so that they can both hear.

"How'd I like…to what?" says Claire.

"Get a new kidney."

"How? From who, I mean? How'd you find out? They found a donor?"

"Let's see. In order, by surgery, from me, and they found me, a four-point match, for your information. Not only that, but I don't have any dreaded antibodies. I still have to have an enormous physical, and some other…stuff, but it'll be okay."

"You were tested?" When Claire says this, Ellie can finally divine exactly what's going on.

"Well I didn't just prick my finger and draw a four in blood by myself." Madalaine's voice is impenetrable—teasing, with maybe a dash of sarcasm. Maddie is often hard for Ellie to read.

"But I didn't know…"

"Your mother didn't want you to know until I'd had at least the first-off test. So, what do you say?"

"Thank you." Claire gives the rote answer that years of maternal training have programmed in as the correct response to that prompt, then realizes that wasn't necessarily what Madalaine was asking for. "Actually, I don't know *what* to say. I can't believe it. Wait…do you mean a week from Wednesday, like less than two weeks away?"

"Yep. You need to go in tomorrow at eleven, just for a couple of hours. I'm going to give blood and they're going to start transfusing you ahead. Plus we'll stockpile some of my blood."

"Aunt Maddie, I don't know what to say. Thank you. I really can't believe this. Nobody knows how much I hate dialysis. Are you sure? I mean, I know how you've felt about me, and…"

"I'm not sure of my own name anymore. Do you think I should go back to Sams?"

"Um…well, to be honest, I guess I'm the last person you should ask…." Claire lets the implication float like a dust mote on the air. "I've actually wondered what my real name should be, I mean I know what it is legally, but…anyway, about the kidney, are you sure?" Anxiety is leaking from her pores into the room, and as hard as Claire tries to keep her voice steady, now, near the goal, she fails on the last phrase.

"I told you, I'm not *sure* of anything anymore, but it's the only thing that makes sense, so yes. We have to talk, you know…your mother."

"Have you talked with her? I thought you…weren't," Claire responds cautiously, ducking her part of it. She pulls away from Ellie almost imperceptibly, and puts the receiver completely to her own ear. Ellie puts a question on her face beneath raised shoulders, but Claire smiles—a fake smile if Ellie's ever seen one, shrugs and gestures so as to say *it's okay*. Ellie takes it as *go away now*, and retreats to the chair. "Has something happened?" Claire continues to Madalaine. Of course, Ellie can't hear the answer.

"I did know about the baby." Claire falters, then settles on, "Are you all right?"

Ellie pretends to be buried in her magazine. Maybe Claire senses that she's hurt because she says, "Hold on a sec, Aunt Maddie," and covers the receiver. "It's okay, come back, she's talking about Bill's baby." Right away Ellie is back, her breath mingling with Claire's, huddling over the receiver.

"Yeah, I think so. They named him Brian William, can you believe that? But…I held him, he looks just like Brian. Exactly."

"Oh. That must be so hard…" Claire murmurs.

"Different from what I expected, really. Then I saw Lydie at the cemetery…."

"And?"

The moment lengthens. Ellie senses, almost viscerally, that Madalaine has tears in her eyes, perhaps already running down her cheeks. The silence is too filled with feeling to approach it.

"I'll call you again, or you call me, okay?" Madalaine says a few beats later. "There's lots to coordinate, but don't worry. I'm going to do my part. I feel…right about it. I feel better. Actually, I feel a little good. And what I want you to do is talk to your mother." With that, and without waiting for a reply, Madalaine hangs up.

"We need to be making plans," Claire tells Ellie later. They've eaten—a credible beef-and-pasta casserole that Ellie made from a recipe Claire found while researching dialysis at the library. It helps her feel some control of her life, she says about the researching, and keeps her focused on what she can do. Ellie had expected Claire to be in an elated mood, but instead she was jumpy, not herself at all. "If I'm going to be in the hospital for a while, and then, if I can go to school on time, well, even a little late, we've got to think about you. And we've got to let…Wayne know about this apartment."

"Aren't you getting a little ahead of yourself? This is major surgery. There'll be weeks of recovery."

"Six weeks," Claire says impatiently, standing and clearing the kitchen table. "Do you want the rest of this salad?"

"No, I'm fine." This, at least, is familiar, this shifting of weight between the two of them, like one person who's impatient at a bus stop bending one knee and then the other. Claire takes Ellie under her wing, then Ellie takes Claire under hers. Ellie hates the idea of Maddie taking her place—either of them.

"Well, I think you should keep this place. Take it over from Da…Wayne, you can afford it if you're full-time. You've got savings, you said." Claire's head bobs emphatically.

"Mama and…" Ellie says, but her mind is scanning whether her recent charts have mentioned anything even remotely connected to moving. Of course, her chart hadn't mentioned moving before she moved in here with Claire, either.

"I know. But look, they've done fine, and if you go back, you'll never leave. Maddie and Mom will help, you know they always have."

Ellie ducks her head. Two slips from Claire, one of them on purpose: she called Lydia *Mom* and she let Ellie know that she knew Ellie hadn't always done everything alone. And another first: Ellie doesn't take Claire on to press the point like a pansy repeatedly closed into a heavy book. It is ragged, best left alone this time.

"I don't know," Ellie says, her body slumped in the straight-back chair that she's pushed away from the table. Presley noses her hand from his spot beside her.

"Well, I do." Dishes clatter as Claire dumps them into the sink like so much unbreakable plastic, which is what they are. The window over the sink—which, with its shade half-drawn against the glare of the setting sun, observes the parking lot like a sleepy eye—needs a good cleaning. While she talks, Claire moistens a dish towel and works on it, but it only gets worse. "That helped a lot," she mutters. "Ellie, I'm sorry. I don't mean to take it out on you. I really do think that you should stay here, for your sake."

"I just don't think you're being realistic about…"

"About the kidney, I know. I could be in the hospital for up to two weeks, but it could be as short as eight or nine days." Claire says the last part in a singsong litany manner, the edge she just apologized for right back into her voice. "I'm talking about you, not me. Could we just concentrate on one thing at a time? Once I'm not stuck with a stupid umbilical cord keeping me here, what I need won't be an issue." This is rare for Claire; she's not explosive, nor given to calling something *stupid* that keeps her alive.

"Everything's all tangled up," Ellie says, stung by Claire's eagerness to leave.

"So it's like a knot in your hair. You have to brush it out."

"Gert told me peanut butter will slide a tangle right out of your hair."

"Oh, for God's sake," Claire says, and turns her back to Ellie, ostensibly to do the dishes. But Ellie is developing a sense about these things. She goes over ostensibly to dry them, but ends up with her arms around her niece.

CHAPTER 43

I am as tangled in this as if my arms and legs were tied together in enormous double knots, no matter what Maddie says. The day after she said she'd give Claire a kidney, I called her to say, *Wait, I can't let you do this*, because I knew I'd made her. And what does she answer? *It's not up to you, Lydie. Get a grip. You're not queen of the universe. You're not even in charge. Trust me on this one. I've found out how few things I'm in charge of, but my body is one of them. See, I thought you were in charge, too, because it looked like you were, and I could blame you, and it all made sense that way.*

"What?" I stammered, trying to follow. I stood in the kitchen and paced enough that I wrapped the phone cord around myself twice. Isn't that ironic?

"Here's the deal. We either think we're in charge of something or we think we're helpless, and half the time we guess wrong. You're not in charge of this."

"But Maddie, I—"

She interrupted, without waiting for the hesitation that was going to come, because I didn't know exactly what my objection was. But she made it sound so—I don't know, haphazard, the way we get through life.

"See, now, I could be guessing wrong, thinking I'm in charge of this. Maybe it's something else entirely pulling the strings. But I think it's me and I'm doing it," Maddie said. And hung up.

I have been trying to sort out that conversation ever since. The balance keeps tipping and I keep trying to add sand in the form of a coherent thought to one side or the other to make it a clear winner, so I can say I know what I'm in charge of. As soon as Maddie said I wasn't in charge of everything, meaning, I guess, that I didn't have anything to do with Brian's death, well, then, I examined the underside of that plate and took on the responsibility I do have, the responsibility I lied about taking when Maddie and I were crying at Brian's grave.

I tried to explain it to John. He came over that night, with yellow roses and a bottle of champagne to celebrate that Claire had a donor, handsome in an open-necked madras shirt and freshly shaved, for my benefit, I knew. I felt bad that he'd gone to so much effort to make it special and there I was dithering about whether it was all right for Maddie to be doing this.

He put the champagne in the refrigerator and went to the right cabinet for a vase. I noticed how easily he moved through my house now, how unlike a guest he'd become and it made me uneasy. I've made no decisions.

"Well," he said. "Don't you think it's up to Maddie, after all?"

"But I got her to do it. What if something happens to her? What about Jennifer?"

"You might think you could make her do this, but I'm not sure you're right. Anyway, you need her help, whether you want it or not."

I fell silent at that, wanting to argue the point, but uncertain anymore what I believed. I pulled out a kitchen chair and sat down heavily in it. A breeze ruffled the kitchen curtain. I could actually smell my flowers on it. The heat's broken some after enormous thunderstorms yesterday, and I've got all the windows open for some real air. That's how I feel, like I just want to get down to what's actually, really real, and I can't tell what it is past one moment. Usually I can tell right when it's happening, but not any farther. Like that one moment in the cemetery, when I took on Maddie's grief and it wasn't for show.

"The thing is, look at the little things we do, how they reverberate. I did ask Claire to watch out for Brian. But Maddie made them late, taking some ridiculous number of pictures. And us—you with a kidney condition, me getting pregnant. We didn't know. *I* didn't know, anyway. Look what's happened to Wayne. I feel…doomed."

John pulled a chair over next to mine and sat. "If you want to, I guess you can trace the whole thing back and make it my fault. I chased you."

"Until I caught you."

"Until I left you," he said. "See? You can't look at it that way. Of course we don't know how things will play out. We're not God."

"There's got to be some way to decide," I said. "It's not as simple as just following some code that tells you what's right and wrong, because I would have decided that it was good to ask Claire to take Brian to the prom with her and Kevin."

John shook his head, not in disagreement, but with a slight shrug, as if to say, *I don't know either*. "Can we have the champagne to celebrate that Claire has a new chance?" he asked. "Even if it's your fault that she has a new chance?"

"Quit teasing me. This is serious."

"You're right. And *still*, we need to celebrate."

I tried to put the question up on a shelf, then, the way I put up breakable things when Claire was little, this one like a troubling, sculptured figure that has the mystery and answer locked inside its mute head. On that shelf, invisible to everyone else, it's watching me, watching me.

Maddie is coming to dinner tonight, before she and Claire have their surgeries tomorrow. Bill and Melody are bringing Jennifer to me later so that she can go to the hospital with us. Maddie actually would have rather she stayed with Bill—so much things change—but Jennifer was insistent. I thought to invite Ellie and Claire, too, but Ellie answered saying just she would come. "But Claire shouldn't be alone," I objected.

"I'll take her to Mama's," Ellie said, and what could I say? I'm not in charge.

I'm making Maddie's favorite foods, my Dijon pork, fresh

corn on the cob from Hadley's farm stand and a rice pilaf. Blueberry pie for desert. A frozen crust, yes, but rolled out and floured, spilling fresh blueberries, and a lattice top. I owe her so much now, it seems almost obscene to make a special dinner, as if I think it will even register on the account.

I'm pleased that she doesn't ring the doorbell, just opens it and tosses a small overnight bag on the sofa while I'm walking to the front door from the kitchen and she's calling me at the same time. She feels a little stiff when I hug her, but she doesn't pull away, and maybe it's my own guilt making me noodle-like in comparison. The gray in her hair has spread, and I see it lacing the parts that were all dark before, but she looks better. More put-together, and she has coral lipstick and mascara, and blusher that makes the darkness around her eyes less noticeable.

"Something smells wonderful," she says. "Here. This is the stuff from my refrigerator that'll go bad if you don't use it, and I put in a tin of cookies for Jen. Put this away."

"What is it?" Actually, what it is is obvious: a sealed envelope addressed to Jennifer.

"Just in case."

"Oh God, Maddie, don't..."

"I'm not. Come on, I'm starved and I can't eat after six-thirty."

"Ellie is coming...."

"That's okay," she says, and then we both laugh, the old conspiratorial laugh. "As long as she doesn't make me listen to 'Hurt.'"

"I already thought of that. I unplugged the tape deck, so I could say it's on the fritz."

"Nice. Remember at that picnic Robbie-Jo had, how Ellie brought that damn boom box and about forty batteries? I thought for sure they'd throw us out of the park." While she speaks she finishes setting the table, which I'd half done. It feels almost normal; I don't know if the reserve underneath is from me or her.

Ellie comes, her usual late self, and with Presley on a leash.

"You know he's afraid to be alone," she says defensively, and slyly, when Ellie's not looking, Maddie and I roll our eyes to each other. Her hair looks a hundred percent better, though, cut the way it is, stylish and becoming, and I tell her that again.

"Lydie, can I ask you something?" Ellie says while I'm dishing out pie.

"What's going to happen with you and Wayne? I'm not just being nosy, I do have a reason."

"Well, just so you know, he's not staying on with me," Maddie sticks in. "I've told him that I'd appreciate his staying on for a couple of weeks after I get home from the hospital, because I'm not supposed to lift—"

"I'll come do anything you need..." I interrupt.

"I know, but you know how he is. He wants to, because of Claire and...oh hell, let's not get into that."

But I don't drop it right away. "I know. He's paying for the apartment, he'll move your refrigerator, he just won't talk to me. I *have* tried," I say to Maddie. "Ellie, he *always* knew, in case that isn't the way you heard it."

"Gert says that people know what they want to know," she says cryptically, scraping her fork across her plate. "This is great pie. Anyway, I was wondering if you know if Wayne's going to keep the apartment for himself."

"I'd be the last person to know," I say. "Has he said, Maddie?"

"He's about as talkative as ever," she answers with a shrug.

"Because, Claire and I were talking and I'm sort of thinking of keeping it, taking over the rent I mean, and maybe...well, it's just an idea."

"Has Claire said she's staying with you?" I say cautiously.

"She's still set on going to that college. I don't know if she'll make it on time. I guess she can go after Christmas if the transplant..." Ellie says.

I'm digesting that, wondering what to do about the bill for

the first tuition installment and trying to sort through the said and the unsaid when the doorbell rings. I open the door expecting the newspaper boy or Hank Schultz with tomatoes from his garden. Instead, it's Claire, my Claire.

"Hi," she says. "Ellie said you invited me. Grandpa drove me over."

"You don't need an invitation, ever."

"I already ate," she says, though she looks shadow-thin in her shorts and red tank top.

"Did Maw Maw give you—"

"Yes," she interrupts with something between a smile and irritation.

I want to ask about her medicines, but sense that it would push the barrier she's erected around herself.

"Claire, come in here," Ellie calls from the kitchen. "I'm so glad you decided to come."

Claire responds to Ellie's call with a smile. "Coming," she says, and, as if there's a force field around me, she keeps a distance as she makes a quarter circle around me to head for Ellie's voice. "Aunt Maddie said I should talk to you," she stops to say.

From behind Claire, following her in, I see Maddie look at her and nod. It seems fraught with the unspoken, but I can't decipher it.

"Sit down, honey," Ellie says, sounding for all the world like me.

Then Maddie says, "There's pie. Want some before Ellie has thirds? We only have another half hour of eating time left, so get busy."

I am outside their circle; whether it was created in the last fifteen seconds or has been rounding itself toward completion for weeks, I have no idea. Claire sits down and Maddie cuts a piece of pie. She lifts it onto her empty plate, complete with blueberry stains from her own piece, licks off her fork, wipes it on her paper napkin and hands it to Claire, who says, "Thanks." I stand a couple of feet away, braced by the doorjamb, utterly out of place. It's early twilight, soft, and even cool. My sisters and daughter look like a scene in a movie: the yellows and ambers of the kitchen, Maddie and Ellie's white blouses subdued by the gold tones of the window light. There are small white candles in brass holders that I've lit in the middle of the table, a bouquet of dahlias and marigolds between them, the scene accented with Claire's red shirt, the darkness of their hair, but all of it blending as if seamlessly composed. Their conversation almost recedes, as though I'm a camera panning back and out. I hear Claire say *When we first moved I thought I was going to have to be the world's first living heart donor because I cleaned the toilet, which you'd think she'd appreciate. But no, just because I left the bleach in it to soak, see, when Ellie peed in it, the water turned sort of red and she thought it was bloody and she'd caught kidney failure from me.* Ellie pretends to get huffy and says, *What kind of idiot cleans a toilet with bleach?* and their laughter merges and separates and merges again. At first, for a moment, I am jealous. But I let their words and laughter blur and become the soothing music of a river moving past me. I put my anger and jealousy on the current's back and send them on to the sea where I've been twice in my life. I'm grateful that Ellie and Maddie and Claire have each other, and let go a little, as if I knew I were dying and that they'd be all right.

It's Maddie who says, "Hey, Lydie, what're you doing, trying to hold the wall up? Come sit down."

When Maddie says that to me, she turns and slides her chair a little, as if to make room. I hesitate a moment, and see her look at Claire.

"Yeah, Mom, come on. You didn't even finish your pie, and I'm about to fight both you and Ellie for seconds," Claire says. She gestures at my chair, as if I didn't know where I'd been sitting all these years, right beside her.

CHAPTER 44

Wednesday, *the* Wednesday. Lydia and Jennifer wait in a special lounge with Claire, who won't even be prepped until after Madalaine has been finished, as Dr. Douglas put it. (Madalaine pointed out the unfortunate word choice to Dr. Douglas, who stammered in embarrassment, but Madalaine had been teasing. Nobody thinks she could be teasing anymore, about anything.) Madalaine left them in the lobby when she checked in at 6:00 a.m.; the woman—impossibly young, she couldn't be but Brian's age—had seemed almost reverential as she stood and came around her desk to point the way to Same Day Surgery.

On Monday, Madalaine had an arteriogram, and something the technicians called an IVP. Madalaine has forgotten again what those initials stand for, although they explained everything to death. She dreaded those final tests, but they'd turned out to be nothing but boring. Last night, she and Ellie had dinner at Lydie's, and Madalaine spent the night with Lydie so Lydie could take her to the hospital at six in the morning. They teetered back and forth with each other in bursts of conversation and silences that reached just enough into the space between them that then they'd both speak at once, and then retreat with excessive exhortations. "No, you go ahead. What were you saying?" Then Claire came, and Madalaine knew that it was because she'd asked her to.

"Wednesday's child is full of woe," Madalaine recites cheerfully a half-hour later as she's prepped for surgery. "I was born on a Wednesday, did you know that?" The first shot, the one she gets before the epidural, is kicking in.

"Oh come now," says the woman in a shower cap and green

scrub suit who's shaving Madalaine's pubic hair. "Look at what a wonderful thing you're doing. We don't have many donors who aren't siblings or parents."

"That's because there aren't enough lunatics and it's hardly legal." Madalaine has swung from terrified to relaxed—and back to terrified. Still, there's been a strange near-ecstasy, as if it all comes down to being able to do one, clear upright thing for redemption, this is it, and yes, yes, she's doing it, yes.

The voice wafts up to Madalaine around her own legs to primly correct her. "Now if it weren't legal, Dr. Douglas wouldn't be doing it, and neither would Dr. Macao. He's wonderful."

"Everybody's wonderful, I'm wonderful, *you* must be wonderful," Madalaine says mockingly, but the teasing part gets lost in her thickening throat.

"Well, thank you," the nurse answers seriously. "I don't know that I deserve that, but you and your doctors do. You certainly have gorgeous blue eyes, like an angel."

"Yeah," says Madalaine, closing them.

"It's all over, you're fine. You're in the recovery room. I'm Sharon. The operation went great. How do you feel?"

The voice seems to surround Madalaine, the source indistinct. She has to figure out how to open her eyes. There's no particular pain, just a sense of missing time. A slit of light troubles her and she shuts it out. "Sick," she whispers as nausea becomes consciousness. "Sick."

"I know," the voice says. "That's normal. Nothing's wrong, don't worry. Claire is about to go into surgery."

"Sick."

"That's called referred pain," a nurse says. "Just some superficial nerves that serve the leg. They have to be cut for the surgery." The side she's lying on is the only part of her really asleep. It wants her to turn over, but Madalaine can't. A machine to one side of the bed beeps and the nurse appears again. "Your sister is here," she whispers. "And your mother and daughter."

"Son. Where's my son?"

"I'm sorry, I don't think he's here," she says, and Madalaine remembers. She pushes the morphine pump, willing her right forefinger, which seems attached to another body, somewhere else. She circles the cosmos again, for Brian.

Madalaine opens onto Lydia's face, her fingers squeezed too tightly in Lydia's hand. "Hey, there," Lydie says. "You did it. You did it. Claire's okay. She's already produced a little urine. I just came from her room, Ellie's with her now. I brought Jennifer with me, she's out at the nurse's station, and she's fine. I thought I should see you first, but I'll get her in a minute." Lydia suddenly stops, as if conscious of talking too much, and adds, "How're you doing this morning?"

"Don't let Ellie in here," Madalaine says, but without impact because she manages a smile. "Blood...blood...and throw up. Ellie's hell."

"You have a point. I'm still not sure how she helped Claire with dialysis, what with her eyes scrunched into tiny little slits," Lydie laughs, pushing down her reaction to Madalaine's appearance, which is cloudy-eyed and white, except for the dark smears around her eyes. "Probably Presley really did it."

"Presley in Claire's room?" Madalaine bends her elbows, braces her hands on the bed and begins to pull herself up. Pain. She grunts and lies back down after a brief effort.

"Nope. I do believe she may have left him briefly unattended. Brace yourself. They told me your catheter is out and they're getting you up to pee and walk pretty soon."

"No way. My vacation. Not moving. Let them wait on me hand and foot, pee for me, too. Gimme my catheter back."

Lydie's face straightens into seriousness. "Maddie. Just now, while we're alone...thank you for my daughter. Nobody but you can really understand that gift. I know I don't understand it the way you do, either, but you've got to know it's all I think about."

"Good. It's good, then. Something good."

"Yes. It's good."

CHAPTER 45

How unfathomable it all is, how layered, how tilted, how hidden, how tangled. Solitary, connected, guilty, pure: our minds mysteriously mix with other forces that we sense but cannot see or touch, and somehow, blindfolded, we create our lives. I almost said *blindly* instead of *blindfolded*, and I find I can't choose between the words. *Blindfolded* says there's an obstacle to vision that's somehow, someday removable. Maybe there's such a thing as a large context in which one could see how it all fits, how one thing leads to another and then branches out like a vine rooted at your feet and spreads like a maze to the horizon. Blindly? Well, I guess that would be like standing in the middle of the vines while they're twisted around your ankles, extending as far as you can see in any direction; you can't see where they're rooted or where they stop, but you must find your way through them, home. I'll go with *blindfolded*, and hope it's right.

Maybe Brian knows which it is, or maybe poor, lost Kevin. I surely don't. I'm inclined to believe now that it's all for good, somehow, in the end, but then I think of those two and I rock back on my heels to uncertain again. But I think of picking berries over at Aggie and Zeke's when I was little. They used to give me a bowl and take me into their five long rows of raspberry bushes when they were gathering fruit for the preserves Aggie made every July. Once I'd filled the bowl, I was allowed to eat my own fill until it was time to go back to the house. Even though the rows were taller than I by a good deal, and prickly branches grabbed at my hair and skin, I loved the berries, both the way they gave right up and plopped into my hand if they were ripe, and the soft feel of their flesh. And the taste of them, sun-warm and foreign! After I'd done it awhile, I learned that if I went backward through a row I thought I'd just picked clean as morning, I'd see lots that I'd missed. One day, I told Aggie my discovery, thinking to impress her.

"Heavens to Betsy, child. Didn't I tell you that before? I thought I did. And here's another trick. Look away, and take a step backward. Then look at a bigger section than the ones right in front of your face. You'll see ones you'd swear weren't there a minute ago."

So I try to do that, walk backward in my mind over where I've been, or step back and look at a bigger part. Maybe someday I'll see Brian and Kevin hanging there, ready to understand, full of good, ripe after all.

Wayne and I have agreed to divorce, but look at this piece of the puzzle: he came to see Claire every day in the hospital and she's calling him Dad, again. He did decide to keep Ellie and Claire's apartment, and so did Ellie, so at the moment they're living there together, Wayne in one bedroom, Ellie in the other. He says her cooking's not bad, which Maddie and I found astonishing, especially when he denied that they ate grilled-cheese sandwiches and tomato soup every night. Ellie says they're looking for a small duplex, so they can help each other out. She was worried that I'd be mad, but I told her I'd be glad if they do. Wayne's a good man. Maybe he and Ellie can learn to be alone together. Gert thinks it's a good idea, so it must be.

I don't know about John. I'm a different woman than the one who fell in love with him nearly twenty years ago, the woman who believed that love always takes you where you should go. Certainly, I love him, and we are bound together to the death and perhaps beyond, but whether we will have another long, long silence between us while we live apparently separate lives, I don't know. John, of course, wants us to marry, but I can't see that far. I don't know that I want to marry anyone again. For now, the only promises I will make are to Claire.

Claire moved back in with me after she and Maddie were both recovered from surgery, when Wayne needed another place to light for at least a while. She's not met John yet. She's unyielding on the point, but John is patient and says, "Give her time."

And she has time, I hope. She's gone to school now. A semester late, but she made it. I know because Wayne and I took her. The college made an exception, let her come in the middle of the year and room with another freshman whose roommate had dropped out. Ellie wanted to go with us, but there honestly wasn't room. As it was, the car sagged with boxes and suitcases and lamps and the like. "All of you can come the next time there's a parents' weekend," Claire said when she hugged her goodbye, and I deflated at first, and then realized, *No, she's right.* Ellie's had a part in giving her life.

When Claire hugged Maddie goodbye, it was fierce and private. I understood that right away. "You know how careful you have to be," Maddie said, gently, not lecturing, holding Claire's face between her hands. "Wash your hands a lot, and don't forget a single pill, hear me?" Of course, Claire's on the immunosuppressant drugs she'll have to take the rest of her life. So far, so good, though. The kidney works. She'll need another one sometime, and then, doubtless, another. Dr. Douglas says it's unpredictable how long any transplant will last. I try not to think about it now, that uncertainty. It's like setting out for Graceland, something Ellie wants us to try again. Maddie says she's game if I am.

How can we all be so alone in our own skins, while so inescapably unified that just to live, we each draw in air that another of us has already exhaled?

I'm in school myself. I've got enough credits now that I have to declare a major. I have to choose a direction even though I still don't know what leads to what, and where, or if, anything ends.

NEXT READER'S GUIDE DISCUSSION QUESTIONS

1. Lydia seems to see herself as the most in-charge sister at the beginning of the novel. Do you think she was correct in her assessment? How you do analyze the power dynamics of the sisters' relationships?
2. How do you feel about the men in the novel? Are they dominated by the women? Which male character shows the most strength? Does one please or disappoint you more than the others?
3. How do you feel about the choices Lydia made? Did she do the right thing by defying Wayne's wishes and calling John?
4. As you read, were you sympathetic with Claire's rejection of her mother, or did you feel that she was too judgmental? If you initially felt she was justified, did your opinion soften by the end of the novel?
5. Do you think Madalaine's decision regarding donation is independent, or do you think she was manipulated? Is Lydia's guilt appropriate?
6. What do you imagine some of the main characters will do after the novel ends?
7. What is your opinion about leading life blindly versus blindfolded?

Experience entertaining women's fiction about rediscovery and reconnection—warm, compelling stories that are relevant for every woman who has wondered "What's next?" in their lives. After all, there's the life you planned. And there's what comes next.

Turn the page for a sneak preview of a new book from Harlequin NEXT.

CONFESSIONS OF A NOT-SO-DEAD LIBIDO
by Peggy Webb

On sale November 2006, wherever books are sold.

My husband could see beauty in a mud puddle. Literally. "Look at that, Louise," he'd say after a heavy spring rain. "Have you ever seen so many amazing colors in mud?"

I'd look and see nothing except brown, but he'd pick up a stick and swirl the mud till the colors of the earth emerged, and all of a sudden I'd see the world through his eyes—extraordinary instead of mundane.

Roy was my mirror to life. Four years ago when he died, it cracked wide open, and I've been living a smashed-up, sleep-walking life ever since.

If he were here on this balmy August night I'd be sailing with him instead of baking cheese straws in preparation for Tuesday-night quilting club with Patsy. I'd be striving for sex appeal in Bermuda shorts and bare-toed sandals instead of opting for comfort in walking shoes and a twill skirt with enough elastic around the waist to make allowances for two helpings of lemon-cream pie.

Not that I mind Patsy. Just the opposite. I love her. She's the only person besides Roy who creates wonder wherever she goes. (She creates mayhem, too, but we won't get into that.) She's my mirror now, as well as my compass.

Of course, I have my daughter, Diana, but I refuse to be the kind of mother who defines herself through her children. Besides, she has her own life now, a husband and a baby on the way.

I slide the last cheese straws into the oven and then go into my office and open e-mail.

From: "Miss Sass" <patsyleslie@hotmail.com>
To: "The Lady" <louisejernigan@yahoo.com>

Sent: Tuesday, August 15, 6:00 PM
Subject: Dangerous Tonight
Hey Lady,
I'm feeling dangerous tonight. Hot to trot, if you know what I mean. Or can you even remember? ? Look out, bridge club, here I come. I'm liable to end up dancing on the tables instead of bidding three spades. Whose turn is it to drive, anyhow? Mine or thine?
XOXOX
Patsy
P.S. Lord, how did we end up in a club with no men?

This e-mail is typical "Patsy." She's the only person I know who makes me laugh all the time. I guess that's why I e-mail her about ten times a day. She lives right next door, but e-mail satisfies my urge to be instantly and constantly in touch with her without having to interrupt the flow of my life. Sometimes we even save the good stuff for e-mail.

From: "The Lady" <louisejernigan@yahoo.com>
To: "Miss Sass" <patsyleslie@hotmail.com>
Sent: Tuesday, August 15, 6:10 PM
Subject: Re: Dangerous Tonight
So, what else is new, Miss Sass? You're always dangerous. If you had a weapon, you'd be lethal. ?
Hugs,
Louise
P.S. What's this about men? I thought you said your libido was dead?

I press Send then wait. Her reply is almost instantaneous.

From: "Miss Sass" <patsyleslie@hotmail.com>
To: "The Lady" <louisejernigan@yahoo.com>

Sent: Tuesday, August 15, 6:12 PM
Subject: Re: Dangerous Tonight

Ha! If I had a *brain* I'd be lethal.

And I said my libido was in hibernation, not DEAD!

Jeez, Louise!!!!!

P

Patsy loves to have the last word, so I shut off my computer.

* * * * *

Want to find out what happens to their friendship when Patsy and Louise both find the perfect man?

Don't miss
CONFESSIONS OF A NOT-SO-DEAD LIBIDO
by Peggy Webb,

coming to Harlequin NEXT in November 2006.

HARLEQUIN®
Next™